Kay Brellend, the third of six children, was born in North London but now lives in a Victorian farmhouse in Suffolk. Under a pseudonym she has written seventeen historical novels published in England and North America. This is her fifth novel in the Campbell Road series and was inspired by her grandmother's reminiscences about her life in an Islington slum.

KAY BRELLEND

East End Angel

HARPER

Harper
An imprint of HarperCollins*Publishers*
77–85 Fulham Palace Road,
Hammersmith, London W6 8JB

www.harpercollins.co.uk

A catalogue record for this book
is available from the British Library

ISBN: 978-0-00-746419-7

Set in Meridien by Palimpsest Book Production Ltd, Falkirk, Stirlingshire

Printed and bound in Great Britain by
Clays Ltd, St Ives plc

MIX
Paper from
responsible sources
FSC C007454

For Mum and Dad, with everlasting love and gratitude
for your hard work and sacrifice.

CHAPTER ONE

February 1936

'Have you killed her?'

'Don't care if I have,' the big man growled. 'The slag deserves to be six feet under for what she's done.'

'What could she have done to deserve this?' the young woman bellowed.

Kathy Finch weighed seven and a half stone and stood five foot three in her shoes, but she was trying to wrestle the brute away from the prone bloodied body of his young wife. He swatted her aside as easily as he would an irritating moth.

Kathy regained her breath and balance, then launched herself at the stevedore again. This time when she grabbed his hairy forearm he allowed her to pull him back, having delivered a final lazy stamp to the figure on the floor.

Ruby Potter had curled into a foetal position in a vain attempt to protect herself and her unborn baby from her husband's boots. But whereas moments ago she had

1

been gamely fighting back – punching and slapping at his thick shins – now she was motionless, her face fallen away to the wall.

Satisfied with the punishment he'd inflicted, Charlie Potter sauntered off to get his donkey jacket from a filthy armchair. The child sitting on it barely flinched as the coat was whipped from under her.

'I think you know right enough what she's done, miss,' Charlie finally answered Kathy. 'Don't come the innocent with me. Ruby talks to you about all sorts of stuff. I've heard her.'

'She talks to me 'cos I'm her midwife!' Kathy yelled. She'd dropped down beside Ruby and was feeling her limp wrist for a pulse. She swivelled on her knees, aware that at any time the vicious bastard could again let loose his temper and she might be on the receiving end. She felt ire well up inside. She'd go down fighting, like Ruby had.

She'd no idea what had led up to this beating, having arrived after it had started. At the sound of the blood-curdling commotion, she had raced down the passageway and burst into the room, but by then her patient was already on her knees. The punch she'd seen Charlie deliver had looked savage enough to fell a horse. It had certainly put Ruby out like a light.

Kathy's eyes slewed to the chalk-faced child sucking her thumb and watching everything with unblinking intensity. She knew she herself was relatively safe, but a maniac such as Potter, who believed his family were his chattels to do with as he liked, wouldn't think twice about laying into his small daughter if he thought she was being insolent.

'You'd better get out of here! I'm warning you . . . I'm

calling for an ambulance and then I'm getting the police.' Kathy's fear was subdued by fury.

Charlie Potter swooped on Kathy, pinching her chin between his calloused fingers. Her neck strained as he hauled her up using just those remorseless digits until she was on her feet and gritting her teeth in agony. When standing in front of him she tried to jerk back from his leery gaze but the pain increased so she settled for despising him with china-blue eyes.

'If she's a goner, I've got friends who'll say I was with them. I've got other friends who'll turn things bad fer you.' He patted her cap and gave her a tobacco-stained grin, making her recoil from his stinking breath. 'Just 'cos you're friendly with the coppers don't mean nuthin'. My friends have got mates in the constabulary 'n' all, if you get my drift. So you think on, miss. You've been about long enough now to know how we do things round here.' His crafty eyes slipped over her slender figure beneath her gabardine mac. 'We don't need you comin' round, interfering. I've told you that before. Ruby's got all the help she needs with friends 'n' family.'

'Leave her be!' The weak command came from behind and Kathy spun around so quickly and violently that Charlie's fingernails scored her skin.

'Are you all right?' Kathy crouched, her roving hand immediately testing Ruby Potter's distended belly. A tiny undulation beneath her fingertips made her whisper a relieved prayer. She turned to glare at the thug behind. There was no flicker of remorse or thankfulness at this sign that his beating hadn't proved fatal. He simply scowled, pointing a menacing finger at his battered wife that promised more was to come. A moment later, he swaggered out of the room.

'Help me up, will you, Miss Finch?' Ruby asked wearily once she'd heard the front door crash shut.

'You stay there. I'm just going out to call an ambulance for you, Mrs Potter,' Kathy blurted.

'No! Don't do that. It'll just make things worse if busybodies get to hear what's gone on.'

'But . . . your face needs stitching,' Kathy said gently, not wanting to upset the woman. The gash on her cheek was sure to leave a nasty scar if left unattended. Ruby looked a dreadful state, and the shame of it was that she'd probably been quite a pretty woman in her time. Kathy glanced at her patient's tangled dark brown hair and pallid complexion. From Ruby Potter's medical notes, Kathy had gleaned that the woman was only six years older than herself. Had she not read her age as twenty-six she'd have guessed her to be in her mid-thirties.

The child jumped down from her seat now she knew the coast was clear. As Kathy gripped under Ruby's arms and strained to lift her, little Pansy shoved her mother on the posterior, trying to do her bit to help.

There was an iron bed set against one wall and, settling Ruby on the edge of the grimy mattress, Kathy gently tilted her chin to get a better look at the damage Charlie had inflicted. 'You should get yourself seen to at the hospital,' she urged.

'Can't you do it, miss?' Ruby pleaded.

'I can't stitch you up.' Kathy had guessed that might come. She was a qualified nurse, but had not been trained to close wounds.

Kathy did her rounds in this poverty-riddled quarter of London, where slum conditions and rough people made the job unpredictable. But she was determined to continue in her vocation, no matter how unpleasant it was at times.

For every vile brute like Charlie Potter there were twice as many salts of the earth around Whitechapel who were terribly grateful for the work she did.

'Don't care how it looks. Just don't want no germs getting in. I'd be grateful if you'd do what you can.' Ruby attempted a smile but it simply made blood leak again from the corner of her mouth. 'Don't want to get you into no trouble, of course, Nurse Finch,' she mumbled, lifting a corner of her pinafore to dab her face.

Kathy shook her head to herself, delving into her nurse's bag to find something with which to clean up her patient. 'I don't carry any equipment for stitches . . . sorry . . .' Kathy knew if she did she'd probably flout rules and risk her job for Ruby Potter's sake. As she looked at the pathetic spectacle sitting with hunched shoulders on the bed, she felt tempted to run after Charlie Potter and let fly with her fists, even though she knew it would make her no better than he.

'Make Nurse a cup of tea, Pansy.' Ruby's fat lips made the words sound slurred, as did the muffling edge of the pinafore she was again pressing to her face to stanch the bleeding.

The little girl shook the dented kettle and, satisfied it had water in it, set it on the hob grate, then squatted down in front of the fire to wait for it to boil.

'Probably got no bloody milk. Suppose that selfish git's used it all in his tea,' Ruby muttered. 'Christ, me head aches . . .' She clutched at her forehead and closed her eyes.

Pansy jumped up and found a milk bottle. She swung it to and fro to let her mother see there was a little bit sploshing about at the bottom.

Kathy wetted some lint under the tap and dabbed it

on Ruby's face, rinsing and repeating the process. She drew from her bag a clean piece of wadding.

'Suppose you're wondering what set him off this time,' Ruby mumbled.

'Your husband seems to think I know all about it. He thinks you confide in me.' Kathy's clear blue gaze drifted from the split cheek she was tending to Ruby's brown eyes.

'He's jealous.'

'Even so, he has no right to beat you unconscious.'

'He's got a right to be jealous, though,' Ruby replied sheepishly.

'I know he has,' Kathy sighed. Gossip was going around the neighbourhood that Ruby Potter was a shameless baggage. In Kathy's opinion, the woman was a fool not to have run off with the other fellow rather than stick with a brute like Charlie. But young and single as Kathy was, she realised life wasn't that simple for the likes of Ruby: the woman's boyfriend was quite likely to be married too, possibly with a brood of children and no money and no job. Charlie Potter was considered one of the lucky ones to be working at the docks, and Kathy had heard him loudly impressing that on Ruby on previous occasions when she'd visited.

But Kathy couldn't condemn Ruby for wanting a man – any man – to show her some love and tenderness.

'All the men round here would've done the same,' Ruby volunteered in her queer voice, breaking into Kathy's brooding. 'Sal Turpin got a fractured skull off her old man when he caught her with a fancy man. Ended in hospital, she did, and her kids got took away.' She raised her eyes and gave Kathy a meaningful look.

'There's no excuse for any of them to act like savages,'

Kathy replied. 'What are you waiting for, the pair of you? Pine boxes to leave in?'

'Where shall I go with no money and three kids?' Ruby grunted an astonished laugh. 'Got one under me feet, one at school and one in me belly.' She shook her head. 'Ain't that easy, Nurse Finch, fer the likes of us. You take it from me, 'cos you'll never know, will you? Nice clever gel like you'll have a doctor or someone posh like that walking you up the aisle.'

Kathy felt a flush warm her cheeks. Ruby was being either sarcastic or diplomatic. She liked the woman, so gave her the benefit of the doubt and decided Ruby probably didn't want to accuse her of being a copper's nark to her face, as some folk did. It had soon got around in the district that Nurse Finch was walking out with a local constable. And nobody liked him: it was David Goldstein's job rather than his character or his Jewish roots they took exception to. East End working-class people roundly despised the police.

'Go on, just do it . . . start on me cheek, if you like,' Ruby suggested gamely.

Kathy continued working as gently as she could on Ruby's face, wiping blood and pressing together edges of skin. She knew the woman was trying not to flinch. She knew too that Pansy had come closer to watch her tending to her mother. When Kathy allowed her eyes to dart quickly to the child, she noticed Pansy's eyes were bright with curiosity rather than fright.

'Got that tea made, Pansy?' her mother asked, grimacing against the pain in her face. 'Can hear the kettle steaming.'

The girl trotted off and splashed hot water onto tea leaves. She put milk into chipped cups a drop at a

7

time so as not to waste any, just the way she'd been told.

'Don't forget to give it a good stir, Pansy. And don't spill none in the saucer fer the nurse.' The curt warning made the child turn large eyes on the adults.

'She's always very quiet,' Kathy remarked without looking away from her delicate work of patching up Ruby.

'She natters sometimes,' Ruby said, flinching at the sting in her lip.

Kathy had done what she could and started packing away her things.

'She keeps shtoom when strangers are around.' Ruby gingerly touched her face, feeling for the damage. 'Then when Peter gets in from school he never stops, so poor Pansy don't get a word in edgeways, even if she wants to.'

'When is she going to school?'

'No rush . . .' Ruby said, sounding defiant.

Kathy guessed that Pansy was already of an age to attend school. She was small and slight from under nourishment – as were most of the local children – but Kathy suspected she was over five years old. She bent to smile into Pansy's face. 'Is that my tea?' Kathy tipped her cap at a chipped cup and saucer with an unappetisingly weak brew in it.

Pansy nodded.

'Thank you.'

The little girl's response to unwanted attention was to shuffle towards her mother and press against her.

'If you lie down, Mrs Potter, I'll listen to the baby's heart before I go and make sure there's nothing amiss.'

'Ain't no need, Miss Finch; I can tell you the little

8

blighter's strong as an ox. Lays into me almost as hard as its father does . . .' Her words faded away.

Ruby knew for sure, even if Nurse Finch did not, that Charlie Potter wasn't this baby's father. Charlie knew, of course, and that was what was making him nastier than usual. He could count months as well as she could and knew he'd been away courtesy of His Majesty when the baby was conceived. He'd been lucky to get back his old job at the docks following six months behind bars. Anyhow, her husband would know for certain when it was born; Ruby feared the child would look foreign, being as the man who'd knocked her up was Chinese.

'You promise me you won't say nuthin' about this commotion?' Ruby pleaded, eyes widening. 'You won't tell Dr Worth, will you? The authorities will poke into me business. Then what've I got left if I lose me kids?'

Kathy could see Ruby was close to crying. The woman had taken a beating off her husband without shedding a tear, yet might weep now but for having her vow of silence. Around here, the disgrace of interference from the hated authorities was deemed worse than being married to a brute. Kathy sighed agreement. 'Now I'm here, I'll just take a look at you and make sure everything's all right with the baby,' she insisted.

'Never had none of this fuss and bother with me other two,' Ruby muttered, easing herself back gingerly on the bed. 'Me mum's friend Ivy from across the street took care o' me before when I was due with Peter and Pansy.'

'Things have changed, Mrs Potter, and people like Ivy Tiller mustn't deliver babies unless they want to get into trouble.'

Kathy was used to coming up against resistance from

women – and their husbands – who had been used to calling in local handywomen to care for them during labour. Rather than risk arrest, most of the unofficial midwives adhered to the ruling, if grudgingly. Kathy sympathised with those women: their livelihood had been bound up in their unofficial profession. Times were hard for everybody and jobs not easy to find.

Kathy listened to the strong heartbeat, amazed at how resilient these working-class wives were. Her own father had been a bully, yet, absurd as she knew it to be, Kathy considered him better than Charlie Potter because his brutality had been controlled. Potter didn't give a damn about the consequences of beating his wife. He believed his criminal acquaintances protected him from trouble. Eddie Finch had not risked drawing attention to himself, or his career fencing stolen goods in Islington, with a charge of wife battering.

He'd floored Winifred with his punches but had refrained from following them up with a kicking while she sprawled defenceless. Like Ruby Potter, Kathy's mother had no intention of allowing outsiders to know her business. Winifred Finch's greatest terror had been giving the neighbours a reason to gossip about her, so she'd hide indoors until her bruises had healed rather than go out and face knowing looks.

Dwelling on her family prompted Kathy to glance at her watch. She'd told her sister, Jennifer, she might call in and see her later on, but time was short and she had a postnatal visit to make to a woman still confined to her bed in the Lolesworth tenements. Besides, after the disturbance with the Potters, Kathy didn't think she could face going into Jennifer's and bumping into the unsavoury characters she kept company with.

'Baby seems fine, surprisingly enough,' Kathy said, having concentrated for some time on the rhythmic thud in her ear. 'There's a nice strong heartbeat.'

'Hear that, Pansy?' Ruby turned to her daughter, standing by the side of the bed. 'Your little sister is doing right as rain.'

Pansy wagged her small dark head.

'You want a girl, do you?' Kathy asked, picking up her bag in readiness to leave.

'Don't want no more men about the place, that's fer sure,' Ruby said. 'Peter's already getting his father's swagger about him . . . he's only eight 'n' all.'

'Will you come to the antenatal clinic next time for a checkup at the surgery? It's on Wednesday afternoons at two o'clock.'

'If I can,' Ruby said, as she always did.

Kathy knew that she wouldn't turn up. If the pregnant women in the dilapidated cottages around Fairclough Street would just attend the local clinic for a quick checkup, it would save her the job of home visits.

Kathy gave Pansy a wave as she went towards the door. Glancing over a shoulder, she saw that Ruby was, head in hands, sipping the weak cup of tea that had been left untouched on the table. She felt a surge of hatred for Charlie Potter and all his like. It was wasted passion. The women would never leave. As Ruby had pointed out, they had no choice but to stay with the brutes and take a bit of happiness where they could with other men.

CHAPTER TWO

'What have you done to your hair?'

Blanche Raven turned her head, inspecting her new hairstyle in the hallway mirror. She was pleased with the permanent wave she'd had put in, even if her mother wasn't, and she guessed from the tone of her voice that Gladys didn't like it. But then her mother could find fault with anything, and sound sour when discussing the weather on a fine day.

'Is Dad in?' Blanche asked, ignoring her mother's question. She was after a sub off her father, having just spent all her wages at the hairdresser's. She knew asking her mother for a few bob would be a dead loss, even though Gladys was flush, having just got paid for her job as a machinist.

'Your father's gone out. I think he's meeting Nick, 'cos he heard he might have a job for him, but of course, I don't get told all of it.'

The mention of her estranged husband made Blanche prick up her ears. She'd only been in minutes but she buttoned her coat ready to leave the house again.

Gladys Scott eyed her daughter grimly. 'Thinking of going chasing after Nick again, are you? Won't do you no good, my girl. He still won't take you back, and you know it.'

'Oh, shut up, Mum,' Blanche muttered, crashing the front door shut behind her. She hunched her shoulders against a sense of dejection and the bitter February wind. She feared her mother was right. Nick had given her the brush-off earlier in the week when she'd turned up at his place with seduction on her mind. She'd felt humiliated when he'd practically bundled her out of the door and told her to go home. He hadn't even offered her a lift in his flash car and she'd had to catch the bus.

Hearing a bus wheezing to a stop at the corner of Bethnal Green Road, Blanche trotted towards it and managed to jump on just before it pulled off. She settled down on a seat next to a fat woman with a basket on her lap. The woman gave her a glare, even though she was taking up most of the seat with her porky backside.

When it reached her stop, Blanche got off the bus and walked briskly in the direction of the Grave Maurice pub. She was hoping that Nick would be in his local, as he usually was at dinnertime, and that her dad would be with him. Nick was more tolerant of her company when her father was around because the two men liked one another. If only she'd listened to her father's advice rather than her mother's, she'd never have let Nick Raven slip through her fingers.

Blanche dawdled outside, peering through the pub windows. She was itching to creep inside and see if Nick and her father were propping up the bar, but she had been brought up right – as her mother would term it – and knew it wasn't nice for a young woman to enter such a rough house on her own. Besides, Nick didn't like pushy women – he'd never got on with her mother – and wouldn't appreciate Blanche marching in on him now if he was with pals. But Blanche didn't fancy loitering outside freezing to death so she had a decision to make.

'Who you after, then?' A burly fellow had just emerged from the pub and seen her on tiptoe, trying to peer into the saloon bar over the frosted-glass pane. He gave Blanche an appreciative top-to-toe look. She was a pretty brunette, and her ample bust and curvy hips were undisguised by the heavy winter coat she wore. He thought she seemed familiar but couldn't bring to mind where he'd met her before.

'Me dad and me husband, Nick Raven,' Blanche answered. She was always proud to let people know who she'd married. 'I think they might be having a drink inside.' Despite the fact he looked like a low-life navvy, Blanche preened beneath the fellow's leer, unconsciously patting her crisp dark waves.

'Yeah . . . they are in there.' Charlie Potter gave her a grin. Now he knew why he'd not immediately recognised her. Blanche Raven had cut her long hair short and put on a bit of weight since the days when she'd been Wes Silver's bit on the side. 'Well, depending on which old man you're after, could be you turned up just in time, luv. Nick's got an admirer moving in on him.'

'Oh, has he!' Blanche snapped and, chin high, stormed past, bristling as she heard laughter following her.

She pushed open the pub door and, once her eyes adjusted to the smoky interior, spied the men she was after. Her husband was leaning on the bar just yards away. The place was crowded but his height and fair hair made him easily recognisable. Her short, balding father wasn't quite so quickly located at his side. Blanche heard his gravelly laugh before she spotted him perched on a stool. She was relieved to see that there didn't appear to be any women with them. Not that she'd have been surprised to see Nick with somebody else. He made no secret of the fact that he'd had affairs since they'd split up.

Blanche pursed her lips indignantly. Perhaps the navvy had thought he was being funny trying to rile her. She reckoned he'd known her identity even before she told him she was Nick's wife, although she couldn't place him. Nondescript old scruffs like him were ten a penny round these parts. Blanche was glad people knew of her association with Nick, despite the fact they'd been separated now for over three years.

Her father had turned and spotted her. He gave her a frown but raised a hand in greeting. The movement drew Nick's attention. Blanche noticed he didn't seem so pleased to see her; nevertheless, she weaved through the crowd to join them.

'What'll you have, Blanche?' Nick asked mildly.

Blanche had to give it to her husband: even though she'd done the dirty on him, he'd always remained generous and polite to her. In fact, she knew if she had an opportunity to ask him for money before they parted, he'd probably hand over a note to her.

'Gin 'n' orange, thanks.' Blanche gave him a coy smile.

'What you doin' here?' her father demanded in a whisper when Nick turned away to get her drink.

'Mum said you was with Nick . . . getting a job . . . so I thought I'd come and see you both,' Blanche muttered defiantly.

15

'Well, I'm more likely to get me job if you ain't around,' Tony Scott retorted, but not too unkindly. He knew his daughter had a renewed hankering for Nick, and he knew why that was. He feared she was wasting her time, but nevertheless wished the couple would get back together. At least then he'd have a bit of a peaceful home life.

Nick Raven was doing all right for himself now. He might not have been when he did the decent thing and married Blanche, having got her pregnant. Then Nick had been driving a lorry for a pittance and his son-in-law's lack of cash and prospects had been the problem where Tony's wife and daughter were concerned. Blanche had acted as though she was doing Nick a favour by agreeing to marry him rather than the other way around.

Nick was now on his way up and Blanche would have been going places with him but for her greed and her mother's influence. Tony knew that it had been with his wife's encouragement that their daughter had started an affair with Wes Silver. Wes was an important fellow around this manor, with a haulage company and gambling clubs, and a reputation for putting people out of business or in hospital if they crossed him. Wes also had a wife and a couple of kids and, when push had come to shove, he'd chosen to stay put. May Silver was too useful to him to be dumped for a younger woman. A lot of people, Tony included, believed May ran the show where Wes's business was concerned and he merely provided a bit of bought-in muscle and credibility.

Tony knew it was sticking in Blanche's craw that her husband's lack of emotion made it seem Wes Silver had actually done him a favour by sleeping with his wife and breaking up his marriage.

'There you go . . .' Nick slid a glass of gin and orange towards Blanche.

She pouted him a thank-you kiss.

'Done something different to your hair, ain't you?' Tony asked, to break the silence that had settled on them since his daughter's arrival. He could tell Nick was pissed off by Blanche's presence, and he knew why. A young blonde seated at a window table had been quite obviously giving his son-in-law the eye, and Nick had been encouraging her with subtle glances. Tony knew her name was Joyce Groves and that she worked in the café up the road. For a moment, Tony had thought trouble might start. Then he'd realised that the fellow sitting with Joyce was her older brother rather than a boyfriend. He recognised Kenny Groves from way back, when he'd been in the same class at school as Blanche.

'What job you getting then, Dad?' Blanche asked, her tongue loosened by a few quick gulps of gin.

'Ain't really spoke about that just yet,' her father answered, glaring from beneath his brows. 'Ain't long been in here so not had a chance.'

'Well . . . I've gotta be off in a minute,' Nick said, looking at a fancy wristwatch. 'Got to see some bloke in Shoreditch.'

'No, stay and have another. My round . . .' Tony Scott knew if Nick went off without offering him a job, he'd swing for Blanche for turning up and ruining his chances.

'Can you start on a house in Commercial Street in the morning?' Nick asked. 'It needs decorating from top to bottom, interior and exterior. I know the weather's a bit against us for outside work but—'

'Course I can,' Tony snapped at the offer of employment. He was a painter and decorator by trade but, lately, he had been picking up any sort of work he could find just to keep some wages rolling in. Although Gladys did piecework, sewing coats for a Jew boy, she never let him forget it was her regular money keeping them all afloat. 'Be glad to start this afternoon on the preparing, if yer like,' Tony burbled, keen to get his foot in the door.

'Be obliged if you'd get going straight away, as I've got tenants lined up ready and waiting to move in.' Nick took a notebook from an inside pocket and ripped out a page. Having written down the site address, he handed it over, upending his glass and draining it in a swallow. 'Gonna get off now . . .' He started towards the door.

He'd only managed a yard or two when Blanche rushed up to hang on his arm.

Nick kept going, trying to curb his impatience when his wife wouldn't take the hint and leave him alone.

Outside the pub, he turned up his coat collar, then removed Blanche's hand from his arm. 'What do you want?'

'Thought you might like to go to the flicks tonight?'

'No, I don't want to go to the flicks with you tonight or any other night,' he said mildly. 'We've been through this. We ain't married now, Blanche . . . well, we are,' he corrected himself, 'but it's over between us and has been for a long time.'

'Don't need to be.' Blanche moved closer, rubbing her hip against his thigh. 'I'll come over yours 'n' show you it can be like it was between us.'

'Right . . .' Nick drawled. 'Well, I'd need to be some sort of demented mug to want to go back to that, wouldn't I?'

Blanche slid her arms about his neck, gazing up into his

18

lean sarcastic face. 'Be better this time, Nick, promise . . .' She turned her head as she noticed she'd lost his attention. A young blonde woman was on her way out of the pub with a man Blanche thought she recognised. She'd been at school with Kenny Groves but she realised the years hadn't treated him kindly. In her opinion, he looked a good decade older than she did. Blanche could see that the petite blonde was more interested in Nick than the fellow she was with, and after a second she realised it was little Joyce, Kenny's younger sister. She felt like flying across and slapping the little cow's face because it was obvious she was giving Nick the come-on. Blanche understood why that was: at twenty-seven, her husband was only two years older than she and Kenny, but he had an air of confidence that made him seem mature and powerful. Nick Raven was also tall and good-looking, and able to afford quality clothes to show off his muscular frame.

'Know her, do you?' Blanche snapped. Her female intuition was telling her that Nick was not immune to Joyce's charms.

'Not as well as I'd like to.' He removed her arms from his shoulders. A moment later, he was heading off towards his Alvis parked at the kerb.

Suddenly Nick halted and strolled back towards Blanche, hands thrust into his pockets. Now he ignored Joyce giving him a come-hither glance over her shoulder, concentrating on his estranged wife. 'We need to talk about the divorce, Blanche.' He gazed into the distance, hoping she wasn't about to get hysterical as she usually did when he mentioned putting an official end to their marriage. In the past he'd backed down rather than upset her and her family. But enough time had passed and he knew he would never again love her or want to live with her. In truth, he wasn't sure if he ever had loved her or wanted to live with her. But four years ago he'd been determined to do the right thing by their unborn child and meet his responsibilities. Not that he could be certain it had been his child . . . and he never would know, as she'd miscarried the little mite at about five months. They'd been married when that happened. The booking at the town hall had been just six weeks premature because Blanche had insisted she wanted to have a ring on her finger before she got a pot belly. In the event she never did get fat but she got her ring and Nick had wondered, once they were all over the turmoil of losing the baby, what the hell he'd done.

Now Blanche shot backwards, clearly not going to listen to any talk of divorces. She knew if she could just get Nick to sleep with her, make her pregnant again, he'd never leave her. He'd stood by her before when she'd been carrying his child and she reckoned he'd do so again.

Nick smiled acidly as he saw her stumbling towards the pub. He'd learned that if there was one sure way to shake Blanche off it was mentioning putting their divorce into motion.

'Ain't talking about it. You know how I feel.' Blanche pointed a shaking finger at him. 'When I took me vows they was for keeps.'

'Yeah? Which ones exactly?' Nick asked sarcastically, following her to the pub door to prevent her entering. 'Weren't the vow of fidelity, was it?' He pulled her roughly to one side so people could exit the pub. 'Now I've told you I can get a divorce on the grounds of adultery – come to think of it, so can you now. But it'd be best if we keep it all nice and friendly, for everybody's sake.'

'We can make a go of it. Why you being horrible?' Blanche gazed up at him, bottom lip wobbling. 'I've said sorry. So I made a mistake – we all make mistakes, don't we?'

'Right 'n' all . . . I made one when I married you,' Nick said, but not nastily. 'It weren't ever right between us and you know it. It ain't ever going to be right between us, and you need to accept that, Blanche. Find yourself somebody else,' he added quite gently. 'Don't pin your hopes on me changing me mind, 'cos I never will.'

Blanche ripped her arm out of his clasp. '*You're* me husband.' Her mouth was set stubbornly as she whipped past him, diving into the pub to find her father before Nick could say anything else to upset her.

Tony sighed as he saw his daughter storming towards him. 'Ain't having any of it, is he?'

Blanche ignored her father's pessimism, polishing off her gin and orange, sniffing back angry tears.

'Anyhow, why aren't you at work?' Tony asked. 'Ain't your afternoon off.'

'Old Emo gave me the day off 'cos I had bellyache.' Blanche worked in a dress shop in Whitechapel High Street and her boss was the Jew who employed her mother as a machinist.

'Yeah, you had bellyache all right,' her father mocked. 'You think that crafty old git ain't gonna know you got yer fancy hairdo on his time?'

Blanche shrugged. 'Don't see it matters anyhow. Emo never pays me if I don't turn up and do me shift.'

'You'll lose that job,' Tony warned. 'Then your mother'll have something to say.' He hopped off the stool, having

21

drained his glass, and thumped it down on the bar. 'She's already warned you you're out of the door the moment you stop paying your way. I ain't going to argue with that. You were lucky we had you back home when Nick kicked you out, considering what you done.'

'Don't care if Emo does sack me,' Blanche said. 'Don't care if Mum throws me out neither. It's me husband's job to keep me. So I'm gonna make sure that's what Nick does,' she muttered defiantly beneath her breath as she followed her father to the door of the pub.

Once he'd got in his car Nick pulled a packet of Weights from his pocket and lit one. While dragging deeply on the cigarette he made a mental note to see his lawyer about starting divorce proceedings. He drove off round the corner and noticed Joyce Groves standing at a bus stop. Her brother had disappeared. She stepped closer to the kerb as she spotted Nick's Alvis approaching so he couldn't miss her.

Nick drove on and didn't bother looking in his rear-view mirror to see how she took that. He'd seen her about for a while and fancied her enough to give her reason to think he'd do something about it. But this afternoon he'd lost the urge for a woman following his talk with Blanche. He knew he could be a hard-nosed bastard when dealing with business matters, and just wished he could find the same attitude when dealing with his estranged wife. He wasn't sure why he felt lethargic about the divorce process. It wasn't as though he couldn't find the money for the lawyer. He liked his father-in-law but not enough to want to keep hearing Tony call him 'son', and as for that dragon Tony was married to, he'd happily never clap eyes on Gladys again.

In his mind Nick cancelled the meeting with his lawyer. What did it matter if he remained married to the silly cow? He'd already made up his mind he wasn't ever taking on a wife again, and at least the women he slept with knew not to expect too much of him while Blanche was hanging about in the background . . .

CHAPTER THREE

'For goodness' sake, Jennifer! Can't you clean this place up, once in a while?'

'Why?' Jennifer Finch was in the process of rinsing out her stockings and underwear. Turning from the sink she sent her sister a sullen look while listlessly dunking the smalls in a metal bowl. 'This dump won't look no better without the dust, you know.' Lethargically, she glanced about.

'It's not a bit of dust that's the problem, Jen, is it?' Kathy retorted.

Jennifer had a couple of ground-floor rooms in a converted house just off Mare Street in Bethnal Green. The upstairs was unoccupied as the landlord had refused to mend the leaking roof and make it close to habitable. On arrival today, Kathy had found her sister's flat in a state, as usual. Jennifer was always promising to have a spring clean, but never did. The only place that ever seemed slightly tidier was Jennifer's bedroom, and Kathy reckoned that was to impress her scummy punters.

Jennifer's sitting room had once been separated from

the kitchenette by a partition wall. The landlord had knocked it down to a low level so now a few old cupboards, a small cooker and a butler sink with wooden draining board were on view.

The faded wallpaper had come unstuck where rain had penetrated through the ceiling and bay window, and now drooped, exposing cracked plaster beneath. The furniture wasn't ancient but Jennifer didn't take care of it and in the year since she'd moved in the upholstery had become stained. The square oak dining table was covered in odds and ends, and there was crockery on the floor. On top of a small radiogram was a smeary glass standing in an overflowing ashtray. The air inside the flat was heavy with the mingled odours of tobacco smoke and mildew. Jennifer rarely opened the windows in case Dot Pearson, who lived next door, was snooping on her, so there was a perpetual unpleasant fug clinging to everything.

Kathy shrugged out of her coat and, rather than lay it on the dirty sofa, hung it over a fiddle-back chair. She picked up the stack of dirty plates from the rug. The top one had remnants of newspaper and a fish supper stuck to it. She plonked the crockery on the draining board. Her sister ignored the angry crash and continued wringing out her washing.

'I've told you before, you'll end up with food poisoning, you daft ha'p'orth, if you don't keep things clean.'

'Good . . . hope I get raging bellyache and die. It'll save me sticking me head in the gas oven,' Jenny snarled.

Kathy grabbed Jennifer's arm, spinning her round. 'Don't talk stupid.' She stepped back as she smelled the alcohol on her sister's breath. Immediately, her eyes slewed to the tumbler balanced on top of the radiogram.

'You've been boozing again.' She sounded more upset than angry, and Jennifer had the grace to blush.

'So what if I have?'

'You promised you'd lay off it.' Kathy swooped on the dirty glass and gave it a sniff, recognising whisky.

'Did I now?' Jennifer narrowed her crusty eyelids. 'Well, if you had my fuckin' life you'd need a drink 'n' all.' She grabbed up the bowl and went outside to peg the washing on the line in the misty backyard. When the few scraps of cotton and silk were hanging limp in the still March air, she turned back to her sister. 'Oh, just leave it. I'll do it when you've gone.' Jennifer seemed irked that Kathy had begun washing up the plates in the stained butler sink.

'Have you been bathing your eyelids with warm salt water, like I said?'

'If I remember, I do it.' Jennifer still sounded irritated.

Kathy raised her eyes heavenward at her sister's attitude.

'You said you'd bring me some stuff over to clear it up.' Jennifer came in, shutting the back door. She was constantly conscious of eavesdroppers the other side of the fence. She was sure Dot Pearson and her cronies thought they were better than she was. Jennifer grudgingly admitted to herself that on the whole they *were* better than she was, but she didn't want anybody rubbing it in.

Kathy pulled a small brown bottle and a pack of lint from her bag. Having unscrewed the top, she upended the antiseptic onto a scrap of lint then wiped it over her sister's closed eyelashes. She handed over the jollop. 'Do it morning and evening till it clears up. And boil your flannels and towels and your bed linen or the infection

26

won't go.' Kathy rubbed together her hands under the icy running tap and flicked them dry rather than risk using the length of frayed greyish cotton hanging on a hook. She knew she was wasting her breath with Jennifer. Her twin regularly promised to alter her way of life, but nothing changed.

Filthy sheets remained on the bed for months on end before seeing the inside of the copper situated outside in the ramshackle washhouse. Considering her twin's profession, Kathy felt sick, knowing Jennifer slept on the detritus shed by strangers' bodies . . .

'Seen anything of Mum and Dad?' Jennifer asked.

'I haven't been over to Islington for weeks.'

Despite Jennifer having been banished from darkening Eddie and Winnie Finch's doorstep many years ago, she still asked after her family with poignant regularity.

'Wonder how Tom's doing?' Jenny mentioned their younger brother.

'Last time I spoke to Mum, she was on the warpath with him 'cos he's good pals with the lads who live round in Campbell Road.'

'Perhaps I won't be the only bleedin' disgrace in the family after all.' Jenny's giggle held a hint of malice.

'It's not a joke, Jen, is it, if he gets himself in bad trouble? Tom's got to find a job soon and he won't have any luck if he keeps larking about. Work's hard to come by.'

'Oh, pipe down, Miss Goody Two-Shoes.' Jennifer's complaint was tinged with amusement. Hearing about their brother's bad behaviour seemed to have brightened her mood.

'Did Mum mention me at all when you last saw her?' she asked hopefully.

'She never does, you know that.' Kathy knew her brusque reply had hurt her sister but Jennifer seemed unwilling to change her seedy life in an attempt to win back her parents' trust.

'Don't want no tea, do you, Kath? 'Spect you've got to be off.'

'Trying to get rid of me already?' Kathy raised her eyebrows. Jennifer didn't look in a fit state to be receiving punters and that was the usual reason she'd tell her to go. Even dockers might expect a brass to make some effort with her appearance. Jennifer's fair hair was matted and the old dress and cardigan she had on didn't look as though they'd seen an iron in a long while. Kathy reckoned her sister hadn't washed, or combed her hair, since she'd climbed out of bed. In fact, she looked as though she could do with a hot bath and Kathy told her so.

'Better get meself tidied up.' Jennifer tried to separate the tangles in her hair with her fingers. 'Bill's coming over this afternoon.'

'Well, in that case, I am going.' Kathy hated Bill Black and had done so since he had corrupted her sister when she was just fifteen and set her on the road to ruin.

'Got any money before you go?' Jennifer wheedled as Kathy picked up her coat. 'I could do with getting a bit of grub in . . .'

'If I thought you'd buy food with it, I'd lend you a couple of shillings.' Kathy gave her twin a challenging stare. 'But you'll spend it on fags or booze or drugs, won't you?'

'I won't, I swear. I'll buy meself some chips and a loaf of bread.' Jennifer blinked her diseased eyelids, giving her sister a winning smile.

Kathy had been treated to such solemn vows in the past. 'Ask Bill to get you some shopping when he turns up.' It twisted her guts to be hard-hearted but she'd lost count of the times her sister had pleaded for money because she was hungry, then spent it on one of her addictions.

'He won't give me nuthin',' Jenny spat. 'He's probably expecting me to give him something. But I've not had no work. Who's gonna want me looking like this?' She scratched at the crusts clumping together her eyelashes.

'Leave it alone! You'll make it worse.' Kathy yanked at her sister's elbow, dragging away her hand.

Kathy's bubbling exasperation was threatening to explode. Her sister had been on the game for years, yet Kathy could never quite relinquish the hope that Jennifer would make a fresh start. 'Why don't you clean the place up, and yourself too while you're at it?' Kathy thundered. 'Look for a proper job and stop wallowing in self-pity!'

'Oh, fuck off!' Jennifer flung herself down on the sofa. 'Bleedin' sick of you and your holier-than-thou crap. Go on, piss off. I know you want to. You only ever come here to crow and look down yer nose at me. If you really wanted to help, you'd give me a few bob so I don't starve. You can see I can't work looking like this.'

'If you didn't associate with scum, you wouldn't look like that, would you?' Kathy bellowed. 'Where d'you think you get the germs from?'

'Oi, oi. What's going on? You gels having a bit of a barney then?'

Kathy spun on her heel to see a flashily dressed stocky man letting himself in with the key that hung through

Jenny's letter box on a bit of string. She picked up her coat and immediately shrugged into it.

'Don't go on my account, darlin',' Bill Black said with a foxy smile. His eyes lowered to look her over beneath the brim of a fedora shading his swarthy features.

Bill was well aware Kathy Finch despised him. Whereas he thought she was very comely, especially in her nurse's uniform. He'd fantasised many times about ripping that off her. But he realised it must be her afternoon off as she was dressed in civvies. Jennifer had told him that her sister often came round, nagging at her to reform her ways. Bill didn't want Jennifer doing that; she might be a pain in the arse with her constant whining, but she had her uses. That was why he'd stopped by . . .

'I'll see you in a week or two,' Kathy told Jennifer. She stared coldly at Bill, until he shifted away from the doorway. She'd been at Jennifer's before when he'd turned up and brushed against her to cop a feel. He wasn't doing that again!

'You come to see me or her?' Jennifer barked, surging up out of the armchair in a fit of pique on noticing Bill giving her sister the eye.

Bill removed his hat and sauntered over to smooth Jenny's dark blond hair. It felt greasy beneath his palm. 'Don't be a stranger now . . .' he called out, riling Kathy, who banged the door shut.

Bill glanced at Jennifer with distaste. At the best of times she looked a mess but next to her pretty sister it was even more obvious. 'Fuck's sake, Jen, what you done to yerself?' He stared at her mucky lashes, nose wrinkled.

'Got fassy eye, ain't I,' Jennifer snapped. 'Probably

caught it off that last punter you brought me in. He stank to high heaven.'

'Get the bath in, shall I?' Bill suggested. He had a hole in his finances and could do with some money. A deal on some stolen goods he'd fenced had gone sour on him and he'd lost twenty quid.

'Got a few bob to lend me?' Jennifer asked sullenly.

'You must be joking, gel.' Bill snorted in disbelief. 'I was going to ask you for a sub.' He gave her rump a playful slap. 'Once you're done up to the nines, we'll go out and see if we can find you a punter who's two parts pissed and won't notice you look a bleedin' sight under the war paint. Then we'll roll him.'

Jennifer huffed dispiritedly, but she'd sooner risk fleecing a customer than have to service him, the way she felt. She'd taken laudanum on top of the whisky she'd drunk earlier and reckoned she might throw up.

CHAPTER FOUR

'What's happened to you?'

'Had a trip, that's all . . .'

Nick came further into the shop and looked about. It was obvious that the display shelves had been broken and he was pretty sure his mother hadn't done it falling over. Neither had she put a dent in the counter where the till drawer was, or chucked flowers about the place and overturned buckets of water. 'All this damage happened when you had that accident, did it?'

He strode back to his mother and tipped up her chin to get a better look at her bruised face. She was an attractive woman in her mid-forties, who kept herself trim and well groomed. 'Who's been in here?' he demanded.

'Not as many customers as I'd like, son, I can tell you that.' Lottie Raven's forced humour faded away. 'Oh, all right, might as well tell you. A bloke came in causing trouble. I told him to take a running jump and he didn't like it and had a paddy.'

'What's he taken? Did you recognise him?' Nick barked

out, feeling murderous. His mother's complexion had reddened in embarrassment.

Lottie shook her head, averting her eyes. Her son might be a cool character but, since he'd been a little lad, she'd known when his temper was up. The brute who'd turned nasty on her was one of Wes Silver's sidekicks. She didn't want Nick getting into a fight with the likes of him.

Nick had never outwardly blamed Wes for stealing his wife but Lottie had always thought it best the two men kept a distance from each other. She'd never forgive herself if her only child got hurt after she complained about something as silly as a drunk trying to touch her up. So Lottie was keeping quiet about Charlie Potter being a bloody nuisance.

The creep had been in before and asked her to go for a drink with him. Lottie knew she'd sooner dive under the nearest bus than have anything to do with the swine romantically. She'd never liked him thirty years ago when they'd been kids at school together, and she certainly couldn't stand him now they were middle-aged.

He'd come in the shop a short while ago, reeking of booze and rambling on about old times, then tried to slobber on her. Charlie thought because she was a war widow, and wore a bit of powder and lipstick, that she was hungry for a man in her life. Lottie could have laughed in his face at his arrogance. He thought she kept turning him down because she was jealous of his wife. Lottie just couldn't make the conceited fool believe that poor Ruby Potter had her heartfelt condolences, not her envy.

'Who was it, Mum?' Nick demanded, picking up an overturned bucket. 'You know I'm gonna find out eventually. You might just as well tell me.' He tried to wedge back in place a shelf hanging off its bracket.

'Just a randy gorilla, son,' Lottie said. 'No need for you to worry. I can look after meself. You know that.'

'He tried it on with you?' Nick sounded astonished. 'I thought he was after stealing from the till.'

'Well, don't sound so bleedin' surprised,' Lottie retorted. 'I admit I'm no spring chicken, but I ain't that long in the tooth either.'

'Have you reported him to the police?'

Lottie looked at her son as though he were mad.

'Didn't think so.' Nick grunted a mirthless laugh.

'He's long gone now,' Lottie said brightly. 'No need to fret. I gave him what for and a slap in the chops and he took off.'

Nick looked thoughtful. 'Has he been in before?'

Lottie mumbled something, disappearing to find a mop to soak up the water pooling on the lino.

'He wouldn't have come in just to lunge at you. I've heard that Wes has started sending thugs round local shops, fundraising for the Fascists. Or so he calls it. Sounds like a protection racket to me. I'll pay Wes a visit and find out . . .'

'He didn't ask for nuthin'! Well, he did, but he weren't getting that.' Lottie flung aside the mop and shot after her son as he headed for the door. 'I can tell you straight, Wes won't know about it . . .' She bit her lip, seeing her son's expression change.

'Something you haven't said, Mum?' Nick recognised his mother's evasiveness.

'Oh, all right, I did know him. It was Charlie Potter.'

In a way, Lottie felt relieved to get it off her chest. The lecherous brute might return to do more damage, or wait for her outside when she shut up shop in the evening. She'd far sooner that her son sorted things out with Charlie than pay a call on Wes and create an almighty ruckus. Lottie didn't want a feud now Nick was doing all right for himself. He'd bought the lease on this shop just six months ago and set her up in business. Although trade was slow, she was enjoying her little bit of wages, and being her own boss.

'Potter?' Nick scoffed. 'He's married and even if he weren't, you're way out of his league.'

'I've tried telling him that,' Lottie said drily. 'He never has listened . . .'

Nick gave his mother a quizzical look as she let slip that there was more to it than a solitary incident.

'It goes back a bit, to when we was at school together.' Lottie turned away, hoping Nick wouldn't press her for any more information.

'And?' Nick sounded obstinately interested.

'Charlie used to like me before me and your dad got together,' she grudgingly relayed. 'But I never had nothing to do with him. Then he got married to his first wife.' Lottie shook her head. 'She was all right, was Miriam, and seemed to keep him in check, but they'd only been married a few years when she died in the Spanish-flu epidemic after the Great War. Charlie dropped out of sight for a good while, then turned up again when you was about eighteen, I suppose.' She frowned at the memory. 'I bumped into him one day on Petticoat Lane and we did a bit of reminiscing. He told me he'd just got married again to a girl a lot younger than him, and was back living locally.' Lottie shrugged. 'Didn't see no more of him. Then a few months ago, out of the blue, he was passing the shop and spotted me inside. In he came, so I put the kettle on and we had a cuppa. Since then he's got it into his head that I've taken a fancy to him. I've never given him reason to think it.'

'I'll give you a hand to clear up,' Nick said. 'I'll get Blanche's old man to come over tomorrow and fix those broken shelves.'

'Thanks, son.' When Nick glanced at her grazed chin, Lottie touched the sore place, grimacing. 'Better go and have a gander in the mirror and see what sort of state I look.' She headed off towards the back of the shop, where there was a small washroom and kitchenette.

'Put the kettle on while you're out there,' Nick called out. 'I'll have a cup of tea before I shoot off.'

Lottie came out of the back room, teapot in hand. She'd suddenly realised that her son seemed to be taking things a bit too well, and that made her suspicious.

'Promise me you won't go stirring things up with Wes Silver; I've told you I'm all right. Probably it was me own fault for inviting Charlie in for a cup of tea.' She nodded at the fragments of glass. 'It was me broke the vase. I threw it at him to hurry him out of the door.' Lottie frowned. 'Have a word with Charlie if you like but don't make a meal out of it,' she said quietly. 'He'll take it out on his wife and kids if you do.' Following her son's nod of agreement, she added, 'Bastard didn't buy nuthin' either.'

'Not exactly the sort to buy his missus flowers, is he?' Nick pointed out sourly. 'Ain't got all day to wait for that tea,' he chivvied to get rid of his mother. He wanted to be left alone with his thoughts. He found the broom behind the counter and started sweeping.

Nick knew his mother was rattled by what had

happened and knowing she'd been upset made him livid. It had been just the two of them since he was five years old; his father had been one of the earliest casualties of the Great War. His mother had said she'd never wanted a second husband because no man would match up to the first. William Raven had volunteered to fight and gone off to France, never again to see his wife and son. Nick couldn't recall his father clearly, no matter how hard he strained his memory to do so. To him, William Raven was a man in a faded photo who'd got a brace of war medals. Nick had those things in a drawer and still looked at them from time to time. Charlie Potter must be nuts to think he could ever replace somebody like that in his mother's life. When Nick caught up with the bastard, he wouldn't know what had hit him . . .

'I don't want you anywhere near Charlie Potter.' David Goldstein was frowning. 'Can't another nurse do that district and see to his wife?' He took Kathy's arm as they approached the road to cross it.

They'd just emerged from the Rivoli Cinema on Whitechapel Road, where they'd enjoyed seeing Errol Flynn swashbuckling as Captain Blood and were now on their way to get a bite to eat in a nearby café.

It was the first time Kathy had seen her boyfriend in over a week as their work shifts had clashed. The incident at the Potters' house had been some time ago but it had stuck in Kathy's mind so she'd recounted to David a diluted version when they were queuing up earlier to watch the film. It had obviously stuck in his mind too for him to mention it again hours later.

'It's just Eunice and me covering the district, and she moans about taking over for me on my days off. The Potters couldn't afford a doctor for emergencies, let alone anything else.' Kathy added wryly: 'Getting pennies out of some of the poor souls for their maternity care is more than they can manage. Their husbands don't like shelling out to feed their own kids, never mind to pay for a midwife.' She had not told her boyfriend that Charlie had manhandled her. It would set the cat among the pigeons because David might confront Potter in his official capacity.

'Do you want me to put in an appearance?'

'No!' Kathy squeezed his arm. 'Ruby would never again trust me. She hates interference, even from the neighbours, and I gave my word not to blab about it.' She gave David a stern look. 'I let you in on it as I know you'll keep it to yourself.'

'Course I'll keep it to myself,' David reassured, dropping an arm about Kathy's shoulders. 'There are plenty of Ruby Potters about in the East End, I'm afraid. I couldn't help them all, even if I wanted to.' He sighed. 'They all lie about tripping and falling to cover up for the old man anyway. If they don't they get another pasting when he comes home.'

David had been walking the beat around Whitechapel for two years and had got to know the ways of the poorer residents. The women were rough but usually decent enough; their prime concern was pulling ends together because they were married to men who handed over a minimum of housekeeping to keep the rest of their wages for the pub. But Potter was a case apart. In a part-time capacity, working for Wes Silver, he was a hired thug and had served time for battery. He was well known to the constabulary at Leman Street where David was based.

'Don't have the best jobs in the world, do we, sweetheart?'

'I like my job!' Kathy protested with a chuckle, as she preceded David into the snug atmosphere of the café.

'Wish I could say the same,' David muttered, leading the way to a table.

CHAPTER FIVE

'Can you come quick, Nurse Finch? Me mum's in a right state and she's sent me to fetch yer.'

Kathy rubbed her bleary eyes, trying to focus on the panting boy hopping from foot to foot on her front step. Moments ago, she'd stumbled out of bed on hearing a furious hammering on the door. She'd been summoned before to deliver babies at night, but usually she opened up to find the woman's husband prowling the path, sucking on a roll-up. Having recognised Ruby's son, Kathy snapped to attention, gesturing he come in.

Beneath his threadbare coat, Peter's thin chest was pumping and he could barely draw enough breath for his next words: 'Me mum's bleeding and she says you're to come.' He clutched at his sides as though assaulted by a stitch. Pulling a pair of women's bloomers from his pocket he thrust them at Kathy. 'She reckoned you'd want to see,' he mumbled, turning about to hide his red-faced confusion.

Kathy examined the show of blood on grimy cotton that often heralded the start of labour. She'd been sure the Potter baby wasn't due for at least another month. It was the woman she'd visited yesterday in Flower and Dean Street who was fit to burst at any moment.

'Is your father at home getting things ready?' Kathy demanded, blinking at the clock on the wall; it was almost half-past one in the morning. She had a feeling, whether Charlie was at home or not, she would find the house in a terrible state with no smell of carbolic soap in the air to reassure her the place was ready for the birth.

Peter shook his head. 'Dunno where he is. Ain't seen him for a few days.'

At this hour in the morning, if Ruby was in premature labour, even a man such as Charlie Potter might be of assistance in boiling water and finding old newspapers to spread around. It was a primitive but effective way of protecting bedding and clearing up quickly afterwards. 'Go home, Peter, and stay with your mother. I'll be along as soon as I've got my things together.' Kathy could tell the lad was scared witless and on the point of bawling. 'Off you go now!' she ordered sharply, trying to snap him out of it. 'Quick as you can! Is there a neighbour you can call on to help with your mother until I arrive?'

Peter shrugged, bottom lip wobbling.

'Knock up the woman your mum is most friendly with and ask if she will help you. I promise I'll be along just a few minutes after you get back.'

Peter hared down the front path and turned towards home. Kathy immediately closed the door and rushed to get dressed. She felt a *frisson* of uneasiness. Ruby Potter had had two children. She obviously knew the signs and stages of labour. Also, Ruby would not invite interference

41

unless she had no choice. Kathy didn't think the woman would have sent her son along at this time of the night unless she felt it was a genuine emergency.

Kathy wheeled her bike out of the shed, secured her case on it, then set off energetically through quiet gas-lit streets, glistening with springtime frost. Nervous exhilaration always set in whenever she was summoned to deliver a baby. But this time she felt anxious too. She didn't relish the thought of Ruby being alone with just her young children at such a time, yet she knew it might be best if Charlie weren't present. The vile beast might refuse to co-operate or help in what he'd consider to be none of his business. Kathy sighed, her breath freezing into a white mist, which she pedalled through. She feared the baby wasn't Charlie's, and knew Ruby did too. The last thing Kathy wanted was a violent outburst when she and Ruby were vulnerable and preoccupied with bringing the poor little mite into the world.

Kathy increased speed, though her aching legs felt on fire. She remembered Ruby recounting that Ivy Tiller had delivered her two previous children. Despite her own rigorous schooling, Kathy accepted that such people as Ivy, skilled through experience rather than textbook training, could be of invaluable help in some cases. No midwife, no matter how adept, knew if things would go to plan when the time came. On those occasions, another pair of hands was greatly appreciated. Kathy hoped there was such a woman in the street where Ruby lived and that Peter might be able to find her.

On turning the corner of Fairclough Street, Kathy was relieved to see a woman hovering in the Potters' doorway, peering out. She recognised her as Mrs Mason, who lived on the end of the terrace of brick cottages.

The neighbour waved urgently as soon as she spotted Kathy wheeling into view.

'Thank goodness you're here, Nurse. She's delirious. Keeps cursing and telling me to get her mum, and I know she's been dead for years.' Peggy Mason retied her apron strings. She'd hurriedly dressed when Peter banged on her door and was feeling flustered.

Kathy parked her bike against the front wall, sped inside the house and into the back room, to find Ruby writhing on the bed. Little Pansy was crouched on the floor; her brother was clinging to his mother's hand in a sweet attempt to comfort her.

'Would you be able to stay and give a hand, Mrs Mason?' Kathy asked quickly. She judged the birth might not be far off and prayed she'd have time to carry out basic preparations to keep mother and baby safe from infection in this insanitary dump.

'For a while, I can,' the woman agreed with scant enthusiasm. 'But I've five kids of me own indoors and me husband's off to work down the railway yard at four. He'll expect something to eat before he sets off.'

Kathy bit back the retort that perhaps he might manage to get it for himself just this once as it was an emergency. But she knew these women were expected to act as skivvies to their menfolk. Her own father had held the same attitude and had stubbornly sat on his backside while her mother darted about like a blue-arsed fly.

'Put some water to boil, please, and gather up any newspapers and old linen that you can find. Clean rags, mind, if there are any,' Kathy added, optimistically. 'There should be a birth pack here somewhere. I left it last week . . .' Kathy whipped her attention to Ruby as she heard the woman whimper.

'Just going to have a wash, then I'll examine you properly, Mrs Potter,' Kathy soothed, gently testing Ruby's rigid abdomen with her fingers. 'Peter, would you take Pansy back to bed then do whatever Mrs Mason tells you to do to help?'

The boy leaped up, dragging Pansy by the hand and scurried into the hallway.

'Where's Charlie, Nurse Finch?' Ruby croaked.

'I don't know,' Kathy replied. 'Peter says he hasn't seen him in a while.'

'Can I push it out, Nurse?' Ruby let out a groan. She folded forward, panting, while Kathy tried to restrain her thrashing.

'No! Don't push just yet. Not till I've had a proper look.' Kathy lifted Ruby's nightdress, dreading to see any sign of a head just yet, before she'd even had a chance to have a scrub with carbolic. A satisfied sigh blew through her lips. 'There's time yet, Ruby, I know there is. You're doing fine, promise you are . . .'

Ruby's scalp ground into the pillow. 'Knew I should have let Ivy take care of me. She'd have let me push it out straight off. It's all your fault . . . interfering bitch,' she ranted in pain-induced hysteria. 'Where's Peter?' Again, Ruby struggled to sit up. 'Go and find your fucking father, Peter!' she bellowed. 'He'll be at the Railway Tavern, the bastard. He can do his duty by me even if he don't want the fucking kid.'

'It's way past closing time, Mrs Potter.' Kathy glanced at Mrs Mason, who'd stopped filling pots with water to gawp at the commotion.

'Nurse is doin' her best for you, luv.' Peggy approached the bed and patted at Ruby's hand, while mouthing at Kathy, 'She don't mean nuthin' by it, Nurse Finch. She's just . . . well, you know how we women are at times like this.'

Kathy did know. She'd had far worse abuse from women deranged by agonising labour. And poor Ruby had far more torturing her than the pain in her belly. Her thug of a husband was about to discover if the baby she had carried for eight months was his. 'Please see to boiling the water and finding clean rags,' Kathy ordered briskly, noticing Peggy standing idle.

Mrs Mason sent Kathy an old-fashioned look but returned to the stove.

'You are being a great help . . . thank you.' Kathy felt guilty for allowing anxiety to make her snappy. The last thing she wanted was the woman going off in a huff, leaving her with just Peter to give a hand. 'Are we able to get some more light?' Kathy glanced up at a solitary gas lamp shedding a weak glow over the disarray in the room.

'There's an oil lamp in our bedroom,' Peter volunteered. He'd left Pansy in there on the bed, but now trotted back to the room to get the light.

'Don't want no more fuckin' light; want me husband,' Ruby moaned, swiping a hand across her sweat-soaked brow.

'Told you she was delirious,' Peggy muttered sarcastically. She lived close enough to the Potters to have heard the commotion that blew up regularly between Ruby and Charlie. She'd seen the poor cow sporting her bruises too. If she'd not gleaned from local gossip why she was getting them, she'd have heard Charlie bawling out that his wife was a dirty scrubber.

'Do you know where Charlie Potter might be, Mrs Mason?' Kathy asked.

Peggy raised her eyebrows, pursing her lips. 'No I don't, and I don't want to neither. In my opinion, she's best off with the likes of him out the way. Neither use nor ornament, that one.' She turned back to the sink and filled more pots from the rusty cold tap, in readiness to lug them over to the stove.

'You're not an easy man to find . . .'

The drawling voice had issued from a nearby alleyway and Charlie Potter spun about to squint into blackness. He'd been drinking but was not as inebriated as he might have been. He and some workmates had spent the evening being entertained by a few dockside whores, so his rolling gait was due as much to being shagged out as drunk. 'Depends who's looking fer me whether I get meself found,' he snarled.

Nick stepped under the gas lamp so Potter could see him.

Charlie licked his lips, cocking his head to a belligerent angle.

'And what d'yer reckon you're playin' at then, Raven?'

'Reminding you of your manners around my mother,' Nick replied smoothly. 'Just a friendly warning: stay away from her.'

'Or what?' Charlie threw back his greasy greying head, roaring a laugh. 'What you gonna do, son? You couldn't even keep yer own missus satisfied. You had to let Wes see to her for you. Don't reckon you'll have much better luck in keeping me away from yer old mum. Not when Lottie likes me so much.'

Charlie swaggered closer to the younger man, top lip curling. He knew that Nick Raven was going up in the world and had a reputation for being able to handle

46

himself. But Charlie was confident his association with Wes Silver made other men give him a very wide berth. As this bloke's wife had regularly dropped her drawers for his boss until Wes gave the silly tart the old heave-ho, he reckoned Nick was a prat showing his face, let alone confronting him.

'Do yourself a favour 'n' piss off before I get right narked.' Charlie tried to saunter on by but found his path blocked.

'Yeah . . . I will . . . as soon as you tell me you're gonna stay well away from Lottie in future.'

Charlie sighed, took a look to the left as though to disguise the fact his right fist was coming up.

Nick stepped sideways and folded Charlie over with a thump in the guts before his opponent could hit him. He was an easy target: too old, too thick, too flabby. Charlie Potter was of a breed of men who thought their hard reputations, won a decade ago, protected them. But he was a nothing. In fact, Nick felt bad for having to do this to a bloke old enough to be his father. A moment later, when Charlie lumbered at him, swinging a right hook, Nick didn't feel so bad about flooring him with a couple of swift jabs.

Charlie collapsed onto his shoes and Nick tipped him off with faint disgust. Up close, he could smell the rank odour coming off him: stale sweat and cheap women. But he nevertheless dragged him to his vehicle and stuffed him onto the front seat. Despite it all, Potter was a family man and his mother felt sorry for Ruby, so he supposed he ought to drop him somewhere near home . . .

Nick leaned across Charlie to push open the car door and was about to put his boot against his passenger's comatose form to tip him out. He hesitated, having noticed Charlie's front door was open and a child was on the threshold silhouetted by a weak light. The little girl appeared to be pointing at him as though she knew her father was slumped beside him. Nick glared at Charlie, wishing he'd not bothered bringing the bastard back home to dump him on his own doorstep. He should have left him where he fell in the gutter. It seemed odd at this time of night but if the kid was waiting up for her old man to come home, he could hardly kick him onto the cobbles in front of her.

Cursing beneath his breath, Nick got out of the car and strode over, hoping to shoo her inside before offloading Charlie. She looked frozen standing there, white-faced, in just a thin cotton shift. A bloodcurdling scream met his approach as though somebody was being murdered. Nick whipped the perished child into his arms so he could get past and into the house.

'You a friend of Charlie's?' Peggy Mason gawped at the tall stranger hovering in the doorway, holding Pansy in his arms. She didn't think he could be pals with Charlie as he seemed flash and well-to-do. She had a brainwave. 'You a doctor, come to help?' Peggy was optimistically hoping to nip off home. She'd done her stint, she reckoned. She'd been at the Potters', running herself ragged, for two hours, and still no sign of an end to it all.

Nick shook his head, frowning. 'What's going on?' He put the child down but instinctively prevented her from getting any closer to the half-naked woman squawking on the bed.

Peggy knew an opportunity when she saw it: doctor or no doctor, friend of the family or no friend, she had a husband who had to get to work and would create merry hell unless she got him tea and toast before he left. Plus, her youngest was overdue for his feed and she could feel her breasts leaking milk.

'Somebody else here to help, Nurse. I'm just popping off to see to me little 'un so Bert can do his shift. I'll come back later if I can . . . all right . . . ?

Kathy had been crouching over Ruby, gripping her hands and calling encouragement but she straightened as her patient fell back, eyes closed. Pushing a blonde curl off her brow with the back of her wrist, Kathy gazed at the fair-haired man stationed by the door. 'Are you a friend of Mr Potter's?' she asked. 'Do you know where he is?' Her weariness was making her feel light-headed. But she had to keep strong and alert for Ruby. From her palpations, she knew the baby seemed small and was having a terrible job fighting its way into the world. She frowned at the fellow's silence, realising he was probably dazed from what he was witnessing.

Her patient let out a shattering groan and Kathy turned back, snapping over a shoulder at the newcomer, 'Oh, it doesn't matter who you are. Now Mrs Mason's gone, could you just make yourself useful? It is a matter of life and death, so please don't stand there like a spare part.' From experience, Kathy knew sometimes the best way to deal with people in shock was to boss them about. She'd done it before to good effect with zombie-like husbands. 'Peter is about somewhere and will take care of his sister, so just come here and help me, please.'

Nick stared at the scene in front of him feeling as though he'd stumbled into bedlam. An ashen-faced boy appeared, struggling with a heavy pail of water slopping about. For some reason, the expression of terror on the lad's face galvanised Nick into action and he took the bucket from him. 'Fuck's sake!' he growled.

Kathy swivelled on her knees, for some reason infuriated by hearing him say that. 'Yeah . . . precisely!' she forced through her gritting teeth before again urging Ruby to grip her hand and push.

CHAPTER SIX

Nick didn't know much about newborn babies. He'd never seen the tiny girl his wife had lost. It had all been done and dusted by the time he got home from work. He remembered thinking that Blanche had seemed to get over it quickly.

He did know that they all seemed to come out with their faces screwed up. He'd seen his cousin's triplets when they were a few days old. He glanced over the young nurse's shoulder as she gently tended the swaddled infant, laying it in a drawer that had been whipped out of the chest in the bedroom to serve as a makeshift crib.

He glanced at the grey-faced mother, then at the baby. The light was bad but Nick knew the kid didn't resemble Charlie either, squashed face or not. The tiny boy looked foreign. Thinking of Charlie made Nick realise he ought to check on him. He could still be unconscious; on the other hand, the weasel could've come to and done a runner rather than get drawn into this chaos. Nick had felt like doing the same thing, but then he wasn't the kid's father and shouldn't be here at all. He took another glance at the baby's sallow skin and almond-shaped eyes. Charlie wasn't the kid's father either, which meant the poor cow recovering on the bed had a bad time in front of her . . .

Kathy was aware of him leaving and turned her head to say thanks. She realised in all the commotion she'd not even asked him his name. But he'd moved too fast and had disappeared so the words withered on her lips. She wiped the poor little mite's mouth of vernix. He was small; perhaps about four pounds, although she'd not yet weighed him.

Once she was satisfied that the baby was settled, Kathy turned her attention back to Ruby. 'Nearly all done, Mrs Potter,' she encouraged. 'You've done the hard part, just the afterbirth to deal with now.'

'She all right?'

Kathy jumped at the masculine voice behind. 'I thought you'd gone.' She herded him towards the door to give Ruby some privacy. At close quarters, and having the time for a proper look at him in the lamplight, she noted he was far younger than Charlie Potter. He was a good-looking man, too, she realised.

She twisted him an apologetic smile. 'Sorry for shouting at you earlier, and thanks for helping.' She was aware he was watching her steadily. 'Are you a neighbour?' Kathy didn't think he could be: he looked too wholesome to be a local resident. But then you never knew who might have bad luck and end up renting a cheap place to doss until they got back on their feet. She'd grown up in a family who'd known its fair share of hard times.

'I'm acquainted with Charlie.' Nick's smile was barely there.

'Do you know where he is? His wife has been asking after him.'

They had whispered but Ruby had heard her husband mentioned and hauled her exhausted shoulders off the pillow.

'You've seen Charlie? Where is he?'

Nick shifted sideways to avoid two pairs of eyes. 'He's just outside. When he comes round, I'll bring him in.'

'He's been outside all this time?' Kathy demanded in astonishment, glancing at Ruby, who was grimacing in pain. Kathy knew the afterbirth was on its way and soon Ruby's labour would thankfully be over. 'Is he drunk?' she hissed.

'He's out like a light, all right,' Nick said, his eyes drawing to the half-empty pail by the sink. His lips twitched as he picked it up.

A moment later, he was back, dragging a dripping wet and dazed Charlie Potter by the arm. 'Say hello to the new arrival,' Nick muttered, shoving him towards the bed. He went out again, closing the door after him this time.

Nick wasn't sure why he was hanging around. He felt drained and hungry and ready for an hour or so's kip. Yet still he sat in his stationary car, smoking, an eye on the Potters' doorway. As his gaze travelled up over rooftops to a pale pink streak spanning the sky, he guessed it must be after five o'clock. Dawn was breaking on a new day but for a poor little kid and its mother there was nothing but trouble on the horizon.

She came out at last, carrying a small instrument case, closing the door carefully behind her. Nick got out of the car, striking a match and putting it to another cigarette.

'Want a lift anywhere?' She looked fit to drop but,

exhausted or not, she was pretty, no doubt about it, and young. 'You old enough to be doing a job like that?'

Kathy gave him a quizzical look but felt too spent to come back at him that she'd qualified a good six months ago as a midwife, and as an SRN before that, thank you very much. She chose to ignore his remark.

He'd been a great help, she realised, had done everything she'd asked and stayed discreetly out of the way when not needed. 'Didn't think you'd still be hanging around.' She glanced past at his big car parked at the kerb. And she'd thought he might be down on his luck!

Nick noticed the direction of her gaze. 'Can I give you a lift?' he asked again.

'I've got a bike, thanks.'

'How did Charlie take it all?' Nick asked casually, blowing smoke arrow straight into the air.

Kathy shrugged, just as evasive. She knew they were both skirting around the obvious in not mentioning that the child had Oriental features. Charlie hadn't said anything either. Once he'd digested the news that his wife had had her baby, the pig hadn't even glanced at the tiny boy for more than a second. He'd simply stomped off to sleep with the children in the other room. Kathy had wanted to stay with Ruby to protect her. But Ruby wanted her gone and had told her so. Besides, Kathy now felt too weary to be of any more practical help. But she'd impressed on Ruby that after a rest she'd be back in the afternoon to check on her and the new arrival. She'd spoken loudly enough to ensure that Mr Potter heard every word of it through the wall.

While Charlie had been drying off his wet face with savage arm swipes, Kathy had noticed blood on his cheek, even if his wife had not. Or perhaps Ruby had grown used to her husband coming in looking as though he'd been in a fight. A thought occurred to Kathy and she glanced up into the handsome face beside her. She couldn't spot anything other than it needed a razor.

'Did you bring Mr Potter back home? He looked as though he'd been in the wars.'

'Yeah, I brought him,' Nick said. For some reason, he didn't want this sweet little thing to know he'd whacked Charlie. 'If you're all right for getting home, I'll be off meself . . .'

Kathy suddenly frowned. While she'd been standing there, talking to him, cogitating on the night's events, she'd taken a look about for her bike. Now she swivelled agitatedly on the spot. 'My bike . . .' She pointed to the wall. 'I'm sure I left it just there.'

Nick grunted a laugh. 'And you expected it still to be there?'

What little colour was in Kathy's face ebbed away as she realised, stupidly, she'd rushed inside the house many hours ago without securing the bike with the padlock. The consequences of the theft were immediately worrying her. She'd never get around as quickly as she needed to without transport. She didn't think Dr Worth would like laying out for a new bike for her and she couldn't afford to buy one herself out of her wages.

'You've been hanging around here for a while,' she blurted. 'Did you see anybody take it?'

'There was a fellow cycling round the corner into Brunswick Street when I turned up in the early hours.' Nick recalled that little Pansy, as he now knew her name to be, had been pointing in the fellow's direction. No doubt she'd been disturbed by someone stealing the bike and had gone outside, feeling curious.

'Oh, damn! That was ages ago.' Kathy stamped a foot in angry frustration before pacing to and fro. People were stirring – a milkman was clattering about at the end of the grimy terrace – but she knew she'd have no luck getting answers from anybody, no matter how many doors she hammered on. Nobody round here ever grassed up neighbours for fear of retaliation. The selfish thief probably wouldn't even keep the damn thing but would sell or pawn it. She felt tears of exasperation prickling behind her eyelids.

'Come on . . . I'll take you home,' Nick said gently, propelling her by the arm towards his car. 'Don't matter how long you stay here in a paddy, you'll never find it now.'

Kathy felt lulled by the motion of the vehicle as soon as they set off. She had to jerk herself awake on hearing a male voice penetrating the fog in her mind.

'You're home.' Nick nodded at the detached Edwardian house that Dr Worth once had lived in and now used as his workplace. At the back of the building was a small single-storey annexe, which was offered to the practice nurse as living quarters.

'Oh . . . thanks . . . thanks.' Kathy struggled upright and grabbed her case from the floor. She hesitated. She still didn't know this man's name. She'd started drowsing almost as soon as they'd set off and now felt rather rude and awkward. He'd shown consideration in leaving her to sleep. 'Sorry . . . I should have asked your name earlier on.' She stuck out a small hand. 'I'm Katherine Finch.'

'And I'm Nicholas Raven.' Nick shook her outstretched fingers.

'Well . . . nice to meet you.' Kathy gave a bashful

laugh, withdrawing her hand. 'And sorry for ordering you about like that . . .'

'Don't worry, I'm glad you did, 'cos I didn't have a clue. Anyhow, I reckon I could put up with you ordering me about a bit more.'

His eyes travelled over her, making Kathy blush. She felt a tightening in her gut that would have been pleasant had it not been tinged with uneasiness.

Nicholas Raven might not be dark-haired and swarthy; in fact, despite his name his hair was lighter than her own and his complexion fair. Yet in a way, he reminded her of Bill Black as he had been when Jennifer first came to know him: all smooth talk and expensive stuff. It had turned out that beneath Bill's brash charm lurked a vile criminal and he'd caused dreadful trouble for the Finch family.

If the two men were similar in character, Kathy knew she'd never want to clap eyes on Nicholas Raven ever again. As he was acquainted with a thug like Charlie Potter, she reckoned she was wise to be suspicious of him.

'When's your day off?'

Kathy kept her eyes on her case, resting on her lap. 'Don't get one. Just an afternoon off and I'm on call all the time. When I get a bit of spare time I see my friend, David.'

'Right . . .' Nick said. He smiled as deep blue eyes peeked at him from beneath thick, dark lashes. He wasn't used to getting knocked back by women. But then . . . she was just a girl, no matter what she did for a living or how bloody hard she worked at it.

'Sorry . . . manners . . .' he drawled as she still sat there, no doubt waiting for him to open the car door for her. He got out, smiling, and did the honours with lazy courtesy.

Kathy knew he was mocking her and she felt her hackles rise. Having given his hand another businesslike shake, she added a curt smile. 'Thanks again for all your help. Goodbye.'

She went quickly up the side path of the imposing house, towards her apartment. She glanced at the shed. Normally, it would have been the first place she would go on arriving home. But there was no need this morning, with no bike to lock away. She'd have some explaining to do to Dr Worth when he arrived to open up the surgery later. So lost was she in her troubling thoughts that she didn't even hear the car pull away. She'd forgotten about Nicholas Raven already.

CHAPTER SEVEN

Wes Silver liked to think he was a debonair man. He also liked to think he was thoroughly English, so when someone called him a fat Yid, he wasn't happy. If he were a Hebrew, he wouldn't be collecting funds for Mosley's party, would he? In a surprisingly mild voice he put this argument to the man bleeding on the floor.

The fellow groaned, jack-knifing his knees to his chest to try to protect his groin from painful contact with Charlie Potter's boot again.

In Wes's mind, he wasn't Jewish and took great pains to impress that on people who cast aspersions just because his grandparents had been called Silverman. They'd attended the synagogue until the day they'd died, so he'd heard his mother say, but Wes considered that a minor detail and no concern of his.

His Irish tinker mother hadn't had a religious bone in her body. The Silvermans had failed to persuade her to get one in order to regularise her relationship with their son, so Abe Silverman had taken off to find a nice Yiddish wife when his son was three. But not before he'd had

Wesley circumcised. Wes hated him for that more than anything, but had believed his mum when she'd told him the crafty git had gone behind her back to get it done when she was out one day. So Wes had loved his mum till she abandoned him. Mary Dooley had gone back to Ireland to live in a caravan with her new fellow when Wes was sixteen. He'd found it hard to bear, although he wouldn't have gone with her even if she'd asked him to. So now, Wes hated the Jews and the Irish. In his eyes, Mosley was a hero and Wes was keen to act the disciple and spread the word.

'Now, Cyril,' Wes addressed the whimpering fellow clutching his balls. 'Why are we having to do this when life could be easy?'

'Ain't givin' you a penny for any causes,' the fellow bubbled through his torn lips. 'Ain't political, am I? Don't believe in nuthin' except putting grub on me kids' plates.'

'Good man.' Wes nodded, strolling to and fro. 'Trouble is it's not what I want to hear, see. 'Cos I *am* political and I *do* believe very strongly in getting all the foreign parasites out of the country. Now I find your attitude troubling, you being a family man with a business to run. You know the Jews are trying to take over everywhere, don't you?' He broke off as a bell clattered and a woman holding two young boys by the hands started to enter the shop. She wasn't a customer, she was the wife of the battered shopkeeper.

'Ah, Mrs Butler . . . glad you're back, dear.' Politely, Wes removed his homburg and dropped it on the counter. 'I've been explaining to your husband how you've been actively supporting the cause but he thinks I'm lying.'

Mabel Butler turned white and shoved her kids back outside the door in an attempt to protect them. She

60

ignored her groaning husband and rushed to the till, opening it and thrusting two pound notes at Wes.

'See? Easy as that, Cyril,' Wes said, folding the money. 'Now I could have taken it, couldn't I? But I don't steal. You remember that in case you're feeling daft enough to accuse me of any such nonsense to the boys in blue.'

'Wouldn't ever do that, Mr Silver,' Mabel assured hoarsely. 'Never, ever . . .'

'That's the spirit,' Wes said, patting her arm. 'It's a shame your husband hasn't your sense or good manners. Called me a fat Yid, he did; now that's not nice, is it?'

Mabel's head quivered in denial and she poisoned her prone husband with a darting glance.

'I live well, so I'm well built.' Wes used both hands to pat his girth. 'People get jealous. You jealous of me, Cyril?' Wes's humour had evaporated as quickly as it had fomented. He seemed keen to have an answer and the air of menace in the shop strengthened.

Charlie knew his boss liked nothing better than to be envied. If the fellow on the floor didn't come up with the right answer, he'd have to stamp on his privates again.

'You must be joking.' Cyril managed a sneer. He might have been down but he wasn't yet out. 'Never in me life want to be anything like you . . .'

Charlie sighed. He didn't even have to look at his boss for confirmation, he just swung his boot.

Wes nodded at the two lads dodging to and fro to peer in through the drapery display in the window. 'Nice kids.' He raised his voice to be heard over the coughing groan coming from Cyril Butler, rolling on the floor. 'You look after them now, won't you . . .?'

Charlie Potter nodded sagely, endorsing his boss's advice, crossing his arms over his chest.

'Well, come on, Charlie . . . places to go . . . people to see,' Wes chivvied playfully. He picked up his hat from the counter, tipping it at Mabel Butler before plonking it back on his sleek black head.

'How's your missus?' Wes asked as they walked off towards the greengrocer's shop on the corner. Within the premises was another local merchant who had felt disinclined to hand over his contribution to fund party politics, thus necessitating Wes arriving in person to explain to him the gravity of the situation. 'Saw your Ruby not so long ago and she looked a bit peaky, I thought. Hope everything's all right at home, son.' Wes gazed up at his sidekick's tense profile, noticing the lines on his face and the grey at his temples. Charlie was some four inches taller than he was and six years older. Nevertheless, Wes liked to think he was his superior in every way.

'She's dropped the nipper already,' Charlie muttered, keeping his eyes on passing traffic.

'Yeah?' Wes waited expectantly.

'Bleedin' kids . . .' Charlie grunted, stuffing his hands in his pockets. 'Fuckin' pain in the arse . . .'

'Well, that's one way to make sure you don't get her up the duff in future, Charlie.' Wes smirked. 'Either that or take your business elsewhere when you're horny, son.'

Charlie tightened his lips. It wasn't the first time his boss had implied his wife was a brass. Although Charlie knew Ruby had been on the game before they met, he liked to think she'd laid off the profession since.

The fact that there was a little bastard at home who had yellow skin and slitted eyes naturally knocked sideways that fond notion. Charlie had knocked Ruby sideways when he'd first found out she was expecting. He could work out easily enough that he'd been locked up when she'd got herself in the family way again. What he couldn't understand was why she hadn't got rid of it. Soon after Pansy's birth his wife had got pregnant. She'd not told him how she'd stopped her belly bloating but he'd guessed she'd done a job on herself. This time she'd kept the kid, yet she must have known that when he got out of prison he'd go berserk. The idea that Ruby might not be as frightened of him as he liked to believe had enraged Charlie almost as much as the image of her opening her legs for a Chinaman while he'd been wanking on a prison bunk.

She'd wailed at him she'd been so skint without his wages coming in that she'd had to do whatever she could to earn a few bob to feed them all. It was probably true, but the excuse cut no ice with Charlie. He'd simply clumped her again and would've kept on but for Peter getting in from school and jumping on his back, howling. So he'd had to chastise his son with his fists as well. And that was a shame because he liked the boy. Peter sometimes reminded him of himself at that age: mouthy and brave . . .

'So . . . what is it, then? Boy or gel? Look like you, do it?'

His boss's jolly questions interrupted Charlie's thoughts, putting his teeth on edge.

Wes already knew the answers to his questions, but he liked to wind Charlie up. Ruby's new kid looked Chinese, so he'd heard. Wes was relishing the irony of it all. They were out and about canvassing to collect for the Fascist Party and rid the country of immigrants and there was Charlie with a Chinese baby under his roof. In a couple of years' time, it would be calling him Dad. Wes slanted a contemptuous look at his henchman but felt quite sorry for him. Charlie would be a laughing stock amongst his workmates on the dock if he let the cow get away with it.

'Up 'n' about again, is she, Charlie?' Wes prodded. 'Don't do to let women get away with shirking for too long. I had my May back on her feet as soon as the midwife walked out the front door. Get lazy, see, don't they, if you don't watch 'em . . .'

It was Charlie's turn to hide a snigger. He knew that Wes's old woman ran rings round him. If May wanted to sit on her fat arse all day long then that's what she did. Wes was just happy his wife had a brain on her so the two of them could share it.

'In we go then . . .' Wes lilted out as they came abreast of the greengrocery display piled up outside the shop. 'Another nonce, Charlie, who needs telling that all the immigrants are taking our jobs and our women. What bloke's gonna put up with a foreigner humping his wife . . . eh?' Wes's crafty glance revealed that he'd successfully touched a nerve about Ruby's Chinaman. Sometimes, Wes felt bad about tormenting his sidekick but he had to carry on because it made Charlie so much better at doing his job.

Charlie burst in through the doorway, sending boxes of apples flying, making the greengrocer spin about at the commotion. The last thing the fellow saw before his face was rammed onto the wooden counter was Charlie's snarl.

Joyce Groves raised herself by digging an elbow into the feather pillow, while twirling her champagne flute by its stem. 'What you doin'?' she asked. She eyed the broad back of the man sitting on the edge of the bed. Reaching out lazy fingers, she trailed them to and fro over ridges of muscle.

'Making sure you don't get pregnant,' Nick said as he took the French letter out of the packet and put it on. Joyce put her glass of champagne down on the bedside table and flopped onto her back. Nick turned, sinking back onto the mattress, then rolled to drag her into his arms. He covered her in a swift precise movement and kissed her. Immediately, Joyce wound her arms around his neck, hooking her calves over his.

'Looking after you, see,' Nick growled against her hot eager mouth. 'You want to show me how grateful you are for that?'

Joyce wasn't grateful but she bucked and squirmed as he started to arouse her and soon she forgot to feel annoyed that he might have rumbled her little game.

Afterwards, she lay back, luxuriating in sensual lethargy, and thought she could grow used to this life . . . expensive hotels and fancy food and drink. Nick had treated her to a night in a West End hotel and they'd seen a show and had a fantastic dinner of lobster and fillet steak. She glanced at the breakfast tray that held the remnants of their meal of eggs and smoked haddock, and another half-empty bottle of champagne. She felt quite like a princess, and she wanted her prince to make it a permanent state of affairs. She didn't want to go back to working in a greasy-spoon café that catered for workmen in overalls who pinched her backside every time she walked past.

She watched Nick through half-closed eyelids as he strolled to the window to stare at the street scene while fixing his tie. He'd been up and about as soon as his passion was again spent. The strength of his lovemaking this morning had left a pleasant ache throbbing at the apex of her thighs and she stretched in cat-like contentment against the silky sheets, thinking.

She knew the reason Nick used johnnies was to protect himself rather than her. She'd heard that his wife had used the trick of getting herself pregnant to get a ring on her finger. Joyce had hoped to use the same ploy. But it seemed he wasn't going to fall for it second time around – more was the pity.

She'd liked Nick since she'd been a school kid. He might be seven years older than she, but she'd noticed him right from the start. She knew he hadn't been aware she existed, but now she was old enough – and attractive enough – to put herself in his way, she was about to make sure that changed.

'I'm going to settle the shot,' Nick said, turning about and digging in his trouser pocket for a packet of cigarettes. 'Give you an hour or so to get yourself decent . . .' he raised a mocking eyebrow at her dishevelled appearance, 'then we'll head back home.'

Joyce twisted onto her belly, an ardent look slanting from beneath her lashes. 'Sure you don't want to stay another night? I'll show you I'm not decent at all.'

'Got business to get to.' Nick shrugged into his suit jacket. 'Look lively, Joyce,' he added briskly, 'or you'll be catching the bus back to Whitechapel.' He smiled but Joyce didn't. She'd been seeing him for a few weeks now and knew he wasn't joking. He'd walked out on her before when she'd angled to keep his company for longer than he was prepared to allow her to have it.

In a short while, Joyce had learned that Nick Raven

could be a cold man, despite the fire in his loins. And if he were not so generous in bed and out of it, she'd think he really didn't like women very much.

'Let's see how the little fellow's doing,' Kathy said, picking up the wrapped bundle and looking into small closed features. Ruby's baby was now a fortnight old and had not yet put on any weight. His complexion was smoother and it was clear he was a handsome child, despite his frailty. He had a mop of neat black hair and long ebony eyelashes.

When Kathy had arrived at the Potters', she was relieved to find Charlie was out. The last time she'd come on a postnatal visit, he'd been home and had sat in the chair watching her from beneath his brows with a mean expression. This afternoon, little Pansy had opened the door to her and nodded solemnly in answer to Kathy's question about whether she was helping her mum to look after her new little brother.

'Have you named him yet, Mrs Potter?' Kathy asked, laying the boy down so she could unwrap the swaddling layers of threadbare sheeting and examine him. He was wet but, that apart, seemed clean and cared for as he had on her previous visits.

'Might call him Paul . . . I like names beginning with P so they go with Potter,' Ruby mumbled.

Kathy smiled, thinking Charlie probably held no such fondness for that theory this time round.

'Have you clean nappies? He needs changing.' Kathy glanced about the messy room.

Without her mother instructing her to do so, Pansy got up and fetched a scrap of towelling from a chair back where it had been hanging to air.

Thankfully, it was dry, and Kathy cleaned the child's bottom and powdered it, then fastened the square of cloth around his hips.

'Have you had any help from family?' Kathy asked. She knew that Ruby's own mother had passed on as Mrs Mason had brought up the subject on the day the little boy had been born. But Kathy recalled that Ruby had once mentioned her mother-in-law lived in the locality.

'Nobody's been over,' Ruby said sourly.

Kathy nibbled her lower lip. She guessed people were shunning Ruby because she'd been caught out committing adultery. 'Perhaps in a few months' time, when things settle down,' she said kindly.

'Things ain't gonna settle down, are they?' Ruby laughed bitterly, nodding at the baby. 'Let's face it, he ain't gonna look any different in a week, or a year, is he?'

'And how have you been?' Kathy changed the subject, sticking to routine, although she was feeling frustrated at being unable to help Ruby in her predicament. 'Are you breast-feeding without trouble?'

'Got an abscess, I think,' Ruby muttered. 'It feels hot and painful. I'll bind meself up to stop the milk.'

'Let me see . . .' Kathy gently examined the inflamed skin Ruby had exposed. 'There's no need to stop feeding. We can sort that out with—'

'Don't want nuthin'. Gonna put him on the bottle.'

Kathy glanced at the woman's averted face and guessed she was repeating what her husband had told her to say.

'Perhaps you should tell your husband how much formula milk costs,' Kathy said briskly. The mean wretch wouldn't want his wife spending on anything she could get free from her own body.

'Get yer bike back, did yer?' Ruby asked, quickly buttoning up her blouse.

'Doubt I'll see that again. I came on the bus today. But I hope my boss will sort something out for me.' Kathy had got a ticking-off over losing the vehicle, so she wasn't feeling optimistic about a replacement bike being soon forthcoming from Dr Worth.

'Trouble all round that night, weren't it? And it ain't done yet,' Ruby said gloomily. She glanced at the baby, sleeping soundly. 'Poor little mite don't know what he's in for . . .'

CHAPTER EIGHT

'Still knocking about with that Yid copper, are you?'

Eddie Finch barked the question at his daughter before she'd even got her coat off. He knew that Kathy had been at school with David Goldstein, but since he'd found out from his wife a few months back that they'd become romantically involved, Eddie had taken violently against David.

'I've told you, Dad, we're just good friends,' Kathy answered wearily, shrugging out of her mac. To shut him up constantly harping on over it, Kathy had decided to make out that her relationship with David was platonic. She wished now she'd kept the news to herself when her mother had asked if she'd yet found herself a nice young man to take her out when she got time off from the surgery.

'You make sure it stays "just friends".' Eddie folded the paper he'd pinned beneath his elbows while studying the football results at the parlour table. ''Cos I don't want no rozzers in my family, and I don't want no Jews either.'

'Well, I doubt you'll have any because David's parents aren't any keener on me than you are on him,' Kathy announced, tempted to add that Eddie's chosen career handling stolen goods wouldn't improve their attitude towards her, if ever they – or David, for that matter – found out about it.

Eddie's jaw dropped and the chair he'd rocked onto its back legs thumped down. It had never occurred to him that his daughter – the one he was proud of – might be unwelcome anywhere. 'They'd be fucking lucky to have you!' he snapped, outraged. 'Who'd they think they are? Bleedin' royalty?'

Despite herself, Kathy was touched by her father's championship, so she gave him a rueful smile. She had often felt like saying something similar to her boyfriend about his bigoted parents. Of course, hers – her father especially – were equally prejudiced, but still, Kathy felt miffed that Mr and Mrs Goldstein didn't want their son seeing her.

She was also annoyed with David for making out they had split up. He seemed eager to keep on the right side of his wealthy parents, although he insisted he was only resorting to fibs for an easy life. Kathy was equally fed up with the nagging she got, but he was telling a dirty big lie, whereas she was using little white ones to deflect her folks' criticism.

He'd told Kathy he'd stuck to his guns and joined the police force rather than let his father browbeat him into studying accountancy to deal with the family firm's books. In Kathy's eyes, it begged the question why he'd not felt so passionately about stopping his mum and dad dictating his love life.

'Give the girl a chance to sit down and have a cup of

tea before you start on her, will you?' Winifred Finch glared over her bony shoulder at her husband while putting the kettle on the gas stove. She beckoned Kathy into the kitchen, away from Eddie, who had now gone to mooch about in the front parlour.

Winnie would sooner Kathy settled down with a nice Christian boy so they could get married at the local church. But as long as the fellow her lovely daughter chose treated her right, and had a bit of money and a job, then he was halfway to being acceptable as a future son-in-law as far as Winifred was concerned. Besides, her husband should give praise where it was due instead of finding fault. In Kathy at least they had one child who wasn't an embarrassment but a positive reason to boast.

It got Winnie's goat that the neighbours were constantly tattling at her expense because she'd got two trouble-some kids. Kathy's twin had been gone from home for five years yet the nosy cow next door still tried to bring Winnie's wayward daughter into any conversation so she could gloat. Yet Winnie knew for a fact that Cissy Dickens' son had turned queer in the army.

'Your father's right, though, Kathy,' Winnie muttered beneath her breath so her husband wouldn't know she agreed with anything he said. 'There ain't a family anywhere that's too good for you to fit in it. You remember that.' She gave a crisp nod.

'It's just the religion thing, Mum,' Kathy explained. 'I expect David's people are quite nice on the whole.'

'Yeah . . . and so are we,' Winnie announced more vocally.

Kathy raised her eyes heavenwards, wishing that were true so she could voice an endorsement.

72

Winifred was aware of her daughter's wry grimace, and what prompted it. But she held her tongue, wanting to savour this visit from Kathy. She looked forward to seeing her and wished her daughter would come over more often to relieve the monotony of her depressing life. But she accepted Kathy worked long hours in a demanding profession that gave her little free time.

Rich Jews with their own business or not, the Goldsteins wouldn't find a girl to give them lovelier grandkids. Winnie glanced at her daughter's perfect profile: creamy complexion and golden hair. Neither required the artifice of powder or bleach. Kathy was a beauty with a smashing character; she'd always been one of the nicest, prettiest girls in the neighbourhood, even as a child. Winnie knew that wasn't just her being biased; folk had always commented on Kathy's attractive nature and looks. Her daughter had been raised in an area where hardship sullied people, turning them mean and selfish, yet her Kathy had risen above it to shine like a jewel. Winnie spontaneously showed her pride and appreciation by giving Kathy a brief peck on the cheek.

'How have you been, Mum?' Kathy quickly enquired at the rare and unexpected show of affection. She repeated her question with more volume as Winifred simply clattered the tea things on the wooden draining board.

'Same as ever,' Winnie muttered eventually. 'Nothing much changes here, love; wish it bleedin' did.' She peered past her daughter into the parlour as her husband, bored with dawdling about, shouted he wasn't having tea, he was off out.

Kathy realised her mother's doleful tone hinted at

Tom still causing problems. Her brother was Eddie's favourite, although the boy seemed to be turning into a right tyke. Kathy avoided discussing him in her father's hearing because he wouldn't hear a word against Tom. His affected air of obliviousness to Tom's mischief then set Winifred off. The last time Kathy had come over to Islington on a visit, she'd given up trying to referee her parents' argument and had got up and gone home, leaving them to it.

'Where's Tom?' Kathy asked, sipping tea. The house was too quiet for her young brother to be in his room. When indoors, he would dash down to see her as soon as he heard her arrive.

'Gawd knows.' Winnie shrugged dispiritedly. 'He's probably messing about with those sods in Campbell Road, just to rile me.' Now her husband had vacated the space, Winnie picked up her cup and saucer and shuffled through into the parlour, sitting down at the small square table. 'Your brother's on the road to ruin, Kathy, same as the other one.' Following that ominous announcement, Winnie cradled her cup between her palms, gazing into the weak brew. 'Your father don't seem willing or capable of doing nuthin' to stop it. Tom don't listen to a word I tell him . . . not any more.' She lifted her cup and gulped, rattling it back onto the saucer. 'You know he hasn't done so since all that bad business years ago.' Winnie lifted an edge of her pinny to dab at her glistening eyes.

Kathy knew exactly what her mother meant by 'all that bad business'. She also knew the person her mother blamed for setting in motion the disaster: Jennifer. That's why her sister's name was taboo and she was only ever referred to as 'the other one', if mention were made of her at all. It was as though her twin had ceased to exist.

Jennifer had done wrong, Kathy would be the first to admit that. But what had happened hadn't wholly been her fault. Eddie and Winnie had to take their share of the blame but neither of them seemed to have the courage to lance that particular boil. In Kathy's opinion, until they did the wound in the Finch family would never heal.

'I like your hair shorter.' Winnie sniffed back tears. Fondly, she leaned forward to touch a blonde curl resting on Kathy's cheek as her daughter took the chair opposite at the table.

'Keeps it neater under the cap when it's in a bob,' Kathy said.

'Well . . . it looks nice.' Winnie stirred her tea and a silence developed between them.

Kathy took a deep breath, summoning up courage. 'About Jennifer, Mum . . .' she blurted out awkwardly.

'We don't mention that name, you know that, miss.' Winnie's startled glance leaped to the door as though she imagined Eddie might have overheard and would burst in, ranting and raving.

Kathy toyed with her spoon. Too many times she'd backed down, not wanting to cause upset. But she'd cleared the first hurdle in mentioning Jennifer. The wistful look in her twin's eyes when she'd seen her a few weeks ago still haunted Kathy. She was sure it was Jennifer's greatest wish to be reconciled with her mother, if not her father. In Kathy's opinion, the savage punishments their father had meted out had driven bad into Jennifer rather than out of her. Kathy knew one of the reasons her sister had run off with Bill Black was to escape her father's fists. But the incentive of a meeting with Winnie might finally motivate Jennifer into making changes in her miserable life.

'I saw Jenny a week ago. I've seen her a few times, Mum, and she asked how you were all keeping . . .'

Winnie shot upright, her face whitening in shock and anger. 'I'm gonna pretend I didn't hear that,' she croaked. 'So don't you say no more. Yer father always asks what we talked about after you've gone. Don't go putting me in a position where I'm to lie to cover up.' She scrubbed her hands nervously on her pinafore.

Winifred hadn't spoken to her other daughter for five years. She'd spotted her on a couple of occasions in the distance but had managed to hurry in the opposite direction, avoiding any awkwardness. Now Winnie wondered if she would recognise Kathy's twin if she walked past her in the street.

'I know she'd like to see you, Mum,' Kathy continued determinedly. 'I think it might get her back on track.'

'Ain't nothing gonna put that one back on track,' Winnie hissed, finger quivering close to Kathy's nose. 'She's too far gone . . . has been fer years . . .'

'How d'you know that if you've not spoken to her?' Kathy asked, keen to keep the dialogue going. 'If you just see her for half an hour and have a talk, I'm sure it'd help her.'

'Won't help me, though, will it, when yer father finds out and goes bonkers? Didn't help Tom, did it, when the little cow went off with Bill Black and all hell broke loose?' Winnie's voice had risen hysterically and she'd grown so rigid she teetered on her tiptoes.

Kathy let her hand drop back to the table when Winnie dodged away from her comforting fingers.

'Don't just write Jennifer off, Mum . . . please. She's our flesh and blood.'

It was as though Kathy's appeal went unheard. Winnie had turned her back on her but muffled sniffling was audible. Kathy sighed, knowing she was defeated for now. Her mother's fears about Eddie's reaction were valid. If her father discovered that she was in touch with her disgraced twin, Kathy suspected she, too, would be banished from darkening his doorstep. She sipped luke-warm tea, wondering why she persevered with trying to preserve her family ties when it all seemed so hope-less. But some sense of duty and affection sent her regularly to visit her parents, and to check on Jennifer. Kathy genuinely cared about them all – Tom especially – despite the fact that at times she felt they were all driving her mad.

'Sorry, Mum . . . shouldn't have gone on about it like that.' Slowly, Kathy pushed herself upright to put an arm about her mother's shaking shoulders.

Winnie elbowed herself free. 'I'll fetch us some biscuits and put the kettle on again.' She had her pina-fore up, dabbing her eyes. Behind it she attempted to sound jolly. 'Got some custard creams and a few bour-bons, if yer father's left us a few in the barrel, that is . . . greedy pig . . .' Winnie hurried away into the kitchen and automatically thrust the kettle under the squeaking tap. But her mind was lively with distressing memories as she added fresh tea leaves to those stewing in the pot.

When barely fifteen years old, Kathy's twin had begun acting like a little tart, showing them up something rotten. She had been slyly seeing Bill Black despite him being ten years older than she was, and her father's business partner. The dreadful affair had resulted in her running off to live with Bill in Lambeth, stealing all her father's savings to take with her. The resultant feud between Bill and Eddie had had devastating consequences for them all. But it was the fact that Tom had got drawn into it that saddened Winifred the most. She was sure that the episode had sent her son off the rails . . .

'It's all right, Mum, don't bother making another cuppa for me . . . I'm off out.'

'You're not going already?' Winnie spun about, her lined features crumpling in disappointment. 'You've only just got here, Kathy,' she said plaintively. 'Can't you catch a later bus back to the East End?'

'I'm not going home, Mum,' Kathy reassured quickly, hoping her mother didn't think she'd go off in a huff because they'd almost quarrelled. 'I thought I'd take a walk up the road and see if I can find Tom. I haven't spoken to him for a while. He was out last time I came over.'

'Oh . . . if you want to then.' Winnie would sooner keep her daughter's company, but at least Kathy wasn't yet heading home. 'If you do catch up with him, give him a talking to, will you, dear? He might listen to you,' Winnie added optimistically. 'Tell him his tea's ready. It might bring him home, if his belly's grumbling.'

Kathy buttoned her coat as she walked around the corner, then plunged her chilly hands into her pockets. It was late April – Easter had come and gone – yet the weather was still cold. In the mornings, when off to do her rounds, she'd stand at the bus stop, stamping her frozen feet to try to warm them. At least when she'd had her bike she'd not noticed the chill: the exertion of pedalling had soon got her circulation going . . .

Kathy glanced up on hearing someone hail her. She raised a hand to Cissy Dickens, swinging a shopping bag, no doubt on her way home with a few groceries. The woman had stopped expectantly on the opposite pavement but Kathy kept on walking, knowing it was gossip she was after.

Her mother was right to suspect the inquisitiveness of her neighbours. Local women with their heads together had been a common sight when Kathy had been living at home. They'd had plenty of grist for the mill from her family. The noise of fights and arguments had issued forth with depressing regularity from the Finch household. But then Cissy often let fly with pots and pans and choice names when her old man stumbled in drunk Sunday dinnertimes.

Her father tippled only infrequently and usually at home. Winnie's sour explanation had been that her husband was too mean to add to the brewery's profit, and besides, he had no friends to go to the pub with. Considering the amount of local families who'd been impoverished by alcohol, Kathy reckoned her mother should give thanks for small mercies on that score.

Kathy carried on into Paddington Street, heading in the direction of Campbell Road. There'd been no sign yet of Tom and she expected to find him, as her mother had predicted, in the Bunk, as it was commonly known. It was also known – with good reason – as the worst street in north London, due to its reputation for housing all manner of rogues and vagabonds needing a cheap place to doss.

Not all of the Bunk's residents were passing through, though; some had lived in the street for a number of years. Kathy knew many of them were good souls who had very little but willingly went short to help others. In the distance she could see just such a person. She immediately broke into a jog, waving, because she'd not seen Matilda Keiver in a long while and it looked as though the woman was about to disappear indoors and deny her the chance of a chat.

CHAPTER NINE

'Hello, Mrs Keiver, how are you doing?' Kathy called breathlessly, coming to a halt by some iron railings fronting a tenement house.

The road in which her parents lived was hardly posh but it was a definite step up on the neighbourhood in which Kathy now found herself. Campbell Road was wide, stretching away into the distance in one direction as far as the eye could see. Looking the other way, Kathy could see a bus crossing the junction with Seven Sisters Road. The tall houses flanking the street were much of a muchness whichever side of Paddington Street they occupied. The majority received little maintenance from their landlords, although the rent collectors called round regularly. Some properties no longer had front doors, just gaping openings hinting at the decay within. Poor wretches desperate to keep warm in winter used anything to hand as firewood, including the fixtures and fittings. Years ago, Kathy had visited Mrs Keiver's daughter Lucy at home in this very house and therefore knew how dilapidated were the rooms.

'Not seen you in a long while, luv.' Matilda's face split in a grin as she emerged again from the house, blinking, to join Kathy in the weak spring sunshine. 'I can see you're doing all right fer yourself, then. Over in Islington to see yer mum, are you?' The middle-aged woman gave Kathy's wholesome appearance a top-to-toe squint.

Kathy sensed the woman's beady blue eyes assessing her, and knew Matilda was busily working things out in her mind. Matilda Keiver was a plain speaker and didn't make apologies for it.

'So . . . what you doing round in the Bunk, Kathy?' Matilda asked. 'After your brother, are you? I know Winnie would sooner he stayed clear of the street and all us bad influences.' She pulled a comical face, mock-affronted.

Matilda did indeed know that Winifred Finch had always thought herself better than the Bunk's residents, but, although they'd had their differences in the past, Matilda didn't hold the woman's attitude against her. She knew that the Finches had had a rough ride over the years, just as she had herself. Matilda had a feeling Winnie and Eddie might have more trouble in store if their son didn't straighten himself out.

'I am after Tom. Seen him, have you, Mrs Keiver?'

'He was about earlier, larking about with Davy Wright.' She glanced towards the Wrights' house further up the street. At present there was nobody around outside. 'I know your mum don't like him knocking about with Davy.' Matilda pulled a face. 'Gotta say, I'm with her on that one. I've told Davy he's got a bit too big for his boots lately.'

'Been showing off, has he?' Kathy recalled that Davy had been a bit of a cocky lad. He came from a very poor family, even by Bunk standards. Despite his cheekiness, she'd always found him likeable.

'Yeah, he's showing off all right.' Matilda sighed. 'Not that I ever had no boys to bring up, but I know that's how lads get once they get the urge to find a girl.' She frowned. 'Got caught smashing the winders round in the Lennox Road mission hall. Police got called and he got took to court but don't seem to have learned him a lesson. Still swaggering about, he is.' Matilda narrowed her eyes, wedging some stray auburn locks into the coil on top of her head. 'Feel sorry for his mum, more'n anything. Polly's still pulling that handcart round the streets to try and make ends meet by selling a bit of soda and soap. You'd think Davy would give a hand 'stead of causing trouble for her.' Matilda crossed her arms over her chest. 'If I was Polly Wright, I'd send the little sod off to the East End to live with his father. Let Stan have a go at controlling Davy; see how he likes it.'

Kathy knew that Davy was the youngest of five boys. She knew too that their father, Stan, had run out on the family years ago to set up with another woman.

Tough tale that it was, and sorry as Kathy felt for Davy's mum, she didn't contemplate the Wrights' misfortune for long; there were plenty of cases of similar hardship in the Bunk. Kathy was more concerned with whether her brother might be mixed up in it all.

'Mum hasn't said anything about it to me . . .'

'Don't think your Tom was involved. Or if he was he kept hisself well hid. Just a little crowd of lads from round here got rounded up.'

'I expect Davy will straighten out when he gets a job.' Kathy was relieved she'd nothing to recount – or conceal – when she got back to her mother.

'Reckon Davy already has left school, even if he shouldn't have done. He hangs about in the street most of the day and you know what they say about idle hands . . .' Matilda arched her eyebrows in emphasis. 'Polly was trying to sort him out a part-time job now he's turned thirteen.' Matilda shook her head. 'She's got a task on her hands the way the unemployment is.'

'Are Davy's brothers still about?'

Matilda shook her head. 'Samuel and Douglas ended up inside for robbery. The other two . . . last I heard, they'd hightailed it up North to find jobs as nuthin' doing round here. Can't see that working out for 'em, being as the Jarrow lads are fighting empty bellies.' Matilda leaned back against the railings, smiling at Kathy. 'Enough about the boys, what about you? All trained up now at the hospital, are you?'

'I've left the hospital. I'm working as a district nurse and midwife, working out of Dr Worth's surgery on Old Montague Street in Whitechapel.'

'Ooh, crikey.' Matilda was genuinely impressed. None of her daughters had been scholars but all had been hardworking girls before they settled down to raise families. 'Helped many babies into the world, have you, Kathy?'

'Nineteen, exactly, on my own. If you add on those I did with a bit of help from me supervisor when I was a probationer, it's more like twenty-five.' Kathy chuckled. 'Last one was on Monday: little girl who weighed over nine pounds and the poor mum went a fortnight overdue.'

Matilda screwed up her face, wincing. 'Ooh! Bet that made the poor cow's eyes water.' She announced proudly, 'All my gels was dainty little things. Beth weighed the most at seven and a half pounds. I had old Lou Perkins in to help me each time . . .' She darted a glance at Kathy, knowing that such help was outlawed now. 'Course, that's what you did in them days; no nice young nurses on call for the likes of us. Couldn't afford it, for a start. Old Lou would be happy enough with a bottle of port as a thank-you, or a few whiskies down her, round in the Duke.' Matilda gazed dreamily into space as she recalled youthful days when her first husband had been alive. 'Had all my kids before the Great War, y'see, Kathy. My Jack, God Bless him, was still alive then. Saw all our gels brung into the world, he did. Idolised 'em all, and they adored their dad.'

Kathy was used to women reminiscing with her about their own experiences the moment they knew of her profession. Usually, she was regaled with horror stories about lengthy labours necessitating martyr-like bravery. But Matilda had a different sort of stoicism. Having battled for survival in the Bunk over decades, coping with a difficult labour was probably the least painful of her memories.

'How's Reg?' It was common knowledge Matilda and her second husband weren't actually married, although they'd been living as man and wife for many years.

'Oh, he's much the same; still doing his totting. Keeps him outta mischief and brings in a few bob. And I do mean a *few* bob.' Matilda blew out her lips in a sigh. 'Tough old life, ain't it? Keep hoping things'll get better. Had them Fascists round here the other day causing trouble down by Seven Sisters Road. Bricks got thrown.'

'Mosley's Blackshirts?' Kathy sounded surprised. David often spoke about the Fascist Party recruiting in the East End but she'd not heard they were making a nuisance of themselves in north London too. Her boyfriend had been on duty not so long ago, when he'd had to attend a clash between Mosley's supporters and anti-Fascist protestors in Limehouse.

'They think people like us are interested in listening to all their claptrap 'cos we're poor so must hate all the immigrants.' Matilda shrugged. 'Course some folk round here do side with 'em. I opened up me window and bawled at them to sling their hooks 'cos me husband's Irish. Didn't like that, did they.' Matilda threw back her head, roaring with laughter. 'Bunch of hypocrites the lot of 'em. Don't like the foreigners, so they say, yet they got their ideas off the Germans and Eyeties.' Matilda crossed her arms over her chest. 'Course, I ain't got anything against Mosley's crew any more than the others. I tell the Sally Army to clear off 'n' all when they come round preaching. Never been political and don't like no interference 'cos none of 'em ever really helps the likes of us.' She gave a smirk. 'Wasting their time trying to convert me, or save me fer that matter . . .' She broke off having seen Beattie Evans coming out of her front door. Behind her were a couple of youths. Matilda gave Kathy's arm a light prod.

'There's your Tom, over there with Davy. Me neighbour's probably given 'em a bit of grub.'

Kathy swivelled to see her brother and Davy Wright slouching across the road. Beattie raised a hand in greeting, then headed off towards the corner shop. Kathy knew the middle-aged widow had a soft spot for hungry kids. She also liked a bit of company. Tom had told her before that Beattie Evans had invited him and his friends in to have a cup of tea and a bit of bread and jam when she was feeling generous. All they had to do in return was listen to her nattering on about the olden days until they'd curbed their hunger and could scarper.

'I suppose I'd better get off and see what Tom's been up to.' Kathy could see from her brother's expression that he was torn between acting nonchalant in front of his friend or running up to her. He raised a lazy hand in greeting, leaving it at that.

Before Kathy had got far, Matilda halted her.

'How's your sister doing? See anything of Jennifer, do you?'

'Yeah . . . I see her on and off.' Kathy smiled faintly. 'She's about the same.'

'One day it'll all come right, you'll see.' Matilda gave a kind smile. 'When you see her next tell her I say hello.'

'I will . . . thanks,' Kathy answered gruffly. Matilda had known about the bust-up that Bill Black had caused in their family, as did a good many local people.

'Well, I'd better get inside and sort Reg out something for his tea. He'll be home soon.' Matilda gave Kathy's shoulder a farewell pat. 'Remember me to yer mum, as well, won't you?' flowed back over her stout shoulder as she disappeared inside the dank hallway.

Tom noticed Davy's eyes pinned to his sister's face as she approached. Kathy was pretty, and all the boys, even those like Davy who were a lot younger than she, tended to stare. Some had even made rude comments about her, making him feel awkward.

'Not at work then?' Tom said gruffly by way of greeting.

'Afternoon off . . .' Kathy replied. She gave Davy a smile. He did look different from when she'd last seen him about a year ago. His complexion was spotty and a dark film covered his top lip as though a moustache

87

wanted to sprout. He certainly looked big enough to be out earning a living. By comparison, her brother seemed like a schoolboy.

'Shame you ain't got yer uniform on.' Davy leered at her. 'I'm feeling right dizzy, Nurse, and could do with you examining me all over.'

'Ha-ha.' Kathy gave him a pronounced sickly smile. It wasn't the first time she'd heard something similar from a brash male. Davy Wright was just the youngest to try it on and she felt disappointed that he had. Matilda was right: the lad had changed, and not for the better.

'Shut up,' Tom whacked his friend's arm, shoving him away. 'Goin' home,' he muttered, and started off towards Paddington Street with Kathy, ignoring Davy making a lewd gesture.

'Davy older than you, is he?' Kathy asked.

'Only six months,' Tom replied defensively. He knew what his sister meant: he appeared far younger than his friend now Davy's voice had broken and he'd started growing whiskers. 'Mum sent you round to get me, did she?' he asked sullenly.

'It was my idea to come round to find you 'cos I missed you last time I came over to Islington.' Kathy sensed her brother's moodiness.

'Well, don't go asking me loads of questions 'cos I ain't telling you stuff so you can tell her.'

'What's got your goat?' Kathy grabbed his arm, halting him. 'I've only come to say hello because I'm off back to Whitechapel soon. Wish I'd not bothered now.'

Tom had the grace to blush. He shoved his hands in his jacket pockets, walking on. 'It's just . . . I've had enough of Mum always going on at me,' he threw over a shoulder.

'Not surprised she's going on at you if you're always so bloody tetchy. When you leaving school?' Kathy asked. 'I reckon you need a job.'

'Soon as I can.' Tom brightened. 'Dad said I can go and work for him.'

Kathy muttered beneath her breath. Her father was a criminal who fenced stolen goods for a living and she was amazed that he'd carried on his dodgy activities for so long without serving a spell in prison. As far as she knew, he'd never had any other sort of work and had been ducking and diving since he got demobbed at the end of the Great War. Her mum excused what Eddie did by saying it had been the only work he could find at the time. A multitude of men had returned home to compete for employment. Her father had never once discussed in Kathy's hearing what he did, but she knew the war had ended a long time ago and her father had had plenty of time to sort himself out a decent career. Eddie carried on because the money he made was far more than a regular job would pay.

'Mum knows all about the plan for you to go into the family business, does she?' Kathy tilted her head to read her brother's expression.

'No, she don't! And don't you go telling her. Dad said to keep quiet about it 'cos she'd give us both earache. She reckons I should get a job as a clerk.' Tom's top lip curled, displaying his lack of enthusiasm for a desk job.

Kathy stifled a giggle at the idea that her brother would be accepted for such a position. 'And what about Davy? Is he getting a job?'

'He's got a job,' Tom blurted, then looked flustered.

'What's he doing then?' Kathy prompted.

'He's learning to be a croupier at the weekend over

on the corner there.' Tom jerked his head at the Paddington Street junction. 'Sometimes he's dogger-out for the men instead, but he don't get as much doing that. Earns a packet sometimes when he gets the pitch to himself.' Tom added enviously, 'Wish I could have a crack at it.'

Kathy knew that illegal street gambling had been going on at that spot for decades. She was also aware that some local kids earned tips acting as lookouts for the players. The coppers who patrolled the area soon put a stop to the illicit activities and were known to confiscate the proceeds, if they managed to lay their hands on it and escape. The gamesters in the Bunk didn't take kindly to losing their stakes and were not averse to cutting up rough to ensure they didn't.

'You'd better steer well clear of it or all hell will break loose when Mum and Dad find out.' Kathy sighed. Her father might encourage her brother to join him ducking and diving but he'd be dead set against his son getting involved in anybody else's shenanigans.

CHAPTER TEN

Kathy had been waiting glumly at the bus stop for ten minutes when she noticed a posh vehicle slowing down at the traffic lights. She frowned, wondering why the car seemed familiar. The driver turned his head and saw her just as she was about to look away. He obviously recognised her too because he cocked his head, smiling, then pointed, indicating he would pull over.

The penny dropped and Kathy felt a bit flustered. It was nice of him to stop, she supposed, but it wasn't really necessary. Nevertheless, from politeness, she lost her place in the queue to approach him. She recalled he'd introduced himself but could only dredge up his surname. It had stuck in her mind because of a contrast with his fair hair.

'Hello, Mr Raven,' Kathy greeted him with a smile. Last time they'd met in dim lamplight and she'd been bleary-eyed with tiredness, but she recalled thinking him good-looking. She hadn't changed her opinion on seeing him more clearly. 'Have you got over the shock yet of being my apprentice?'

'Not really,' Nick replied ruefully, coming round the car to join her on the pavement. 'I've been kicking myself for not chucking a bucket of water over Charlie sooner and letting him take over.'

'I'm eternally grateful that you didn't do that,' Kathy declared vehemently. Having that brute snarling on her shoulder at such a crucial time for mother and baby was a truly horrifying idea.

'Came up to scratch for you, did I?' Nick asked throatily, strolling closer.

Kathy glanced up bashfully into a pair of slate-grey eyes. 'You did very well, and I was grateful for your help.' She edged away, feeling overwhelmed by his proximity. 'Mr Potter would have been a hindrance, not a help. He's an unpleasant character.'

'Quite an understatement . . .' Nick remarked drily, looking her slim figure, dressed in civvies, up and down. 'Off duty today then, are you?'

'Just the afternoon off; I've been to see my mum and dad.' Kathy had been about to question him on how he was acquainted with Charlie Potter but he'd neatly side-stepped, managing to change the subject before she'd had a chance.

'Live in Islington, do they?'

Kathy nodded.

Nick glanced past at a turning some yards away. 'Not Campbell Road?'

'Oh, no.' Kathy choked a giggle. 'Don't let my mum hear you say that.' She elevated her eyebrows, feigning alarm. 'Have your guts for garters, she will, Mr Raven, if you imply any such dreadful thing.'

'Not the nicest place, is it?' Nick propped an arm against the bodywork of his car.

'Some good people live there, though,' Kathy returned, recalling her interesting chat with Matilda just an hour or so ago.

Nick drew a pack of Players from his pocket. 'Yeah? I wouldn't have thought a nice girl like you would know anything about that slum. Who're you friendly with up there?' He offered her a cigarette, then when she declined with a headshake lit his own.

'Nobody you'd know.' For some reason, Kathy was reluctant to oblige him with an answer. Mrs Keiver didn't take kindly to being gossiped about. Kathy had heard the woman putting a flea in her mother's ear for tattling behind her back. Winnie and Matilda had long had a volatile relationship although at present they seemed on an even keel.

'I know people who've lived in the Bunk, and still have relatives in the road . . . might be the same family you know.' Nick exhaled smoke with his words, his expression teasing.

'Name them?' Kathy challenged. He might mock her for her attitude but people like him who appeared affluent usually denied any link with such a notorious neighbourhood.

'Rob Wild and his brother, Stephen. They've both moved on to better things but were brought up at that end of the road there.' Nick pointed his smouldering cigarette at the Bunk's junction with Seven Sisters. 'Worst part, that is; people who live up the other end reckon they're a better class.'

He'd correctly stated that Campbell Road's inhabitants seemed to form two distinct camps. Winnie had told her some residents were reluctant to venture across the Paddington Street dissection and into 'foreign territory', as they called it. Matilda had never observed such a rule. In her prime she had been a rent collector and would walk the Bunk top to bottom on her rounds, gaining a fearsome reputation for fighting with men as well as women to extract from them what they owed her guvnor.

'Know the Wilds, do you?' Nick asked.

'Never heard of them,' Kathy said, giving him a deliberately dubious frown.

'Rob's aunt's still there in the road. Been moving up and down from one dump to another, she has, for donkey's years. All her daughters scarpered, though, soon as they could. I expect they're all married now. I think Matilda remarried after her first husband died—'

'Matilda?' Kathy interrupted, the start of a smile curving her mouth.

'Yeah . . . Matilda Keiver, as she was then . . . know her?'

'I've been talking to her this afternoon!' Kathy gasped an astonished laugh. 'She never actually married Reg Donovan, so she's still Mrs Keiver.' Kathy belatedly remembered her rule about not gossiping. 'Small world, isn't it? I thought you were making up knowing anybody.'

'Yeah . . . I know you did.' Nick said. 'Why's that?'

'Why's what?' Kathy felt awkward. She knew he was asking why she thought he'd bother doing something so trivial. And she couldn't find an answer, other than that she didn't completely trust him to be honest. Yet he'd given her no reason not to. 'You being an East Ender, I thought you wouldn't know people round here,' she mumbled. 'Oh . . . my bus . . .' She took a step away, unsure whether she was relieved or sorry to be on her way back to Whitechapel.

She'd lost her place in the queue but was hoping she might squash a place on the vehicle pulling in at the kerb some yards away. It was standing room only inside and Kathy knew that was a bad sign for those who'd been dawdling in the cold waiting for its arrival.

'Bye . . . nice to see you . . . gotta go . . .' she threw over a shoulder at him, trotting away. She slowed down, huffing a disappointed sigh on seeing the conductor put his arm across the gangway to shoo away all but a few of the hopeful passengers. Kathy realised if she'd not lost her place near the head of the queue she'd be on her way home.

'Come on, I'll give you a lift.' Nick strolled up behind her, pitching his dog end to the pavement. 'I'm heading back that way meself.' He gave her a smile on noticing her hesitation. 'What's worrying you, Kathy? I got you home in one piece last time, didn't I?'

An elderly woman in front of Kathy in the queue turned and gave the two of them an extremely old-fashioned look while adjusting her headscarf.

Nick averted his laughing face and, taking Kathy's elbow, steered her towards his car.

She wasn't sure why she'd not objected. Usually if any man – even David – acted high-handed her hackles would rise. But she was glad of a lift home and it was a sensible solution as they were both heading in the same direction. Kathy clapped her gloved hands together. 'Still gets cold in the evenings even though it'll soon be May,' she blurted, feeling self-conscious as they set off.

'Nights are much lighter, though.' Nick bowed to her need for a bit of small talk.

He'd liked her the first time they'd met and not forgotten her. He slanted her a glance, noticing her nervousness, wanting to put her at ease. She was young . . . demure . . . and he found that rather odd considering the work she did.

A previous girlfriend of his, way back, had been a nurse. Lorna had been a confident brash sort with a big bust and a big laugh, and a very generous nature much appreciated by the boys.

Nick's eyes travelled over the petite blonde sitting beside him, hands neatly folded in her lap, head turned to watch passing scenery. He found himself brooding on how intimate a relationship Miss Finch had with her boyfriend . . . then stopped pretty quickly when he found himself veering between resentment and arousal.

'So, Nurse Finch, how come you've got some free time? Does the doctor take over in emergencies when the midwife is needed and you're not about?'

'His wife does.' Kathy turned towards him for a chat. 'Eunice had my job before she married Dr Worth.'

'Married the boss, did she, clever girl?'

'She's trained up same as I am so covers for me when I'm off. Normally, she's the receptionist at the surgery. She hates me having time off because since she's gone up in the world she prefers her cushy number sitting behind a desk. But I insist on me time off. One afternoon and one day at the weekend.'

'Quite right too,' Nick said. 'Not seeing your friend David then this afternoon?'

Kathy shot him a sharp glance, amazed he'd remembered that she had a boyfriend, let alone his name. 'He's on duty. We don't always get the same shifts.'

'On duty?'

'He's a policeman.'

'Better watch what I say and do then . . .'

'Yes,' Kathy replied.

Nick looked at her and for a moment their eyes held. Kathy had a feeling he wasn't just talking about watching his step because he was acting flirtatious. She recalled Charlie Potter's bloodied face and her suspicion that they'd been fighting on the night Ruby had given birth. She realised she knew very little about this man: what he did and the company he kept. She didn't even know if he was married, not that it bothered her if he was. But his wife might get annoyed if she found out this was the second time he'd driven her home with a glint in his eye. Kathy gazed out of the car window, thinking her life was complicated enough so it might have been better to have waited for the next bus after all . . .

'How's the Potters' little lad doing?' Nick asked, as though his mind had been tracking hers back to the night they met.

'He's starting to thrive. His name is Paul and he's nearly two months old.'

A silence developed and, snatching a glance at his frowning profile, she could tell he was mulling that over.

'Charlie's taken to him then, has he?'

'I wouldn't go so far as to say that,' Kathy said slowly. The last time she'd been on a visit to the family Charlie had been nowhere to be seen. She'd gleaned from Ruby's muttered comments that her husband's moods were unpredictable and that put her constantly on edge.

'Do you know who the boy's father is?'

'Ruby never speaks about him . . . just hints. I think he might be a seaman she met at the docks. He's probably long gone, sailing the high seas.'

'Ah . . . right . . . so you know Charlie's missus has a profession.'

'I guessed she does what she has to, to get by,' Kathy retorted.

Nick raised his hands from the steering wheel in a gesture of truce. 'Don't jump down me throat. I'm not moralising . . .'

'Good . . . because perhaps you shouldn't . . .' Kathy said sourly.

'And that means?' Nick asked levelly, tapping a cigarette from the pack of Players and jamming it between his lips.

'It means I think you had a fight with Ruby's husband the night her baby was born and that's why he looked bashed up and was in a foul temper.'

'And what's that got to do with his missus working as a brass?'

'Her husband's meaner to her than usual when he's in a rage over something. I don't suppose he took kindly to getting a beating – or a soaking – off you. When things aren't going right for Charlie he keeps Ruby short of money, she's told me that. So I imagine she does whatever it takes to feed her kids . . . Oh, what do you care!' Kathy felt uncontrollably irritated. 'Stop the car, I'll make my own way back home, thanks all the same.'

'Calm down, Kathy.' Nick sounded vaguely amused. 'Is it all right if I call you Kathy?'

'No. It isn't. Would you stop the car, please, Mr Raven.'

'You can call me Nick.'

Kathy glared at him. He smiled back with easy charm.

'Calm down,' he repeated soothingly.

For some reason, Kathy did start to relax. She felt the tension melt out of her limbs and she threw back her head and closed her eyes, accepting she'd overreacted. 'Sorry,' she mumbled. 'It's just . . .' She didn't know how to explain that for some reason Ruby Potter and her children plucked at her heartstrings in a way that none of the other poor families she'd dealt with ever had.

Ruby, baby Paul and the other Potter children had wormed into her mind and she thought about them a lot between her visits. Kathy realised that her sister's miserable existence probably made her prone to pity women who'd been corrupted into vice by older men. She'd no idea what had happened in Ruby's youth; they'd never spoken about it. But she wouldn't be surprised to learn that, as a girl, Ruby had been abused and exploited as her own sister, Jennifer, had.

'Are you interested in knowing why I had a fight with Charlie?' Nick asked mildly, breaking into Kathy's reflection.

'Yes . . .' Kathy eventually answered.

'My mother and Charlie were at school together. Long time ago, that was. They're both in their forties now. Me mum's got a florist's shop and Charlie's been making a nuisance of himself over there. Seems he thinks she likes him as much as he does her. When she put him straight he got nasty, smashed up the place. So I thought I'd make things clear for him.'

'He's been after your mum? What does your dad say?' Kathy gasped in surprise.

'She's a war widow.'

'Oh . . . sorry . . .' Kathy mulled over what he'd told her. 'Did he hit your mum?'

'Yeah . . .'

Kathy gave a sorrowful shake of the head. 'He hits Ruby. He hurt her badly once; I arrived when he was going at it hammer and tongs. He's a brute so deserved a thump off you.'

'That's what I thought.' He gave her a sideways smile. 'So, can I call you Kathy?'

'Oh, all right . . .' Her amusement quickly faded. 'I wonder if Ruby knows about her husband chasing after women.'

'I reckon she does,' Nick said. 'If she's got any sense she'll encourage him to go off with one of them.'

'Have you come across Charlie Potter since that night?' Kathy asked, keen to probe for a bit more information.

'Nope.' Nick's mouth turned down in a humourless smile. He knew he'd not heard the last from Charlie. The man would be brooding on the run-in they'd had over Lottie and would be biding his time for a gloves-off rematch to save face. But Potter had since left Lottie alone and that was all Nick cared about.

He reckoned at the moment Charlie probably had other things on his mind – like tracking down a randy Chinaman so he could give him a kicking. Nick didn't think he'd have much luck there: Kathy was probably right and the bloke had come in on a boat and had now sailed off into the sunset.

'Did you get your bike back?' Nick asked.

'No sign of it anywhere,' Kathy answered glumly. 'Dr Worth or Eunice give me a lift in their car if it's an emergency, otherwise I have to walk or catch the bus to do my rounds.'

'The doctor's too tight to buy you a replacement?' Nick sounded incredulous.

'Well, it was my fault it went missing.' Kathy stuck up for her boss although privately she thought he was being mean over it. She had offered to contribute half towards the cost of a replacement bike and pay it off a little bit each week. But she knew Sidney Worth was waiting to pick up one for a song, second-hand. Unfortunately, so were a lot of other people who couldn't afford a car and needed to get about. A good used bike for sale was as rare as hen's teeth.

'I'll keep a look out for one for you, if you like.'

'Would you? Thanks,' Kathy said brightly. She had a feeling he meant it too, and was not just making conversation. 'Second-hand,' she warned, 'and if it's got a carrying rack on it, so much the better. Course, a pump, a bell and good tyres are essential . . .'

'Any other requirements, Miss Finch?' Nick asked mockingly. 'Sounds like you really need a new one.'

'Sorry!' Kathy was mortified that she'd sounded demanding. She noticed a quirk at a corner of his mouth and blushed.

'I'll keep me eyes peeled . . . and be in touch.' Nick promised.

CHAPTER ELEVEN

Blanche Raven sidled up to the café window and glanced in through misty glass. She smirked at the satisfying sight of her rival being run ragged. Joyce Groves was whipping to and fro with steaming dinner plates, banging them down in front of people before disappearing in the kitchen. Moments later, she'd return to scurry about serving more meals. Despite her spiteful smile Blanche was seething mad and she was here to make sure the woman messing about with her husband got to hear all about it.

Nick had dated women before but Blanche had never known who they were because those girlfriends had lived further afield. But Joyce had been making sure everybody knew about Nick's involvement with her. Blanche recognised her game: she was after getting an engagement ring on her finger so she could pack in her job as a skivvy to prepare for the big day. Blanche was determined to be the one jacking in her job and having the life of Riley on Nick's money.

A few weeks back she'd cornered Joyce in Petticoat

Lane and had warned her to back off. Joyce had taken no notice, laughing in her face. She might not have acted so brash if she'd been on her own. But the cow had had her brother, Kenny, and a few friends surrounding her in the market. Today her rival was on her own and Blanche was determined to wipe the smile off Joyce's face, with her fist if necessary. Nick Raven was hers; they were married, and that's how it was going to stay.

The proprietor of the café was counting out some money from the till and Blanche watched Les Drake hand it to Joyce, who'd come out of the back room in her coat. It seemed her shift was finished at last. Blanche was glad. It was bloody freezing weather for May and she'd already been hanging around outside for half an hour waiting for the trollop to show her face. She trotted off to hide up an alley that led to the back entrances to the parade of shops, her mouth slanting maliciously. Joyce would try to dart back inside the café if she cottoned on to an ambush.

'Now I've warned you once but you ain't taken no notice, have you?' Blanche barged into view, hands on hips.

Startled, Joyce whipped about. 'Oh, piss off,' she spat at Blanche. She'd got a stinking headache and her toes were throbbing in her court shoes because she'd been on her feet since six thirty that morning when Les opened up. It was now gone three o'clock in the afternoon and she hated doing long shifts with just a half-hour break for her dinner. The customers were mainly randy navvies who touched her up and had the table manners of pigs. They scraped together the cost of the dinner, moaning at Les about the price, then went off and never left a tip for her to boost her miserable wages.

'I'll give you "piss off", you bitch.' The lazy disdain in the younger woman's face was enraging Blanche.

Joyce sensed her opponent about to lunge at her but was too tired to shift out of the way quickly enough to prevent Blanche grabbing a handful of her long fair hair.

Blanche kept her rival's head at an awkward angle while yanking her into the alley. 'I've told you to leave me husband alone, but I saw you cosying up to him again earlier in the week.' Blanche emphasised her words with a tug on Joyce's hair.

'Get off me, you mad cow!' Joyce tried to prise Blanche's fingers away from her scalp. Unable to do so, she punched at them in frustration, worsening the pain in her head. 'He don't want you no more. Why don't you ask Nick yerself if you don't believe me?'

There was nothing more likely to infuriate Blanche than the truth. Every time the post came in the morning she was expecting to see a solicitor's letter bearing news of the divorce proceedings.

'He's married to me and that's how it's gonna stay,' Blanche bellowed, as though hoping it might come to pass the louder she shouted. 'Understand what I'm saying, do you, you stupid scrubber?' She delivered a stinging slap to her opponent's cheek, making her howl.

'Get off me!' Joyce shrieked.

A man came out of the café and, hearing the commotion, strolled over.

'What you two up to then?' Charlie Potter grinned as he saw the waitress who'd just served him being treated like a rat by a terrier. He'd always thought her a bit above herself. She'd banged down his cup and saucer once when he'd pinched her backside in the café, slopping tea down the front of his trousers.

He knew the names of both women and he could guess what the argument was about: Nick Raven. The fellow had been on Charlie's mind lately. Potter never forgot people who got the better of him, especially when women had been watching his humiliation. Nick Raven had made him look a prat in front of Nurse Finch and his own wife on the night the little chink bastard was born.

Chuckling, Charlie pulled the two women apart and wedged his hefty body between them. Joyce immediately dodged sideways and let rip with her nails down the side of Blanche's face, then turned and fled, swearing over her shoulder.

'You remember what I said, you fuckin' bitch,' Blanche yelled, her chest heaving with exertion. She was enraged that Joyce had managed to get in the final blow. 'What d'you think you're doing sticking yer oar in?' she stormed at Charlie. 'I would have floored her.'

'I reckon you would've 'n' all, darlin'. She scarpered pretty quick. Your face is bleeding,' Charlie pointed out to Blanche, grinning. He'd needed a boost because he was almost out of money and had nothing to do but go home and take it out on his wife and kids. Seeing two young women having a scrap had cheered him up nicely.

Blanche flicked him a dark glance, brushing herself down.

'I know you.' Charlie was unperturbed by her contemptuous look. 'You're Nick Raven's wife.'

'That's right,' Blanche snapped. 'That's who *I* am. Shame she don't remember it, the little tart.'

'Ah . . . playing away, is he?' Charlie said, as though it was news to him. He'd known since Blanche started sleeping with Wes Silver that Nick had dumped his wife and not long after started seeing other women. He might hate the bloke but he had to give Nick credit for how he'd played it: cool as you like. No drama, no punch-ups, no nothing; he'd just kicked Blanche out, back to her parents, and carried on regardless.

'Nuthin' will come of it with her, darlin',' Charlie crooned, eyeing Blanche up and down. She was a comely sort with a good pair of tits on her, and he started feeling horny despite her face looking a mess and her hair matted. 'That Joyce ain't a patch on you fer looks, is she? Nick'll come to his senses.' He shifted back against the wall and crossed his arms, watching as she dabbed at scarlet scratches with a handkerchief.

He might be as old as her dad, and a bit rough and ready, but he knew the right things to say, Blanche realised. She peeped at him from beneath her lashes, noticing he had quite a rugged attractiveness. He wasn't that much older than Wes Silver; she reckoned he might be a few years the wrong side of forty. She recalled now that she had seen him with Wes once or twice, acting as his sidekick, but couldn't bring to mind his name.

'Still working fer Wes, are you?' She smiled coyly. 'Forgotten yer name though, sorry.'

'Yeah . . . on and off, I work fer Wes, when I ain't on shift down the docks. Busy man, me . . .' Charlie's chest expanded boastfully. 'Got fingers in lots of pies, I have, luv, 'cos it keeps the money rolling in, see. And we all need that, don't we?' He gave her an exaggerated wink. 'Me name's Charlie, in case yer interested in remembering it this time. Charlie Potter.'

As far as Charlie was concerned, Blanche Raven was a nice classy bird and he wouldn't mind at all getting to know her better. She might fight and swear; she might have dropped her drawers for Wes till he gave her the elbow, and went home to his wife, but in comparison to the rough old sorts like Beverly, who hung about down by the docks and were his usual targets, she was a princess.

Nick might not have cared in the past what his wife got up to but Charlie reckoned he wouldn't take kindly to him shagging his wife. It would also make a point to Lottie Raven that Charlie Potter could have women far younger than her if he wanted to.

'Bit shaky on yer pins, luv, after that set-to? Want me to walk you home, do you?' Charlie crooked an elbow at her for her to hold. 'Take you on the bus, if you like.'

'Not got a car then?' Blanche returned. She knew what he was hinting at, and it wasn't just a bus fare paid for out of the kindness of his heart. But she had her requirements in a man: enough money for a good drink and a decent dinner came top of her list. A car to swank about in wasn't far behind.

'Nah . . . getting an Austin soon, though.' Charlie felt deflated. 'Please yerself . . .'

Blanche stuffed the bloodied hanky in her pocket, feeling a bit miffed. She enjoyed flattery and attention from any man – even one like Potter with little to recommend him. She certainly liked to choose to walk away first from a bit of flirting. 'Let me know when you get that car,' she taunted Charlie as he swaggered off up the road, then smirked when she saw his big hands form fists at his sides.

'It's yer own bleedin' fault you're in deep shit, so don't come crying round here. You won't get no handouts from me.'

Ruby had known she'd get little sympathy from her mother-in-law, but she'd hoped she might get at least a shilling off the woman seeing as when Violet was short recently she'd lent her half a crown, and never got it back. But it seemed that Vi Potter wasn't even going to let her in the front door let alone clear her debt.

"Ere . . . you hang on a mo, Vi.' Ruby tilted her chin to a combative angle, wedging a foot over the threshold. 'Ain't after no handouts. You owe me half a crown and if you ain't got it all to give back you can find at least half.'

'I'm givin' you nuthin'!' Violet spat. 'Go ask yer husband for money.' She pulled the door open wider to sneer, 'Oh, yeah, that's right, you can't, can yer, 'cos if you do he'll probably knock yer teeth down yer throat fer making him a larfin' stock.' Vi looked Ruby up and down with despising eyes. 'Tell yer wot, Ruby, it's a bleedin' shame yer didn't give Ivy Tiller the job of turnin' up and helping out. She'd've sorted you out a bit of graveyard luck with that one.' Vi snapped her head at baby Paul, asleep in the pram. 'But too late now, ain't it, so why don't you go find the Chinaman wot knocked you up and ask 'im to give yer summat? 'Spect he'll want you to give him summat in return, but then yer used to doing that, ain't yer, gel?'

Charlie's mother slammed the door in her daughter-in-law's face. Ruby knew exactly what Vi had been hinting at: a few rogue handywomen could be persuaded to lose an unwanted baby and cover it up as a stillbirth. Ruby was used to her mother-in-law being spiteful, even in front of her grandchildren, but she'd sunk to new depths with that remark. But Ruby let the woman's callousness pass, concentrating on getting some money as none of the kids had eaten yet that day. She quietened Pansy, who was sitting atop the pram coverlet, grizzling. She hammered on the door, ignoring Violet cursing colourfully from behind the panels.

'Give us a coupla bob or I'm not leaving. Me kids are hungry and that good-fer-nuthin' son of your'n don't give a toss about their empty bellies.'

'Good-fer-nuthin' son, is he?' Vi screamed, yanking open the door. 'You've got a bleedin' cheek, you scummy whore.' She launched herself forward, clumping Ruby on the side of the head and making Pansy howl in fright.

Violet was a hefty bruiser of a woman, even though she'd turned sixty-one a few months ago, and she never let anybody disrespect any of her family despite being aware that most of her eight kids were wrong 'uns.

In fact, Charlie, in Vi's mind, had turned out the best of the lot of them. He'd got a good job and had contacts with important people. Wes Silver had come over and had a cup of tea with her in the past. Vi had almost burst with pride at the look on some of the neighbours' faces when his posh car drew up outside and out he got in all his flash togs to knock on her front door.

At Christmas-time, Charlie always brought her in a load of hooky stuff that'd stuck to his fingers when the containers were being unloaded at the docks. Her eldest son looked after her – far better than his useless father ever had. But thankfully, Greg Potter was long gone to meet his maker and her new man treated her better – probably because he knew that he'd get a clump if he didn't.

Stan Wright had moved in with her a decade ago, leaving his wife and young family back in Islington. That had suited Vi: the last thing she'd wanted was to have to raise another woman's brood of kids when her own had all reached an age to be kicked out from under her feet to make their own way in the world.

Ruby had been knocked sideways by Vi's punch but regained her footing and shoved the pram to one side so Pansy, sobbing her heart out, didn't get knocked off the top of it if things turned really nasty. She might not have her mother-in-law's brawny build or vicious nature, but she'd go down fighting for the money to buy a loaf of bread.

'Put something in that or I'll make sure all yer neighbours'll hear what I've got to say about your precious son.' Ruby shook an open hand in front of Violet's face. 'Big man, Charlie, eh?' She lifted up her daughter's lank hair to display a bruise on a temple. 'That's all he's fit for: bullying women and little kids.' From the corner of an eye, she saw a dirty scrap of net curtain twitch next door. 'Go on, shall I?' she mouthed at Vi. 'Can see old Maude's got her ear pressed to the winder so she don't miss nuthin'.'

Violet's lips tightened in rage, but she'd glimpsed her neighbour being nosy too. She hawked and spat onto Ruby's palm. 'You wanted summat . . . have that!' She slammed the door in Ruby's face but a moment later a small silver coin dropped out of the letter box.

'And another, you tight-fisted bitch.' Ruby swooped on the sixpence. And then on the next as it fell at her feet.

'I'll be back tomorrow for the rest, so make sure you've got it ready to hand over,' Ruby bawled against the door panels, pocketing the coins with one hand and wiping slime off the other onto her coat. 'And don't bother pretending you ain't in, Vi, 'cos I'm already on to that one.'

Ruby let the brake off the pram. With a soothing stroke at her daughter's wet cheek to try to quieten Pansy's hiccuping sobs she trudged off up the street towards the bakery.

Ruby had already forgotten about her hateful mother-in-law and was calculating how far she could stretch a shilling if she settled for stale brown loaves, broken biscuits and sterilised milk.

'Get some bickies fer tea, shall we, Pans?' she crooned at her distressed daughter.

Pansy used her knuckles on her eyes to dry them, nodding solemnly. 'None fer Daddy . . .' the girl whispered, making her mother stare at her in surprise. Her daughter rarely uttered a word and answered everything with nods or shakes of the head. It was one of the reasons Charlie set about the girl, because he saw her silence as her defiance. With an enlightened smile Ruby wondered if it was Pansy's way of showing him her hatred; her daughter had come out with that cute remark without any prompting.

'Nah . . . none fer 'im,' Ruby said and, leaning forward, planted a rewarding kiss on the top of Pansy's dark head.

CHAPTER TWELVE

'I warned you you'd end up with food poisoning if you didn't clean the place up!'

Kathy's voice was sharp with exasperation, but as Jennifer retched into the sink, she carefully anchored her sister's hair back from her face in one hand while the other rubbed at her heaving spine till the tension went out of it.

'Shut up going on about it,' Jennifer whined, wiping her dirty mouth with the backs of her fingers. 'Feel dreadful, I do, Kath . . .' she whimpered, stumbling away from the sink to collapse onto the sofa. Drawing her knees to her chest she hugged them, rocking to and fro.

Kathy looked about at the state of her sister's home. Not that it was any worse than when she'd last visited. The living room was pretty much exactly the same: dirty plates with odd bits of food stuck to them were abandoned on the floor and a tumbler was balanced inside an overflowing ashtray. Without taking a sniff inside the glass Kathy knew it would most certainly reek of whisky.

'Has Bill been over here lately?'

Jenny nodded her head into supporting palms. 'Went home this morning, he did, when I started throwing up.'

'Has he got the bellyache as well? Have the two of you eaten something bad, d'you reckon?'

'He's got cast-iron guts,' Jenny mumbled bitterly into her hands. 'He never gets the shits, the lucky thing.' Bill had cleared off as soon as he realised she was feeling poorly. He'd not even offered to go the chemist and buy her some stomach powders. The tight fist begrudged laying out for them. 'Messed meself in bed, I did, Kath.' Jennifer raised her bleary eyes to her sister. 'Couldn't get to the lavvie quick enough. Bill weren't happy . . .' Her voice tailed off into embarrassed quiet.

'Not surprised he's gone then,' Kathy finally said.

'Got anything to give me for it, have you, Kath?'

'Yeah . . . a bar of carbolic and a kick up the backside.' Kathy stared grimly at her sister, feeling little sympathy for Jennifer's plight. In fact she was surprised her sister didn't come down with sickness and diarrhoea more often. It was several months since Jennifer had last had an upset stomach, and it hadn't been as chronic as this bout. Kathy sensed her irritation mounting and knew for two pins she might box her sister's ears in the hope it might knock some sense into her. To calm herself down she left the room, heading off to inspect the mess elsewhere.

'Ain't you got no medicine with you?' Jenny's mournful cry went unanswered by Kathy as she opened the door to her sister's bedroom. 'Got any laudanum, have you?' met Kathy's ears as she reluctantly entered, to be met by the sight of tatty, stained sheets. A musky fug of stale male sweat and faeces made her gag then hold her breath. But she was grateful to see that a brown stain was all that remained of her sister's accident. Gingerly, Kathy ripped the bedding free by handling just the very edges of the sheets, manoeuvring them together with her feet before kicking the ball towards the door. It was her afternoon off and if she'd known the task in front of her when she reached Jennifer's she'd have brought a rubber apron and gloves.

'I'll put the sheets in the copper out the back for you, and do the washing up, but that's all the clearing up I'm going to do. The rest can wait till you're feeling better.' Kathy came back into the living room, still rolling the linen in front of her with the soles of her shoes. 'You can peg this lot out later. It's a nice afternoon and should dry. If you want it ironed you can do that yourself too.' She gazed at Jennifer but her sister had buried her head in a cushion, making Kathy sure she wasn't heeding a word she said.

'If being sick like this won't teach you a lesson, then God knows what will. I give up.' Kathy sounded defeated.

With one eye flickering open, Jennifer watched her sister as she approached the back door, hoofing the dirty sheets in front of her. 'Seen anything of Mum?' she moaned, clutching her belly with both hands as a griping pain knotted her insides. Whenever she felt ill or anxious about something she instinctively craved her mother's comfort, despite the unlikelihood of getting it. She'd not spoken to Winifred in over five years.

'Saw all of them last week,' Kathy called from the back step. She lifted the dirty linen on her shoe and let it drop onto the concrete. She knew that once she reached the washhouse – just yards away – she'd use the wooden tongs to drag the filthy cotton into the tub.

Having got the copper filled and alight, Kathy fed the washing in, plunging it down into the steamy interior, adding more soda crystals and Sunlight soap shavings and mixing it to a froth. She gathered up the dirty towels that she found lying about indoors and dunked those in too. Suddenly bursting with zeal she carried on hunting, unearthing dirty underwear from under Jennifer's bed. Soon every piece of grimy cotton she could find – even men's pants – had been jammed in and there was barely room for her to agitate the suds with the wooden tongs.

Finally, Kathy came inside, blowing wispy tendrils of hair from her perspiring brow, and rummaged in the cupboard under the sink for the carbolic soap. It was still where she'd put it weeks ago, untouched in its wrapper.

Kathy washed her hands thoroughly and clattered the bar of carbolic down onto the draining board. 'When I go off home later, boil up some water and give yourself a scrub down with that. Are you listening, Jennifer?' Her sister appeared very still as though asleep.

'It stinks,' Jennifer suddenly piped up. 'Bill reckons it reminds him of hospitals. He was in hospital once and he hated it.'

'Well, if he gets a bad infection he might have a spell back inside one. And so might you!' Kathy snapped.

'If you bring me in a nice bar of Pears soap, I'll use that 'cos it smells nicer.'

Kathy picked up the bar of blue marbled soap and threw it into the sink in a fit of frustration.

'What did Mum say? Did she ask about me?' Jennifer sounded peevish.

Kathy came over, drying her hands on a clean hanky dug from her pocket. She knew it was pointless getting in a temper over her sister. Jennifer was Jennifer and had been lost to reason since the age of fourteen, when she first started taking an interest in boys . . . and had caught the eye of Bill Black.

'No, Mum didn't say a word about you; but I did. I told her I had seen you recently.'

Jenny perked up, lifting her head away from the upholstery. 'Yeah? What did she say to that?'

Kathy perched on the armchair opposite the sofa. 'She wasn't happy I'd mentioned your name at all,' she said with brutal honesty. 'Dad went out soon after I arrived so he didn't hear what we talked about,' she added, anticipating Jenny's next enquiry.

Jenny's head sagged back onto its support. 'How's Tom?'

'Driving Mum mad. I can understand why. He's knocking about with Davy Wright and that one's turned into a right tyke.' Kathy half smiled. 'He made a pass at me.'

Hearing about it drew a weak giggle from her sister. 'Cheeky little beggar.'

'He's that, all right . . .' Kathy paused. 'I went round to the Bunk to find Tom just to have a chat with him before I set off home. I saw Matilda Keiver and she asked after you . . . sends her best.'

Jenny smiled on hearing the news.

'Still the same old Matilda, she is, in the same old house. Beattie Evans was out and about too. She's a kind soul. She'd been feeding Tom and Davy up with bread and jam. Then I walked back to Mum's with Tom and when she found out he'd filled himself up at Beattie's, she went bonkers. You know how she hates waste. She'd done Tom a bit of steamed fish and mash for his tea and he told her he didn't want to eat it . . .'

Jennifer went pale and her cheeks ballooned at the description of food she particularly disliked.

'Oh, no!' Kathy wailed. 'Hold on, Jenny, till I fetch the bowl.' Kathy leaped up, racing to the sink, groaning when she heard the sound of Jennifer vomiting behind her. She knew which of them would be clearing that up.

David Goldstein was accustomed to being sworn at because of his job. He was also used to getting abuse because of his faith, even though he was not Orthodox and considered himself no different from any other Englishman. This afternoon he risked getting it from both barrels.

He linked arms with his colleagues as the protestors surged forward. Feeling a dig in the ribs from a fist, he tried to turn but the close formation of the police line prevented him seeing much over his shoulder.

'Hold on tight, Goldie,' David heard his sergeant order as a wave of anti-Fascists rushed at them in the hope of breaking their chain and scattering them.

A well-aimed blow to the backs of David's knees sent him staggering but he quickly recovered as he saw a snarling man taking a kick at his head. He drew his truncheon to protect himself but the would-be assailant had darted away, losing himself in the crowd. 'Commie bastard,' David muttered, dusting himself down and rushing to rejoin his colleagues and help man the barricades.

'Wish Mosley'd hurry up and get this over with,' Sergeant Booth grumbled. 'I'm ready for home 'n' me tea. Let 'em have a free-for-all if they want it, I say.'

'All these shops will get their fronts kicked in if we disappear.'

'Nah, Jews own most of 'em round here. They'll look after their own . . . always do.' Sergeant Booth suddenly seemed sheepish. 'Sorry, Goldie . . . forgot . . . no offence . . .'

It had slipped Booth's mind that his colleague was Jewish. It was an easy oversight: David Goldstein had light brown hair and hazel eyes. He didn't look a typical schmock, in Percy Booth's estimation. Privately, Booth believed that was why Goldie had been offered the job at the Met. He reckoned if David Goldstein had been swarthy with a hooked nose he'd never have got his feet under the front counter at the local cop shop. But Goldie was a pleasant character, good at his job, Booth had to give him that. Nevertheless, the sergeant still found it surprising that the lad had turned down a cushy number in the family firm in favour of doing this. In Booth's opinion nobody in his right mind would give up sitting on his arse all day in favour of being punched and spat at by a mob on a regular basis.

'No offence taken . . .' David finally said through his teeth. Since the Fascist rallies had started a few years ago most of the violence arose out of the antagonism between the protesters and the police. A meeting at Olympia had descended into chaos when Mosley's black-shirted stewards had brutally dealt with hecklers in the hall. The police had been accused of not doing enough to intervene. Privately, David had to agree with that; he'd seen first-hand what had gone on. But he'd followed orders, the same as the rest that day.

'Come on, Mosley, get on your way, for Chrissake,' Sergeant Booth muttered impatiently, aiming a backward kick at a lanky fellow deliberately elbowing him in the neck.

Sir Oswald was standing in his armoured car, addressing his supporters, one arm outstretched in a rigid salute. A roar went up as the followers realised the rally was coming to an end. Mosley suddenly dropped down into his vehicle and it slowly moved off.

'Right, get ready for a final surge, Goldie . . .' Sergeant Booth had rightly anticipated the crowd venting their anger one final time. The Union flags and Fascist colours were being waved frantically with the intention of inciting a reaction from the protestors. 'Just one last charge, son, and we'll be heading home for tea.' Sergeant Booth sounded jolly.

'Not before time,' David muttered, untangling his foot from a discarded flag on the ground. He felt his helmet go flying and, although he didn't know it, his thoughts fell in line with those of his sergeant: he wondered what on earth he was doing putting up with this shit when his parents wanted to give him a generous salary and a nice desk job.

'You ought to be ashamed of yourself . . .'

David swooped on his helmet and put it on, adjusting the chin strap. Turning his head, he saw one of his cousins frowning at him. Samuel Goldstein was the son of his father's only brother. David sighed; it wasn't the first time he'd been accused of being a traitor by family members who hated Mosley and all he stood for. Sometimes the messages came via his parents, and that annoyed him. If any of his extended family had an axe to grind over his chosen career he'd sooner they found the guts to tell him face to face, as Samuel just had.

'I'm not taking sides, Sam. I'm simply doing a job,' David said.

'Yeah, that's what they all say in the midst of raping and pillaging,' Samuel mocked.

A police cordon had enclosed the band of Blackshirts

and was escorting them to the top of the road to disperse. The protestors were drifting away.

'Don't be so bloody melodramatic,' David said wearily, starting off in the direction of the station, the backs of his hands brushing down his uniform. Most of his colleagues had got a lift back in the Black Marias but he preferred not to be wedged in with that lot.

His cousin fell into step beside him. They weren't close friends – not any more. They had been in their youth, but then Samuel had gone on to marry the girl that David had been stepping out with. There'd been no actual falling out; a faint hostility had set in and they'd grown apart as David distanced himself and Samuel settled into married life with Rachel.

'You wait and see,' Samuel warned with a finger wag. 'These Fascists are going to end up causing big trouble, you mark my words.'

'You and your friends aren't stirring the pot organising counterdemonstrations?' David mildly pointed out.

'We have to make a stand against such hatred or we'll be crushed underfoot. Anyway, I wasn't involved.' Samuel adopted an innocent expression. 'I was just passing when it all kicked off.'

David stared explicitly at the dishevelled state of his cousin's overcoat, where two buttons had been ripped off in the fracas. 'Of course you were, Sam. That's exactly what I thought . . .'

Samuel clapped his cousin on the back in appreciation of his tacit support. 'As Mosley likes the Nazis so much, he should piss off to Germany and set up camp over there.' He thrust his hands into his pockets.

'How's Uncle Reuben?' David could sense his cousin's

anger reigniting so changed the subject, asking after Sam's father.

'Doctor's told him to stop drinking so much, other than that he's much the same.' Sam shrugged.

'And Aunt Nora?'

'Driving me and Rachel mad. She keeps going on about wanting her grandkids before she gets any older . . .' His smiled faded. He'd spoken spontaneously, forgetting the subject was a bit awkward with this fellow.

David patted his cousin's shoulder to ease his embarrassment. 'Yeah . . . come on, mate, it's about time. You've been married long enough,' he said, letting Sam know it was time for all to be forgiven and forgotten. He suddenly spotted Kathy across the road, walking ahead of him, and his face split into a grin.

'There's my girl . . .' David was about to speed across the road to speak to Kathy but he didn't want it getting back to his parents that he'd lied about their having split up.

'Very nice.' Sam cocked his head to assess Kathy's rear view and her wavy blond hair glinting in the sunshine. 'Not a regular in the synagogue, I'd say,' he teased.

'You'd be right; so if Mum or Dad grills you on the subject, you don't know anything. Just like I don't know anything about your politics.'

'Understood.' Sam tapped the side of his nose, winking conspiratorially. 'Don't even tell me her name. The less I know about yon fair maiden, the less I've got to forget.'

The men parted with a handshake, then David loped across the road to catch up with Kathy. She spun round, surprised and happy to see him.

'You timed that just right.' David settled in to stroll

beside her. 'Where have you been?' He'd noticed she was out of uniform. 'Thought Thursday was your afternoon off this week.'

'So did I, but Eunice changed it as she's got a hairdresser's appointment on Thursday. I've been to see Jenny. It's as well I did call in; she's quite poorly.' Kathy noticed David's expression registering faint disapproval.

Years ago, it had got around the neighbourhood in Islington that Jennifer Finch had turned out no good and her parents had disowned her. Kathy had wondered if David's folk had taken against her because of her twin's bad reputation. She imagined most people had jumped to the conclusion Jennifer Finch was rearing a bastard on her own because the father had done a runner. Heaven only knew what they'd think about her sister being drawn into a life of shoplifting and prostitution.

When her sister's name cropped up in conversation David seemed satisfied with vague explanations that Jennifer had a few problems in her life. Her boyfriend, Bill Black, was a villain, and there was a possibility David might have come across him in his line of work. Kathy was optimistic they'd not met, as Bill hailed from south London; nevertheless she took care never to mention Bill's name.

'What's up with Jenny?' David suddenly asked after they'd been strolling in silence for a few minutes.

'Bad stomach . . .' Kathy blurted, jogged from her uneasy reflection on the stumbling blocks dogging their relationship.

David lifted his eyebrows in a way that nettled Kathy.

'I've felt queasy recently. Perhaps there's something going round,' she said obstinately.

'You've probably caught something off her.' David

came to a halt at a crossroads, about to head off in a different direction from Kathy, towards Leman Street station. 'See you Saturday? I'll pick you up at seven.'

'I'm not sure . . .' Kathy said. 'I might get Sunday off instead. Best leave it this week.'

CHAPTER THIRTEEN

'A fellow came round to see you this afternoon.'

Kathy had just arrived home and had been about to unlock her front door when her boss's wife had called out to her, halting her in her tracks.

'A man came to see me? Who was it? A patient's husband?' Kathy retraced her steps, noticing Eunice Worth was giving her a rather strange look.

'Don't know any woman on your rounds lucky enough to have a husband like him.' Eunice crossed her arms over her plump bosom. 'He brought you a new bike over.' She cocked her head, still eagle-eyed. 'I told him to put it in the shed.'

Kathy moistened her lips. There was only one fellow she could think of who might get her a bike – other than Dr Worth. And obviously, he had not; neither did Kathy believe he'd made much of an attempt to do so. David hadn't been of much help either when she'd told him about the theft. He'd shrugged and said the most he could do was log it at the station and hope that it might turn up.

'Tall blond man, well dressed, said his name was Nick Raven . . .' Eunice said slyly.

'Oh . . . right . . .' There was no reason for guilty colour to stain her cheeks yet Kathy sensed it was.

'New boyfriend?' Eunice was unable to control her inquisitiveness any longer. Her plucked eyebrows winged over her sharp gaze, demanding a reply.

'Just an acquaintance.' Kathy sounded commendably casual. 'He knew my bike got stolen and promised to keep an eye out for one for me. I'm glad he's been luckier turning something up than Dr Worth has.'

The barbed remark wiped the smile off Eunice's face. She knew very well that her husband had put minimum effort into searching out a replacement vehicle for his district nurse. Eunice's opinion was that Kathy Finch should take more care with other people's property or suffer the consequences, and she'd nagged her husband into sharing it.

'Did Mr Raven leave a note?' Kathy enquired, her mind turning at once to how she was to thank Nick and ask how much she owed him for the bike. She'd no idea where to contact him.

Eunice glanced in irritation over a shoulder as her husband summoned her. The appointments weren't quite finished for the day and two patients remained seated in the waiting room. She would have liked to linger and probe for a bit more information about Nurse Finch's relationship with the handsome fellow, dressed in an expensive suit, who'd turned up in a workman's van to make the delivery.

'He didn't leave anything but the bike,' Eunice said. 'Don't reckon he would have said his name only I made a point of asking for it. Yes . . . I heard you . . .' she hissed at her husband as he again called her because the telephone had started to ring.

Once Eunice had gone back to work, Kathy unlocked the shed and went inside. Her worst fears were proven. The bicycle was exactly what she wanted in size and shape, brand new and gleaming. She sighed, tightening her fingers on cold chrome handlebars. She feared Nick Raven's generosity had a lot to do with the gleam in his eye when he looked at her. So she'd have to give the bloody thing back because she hadn't got the cash to pay for it . . .

Kathy walked along, looking at shop fronts in Vallance Road. Nick had told her his mother had a florist's on this street. She hoped he hadn't been giving her a load of old flannel about how he came to know Charlie. Perhaps Nick's version of Potter pestering his mother in her flower shop, forcing him to retaliate to protect her, had been a concocted tale.

Kathy spotted a possible premises on the opposite side of the road: LOTTIE'S FLOWERS was proclaimed in bold script over the colourful awning. Kathy crossed over and, under cover of admiring hyacinths behind the windowpane, darted glances at the people within. The shop looked quite empty; just one customer handing over some cash for a bunch of tulips. But the woman behind the counter, wrapping the posy, looked to be a possible candidate. Lottie, Kathy supposed the woman to be from the shop name, seemed about the right age to have a son in his late twenties.

Having rallied her courage, Kathy entered the shop, breathing in a wonderful fresh floral scent. She approached a display of waxy-leaved hothouse lilies, their heavy perfume filling her nostrils. They reminded her of funerals so she moved on, browsing the buckets filled with a rainbow of blooms, while waiting for the customer to leave so she might talk to Lottie in private.

'Those make a lovely display.' Lottie Raven came up behind Kathy, nodding at some yellow freesias. 'From a hothouse, those are, grown down Kent way. Won't see them in your garden till the weather warms up . . .'

'They smell beautiful . . .' Kathy was determined not to pose as a customer, raising false hope of a sale. 'Sorry to bother you but I wanted to ask you something,' she blurted as soon as the door closed on the departing customer.

Now they were face to face, she realised the florist was an attractive middle-aged woman who did rather resemble Nick Raven, although her hair was brown, threaded with silver, and her eyes blue rather than grey.

'Ask away,' Lottie prompted.

Lottie didn't get many nurses in; she knew they couldn't afford such luxuries as bouquets on their pay. Apart from orders for weddings and funerals, most of her customers were pampered housewives, or husbands hoping to ingratiate themselves with their spouses on anniversaries. Lottie was coming to realise that she should have set up shop in a more salubrious area if she wanted to make a good living.

'I was just wondering if you're Mrs Raven and have a son called Nick?' Kathy saw at once from the woman's expression that she'd struck gold.

Lottie looked taken aback, then her expression turned speculative. Women liked her son, and plenty were keen to bring themselves to his notice, whether he wanted them to or not. She knew he was presently seeing Joyce Groves, although they hadn't been introduced. Lottie was relieved about that as she'd heard on the grapevine that her son's new fancy was a bit of a calculating madam. The description reminded her of Blanche. Only her daughter-in-law hadn't been clever enough to calculate how well Nick would do for himself once he'd got shot of her. Suddenly it occurred to Lottie that a nurse might be the bearer of bad news.

'Has something happened to Nick? I haven't seen him in days.' Ever since her son had had a run-in with Charlie, Lottie had worried the brute might ambush Nick to get him back.

'Oh, it's nothing like that.' Kathy gave the woman a reassuring smile. 'It's just . . . I don't know how to contact him, so would you give him this next time you see him?' She held out an envelope that bore his name neatly written on the front.

Lottie looked at it suspiciously. 'What is it?'

'It's just a short letter . . . nothing sinister, honestly.' Kathy could tell that Lottie believed it might be, and realised that wasn't a good sign. 'Your son was kind enough to do me a favour but I wasn't able to thank him. I don't know him well so I've no idea where he lives to post it.'

Lottie took the envelope gingerly. She wasn't prepared to give out Nick's address, or his telephone number, without checking with him first. Neither did she want to act as a messenger for a stranger and irritate her son. The simplest way to deter ambitious hopeful girls was to let them know Nick had a wife in the background. If this young lady weren't on the hunt, she wouldn't care either way about him being married.

'Perhaps you ought to tell me your name, dear, and that this is nothing his wife's going to be upset about.' Lottie wagged the letter, giving Kathy a subtle smile. 'Don't want to get in trouble for passing secrets.'

'Oh, no . . .' Kathy finally replied. 'Nothing in that to upset anyone at all. And my name is Kathy Finch.' She was heading for the door before Lottie could ask any more, or return the envelope.

Once outside, Kathy suppressed an urge to return and tell Mrs Raven that if anybody had a right to be upset it was her, because she'd never encouraged Nick's roving eyes to land on her. Lottie obviously knew her son was a philanderer; she'd not seemed surprised at the idea of him playing around behind his wife's back.

Kathy knew if she'd had the vital information about him before she'd written the note, its content would have been quite different. When he came back to see her again, as she'd requested, she'd wrap the bloody bike around his neck if he seemed reluctant to take it.

'Can I come back and live with you, Lambeth way?'

'No you bleedin' can't.'

'Why not?' Jennifer asked the question but already had an inkling of why Bill didn't want her around permanently. She'd caught a whiff of perfume on Bill on previous occasions when he'd turned up on a visit, and today she'd noticed a long dark hair clinging to his sleeve. She hadn't confronted him over whether he'd shacked up with a woman in Lambeth because she could guess the answer, and despite knowing he was no good, Jennifer still loved the man who'd taken her virginity.

At fifteen she'd thought him the most handsome, charismatic fellow, and had believed, just for a little while, that he'd fallen in love with her and would marry her. Then she'd got to know him and realised that every woman he thought might be useful to him was treated to his charm. Jennifer had cottoned on quickly to the fact that she needed to keep her boyfriend in cash to keep him interested. She'd preferred shoplifting to prostitution as a way of earning.

'Let me come hoisting with you round the West End, Bill,' Jenny burst out. 'I'm skint and need money for stuff.'

'Hoisting? You?' Bill answered on a bark of laughter. He grabbed Jennifer's arm, dragging her with him to the mirror over the mantel. 'You seen yerself lately, Jen?' He shoved her closer to the spotted glass, shaking her when she avoided looking at her bedraggled reflection. 'Ain't exactly the sort of customer to be seen swanning about in Dickens & Jones, are yer, gel? Not any more.'

Bill stomped off and collapsed into the sofa, kicking away a dirty plate by his foot. He was angry because once Jennifer had looked exactly the sort of person to be seen patronising such a swish establishment. At fifteen years old, fresh-faced and pretty, done up to the nines in classy clothes, Jennifer had passed herself off on numerous occasions as a well-to-do young lady out on a spending spree on her rich daddy's cash. She'd been a regular in Oxford Street, and if not exactly making purchases, she'd certainly exited top stores like Selfridges loaded down with their luxury merchandise.

Having Jennifer back to her old self was the stuff of Bill's dreams, and hearing her suggest she could still do it simply wound him up. It wasn't just that she looked a mess – he could tart her up if need be – the stumbling block was her mental state. A hoister needed to be sharp

130

and clever, with a ready line in patter if she were stopped. Five years ago, Jennifer could outthink and outrun any store detective. Now she couldn't go a day without drugs and drink, and found it hard to put together a coherent sentence when under the influence. She was a wreck and, unfortunately for them both, it showed.

In her heyday, Jennifer had been the queen bee of Bill's little gang of female shoplifters and had made him a small fortune. Then everything had gone sour on him . . . and he blamed her, and her poxy family for the disintegration of his little empire.

In the past, Bill had had a good business relationship with Jennifer's father. That's how he'd met Jennifer in the first place: dropping off boxes of stolen goods over in Islington for Eddie Finch to fence. Following a dispute with Eddie over priceless jewellery, Finchie had beaten him up so badly Bill had ended up in hospital. Their feud had then escalated into all-out war.

Bill had been humiliated and robbed by Eddie so in a fit of insanity he'd kidnapped little Tom Finch, to try to save face and force Eddie to give back the cash he'd stolen from his wallet. But Bill's act of revenge had turned sour on him. The police had got to hear all about it and Bill had been arrested. He'd done a stretch inside, then come out to find his little team of shoplifters had poached his best contacts and dispersed.

Only Jennifer had remained, not from loyalty to him but because she'd had nowhere to go. Her parents had disowned her because of her association with him, so she'd holed up in his flat while he was in gaol and paid the rent by going on the game.

Now Bill was reduced to small-time larks with characters he previously wouldn't have bothered to acknowledge.

131

Despite his bitterness over it all he couldn't break all ties with Jennifer. When desperate for cash they could pull in a few bob finding her business. Sometimes they'd roll the punter, other times Jennifer had to hold up her end of the bargain to the best of her ability.

Bill looked at her thin figure and tangled hair with faint disgust. God knows what anybody saw in her. These days he only slept with her himself when he'd had a few too many sherbets.

CHAPTER FOURTEEN

'Fucking hell! What's all the commotion about?' Tony Scott bellowed.

He'd been pulling on his overalls over his pants and vest when he'd heard shouting in the room below. Hopping to and fro, he attempted to extract his foot from a knot of crumpled navy twill, finally flinging the overalls on the bed. He hurtled down the stairs and burst in to the kitchen to be met by the sight of his wife wrestling with his daughter.

'Give it here . . . no point ripping it up, you foolish gel . . . let me see it.' Gladys was trying to prise a letter from Blanche's fist.

'It's that bitch Joyce Groves.' Blanche was dancing in rage. 'It's her fault. She's the one done this, Mum, 'cos I gave her a smack and told her to stay away from him.' Paper was waved agitatedly beneath Gladys's nose. 'I'll have her, Mum. I'll swing for her, swear I will. She ain't getting away with stealing me husband.'

Tony snatched the letter from Blanche's fingers before she could crush it. Having seen the name of a firm of solicitors emblazoned in bold type across the top, he knew he wouldn't need to read more than the first few lines to have the gist of the letter's content.

His son-in-law wanted a divorce and, all things considered, Tony couldn't blame him. He was only surprised that it had taken Nick this long to get round to it.

'Sit down, Blanche and have a cup of tea to calm your nerves,' Gladys soothed, sending her husband a frantic look.

Blanche's usually pale, pretty face was scarlet and running with tears and snot. Her mother started to dab at the mess with her hanky but Blanche knocked away her hand in irritation. The next moment the tension seemed to leave her and she collapsed down into a chair at the table.

'Ain't going to work and don't want no fucking tea,' she gurgled at her mother, who was nervously proffering a steaming cup.

'Come on, Blanche, love,' Tony crooned, crouching down by his daughter. In the chaos, he'd forgotten he was wearing only his underclothes and the baggy cotton gaped at his crotch displaying some wiry dark hair. 'It's not unexpected, is it now, dear. You know Nick's been patient over it all . . . can't say he ain't,' he carried on, oblivious to his daughter averting her face from him in disgust.

'Soon find someone else, won't yer now?' Tony added gamely, patting his daughter's knee. 'You can go out and have fun with some friends . . .'

'Why don't you just shut up all that bollocks and go to work?' Gladys hissed, jerking her thumb at Tony's pants and then at the door in case he couldn't understand plain English.

In all of the three years her husband had had to come up with some words of wisdom for his daughter, following the breakup of her marriage to Nick Raven, it seemed that was the best he could manage. And he'd had to expose himself for good measure.

Tony glowered in humiliation, flung the letter on the table and stalked off down the hallway.

Ten minutes later, Gladys heard the front door slam as her husband went off to work in a huff. She turned from the washing-up bowl to Blanche, still seated at the kitchen table, head in hands. Her daughter was in her dressing gown, hair tangled and face grimy with sleep. She would have been late again for work, no matter what had landed on the doormat this morning.

Inwardly, Gladys cursed the postman. If only he'd come at his usual time, after nine, instead of turning up early she could have at least got Blanche off her backside and out of the front door. The lazy little cow was taking more and more time off and Emo Goldstein had already dropped hints about sacking her if she didn't buck her ideas up.

'You've had time enough to get used to the idea of being Nick's ex-wife, my gel.' Gladys had decided that a bit of plain speaking might do the trick where sympathy had failed. 'Having a tantrum over it ain't going to get you that.' She clicked her fingers beneath Blanche's nose. 'Weren't so long ago you didn't want him, or his baby. You wanted Wes Silver instead.'

Blanche narrowed her eyes on her mother. 'Yeah . . . 'cos you told me I could do better for meself than a lorry driver. Only Nick ain't a lorry driver now, is he? And if I'd stayed with him instead of listening to you I'd be doing all right.'

'Don't take that tone with me, young lady,' Gladys snapped, but had the grace to blush because of the truth in the accusation. 'Nick Raven was *your* choice and *I* was entitled to me own opinion on him.'

'It changed pretty quick, didn't it, when things started looking up for him? Can't do no wrong now, can he?'

Gladys bent down so her face was level with Blanche's. She grasped her daughter's chin in her fingers. 'Well, find yerself another man with a bit of standing to give you what yer want. Nick Raven ain't the only one around, y'know. And do it sharpish, miss,' she added. ''Cos you can take it from me yer looks won't last for ever and whining on like this won't get yer nowhere.' Abruptly Gladys straightened. 'For now, get off to work. I meant what I said about you paying your way while you're under this roof.'

Gladys flung off her pinafore and headed down the narrow hallway. She had her sewing machine set up in the boxroom upstairs. 'I'm getting started on the coats; when you see Emo this morning tell him I've run out of black buttons, so he'd better drop me some by.'

Jennifer licked her lips nervously, hovering just inside the entrance to Gamages. She'd not set foot in the store in years. Even when she'd been a regular she'd never purchased anything – not even a bottle of scent. But she'd removed lots of them in her time, and plenty of other lovely stuff too. She was confident she could do so again.

She knew she'd been looking a wreck lately, and this morning had done something about it, sorting out from her wardrobe her 'court clothes', as Bill called the outfit because she'd worn it when she'd been called before the magistrate for stealing when living over Lambeth way. She'd haphazardly run the iron over the plain dark skirt and prim white blouse with a Peter Pan collar, then buffed her best court shoes before setting about the rest of her appearance. Her dark blonde hair had been smoothed down flat and secured with a slide, then she'd powdered her face and put on a bit of coral-coloured lipstick. A dab of Coty L'aimant perfume that had lain forgotten in a drawer finished off her toilette.

If Bill wouldn't take her with him hoisting and give her a bit of cover while she did the necessary, then damn him! She'd go to work on her own. She'd done it before when he'd gone to prison and been successful till she started to drink too much and got arrested in Liberty's in Regent Street with two lacy slips stuffed down her cleavage. The magistrate had let her off with a fine but the threat of a stretch inside had shaken her up enough to make her try her hand at something else to earn a living. Now she wished she hadn't gone on the game because that was a prison of sorts too.

Jenny had walked to Gamages as she'd not had the bus fare. By the time she'd arrived in Holborn she'd been feeling quite energetic, the fresh balmy air of the June day making her feel bright and breezy.

Once she was strolling in the sweetly scented atmosphere of the shop, a familiar fizz of excitement streaked in Jenny's veins. The breath caught in her throat and her stomach flipped queasily. She liked the sensation; she'd always been at her best when scared.

Head high, shopping bag lightly swaying, Jennifer joined the customers browsing nearby counters. Catching sight of her reflection in a mirror her lips twitched in satisfaction. She'd made a reasonable job of tarting herself up and beneath the face powder her complexion looked healthily pink from her walk.

Some Yardley lipsticks were within reach and as soon as the assistant turned to use the till she palmed two from the counter display. It was a small success but she sashayed buoyantly on in the direction of the ladies' lingerie.

Within fifteen minutes, Jennifer had filled her pockets and bag with a selection of cosmetics and pretty silky scraps. She was feeling light-headed with euphoria when a hand grasped her elbow.

'I'd like you to accompany me to the manager's office, madam. Now, no silly business,' the store walker growled, having received a forceful shove in the guts from a small fist.

Jennifer cursed beneath her breath, glancing to and fro and wriggling her arm, but he had a firm grip on her. He was just a regular flatfoot who would stick out a mile to a professional yet she'd not even noticed him. At the age of fifteen she'd have located him within minutes of stepping over the threshold but in her enthusiasm to get started she'd forgotten the cardinal rule of scouting for security guards.

'No trouble now, lass; don't want to make a spectacle of yourself in front of all these folk, do you?'

His Yorkshire brogue was irritating her and Jennifer felt tempted to knee him and run, as she'd seen Bill do with great success on one occasion. The fellow had gone down like a sack of spuds and they'd both got away scot-free, pockets jangling with solid silver. It had been just before one Christmas and they'd shifted the spoons and cruets easy as anything and had a fine turkey feast on the proceeds.

She allowed the Northerner to propel her towards the back of the store, knowing it was useless even trying to clear out her pockets. He'd got her arm in a vice-like grip and besides, she'd stashed away too much stuff to drop it all on the floor.

'Have you telephoned for the police, Miss Weston?'

The lanky woman nodded at her boss. 'A constable from a different station is coming over directly, Mr Thorpe, as our local fellows are busy with an emergency.' The young secretary slid Jennifer a despising look as she exited the room.

Rather than let the snobby bitch rifle her bag and clothing, Jenny had pulled out the pilfered items herself a short while ago. Now she stood quite still before the two men, eyes downcast, her mind frenziedly occupied in searching for a way out of the mess she was in.

Mr Thorpe was a short stout man, dressed in an elegant double-breasted suit. As Jennifer glanced at him, he raised his eyebrows, wordlessly demanding an explanation from her. He took such odious behaviour as a personal insult and was determined all shoplifters suffer the full force of the law.

Jenny had not volunteered a defence so far, even though the tally of her crime was littering the surface of the manager's desk. The sight of it made her simultaneously depressed and elated: if she'd got away with it Bill would have praised her to the skies. But there was enough value in the items to ensure that this time a magistrate wouldn't be so lenient and she'd get hard labour.

'Have you anything to say for yourself?' Mr Thorpe demanded, perplexed as to why the young woman continued with dumb insolence. She wouldn't even give her name. Usually, when caught, female thieves burst into tears, garbling apologies and tales of feckless husbands and hungry babies crying at home . . .

'Yeah, I've got something to say,' Jenny piped up, suddenly struck by an idea as the Yorkshireman again eyed her from beneath a set of wiry brows. She'd noticed him staring at her bosom before, and his hand had lingered a little too close to her backside when he was ushering her into this office. 'I'm glad the coppers are on their way 'cos that one there's a pervert and I'm gonna tell 'em so.' She jerked a nod at the store walker. 'Had a go at getting his hand in me drawers, didn't he, before you turned up. Said he'd let me off if I was nice to him. But I ain't that sort of girl.'

Jenny felt no compunction at telling such a lie. She'd been used by enough men in her young life to resent the lot of them by now and gain satisfaction from getting her own back when she could.

She knew she'd struck lucky when the manager's jowls quivered and his eyes slewed to his employee. Jenny guessed the store walker was a randy sort who might have been disciplined before for trying to cop a feel of a woman.

'Wait just outside, Grayson, while I question this young woman,' Mr Thorpe enunciated. 'I'll speak to you in a moment.'

'I've not touched her, sir!' Grayson protested. 'The lying . . .' he managed to swallow a snarled obscenity on hearing a knock on the door.

'The constable is here, Mr Thorpe.' Miss Weston was back with a policeman in tow.

It was a long time since David Goldstein had come face to face with Jennifer Finch. Nevertheless, he knew her straight away and desperately hoped his expression hadn't betrayed the fact. She was his girlfriend's twin and although they weren't identical, and Kathy was far lovelier, there was enough of a likeness between them for kinship to be obvious.

Jenny had never been introduced to her sister's boyfriend and realised it was because Kathy was ashamed of her. But she remembered David from schooldays, although they'd rarely spoken as he'd been in a different class. He looked a typical copper in her opinion: stern and older than his years. Despite his professional poker face she knew he'd recognised her and she guessed he wouldn't keep this little episode to himself.

Kathy would kill her when she found out what she'd been up to; and of all people, Jenny wanted to keep her sister on her side. Kathy was the only true friend she'd got. Her heart sank and the defiance ebbed from her features. She stared at the parquet floor, cursing that her luck had just run out.

'Are you certain you don't want to bring charges?' David peered again at the array of expensive finery dumped on the manager's desk. He was no expert in women's undergarments and cosmetics but guessed the haul's worth ran into tens of pounds.

'It's not necessary. Bad publicity . . . you understand. Not the kind we want at all.' Mr Thorpe shook his head vigorously. 'It could have been an error of judgement on her part . . . or our part. Grayson can be . . . overzealous . . . at times, you see. Too good at his job.' He chuckled lightly. 'Who knows, the young woman might have bought the items before leaving, if left to her own devices.' Mr Thorpe politely ushered David towards the door.

'Did she say that was her intention?'

'I don't recall.' The manager's plump face wrinkled as he feigned concentration. 'Often the shock of being apprehended is too much for these women; they panic and either become hysterical or clam up, you know.'

'In which way did this one react?'

'Oh . . . a bit of both, I believe.'

Closing his notebook, David put it in his breast pocket. Something wasn't right. He'd been dragged here from East London only to find he'd been sent on a fool's errand. Sergeant Booth had let him have one of the cars to bring the offender quickly into custody. The old boy wouldn't be pleased to know he'd bestowed an unwarranted little luxury on him.

'Right . . . I'll be on my way then and escort Miss . . .' David stopped himself just in time from naming the culprit.

'Oh, she wouldn't give her name . . . too ashamed, I expect.' The manager opened the door, beckoning to his secretary.

Mr Thorpe felt relieved watching the young constable escorting the thief along the corridor until his gaze fell on Grayson, loitering with Miss Weston in the outer office. The two of them had been guarding the woman while he talked privately to the policeman.

It was the third time a female had complained to him about Grayson's unwanted advances. The other accusations had come from members of staff. Sandra in Toys and Deirdre in Shoes had sensibly let the matter drop following a hint that a scandal might result in them losing their jobs. Mr Thorpe had had a discreet word with the store walker following those incidents and been assured by Grayson that his friendliness had been misinterpreted.

Mr Thorpe had had his doubts and now regretted not having sacked the man sooner. A frolic with a female assistant was one thing but there was an uncontrollable hazard in outsiders getting touched up by one of his employees. He felt sorry for Grayson but he'd have to go.

CHAPTER FIFTEEN

'Gonna drop me off home then?'

Jenny's cheeky demand earned her a sour look from David. He'd waited till they were outside the store before giving her the good news that she wasn't to be prosecuted for shoplifting. Her surprise had transformed into triumph, leaving her chuckling gleefully.

'How did you pull that one off?' he casually asked, unable to curb his curiosity.

'I'm sure I don't know what you're talking about, Officer.' Jenny exaggeratedly batted her eyelashes. 'I've been falsely accused by those nasty men.'

'You were going to pay for that little haul, were you?' David suggested sarcastically.

'Who knows?' Jenny answered airily.

'Turn out your pockets . . . let's see what you've got on you then in the way of cash,' he ordered.

'You arresting me after all?' Jenny's impudence vanished. She'd thought she was home and dry moments ago.

David slanted her a glance from beneath the brim of

his helmet. She was quite attractive in a common way, especially when seeming vulnerable, as now.

'Give us a lift, David,' Jenny wheedled. 'I know you're heading my way. Kathy would want you to,' she added slyly. It was time one of them owned up to the fact they had a mutual friend. 'We're almost family . . . aren't we?'

'Shut up. You don't know anything about me and your sister.' David pulled out his notebook, flicking officiously to and fro through the pages.

'That's where yer wrong, see,' Jenny teased. 'Kathy 'n' me are close and talk about things, you know.' She flinched from the sudden anger darkening his face. He might be a copper with a conscience – he knew she'd had a lucky escape and he didn't like it – but she reckoned pushing him too far, even in jest, might be a mistake.

'You fancy your neighbours knowing you've been in trouble, do you? They will if I pull up outside your place.'

'I haven't been in trouble, have I?' Jenny could tell he was almost swayed to give her a lift. 'Anyhow, don't care what any of me neighbours think. The nosy cows can all get stuffed, 'cos I'm innocent.'

'Innocent, are you?' David snorted, approaching the police car parked at the kerb. 'I'd lay money that's one thing you're certainly not.'

Boldly, Jenny opened the back door and slid onto the seat. She leaned forward so their gazes were clashing in the rear-view mirror, daring him to order her out of the vehicle.

David could see just her eyes, realising that they were similar to Kathy's in colour and shape. But Kathy's gaze was clear and direct, whereas her sister's brimmed with artfulness.

'Take me home, Officer, and you can show me your truncheon . . . and your handcuffs, if you like.' Jenny slumped into the seat, throwing back her head to guffaw.

David turned the ignition, head lowered to conceal a half-smile. He hated himself for liking women with dirty laughs and knowing eyes.

Kathy listened to the baby's heartbeat and gave the expectant mother a satisfied nod. 'All as it should be, Mrs Castell.'

The woman had miscarried her last two pregnancies some years ago and had confided in Kathy she despaired of giving her husband the son he wanted. She was considerably older than he, but at thirty-six there was no reason why she couldn't deliver a healthy baby, and Kathy often told her so.

It made a pleasant change for Kathy, doing her rounds amongst the impoverished, to come across people who positively yearned for a child rather than dreading the prospect of another mouth to feed.

'Is it a boy, do you think?' Mrs Castell asked, straightening her clothes.

'Oh . . . I don't know.' Kathy smiled. 'I'd be a rich woman if I could charge expectant mums for correctly guessing their baby's gender.'

'I'd give you a bob to know what mine is. If I end up only ever having the one, I'd like a son,' Mrs Castell said wistfully. 'My mother says she thinks it is a boy. I'm all out the front, y'see.' She gave her distended belly a pat. 'If I was carrying weight on my backside then it'd be a girl, so Mum reckons.'

'I've heard that said.' Kathy confirmed knowledge of the old wives' tale while packing away her things. 'My mum says that a son is a son till he gets him a wife, but a daughter's a daughter all the days of her life . . .' She recited one of Winnie's proverbs. Her mother often used it when Tom was driving her up the wall and she wanted some support from Kathy. 'So some people reckon having a baby girl has big advantages.'

'That saying's true 'n' all.' Mrs Castell stuck her hands on her hips. 'Me mum sees nothing of our Roland, even though he's the oldest. He leaves it all up to me and me sister to fetch Mother in her shopping 'n' so on.'

'Married, is he?' Kathy asked, chuckling.

'Oh, yes!' Mrs Castell's grim tone spoke volumes about her opinion of her sister-in-law.

'Well, I'd better be off.' Kathy clicked shut her case. 'I've a postnatal to do round the corner in Thrawl Street on my way back to the surgery.'

'I'll come to the clinic next time, save you a trip.'

'I'd appreciate it . . . I'll introduce you to the nurse who covers for me when I have days off. She's the doctor's wife and very nice.' Kathy wished she could praise Eunice more enthusiastically.

Kathy was walking briskly, enjoying the sunshine warming her complexion, when she saw her boyfriend behind the wheel of a car. It was so unusual a sight – David rarely got allocated a vehicle to get about in – that Kathy actually stopped in her tracks and waved to attract his attention. She wouldn't have done so had he been

147

with a colleague but he was the only person in the vehicle. She was sure he had seen her but he carried on without an acknowledgement. She realised she must have been mistaken; although he'd glanced her way he'd obviously been too preoccupied to notice her. If they did catch sight of one another during working hours David always went out of his way to intercept her so they could have a chat.

Kathy made a mental note to ask him about the car when she saw him on her day off on Sunday, and carried on in the direction of her next appointment.

Arriving back at the surgery hours later, Kathy found Eunice in a flap over some patients' notes that had gone missing.

'Are you sure Dr Worth hasn't already got them on his desk?'

'If he'd got them on his desk he wouldn't be asking me to fetch them in to him, would he?' Eunice snapped while scrabbling in a drawer by the telephone.

Kathy sighed. Eunice could be a right misery at times. 'Just trying to help,' she said, heading towards the side door that led to her annexe. She'd only popped into the surgery to let her colleagues know she was back from her rounds.

'Sorry . . .' Eunice muttered; she held up some manila folders. 'Found them under this lot . . .' she thumped a pile of telephone directories with the palm of her hand.

'Right . . . good.' Kathy smiled faintly.

'Still got that bike in the shed, have you?' Eunice asked, cocking her head to one side, following Kathy towards the exit.

Kathy simply nodded a reply. Eunice had been grating

on her nerves, constantly probing about the bike. It was nothing to do with her or Dr Worth what she did with the damned thing. They hadn't offered to pay for it. If they had she'd have passed the money to Lottie and would be gladly using the bike to save shoe leather.

'Mr Raven hasn't come back for it, then?'

'Not yet . . .'

'Been a while since he turned up with it.'

'Mmm,' Kathy muttered. She felt her face flushing. Nick Raven had been dogging her thoughts more than a married man should. But once she'd had the opportunity to give him a piece of her mind, that'd stop, she was sure.

'Why don't you make use of it till he collects it? He might not want it.'

"Cos, as I said before, a new bike is out of my price range and I can't give it back second-hand.' Before Eunice could pursue the subject, Kathy nodded at the folders in the older woman's hand. 'Thought your husband was waiting for those . . .' Kathy went out of the side exit and headed towards her front door, frowning at the shed on passing it.

'I saw you earlier in the week driving a car.' Kathy had just remembered the fact and blurted it out to David as they sat in a bustling café, sipping tea. She gazed at him expectantly. When he made no comment, simply pulling a face, she added, 'I thought you'd seen me and would stop. You were on your own so I waved, but perhaps you didn't notice me.'

'I didn't,' David said. 'Ready to see the film?'

'It's a lovely evening. Shall we take a walk towards

Victoria Park instead of being cooped up inside the Rivoli?'

'If you like.' David pushed away his half-finished tea. 'How's your week been?'

'Much the same.' Kathy's expression turned reflective. She thought back over her busy schedule, which had begun at four o'clock Monday morning when a sixteen-year-old miscarried. The girl's frantic widower father had called Kathy out to the Fieldgate Mansions tenements. He hadn't known she was pregnant and thought some dreadful disease had befallen his daughter when she started bleeding heavily. A tiny lifeless form had alerted him to the truth and he'd panicked and called the surgery. As soon as Kathy arrived she knew the man regretted getting official help. He wanted her gone almost before she'd put a foot over the threshold, the shame of the situation having overtaken his anxiety for his daughter. The haemorrhaging mother ended up in hospital, the baby, down the outside lavvie before Kathy had arrived and prevented the poor little mite's undignified disposal.

It was too depressing a story to want to relive it. She turned her mind to more cheerful characters. 'Mrs Castell is six months gone now and doing fine, so far as I can tell,' she recounted brightly. 'It's good to see her so chirpy. Oh, and I called in to see Mrs Potter. Her little lad is bonny . . .' Kathy smiled softly at the memory of the handsome black-haired boy. Paul Potter was gaining weight and his little arms and legs were beginning to plump out. She'd noticed a bruise on Ruby's upper arm making Kathy sure Charlie had again manhandled his wife. But the woman's face had been unblemished – apart from the faint scar that remained from the savage beating he'd given her months ago.

'Seen anything of that sister of yours?' David's gruff question broke into Kathy's brooding. He suddenly picked up his cup again and drained it of tea.

'Haven't seen Jenny since the beginning of last week.' Kathy gave David a thoughtful look. It was unusual for him to mention her twin out of the blue. But she felt happy for him to show an interest rather than seeming bored by any mention of her sister, and was about to tell him so when he interrupted.

'It was good that Fred Perry won at Wimbledon, wasn't it?' He indicated the children playing outside in the street with their bats and balls. Kathy squinted into bright evening sunlight, smiling while watching the squealing children.

Kathy had listened to a radio news broadcast about Fred Perry's victory a couple of days previously. She had never been a sporty type but when living at home at the age of about thirteen Eddie had got hold of a couple of tennis rackets via one of his dodgy associates. Before selling them on he'd allowed his twin daughters to take them to the park for a knockabout. The memory of that soft summery afternoon larking about on long grass with Jenny had stayed with Kathy. She'd often wished her father had allowed them to keep the rackets so they could have relived the lovely day, but Eddie never allowed sentiment to overrule profit. He'd taken the rackets back the same evening, moaning that one had a scuff mark on it.

'Where's the rest of it?'

'What *rest*?' Charlie Potter muttered sullenly.

Wes Silver stared in disgust at the mound of crumpled ten-shilling notes Charlie had dumped onto his desk. 'You must be losing your touch, Charlie boy, if that's all you managed to collect this evening.' He sounded resigned, on adding, 'I'm gonna need to find myself a new right-hand man, 'cos you're not up to the job any more.'

'It ain't as easy as it was getting them to part with it.' Charlie mimed gossips by tapping a calloused thumb against his fingers. 'That lot in Great Alie Street are geeing each other up about forming committees. I had to whack Butler so he'd hand over that ten bob, and his old woman was going on about getting the law on me.'

'So you after me coming out again with you on the rounds so they show you a bit of respect?' Wes banged a fist on the desk. 'No point in having a dog and barking meself, Charlie, is there.'

'Dishing out slaps and threats ain't working no more. Serious damage is needed.'

Wes knew Charlie's complaint had a ring of truth to it. On the first few occasions they had gone round collecting, the local shopkeepers had been in shock, handing over money to keep the peace . . . and their teeth. Some had even been swayed towards supporting the cause. But now they realised they were expected to cough up on a regular basis they were less inclined to be intimidated and had started fighting back.

The anti-Fascists were gaining support from the likes of Mr and Mrs Butler and the other traders. Wes knew some of them were agitating at Mosley's rallies because he'd spotted them in the crowds. Extracting funds from them had turned into a double-edged sword because it had never been his intention to boost the number of his hero's enemies. Nevertheless, Wes calculated that when push came to shove business was more important than politics.

To Wes, ten-bob notes were pocket change. But even small fry had their uses, and he didn't like to lose face or let go of any source of income. He grabbed the notes in a large fist. With a sigh he set about straightening and counting them.

'Eight pounds ten shillings,' he announced bitterly. 'Gonna look a bit of a prat turning up at Sanctuary Buildings and offering that as a contribution for the cause, ain't I? How many dozen Blackshirts will that buy?'

Charlie knew that whatever funds were collected, be it fifty pounds or five, only about half of it ever found its way to Mosley. The rest went home with Wes to his nice big house close to Victoria Park where no doubt May Silver commandeered it.

Charlie watched as Wes folded all the notes and slipped them into an inside pocket of his suit jacket.

'Got me wages?'

'Wages?' Wes parroted, looking affronted. 'Chrissake, Charlie! I'm surprised you had the bleedin' cheek to hand over that little bit . . . now you want some back?'

'I need me money,' Charlie growled, swinging about with fists balled at his side. He was going out drinking later and needed a bit of money to flash about.

Wes sat back in his chair, fingers steepled, staring at Charlie. It wasn't the first time he'd sensed his underling would like to leap across his desk and land him one. Charlie was like one of Fritz's unexploded bombs littering the area: you never knew if he might go off under the right conditions. He removed the notes from his pocket, peeled off two. 'Here . . . take that, if you're desperate . . .' The money was placed on the desk with a magnanimous flourish.

'Thanks,' Charlie muttered, back teeth grinding because he felt self-conscious. He got a decent wage off his shift at the docks, but the amount of drinking, gambling and womanising he did made the extra he earned from Wes a necessity to maintain his way of life. Charlie also prized the standing he got from his association with Wes Silver. So, even though he often felt tempted to let loose his tongue and his fists on his boss, he didn't.

Wes wasn't in the same league as the really big boys: the Sabini brothers or the Solomons and other gangs who ran not just in the East End but had tentacles that stretched into other areas of London and, so it was rumoured, overseas. But on his own little patch in the East End, Wes was feared and respected. Charlie knew it was his job to make sure that continued. He could have collected a bit more tonight if he'd carried on pounding the pavements but he'd wanted to knock off a bit early as he had things planned.

Charlie had already siphoned off a ten-bob note from the takings. Wes probably guessed he regularly dipped in before handing over the money. Even so, Charlie still reckoned he was due his rightful earnings.

Wes watched his minion bringing his temper under control and his lips twitched craftily. 'You seem a bit on edge this evening, mate. Everything all right at home, is it? Ruby and the kids all right?'

'Driving me round the bend, they are, as usual.' Charlie saw what his boss was trying to do: give him an excuse for snapping and snarling. 'Off out tonight for a bit of peace and quiet from the lot of 'em.'

'Best thing that is . . . have a few pints on me . . .'

Charlie turned away, pocketing his wages. His smile turned snide. 'With any luck, I'll be having more than that on you, mate,' he muttered beneath his breath as he went out, thinking about Blanche Raven.

CHAPTER SIXTEEN

'And where d'you think you're sloping off to?'

Davy Wright scowled at his mother. She knew very well where he was off to. He'd been going to see his father in the East End, on a Saturday afternoon, for months. He wished now he'd never told her about how that started.

He'd bumped into his father by chance, spotting him doing a van delivery to Islington just before Christmas. Davy had recognised his father straight away, despite having only been eight years old last time he clapped eyes on Stan Wright. His father had run out on them several years before, turning up out of the blue on a sentimental visit to his four sons. Stan had not stopped long, as his estranged wife threw the poker at him as soon as she realised he was only giving her a couple of half-crowns to help out the family.

After another long absence, Davy had thought his father might pretend he'd not seen him and hop in the van and drive away, but he'd offered him a lift, and given him two bob on dropping him off at the top of

Campbell Road. Stan's unexpected generosity made it worthwhile for Davy to pursue the relationship. His mother gave him nothing and expected him to hand over to her everything he earned from his odd jobs. She'd found out he was acting as a part-time croupier at the weekends during the illegal street-gambling sessions. He'd expected her to go mad but she'd demanded to know what the job paid, so he'd boasted a bit about how well he did. That had been another mistake because she expected something every week now even if he hadn't had work.

So, when Stan had said farewell on Christmas Eve and told him to pop over and see him some time, Davy had taken him up on it, turning up in the East End the very next week.

His father hadn't been so generous on that occasion, or as welcoming, no doubt because the old dragon he lived with had made it clear she didn't want Davy in the house. Father and son had shuffled off together for a walk with Violet Potter bawling down the street after them that Davy could piss off back to Islington because she didn't want any of Stan's kids coming calling. Instead of Davy knocking his dad up in Brick Lane, he and Stan now made a habit of meeting up on a Saturday afternoon by Petticoat Lane market. Sometimes Davy got no more than a chat about his father's wartime heroics in the navy and the cost of his bus fare during their mooch about; other times Stan dipped in his pocket and was as generous as he'd been that time when wishing Davy a merry Christmas.

'I said, where you off to?' Polly Wright gave her son's arm a shake to hurry his reply.

'East End . . . see Dad.' Davy mumbled, pulling away.

He knew he had to toe the line. His mother had warned him that either he coughed up each week or he was out on his ear. Davy also knew there was no way his father would take him in if he and his mother had a bust-up. Violet Potter had made that pretty clear.

'Seein' *him* again, are yer? Well, make sure he sends some money back fer me,' Polly snarled, as she always did if she managed to catch Davy before he set off for the bus stop.

Stan Wright might have run out over a decade ago but she still classed him as her husband. The main reason she'd never taken up with another man was that she resented letting Stan off the hook. That was how he'd see it as soon as he found out another fellow was pitching in his wages with hers. Now Davy had discovered his father's whereabouts, Polly reckoned it was high time Stan made good on what he owed her for bringing up his five sons on her own.

'Where you off to?'

'See me old man.'

Tom Finch had just turned up at Davy's house, football under his arm, to find his friend emerging from his doorway looking cleaner and tidier than he usually did when they had a kick-about on a weekend.

'Thought this week you was going over Sunday to see him,' Tom said huffily. Davy had told him he'd got an opportunity to act as croupier on Saturday dinnertime.

'Going today; nuthin' doing for me on the corner.' Davy sounded disappointed; the job of croupier could be lucrative and therefore sought after by grown men who thought they were more entitled to the pickings than any upstart kids showing promise at it. Davy feared he would soon be elbowed out completely as more men in the street lost their regular employment.

'Fancy comin' over there with me?' Davy asked as they walked up the road. He'd asked Tom before if he fancied a bus ride to Whitechapel but his friend had never taken him up on the offer.

'Me mum'll go nuts.'

'Don't tell her.'

Tom fancied doing something now he was at a loose end. He had a shilling burning a hole in his pocket for the fare. Kathy had come by earlier in the week to visit and had slipped him the coin out of sight of their mother's eagle eye. If Winnie had seen it she'd have had it off him the moment Kathy went home.

'Be back by teatime, will we?' Tom asked, partially swayed by the idea of a trip out.

'Yeah . . . always back by then 'cos me dad's gotta take that old bag down the pub Saturday night.' Davy now knew enough about his father's domestic routine: Violet's rule was that Stan must be home early for his tea so they could get ready to go out on the razzle by six o'clock.

Tom grinned. 'All right . . . just get rid of this and tell me mum we're off to the flicks.' He tossed the football in the air, catching it before setting off up the street at a trot.

'Don't take ages, then, or we'll miss the bleedin' bus,' Davy called after his friend.

'Hello, son, how you doin'?' Stan Wright extended a hand to Tom and shook it. 'Remember your dad, I do. Me 'n' Eddie would have a pint together now 'n' again when I was living in Islington.'

Tom smiled bashfully, trying not to stare at the big bruise on Davy's dad's cheek. Stan had obviously been in a fight and Tom reckoned the man must be a bit of a rough handful although he looked a lot older than his own dad. Stan's hair was almost completely grey and sparse on top, and he had a soft wobbly belly on him, visible beneath his faded check shirt. It was a warm July day and where he'd rolled his sleeves back Tom could see an anchor tattoo adorning one of his forearms. Tom felt impressed that Davy had such a father. His own dad didn't have any tattoos and he was a coward. Tom remembered past occasions when men came round after Eddie to accuse him of short-changing them on a deal. Eddie would get Winnie to say he was out while he hid upstairs, peeping out from behind the bedroom curtains, till the coast was clear.

Stan Wright sensed Tom Finch studying his purple cheek so avoided his son's knowing eye. He was getting sick of Violet branding him for all to see. He knew that daughter-in-law of hers was most of the problem, winding her up by coming over asking for money.

'Where we going then?' Davy asked as they set off, jostling to and fro in the bustling market, smirking at merchants' ribald patter.

'Don't mind, son . . . fancy taking the weight off for a cuppa and a bun in a caff?'

'Yeah . . . great . . .' Davy was happy to take advantage of his father showing off in front of Tom. Usually, Stan's largesse would run to a pie or sausage roll for them both from a street vendor.

'So . . . your dad still in the same business, is he, Tom?' Stan asked craftily. He was aware his question made the boy shift uncomfortably on his chair. When he'd lived in Islington he'd come to hear that Eddie earned well ducking and diving on the wrong side of the law.

'Yeah . . . he's still got his own business. I'm joining him when I leave school,' Tom added proudly.

'Are yer now?' Stan nodded at his son. 'Hear that, Davy? Yer mate's going in with his dad.'

'Shame you ain't got a business, then I'd go in with you,' Davy answered wistfully.

'Wish I did have me own lark set up, son. But me stepson, as I call him, even though he ain't proper family like you, well, Charlie's in partners with a very big noise round the East End.' Stan had elevated Charlie Potter from Wes's underling to his equal.

'Yeah?' Davy sounded interested. 'I'm done with school soon. Any chance you could put in a word fer me with Charlie?'

'Oh, no, son,' Stan said quickly, wishing he'd kept his mouth shut. His stepson wouldn't take kindly to finding out he'd been discussing him. 'Closed shop, it is, if you get me drift . . .' He tapped the side of his nose and gulped down his tea.

Davy looked downhearted; he would have liked to be able to brag to pals, as Tom did, that he was going to work in a family firm. Most of the kids who'd left school at the end of term only had dead-end errand-boy jobs or the queue at the Labour Exchange to look forward to.

'What you up to then?'

Charlie Potter had come up behind the trio seated in the caff and taken the table opposite. Politely he yanked back a chair for his female companion before lounging into his own.

Stan had instinctively shot to his feet at the sight of

his stepson, wondering if he'd been overheard talking about him a moment ago. When Charlie gave him an easy smile, he sank down into his seat, feeling foolish. 'Bleedin' took me by surprise, Charlie, creeping up like that,' he complained, trying to cover his lapse.

'Guilty conscience, mate, that is.' Charlie smirked at the two lads. He gave the waitress a lazy wink as she set down two cups of tea on the table. 'Reckon one of you must be Stan's son. Me muvver's told me about a lad coming over on a Saturday.' He didn't add that Vi had moaned something chronic about it.

'That's me,' Davy piped up when his father sat sullen and silent. 'And this is me pal Tom Finch.'

'Well, nice to meet you both.' Charlie sensed a pair of sharp dark eyes on him. 'I'll introduce you to me friend Blanche now you've done the honours.' Charlie had noticed that Stan had been darting suspicious glances at the pretty brunette with him.

Blanche perked up now she wasn't being overlooked, dimpling a smile. She'd noticed that the older youth had been ogling her bosom while talking to Charlie, so leaned forward, elbows on the table so he could get a better look. 'This your stepfather then, is it, Charlie?' she asked.

'That's him.' Charlie slung a brawny arm around her shoulders, just to let Stan into the nature of his relationship with Blanche. He could tell the old sod was itching to know if he was sleeping with a bit on the side. He wasn't yet, because Blanche was still playing hard to get, but he was confident that once he bought her the dress she'd admired a moment ago, hanging up on a stall in the market, she'd come across. Stan didn't have the guts to make any sly remarks about his wife and kids at home, so, just to rub it in that he'd managed to hook up with a good-looker young enough to be his daughter, Charlie nuzzled Blanche's cheek, making her giggle.

'You lads finished yer teas?' Stan shoved away his cup and saucer. 'Come on, let's get goin' . . .'

'Somethin' I said?' Charlie asked, sounding jolly.

'Don't be daft,' Stan muttered. 'We're off now 'cos Davy and his mate have gotta get the bus back to Islington soon. See you later on then, Charlie . . .'

'Ain't in a rush to get home, Dad,' Davy piped up, drawing a glare from Stan. He ignored it, getting to his feet. If his father wouldn't put in a word for him, he'd do it himself. 'Me dad's told me how well you're doing in yer business. I'm leaving school soon and looking fer a good job . . .' He boldly stuck out a hand to Charlie.

'Told you all about me, did he now?' Charlie cut in, giving Stan a menacing smile. 'That's nice.' He pumped Davy's hand. 'I'll keep you in mind, son, don't you worry about that.'

Davy beamed, then realising his father was already on his way to the door he followed him.

Blanche spooned sugar into her tea and stirred it. 'Fancy a bit of cake,' she announced sulkily.

Charlie looked at her. 'Fancy lots of things, don't yer, gel? Fancy me, do yer?'

'Course I do . . .' Blanche purred in a bid to open his wallet.

She realised that oddly it was the truth. She was coming to like his rough-and-ready ways and was glad he'd made an effort to get in touch with her after they met on the day of her fight with Joyce Groves. She'd come out of work one evening to find him hanging about outside the Goldsteins' dress shop. After a bit of dilly-dallying, she'd agreed to go with him for a drink in a pub, because she was losing hope of her and Nick getting back together.

It had been weeks since she'd received a letter from her estranged husband's solicitor about the divorce and she'd resigned herself to the inevitable. Blanche would sooner have got back with Wes Silver if she couldn't have Nick. But she knew that wouldn't happen either. His wife now had a stranglehold on him, following their affair. Although he was only consolation prize, Charlie Potter had a swagger and a powerful presence that impressed her. She'd noticed when they'd been in the market that people were respectful when he was around, moving quickly aside so he could guide her closer to the stalls and let her see the merchandise. She'd heard rumours about him being a wrong 'un but he could be a gentleman to her. So she reckoned Charlie Potter might do till someone better came along . . .

'Need a new dress if we're going out later. Got nothing to wear . . .' Blanche thought she might as well test how much of a gentleman he was prepared to be. If he paid for it, she knew she'd feel aroused enough to stay the night with him if he again suggested getting them a room in a hotel.

'Don't you get no discount off the clothes where you work?' Charlie had rented an old Humber to pick her up from work last week in the hope of getting her to join him on the back seat. She'd let him get her merry on gin and orange but had turned her nose up at the rest. He'd reluctantly upped his offer to a night in a hotel but still she'd flounced off home. Charlie was starting to think Blanche was hard work and it was high time she let him find out if she was worth the effort.

'Get a discount? You must be joking!' Blanche snorted, having swallowed her mouthful of tea. 'Don't get nuthin' fer nuthin' off that old Jew boy. Pay full price for all of his stuff. Anyhow, it's old-fashioned and I wouldn't want any of it even if I could afford it. I like the dress outside in the market.'

'Yeah, I heard you,' Charlie snapped.

'Gonna get me a slice of fruitcake cake, then?'

'No, 'cos I'm watching your figure even if you ain't.' Charlie gave Blanche a smile, draining his tea in a swallow and wiping his mouth with the back of a hand. 'Never fit in that dress out there, will yer, gel, if you keep scoffing cakes and get fat.'

Blanche gave him a subtle smile as his lustful gaze roamed over her. 'Reckon you might like me better out of it than in, anyhow. You can let me know later, if yer like . . .'

'Yeah, I will.' Charlie stood up. 'Go get it then, shall we, and tonight I'll stand us a stay in a hotel and unzip it for you.' He put his meaty hands on the table and leaned forward to purr, 'No arguments . . . right?'

CHAPTER SEVENTEEN

Nick had felt like bawling his mother out on the day she gave him Kathy's letter. But he hadn't. It wasn't Lottie's fault that she didn't know he'd started to think about a certain girl in a different way from the rest of the women he pursued.

In the past, he'd used the same tactic himself, dropping hints about a wife in the background, when trying to deter a woman on the prowl. But Kathy Finch wasn't on the prowl . . . he was. And she'd known he was interested in her from the day that he'd dropped her home after the Potters' baby was born. It had been months ago, and he'd hoped to forget her. But he hadn't been able to put her out of his mind and had found himself taking longer routes when driving just so he might catch a glimpse of her on her rounds.

He had bought the bike to test the water. He'd thought if she accepted the gift he might get a foot in the door . . . but that was before Lottie blurted out something he should have mentioned to Kathy himself. He would have done so when things between them progressed a bit, and the time seemed right.

He slipped her letter back in the desk drawer. He'd had it for several weeks and done nothing about going to see her, as she'd politely requested. He chuckled wryly, acknowledging his cowardice. He was hoping her opinion of him might have softened over time but he knew he was mistaken. If he thought she might like him enough to care that he had a wife, he reckoned he was mistaken about that too. Probably she just had him down as a randy chancer, best avoided.

Nice girls didn't accept gifts from married men, and he knew he would definitely not be mistaken about the reception he'd get when he eventually turned up. She'd tell him to take the bike back while trying to remain civil. The bloody thing must be stuck in her shed as she wasn't using it. He'd driven past the bus stop in Commercial Street a few days ago and seen her standing there, in her nurse's uniform, with her bag in her hand. She hadn't noticed him as she'd been chatting to a woman in the queue. He'd slowed down to watch her laughing, feeling glad she looked happy, and just as beautiful as he remembered . . .

Once round the corner, he'd pulled up to have a smoke and a think about things. He'd mocked himself for having gone out of his way to bump into her with no success, then when it happened by chance, being too timid to take advantage. By the time he'd turned round and headed back to talk to her, the bus had been and gone, with Nurse Finch on it.

But something good had come out of his mother's

indiscretion: he'd snapped out of his indifference over the long overdue divorce proceedings.

The telephone on Nick's desk rang, breaking into his musing. His father-in-law started giving him a list of stuff he needed from the builders' merchants for work on the Commercial Street property.

'Bit slower, mate, I don't do shorthand,' Nick complained as Tony reeled off his demands for materials.

'Need to get yerself a secretary then,' Tony quipped. 'I reckon our Blanche would be up for the job. Have a word, shall I?'

His son-in-law's discouraging grunt wiped the smile off Tony Scott's face. He finished reading out his list then put down the receiver, brooding on his daughter. He knew Blanche would jump at a chance to have any role in her ex-husband's life, including working for him. Tony was desperate for Nick to show a bit of interest in her. He was resigned to the fact that a renewed romance was out of the question, but if the couple could be friends he'd be satisfied.

The letter from Nick's solicitor about the divorce had sent Blanche into a right state for a few days. But that had been weeks ago; she seemed to have perked up now and that was worrying Tony because he feared his daughter's renewed exuberance was down to the company she was keeping.

Tony had felt uncomfortable raising the matter of the solicitor's letter with his boss. But he had, following nagging from his wife and daughter that it was his duty to try to persuade Nick to withdraw proceedings. Tony hadn't expected to get anything back from Nick but a reminder to mind his own business. He'd been spot on. But Tony knew he'd have to speak to Nick soon on another matter concerning Blanche, in the hope his daughter might heed her ex-husband's advice if she wouldn't take his.

Driving home in a works van one evening, Tony had recognised Charlie Potter hanging about at the top of the road and wondered what the villain was up to. Little had he known at the time that Charlie was waiting on Blanche, who was indoors, getting ready to go out with him.

The following weekend, Tony had seen them together entering a pub and had been shocked at the way Charlie had his arm around Blanche. He'd felt so nauseated at his daughter allowing herself to be pawed by a lowlife that he'd forgotten about playing in the darts match at his working men's club and had returned home.

Tony started packing away his tools; it wasn't knocking off time but he wanted to catch Blanche coming out of work and have another go at talking some sense into her. Gladys didn't yet know that her daughter was seeing a violent thug who also happened to be married. Tony knew that when Gladys found out what had been going on, she'd kick Blanche out.

'Your father in a rush to get you home, is he?' Emmanuel Goldstein continued counting the roll of notes he'd taken out of the till. He stuffed the wad into a canvas bag. 'The man needs a watch. You finish at six o'clock. You should tell him.'

'I know. I do, Mr Goldstein,' Blanche dutifully replied. She'd also noticed her father pacing up and down outside, puffing on a cigarette. She twiddled her thumbs on the wooden counter. The clock on the wall gave the time as ten minutes to six. No customer had passed over the threshold in the past forty minutes and none was likely to. Still, she knew her boss wouldn't allow her out until the dot of six o'clock, even though it was obvious her father had arrived to give her a lift. Not that Blanche wanted the earache she was sure to get from Tony, but she was pleased to see him as it would save her the bus fare home.

'He saw me waiting. Why didn't he let you off a few minutes early?' Tony complained, stamping on his dog end.

'Go and ask him,' Blanche returned, shrugging into her cardigan. 'Ask Mum why the old git sends her back the coats 'cos she's forgotten to snip a few threads off inside the linings. It's how he is, the miser, and I hate working for him.'

Tony wished he'd kept his mouth shut: his daughter twisted everything about to find an excuse to moan about her job.

'And if you've turned up to start bellyaching about me friends, you're wasting your time.' Blanche got into her father's van.

Tony plunged onto the seat beside her, slamming the door and thumping his fist down on the steering wheel. 'Now you listen to me, my gel! Charlie Potter ain't *friends* with anyone, least of all someone like you, who's young enough to be his daughter. He's a bad sort with a wife and kids at home.'

Her father's angry outburst turned Blanche's expression sulky. It hadn't come as a surprise when her new boyfriend had admitted he was married, because men of his age were rarely single. Her mother had told her about the amount of men who'd got killed in the Great War, and how it had left women spinsters because there weren't enough of the opposite sex to go round. In

Blanche's opinion, there was still a lack of attractive fellows to choose from.

She wasn't bothered about Charlie's home life. It wasn't as though she was thinking of stealing him away to settle down with him. She was just having a bit of fun till the right man came along to take care of her properly.

'You listening to me?' Tony noisily changed gear.

'You don't need to worry about me, Dad.' Blanche gave him a winning smile. 'I ain't your innocent little girl now, am I? I'm all grown up. I've been married, and pregnant, and an older man's mistress, so I know what life's all about.'

'You think being a married man's bit on the side's something to be proud of, do you?' Tony glared at her. He'd hated Blanche being involved with Wes Silver and had guessed from the start that it'd all end in tears. He had to admit, though, he'd gladly see Blanche back with Wes rather than knocking about with a piece of scum like Charlie Potter.

'Wes knows that you're hooked up with one of his henchmen, does he? Bet he's laughing his bollocks off about that.'

Blanche shrugged airily, although her father's remark had hit home. She reckoned Wes might be a bit jealous of her seeing Charlie; if anybody was laughing at her it was Wes's cow of a wife. Blanche had come face to face with May Silver just after Wes told her it was all over between them and he was going back to his wife. The older woman had made a point of sneering at her in a way that had made Blanche's fists itch. May would lap up knowing her husband's cast-off was now sleeping with one of the hired help.

'None of Wes's business now, is it, what I get up to? Same as it's nothing to do with you 'n' Mum.'

'That's yer attitude, is it, gel?' Tony pursed his lips, steering the van jerkily round a corner. 'Well, when you get in you can repeat to yer mother what you've just told me, and I reckon she'll tell you where the door is.' He noticed his threat had wiped away Blanche's smugness. 'Think a nobody like Potter'll set you up somewhere, do you, when you get kicked out of ours?' He snorted derision. 'You'll get nuthin' off him except a right-hander every time you upset him.'

'Charlie might look a bit rough but he treats me like a lady.'

Tony gave his daughter an incredulous look. 'And you reckon that'll last, do you, once he's had what he wants? Ask his wife how well he treats her. You ain't special to him, Blanche, and you're a mug if you think differently. Remember this, I can't protect you from somebody like him once the novelty's worn off. So you think on . . .'

Emo Goldstein was on the way to the bank to pay in the previous day's takings when he spotted his son talking to a blonde dressed in nurse's uniform. He sighed, shaking his head to himself, pulling his trilby's brim low over his eyes so he could pretend he'd not seen them together. He knew who she was, and he knew David wasn't telling the truth when he said he'd thrown her over.

Emo had nothing against Kathy Finch personally; he could understand why his son was smitten. She was a good-looker, doing a good job, and would make someone a fine wife. But not his son.

Her faith and her family went against her in Emo's

172

eyes, and David's mother felt even more strongly that their son should choose a well-bred Jewish girl to marry. If only he'd make an effort to socialise more within the community, David would be a sought-after husband too. He was a handsome boy with nice ways; everybody said so. Emo intended that his only son would have plenty to offer a bride . . . as long as she was the right one. Emo wasn't a boastful man but he'd made sure that people knew how generous he intended to be when David found a suitable girl.

He and his wife, Sarah, had believed their son had settled on the perfect wife years ago. But David and Rachel's romance had turned sour before an engagement could be announced.

On reaching the bank, Emo quickly ducked behind a pillar, glad of the shelter as he noticed the couple crossing the road. Peering round the stone, he watched his son and the nurse laughing together. Emo knew if his wife found out he'd seen David with Kathy she would expect a detailed account, including his opinion on how amorous they'd appeared.

Emo frowned, trudging through the bank's doors. His son was a grown man, in his mid-twenties. David would follow his heart and do as he pleased, and his mother would have to get used to it . . . or lose contact with her son.

'How are you, Pansy?'

The small girl nodded, as she always did when unwilling to speak. The solemn signal was her way of letting Nurse Finch know she was all right.

Only Kathy was never sure that any of the Potters were really all right.

She had no official reason to continue to come to see Ruby and the children. The woman's confinement had ended a long while ago. But still she felt compelled to find the time to stop by to check on the family whenever she was passing. She chose times to call when it was most likely Charlie would be out. If by unlucky chance he were in, Kathy stuck to asking businesslike questions about mother and baby, aware of his gimlet glances on her all the while. When the brute was nowhere to be seen, Kathy would stop and sit down for a chat with Ruby.

'Cup of tea, Nurse Finch?' Ruby offered, putting Paul down in his pram. The woman looked pleased to have a bit of company and went to fill the kettle. 'Sit down at the table if you don't mind the mess . . .'

'No tea for me, thanks all the same . . . it's a flying visit.' In fact, Kathy had plenty of time as she'd finished her rounds. But she was very aware of how precious were things like tea and milk to women like Ruby, who had to account to mean husbands for every penny they'd spent before they could prise out of them a bit more housekeeping.

Before taking a seat, Kathy peered into the pram and smiled at the sight of the gurgling baby. His dark brown eyes were wide open and he gave her a gummy smile as she tickled his chin. Kathy's smile faded as Ruby came closer and she noticed a yellowing bruise by her temple. Kathy looked away, ruffling Pansy's hair. It was pointless saying anything about the mark; Ruby would insist she'd banged her head on a cupboard or fallen in the back yard, as she always did when showing signs of a beating.

'Are you helping Mummy look after your baby brother?' Kathy pulled out a chair and sat down.

The little girl nodded slowly, pressing together her small lips.

'Big help, she is,' Ruby said proudly. 'Dunks nappies and puts 'em out to dry, don't yer, Pans?'

Again the child nodded, a glimmer of a smile still present.

'You'll miss her when she goes to school,' Kathy said.

Ruby turned away. 'Best off here with me, she is.'

'But . . . you want her to learn, don't you?'

'I can teach her what she needs to know.' Ruby's voice sounded brittle.

'Surely you'll want her to learn her sums and so on.'

'I can teach her, I said.'

Kathy bit her lip, falling silent. She knew very well that Ruby's education must have been minimal. The woman could hardly read the instructions that had been with the maternity pack she'd received before Paul's birth. There was little hope of her helping her daughter to read and write.

'You'll get in trouble, Ruby,' Kathy said gently. 'The school board people will find out sooner or later . . .'

'Cross that bridge when I come to it,' Ruby snapped. She suddenly looked deflated. 'She's better off here with me. Don't want no mean kids bullying her 'cos of how she is. She gets enough of that here at home.' She suddenly clamped together her lips. 'Better get on now . . . lots to do before Peter gets in from school. He'll want his tea and Paul's due a feed.'

'Still got plenty of milk for him?' Kathy asked.

Ruby chuckled. 'Like a bleedin' dairy, I am. Never had this much with me other two.'

'No more soreness, or cracked nipples?' Kathy remembered that just after the birth, Ruby had had a nasty abscess and had vowed to put the baby on the bottle. But she'd persevered with breastfeeding, no doubt because Charlie had refused to stump up for formula milk.

'Nothing like that. He's a gentle little soul even now he's getting his teeth.'

'Toofpegs . . .' Pansy suddenly piped up and pointed to the pram.

'Paul's getting his teethpegs, is he?' Kathy asked, hoping to encourage some more words from the little girl. But Pansy had withdrawn again and simply nodded.

'See . . . she ain't daft,' Ruby said proudly. 'She's bright as a button, ain't yer, Pans?'

'All the more reason to get her into school. She'll do well, Ruby, and when the time comes Pansy will get herself a good job with good pay.' Kathy watched the woman's expression turn achingly wistful. 'Peter will surely look out for Pansy if she goes to the same school.' Kathy pressed home her point.

'Ain't risking it.' Ruby again sounded intractable. 'He can't be with her all the while. I know how nasty folk are.'

'Yes . . . you do . . .' Kathy sighed, standing up to leave. She felt she had made some headway on the subject of Pansy's schooling and it was best to let Ruby mull things over. It was obvious the woman desperately loved and wanted to protect her daughter. An education would help Pansy escape the miserable existence her mother had and Kathy believed Ruby knew it.

Kathy had reached the door when it opened a few inches in front of her face. Charlie Potter entered and she diverted quickly away from him.

'So, Mrs Potter, if you come along to the surgery you can have Paul weighed at the postnatal clinic.' Kathy felt she had to say something to justify her presence.

'He don't need no more weighing, Nurse Finch,' Charlie said, giving Kathy a grin that left his cold eyes unmoved. 'Doin' all right, is little 'un. Ain't that so, Rube?'

The baby, as though startled by Charlie's voice, started to wail, and Ruby rushed to agitate the pram in an attempt to quieten him.

Kathy looked from Ruby to Pansy, noting the same expression of fear stilling their features. They seemed to be holding themselves rigid, waiting for a sign as to the mood of the head of the family.

'Spoke to you, gel . . . arst a question,' Charlie reminded his wife. 'Tell Nurse Finch how well nipper's doing.'

Ruby jerked to attention, nodding. 'He's doing well . . . we all are . . . Nurse knows that. Told her already, ain't I?'

Kathy despised herself for wanting to rush from the menacing atmosphere and into the sunshine outside. She forced herself to step towards Pansy and ruffle her hair. Then with a sense of hopelessness because there was nothing she could do to make the brute go away and leave them all in peace, she said clearly, 'Glad to hear everything's as it should be.' She slipped past Potter and towards the door. 'I'll be round again soon.' She directed her comment at Ruby but the woman avoided her eye and Kathy closed the door quietly behind herself.

'I reckon you been talking out o' turn again, criticising me.'

'I ain't . . . I ain't said a word about you.' Ruby backed away as her husband advanced purposefully.

'Why's she keep coming here then, poking her nose in?'

'I don't know,' Ruby said with a catch to her voice. 'I don't ask her to. She's just nice like that . . . caring . . .'

'I'll give you fucking caring,' Charlie hissed, his attention diverting as the baby's screams hit a peak. 'Shut that poxy brat up or I will.' Charlie glared at the pram and took a menacing step towards it. 'We was doin' all right before you started whorin'. That little bastard ain't my problem and I want rid of it!' he roared.

'We weren't all right.' Ruby darted to the pram, trying to soothe the baby with her touch while shielding Paul from her husband. 'We've never been all right, and you know it. Ain't Paul's fault.'

'Perhaps if I rearrange his features a bit fer 'im, people might not stare so much and have a good laugh behind me back 'cos me wife's opened her legs fer a Chinaman.' He dived past Ruby and grabbed the howling boy by his clothes. His fist hovered by the baby's boiling, crumpled face, his teeth drawn back in a ferocious snarl. He glanced at Ruby. 'Hate the ugly fucker, I do . . .'

'I'm sorry, Charlie . . . give him here . . . please . . . make it up to you, I will . . .'

'Yeah . . . you will . . .' Charlie thrust the baby at her.

'Go and get in bed, Pansy,' Ruby whispered as her husband kicked at the pram as he passed it, unbuttoning his shirt on his way to the bed. 'Daddy wants his tea.' Carefully, Ruby placed Paul back in his pram, tears sliding down her cheeks.

Pansy climbed onto her grimy bed and crawled under the covers, pulling the blanket over her ears when she heard the thuds and bangs and her mother groaning. When her little brother started to scream louder, she banged her head against the wall that separated the rooms, repeatedly whispering, 'No, Daddy . . .'

CHAPTER EIGHTEEN

'You've got a visitor.'

Kathy simply frowned. She had walked all the way home preoccupied by tortured thoughts of the Potters and had been startled by Eunice pouncing on her as she unlatched the gate.

'He's hanging about in there.' Eunice jerked a nod at the waiting room. 'I told him you were due back any minute.'

Kathy had an inkling of the identity of the caller even before Nick Raven started strolling down the path towards her. She hadn't wanted anyone else to be in on this meeting and wished Eunice would take herself off. She caught her breath as Nick approached, having forgotten just how handsome and imposing he could seem. He was taller and broader than Dr Worth – or David, for that matter – and his fair hair seemed to have a silver glint with the evening sun on it. Had she been more alert Kathy realised she would have recognised his smart car parked a few yards down the road and be prepared for this.

'Oh . . . hello.' Kathy forced out a greeting. 'I expect you've had my letter by now and have turned up about the bike.'

'Mmm. Sorry it's taken me a while to come over. Been busy.'

'That's all right . . . I understand . . .' Kathy glanced at Eunice, still hovering. 'It's in the shed. I'll just unlock it. I expect I didn't make plain the sort of bike I was after; second-hand was all I wanted.' She gave him a flashing glance. 'But thanks anyway for taking the trouble to—'

'Mr Raven wants to donate the bike to the surgery,' Eunice interrupted, suppressing a smirk. 'So it's not just yours, you see, Kathy. We can keep it for the next nurse to use when you leave.'

'Right . . . good . . .' Kathy eventually said, swerving her blue gaze to clash on a pair of narrowed grey eyes. 'How thoughtful of you, Mr Raven.'

'Sorry . . . should have made myself clear when I dropped it off.' Nick dug his hands deeper into his pockets. 'It was my fault the other one got pinched, anyhow, so I ought to replace it. Charlie and me were a distraction to you that night. I expect you'd've remembered to lock the bike if we hadn't shown up a bit the worse for wear.'

Eunice's expression made it clear she'd like an explanation.

'Mr Raven brought Ruby Potter's husband home the night Paul was born and there was a bit of confusion.' Kathy left it at that.

'Oh . . . Potter had been drinking, had he?' Eunice's features registered distaste. 'I recall the family you mean. Came a month early, didn't he, the poor little blighter.'

She turned to Nick. 'A bike is so important with night-time emergencies like ours. Babies won't wait for the buses, you know . . .'

The group fell quiet as the last patient, leaning on a stick, came out of the building and went on his way. A moment later, Eunice's husband followed the elderly fellow down the path, hand extended towards Nick in readiness to be shaken.

Sidney Worth knew of Nick Raven's reputation. A while ago the man had had his picture in the local paper for donating fifty pounds towards the cost of rebuilding the community hall. Sidney knew if he could foster enough support and private funding from philanthropists the project he had in mind might materialise. He wanted to enlarge the maternity clinic into the annexe where Nurse Finch had quarters. Of course, it would mean she and her successors would have to find alternative accommodation . . .

'Eunice has told me about your gift, sir. Much obliged for such generosity.' Dr Worth grasped the fingers Nick had withdrawn from his pocket and pumped them. 'We are always very grateful when local businessmen find it in their hearts to be charitable. The less fortunate of the parish benefit enormously from such gestures—'

'My pleasure.' Nick cut across Dr Worth's gratitude in a voice tinged with irony.

'Well . . . I'll leave you all to it. I have some notes to write up,' Kathy said, giving him a sharp glance.

'There was something else I wanted to speak to you about, Nurse Finch.'

Kathy hesitated; so did Dr Worth and Eunice, until it became obvious that their benefactor was waiting for them to leave before saying anything else.

'I take it you're not going to ask me in.' Nick nodded at her front door as the couple disappeared inside the surgery.

'That's right,' Kathy replied politely.

'I'm getting divorced.'

'Sorry to hear it,' Kathy said.

He gave her a rueful smile. 'Look, perhaps I should have mentioned it sooner.'

'I don't know why you think I'd be interested.'

'I think you do.'

'And I think you know that I told you I have a boyfriend.'

'Ah, David Goldstein . . . that's right. You did tell me about him.'

'I didn't tell you his surname,' Kathy blurted, alarmed that he might have been checking up on her. 'How did you find that out?'

'My ex-wife works for the Goldsteins, in one of their shops. I know they've got a son called David who's a local copper. Wasn't that hard to work out he was probably the one. But I wasn't quite sure till just now . . .'

Kathy's lips parted in surprise, leaving her momentarily dumbfounded. 'Well, small world,' she eventually said.

'Yeah . . . too small,' Nick muttered. 'My mother took to you.'

'I thought she was nice,' Kathy admitted after a quiet moment reflecting on the meeting with Lottie Raven. 'Has Charlie Potter been back bothering her? I didn't think it right to ask her about it.'

'I hope she'd tell me if he had.'

'He's still beating his wife.' The words spurted out of her like vomit.

The dreadful knowledge of Potter's brutality was burning like acid in her gut and the longer she kept it to herself the more the pain became unbearable. Nick Raven was the only person she felt she could talk to about it because it was no secret to him. A member of his own family had first-hand experience of Charlie's sadistic streak.

There had been times when Kathy had yearned to confide her worst fears in David, but she'd realised he might feel duty-bound to tell his superiors and they would intervene. Ruby's lot would then worsen; she might even lose her beloved children.

Nick rubbed a hand over his jaw. 'It doesn't surprise me he's still dishing out right-handers.'

'I suspect he might have hurt the children too, before now,' Kathy whispered. 'I've seen marks on Pansy . . . Ruby says she's clumsy. I've no proof of anything.'

'And the baby? Have you seen bruises on him?' Nick demanded.

Kathy shook her head. 'I made up an excuse to examine him not long ago. He's bonny and seems content.'

Nick stared at her; that he understood the gravity of the situation was clear in his expression.

'I've just come from theirs, actually. I made a point of popping in this afternoon. I often stop by if I think Charlie might be out. Ruby has a bruise healing on her face.'

Nick came closer to her as though to comfort her. 'Have you mentioned any of it?' He raised his eyes, indicating the surgery with a subtle nod.

'Ruby's made me promise not to. She's scared the children might be taken away by the cruelty people.'

'Be the best thing, wouldn't it?'

'Not for her!' Kathy hissed, violently shaking her head. 'I think she'd kill herself if she lost them.'

'If Charlie doesn't top her first, you mean?' Nick brusquely gestured apology for his sarcasm. 'You going to come out with me so we can talk about this some more?'

Kathy gazed at him, disillusioned.

Nick blew out his lips in a gruff chuckle. 'All right, I own up: I want to get to know you a bit better too.'

'No strings attached?'

Nick shrugged, walked away a pace. 'If that's how you want it . . .' he said over a shoulder.

'You don't sound very convincing.'

'Good . . . because if I did, you'd accuse me of play-acting. When's your afternoon off?'

'Wednesday next week.' Kathy answered automatically.

'Right. I'll pick you up after midday.'

'Not before one o'clock. I don't finish till half twelve. I'm going to tell David about it.'

'You do that.' Nick gave her a second long smile before striding towards the gate.

'I was hoping I might bump into you, mate.' In fact, Charlie had been loitering in the vicinity of the bus stop with the intention of intercepting Davy. He knew Stan's son routinely travelled back to Islington at about five o'clock, having spent Saturday afternoon with his father. 'Got a minute for a chat and a cup of char before you get on yer way?'

Davy grinned, delighted to see him. It had been some weeks since they'd met, but in the meantime, Davy hadn't forgotten his dad's stepson. He had often found himself wondering whether Charlie's promise to let him know if a job turned up had been just talk. He was praying it had not.

'Course I've got a minute. I'll catch a later bus home,' Davy burbled.

'Go over there, shall we, and have a cuppa? Fancy a bacon sandwich, do you?' Charlie indicated the greasy spoon caff across the road.

Davy nodded eagerly. His father had been stingy earlier, spending only a few coppers on some grub when they were out walking, and leaving Davy still hungry. There'd been no sit-down in a caff for a bite to eat on a Saturday afternoon since the day he'd had Tom's company. His friend hadn't been over again. Eddie Finch had seen his son getting off the bus when they got back to Islington that evening. Tom's dad had wanted to know all the ins and outs of where they'd been and who'd they'd seen. After that, Tom had said he couldn't be bothered to make the trip again.

Joyce Groves plonked down two cups of tea. 'Bring the bacon sandwiches over in a minute,' she muttered, returning to the kitchen.

Charlie watched her pert rear end disappearing inside the kitchen door. Before it swung shut, out wafted a sound of sizzling and an appetising savoury aroma.

'So what you been up to since I last saw you?' Charlie turned his attention to Davy. 'Been lucky and found yerself some work?'

Davy shook his head. 'Done a few errands fer peanuts, that's about it. Finished school 'n' all, I have, and me mum's driving me mad about getting full-time pay.'

'Got nuthin' but *errands*?' Charlie sounded disgusted.

'Had a good bit coming in from me street betting lark a while back. Up to thirty players a session turned up when I was croupier on the dice,' Davy announced proudly. 'But that's turned sour. I'm getting elbowed out 'cos the men don't like the idea of me getting good at it and takin' over.'

'Street gambling, eh? You don't mind a bit of duckin' 'n' divin' then, Davy boy?' Knowing Stan's son didn't mind operating on the wrong side of the law was a relief to Charlie and made his plans more likely to come to fruition.

'Nah . . . do anythin', I will, s'long as it pays,' Davy boasted, his hopes soaring that he was about to hear some good news about a job.

'How about your pal . . . Tom was his name, wasn't it? How's he doing work-wise?'

'He ain't yet left school so he's just got a bit of sweeping up down the railway yard. Sometimes I get a day down the market. Me mum likes that 'cos I always bring her in a bit of veg even if the geezer don't pay . . .'

'Ain't no real use, though, is it?' Charlie said pessimistically. 'You should be getting proper wages.'

Davy nodded, hoping this was leading somewhere.

'Course, you know why there's no regular jobs, don't you, son?' Charlie stuck out a digit in readiness to start wagging it in emphasis. 'Too many bleedin' foreigners in the country taking all the work, that's the reason. Then there's the Jews got fingers in all the pies . . .' He shook his head regretfully. 'Makes it hard for the rest of us, don't it? I mean, I'm a union man meself but I don't like the way the Commies are muscling in on the act . . .' Charlie sucked his teeth, grimacing.

Davy didn't know much about politics and previously had had no desire to learn. He'd heard lots of similar complaints to Charlie's from the men – and some of the women – living on Campbell Road who blamed their hard luck on outsiders. He realised Charlie was expecting his support on the matter so began nodding solemnly.

'Me guvnor . . . part-time guvnor that is, 'cos I've got regular shifts down the docks – well, he's big in Mosley's crew. Heard of the British Union of Fascists, have you, mate? Trying to put things right fer us all, they are, and me and me guvnor are right behind them. We do a bit of fundraising for the party. Heard of Sir Oswald Mosley, have you, Davy?'

Davy nodded. 'I saw him once. Got a gammy leg, ain't he? His lot come round our way sometimes and give a talk. I'm all for 'em. Same as you.'

'Got his limp fighting for king and country, you know. Youth cadets march at Mosley's rallies. Sensible kids about your age, who know things've got to change. I expect you've seen them decked out in smart outfits.'

'Yeah . . . I have seen 'em.' Davy had thought the Fascists looked good in their black-shirted uniforms. The only shirts he wore came off totters' barrows, bought by his mother. Apart from wanting to earn to keep a roof over his head, he needed good pay so he could start choosing his own clothes instead of wearing the rags she brought in for him.

Joyce Groves crossed her arms and leaned against the doorjamb, watching Charlie and the lad nattering while she waited for Les to finish frying bacon for their sandwiches. She was in a bad mood, and had been for days.

Nick had picked her up outside work one evening last week and her pleasure at that unexpected meeting had soon vanished when he told her it was over between them.

Her subsequent attempts to contact Nick for an explanation had met with a blank. If she phoned him he was civil but abrupt, and the receiver went down after a few seconds. When she'd turned up on his doorstep he hadn't invited her in and had remained unmoved by her seductive appearance and sexual promises.

In her heart, Joyce knew she didn't need him to tell her why he'd called a halt. There was nothing for it but to try to persuade him not to listen to that poisonous bitch of a wife of his. But Nick wouldn't discuss Blanche – or anything else, for that matter.

Joyce had known the cow would go crying to her ex-husband about the fight they'd had, and blame everything on her. She knew the couple weren't yet back living together because Blanche was still hanging about with Charlie Potter. But Joyce was miserably aware that her rival must have had some success weaselling her way back into Nick's life, although she couldn't believe that Nick would be jealous of the likes of Potter.

The first time her brother, Kenny, told her that Blanche and Charlie had been spotted together in the pub Joyce had howled with laughter. In Joyce's opinion, the brass-faced baggage deserved to be brought down a few pegs. Blanche had swanned about like Lady Muck when she was Wes Silver's bit on the side. It was only after May dragged her husband home that Blanche remembered she had a husband of her own.

Joyce's mouth slanted calculatingly. Charlie had noticed her watching him and was staring back. Usually, she wouldn't be seen dead with someone as old and rough as him. She reckoned that Blanche felt more or less the same way about getting involved with the scumbag. But Potter was at the centre of things and could therefore be useful. Joyce had a burning need to get even with Blanche for ruining her chances with Nick Raven.

'Here we are . . . two nice hot bacon sandwiches,' Joyce said, leaning forward to show a bit of cleavage while putting down the plates.

Charlie gave her a shrewd look. Usually, Joyce couldn't be bothered to have a chat with him, but she seemed to be giving him a green light now. Just to make sure he wasn't dreaming, a few calloused fingers travelled to the back of her knee, fondling. She didn't move away, or hiss a curse at him beneath her breath, as she usually did.

Charlie's throaty chuckle made Joyce's hackles rise. But she gave him a flirtatious smile. 'Bacon sandwich is going cold,' she mocked, sauntering off, well aware he was watching her swaying hips.

She went into the kitchen, a sneer curling her lips. She wouldn't mind leading him on, letting him think he might get lucky when there was no chance she'd ever sleep with him. She was younger and prettier than Blanche and any man would choose her over Nick's ex-wife. Then when Charlie kicked Blanche into touch, making her look a stupid cow, Joyce would tell Potter that he could go and get stuffed, and laugh as she did it.

CHAPTER NINETEEN

'What d'you want?'

'What d'you think?'

Jennifer started to push the door shut but David prevented her slamming it in his face by ramming a hand against the panels.

'I told you not to come here again. It was a mistake,' Jenny said hoarsely.

David's harsh chuckle was filled with self-loathing. 'Yeah . . . it was a mistake, all right, but it's too late now.' He shoved the door, sending her skittering backwards a few paces, then walked inside, closing it behind him. He knew she was on her own because he'd waited in shadows for her previous visitor to leave before approaching the door. He'd given her ten minutes and was hoping in the meantime she'd washed and tidied herself up. Looking her over, he saw there was nothing to suggest she had. She looked a dirty slut.

David was out of uniform, dressed in an overcoat and wide-brimmed hat, despite the fact it was a late summer evening. He could have laughed at his own stupidity;

191

it wasn't an effective disguise and anyone who knew him by sight would spot a local copper calling on a prostitute . . . who happened to be his girlfriend's twin.

He now knew why Kathy . . . sweet, beautiful Kathy . . . was always so careful in choosing her words when answering questions about her sister.

Jennifer had told him herself why she was the black sheep of the family when he had brought her home after her shoplifting spree. It had been the last time he'd seen her looking clean and presentable. He knew she wouldn't have opened up that afternoon if she'd put the kettle on, as she'd said she would when she asked him in, Instead, on entering the disgusting dump she lived in, she'd headed straight towards the bottle of Scotch. She needed a nip to calm her nerves after the run-in with Grayson, she'd said. David now knew Jennifer Finch didn't need any excuse for a drink. She'd offered him the whisky, then when he'd declined because he was still on duty, taken two swift refills and shot them back in single swallows.

David knew he should have resisted the urge to go in when she offered him tea and conversation because she had something she wanted to get off her chest. But curiosity about her had overwhelmed him and it had been his downfall.

There was a sort of hideous fascination for him in the squalor of the way she lived, as there was in the fact that she reminded him of Kathy at times when she glanced at him from under her lashes with those big blue eyes. But Kathy's modesty was genuine, with no hint of a saucy challenge that made him feel she was begging him to tame her.

A typical drunk, Jennifer had got pushy and sulky when he refused to join her in 'a small snifter', as she called it. As soon as the touching started he'd known she'd the power to make him stay and it hadn't taken her long to set him straight about her profession and get him to agree to do whatever she wanted. Because she'd let him do whatever he wanted.

And he'd loved every minute of sordid pleasure that had left him naked, dripping sweat on a bed covered in filthy sheets. And he was back to do it all again, for the third time. David knew to his shame that Jennifer was as addictive to him as the Scotch was to her.

When he left her after their first encounter he'd been trembling. He'd driven past Kathy, seen her waving and smiling at him, and felt as though it was some divine retribution for his vile sin. By the time he got back to the station he was ready for a hot bath and had told Sergeant Booth he had to go home because he was feeling sick, as though he might have caught something. It hadn't been a lie; he was aware it was likely he'd get the clap, or worse, off Kathy's whore of a sister. Still he couldn't stay away.

Jenny tightened the belt of her dressing gown about her shivering form. She wasn't frightened of him; it was the anticipation of what was to come making her quake. Only Bill had ever managed to make her feel this horny, and he never bothered pleasing her much any more. He didn't even come over to please himself: she'd not seen him in a while and imagined the brunette in Lambeth had her claws sunk in him.

They stared at one another. David could see her swaying a bit and her eyes were glazed. He knew she'd already taken what she needed. Now it was his turn.

He got the cash out of his pocket and let it fall to the table. The handcuffs followed, dropped with a clatter.

Jenny's eyes whipped to them and she licked her lips, her sudden intake of breath perking up her breasts. She began untying the belt of her dressing gown as she sauntered past him towards her bedroom.

His wife was running in his direction to meet him when behind her Nick glimpsed a uniformed policeman entering the shop Blanche had just left. All things considered, he found it odd he'd never before set eyes on David Goldstein. Or perhaps he had seen him around the neighbourhood but not registered him as Emo's son. The copper was removing his helmet and, hatless, Nick could tell that David Goldstein wasn't swarthy like his father.

'What you doing here?' Blanche excitedly launched herself at her husband. He was leaning against a wall smoking, obviously waiting for her. They'd not seen each other in months and the only communication between them had been the solicitor's letters. Blanche was hoping Nick's unexpected appearance meant he might be persuaded to call off the divorce.

Nick ground the dog end beneath his shoe. He'd promised Tony he'd have a word with Blanche about getting friendly with Potter. He felt undeniably irritated to have taken on the duty, as he'd married the man's daughter out of decency, then had her cheat on him within a year. But he'd been fond of Blanche once and he wouldn't like to see her beaten up by the maniac who'd set about his mother and regularly beat his own family.

'Tony tells me you're seeing Charlie Potter.'

'Shame me father can't mind his own business, ain't it?' Blanche's mouth drooped sullenly.

'You're lucky he's not yet told Gladys,' Nick replied evenly. 'Tony reckons your mother'll have you out on your ear the minute she finds out you're knocking about with a nutter, and I think he's right.'

'Gonna take me in when she does?' Blanche suggested coyly.

'No; and neither will Charlie. He's got a wife and kids.'

'So what? Wes had a wife and kids.'

'Yeah . . . he also had a bank balance that'd cover two homes.' Nick's lips twitched in sour humour. 'Till May told him different, that is.'

'Oh . . . just piss off, will yer? You've only come here to gloat.' Blanche didn't like to be reminded of how Wes had dumped her when she'd sacrificed everything for him. She especially didn't like to hear it from the husband she'd lost in the process.

'Ain't gloating, Blanche.' Nick didn't think Blanche would take much notice of anything he said; she never had in the past if it contradicted what she hoped to hear. 'Yer dad's worried sick about you and I can see why.'

'Can you?' Blanche snapped petulantly. 'Surprised you give a monkey's.'

'I wouldn't be here otherwise, would I?'

'Mean that?' Blanche asked, stepping closer and clutching Nick's arm.

'Listen . . . I know Charlie Potter. Me mum knows him too and wishes she didn't. He ain't the charming life and soul of the party he likes to make out. He uses his fists on women when he can't get what he wants. Tony and me don't like the idea of you getting hurt. That's all there is to it.' Nick removed Blanche's stroking hand from his sleeve.

'You still going through with the divorce?' Blanche angled her face up to his.

'Of course; that's nothing to do with any of this, is it?' Nick said, curbing his impatience. He'd known that coming to see Blanche might give her false hope on that score. 'I'm just here to give you a friendly bit of advice. It's up to you if you take it or not.' Nick dug in a pocket, then offered the pack of cigarettes to Blanche before taking one himself.

When he'd lit the Weights they stood smoking in silence for a moment.

'How does Lottie know Charlie?' Blanche asked after a short contemplation.

'They went to school together, and me dad too.' Nick blew smoke sideways. 'Potter's had a fancy for my mum since they were kids, by all accounts.'

'Lottie!' Blanche snorted a giggle. She'd never known her widowed mother-in-law to have a man in her life. She certainly didn't imagine Charlie would go for a woman that old, even though she had to give it to the woman for keeping herself in shape.

'Yeah, Lottie,' Nick answered acidly. 'She's the same age as Charlie. He's old enough to be your father.'

Blanche flicked ash. 'Don't matter to me how old he is. I like older men.'

'Yeah, I noticed. Want a lift home?' Nick strode towards the car at the kerb. He'd had enough of trying to talk sense into his ex-wife.

Blanche trotted after him, hanging on his arm. 'I'd give Charlie up tomorrow if you 'n' me got back together, Nick.'

Nick stuck the cigarette in his mouth and jerked open the passenger door for her, a weary headshake his only response to her suggestion.

'Still seeing that ugly mare Joyce Groves, are yer?' she spat, stubbornly hanging back, making him wait.

'You getting in, then?'

Blanche threw her arms about his neck, nuzzling into his cheek. 'She's no good for you, Nick. I am. Fresh start, that's all we need. I'll make it all up to yer, swear on our dead baby's soul . . .'

'Fuck's sake! Shut up! How many times do I have to say it?' Nick disentangled himself and strode round the car. 'Get in or catch the bus.'

Blanche knew he'd drive off and leave her. She could see that she'd pushed him too far so she collapsed into the seat, banged the door shut, and started crying.

Nick got a handkerchief out of his pocket and chucked it onto her lap. 'Stick around with Potter much longer, Blanche, and he'll really give you something to bawl about, don't you worry about that.'

'You coming with me or not on Saturday?'

'Nah . . . only get the third degree off me mum, won't I, if she finds out.'

'Woss up with yer?' Davy grumbled. 'Thought you was after earning a bit of money.'

'I am!' Tom grimaced in emphasis. 'But she'll want to know everything, and drive me up the wall.'

'Charlie's said he's gonna pay us five bob each, and he'll stand us a feed in the caff before we come home. All we've got to do is hang about outside some shops dressed up in black shirts like we belong to Mosley's crew. Won't get wages no easier'n that, will we?'

Tom knew his friend was telling the truth because he'd brought a couple of the smart shirts back with him from the East End last week and told him all about the

197

youth cadets. Davy had offered him a shirt to keep but Tom had refused it although he could do with a new one. He knew his father might not mind about him getting involved with the Fascists; Eddie regularly moaned about the immigrants and Jews, and Tom had heard his father praising Sir Oswald Mosley. His mother's attitude was that all politicians were crooked and it was best to have nothing to do with any of their sort. Tom didn't think that even a brand-new black shirt would change her mind about that.

Tom wasn't that bothered about having the shirt either. But he couldn't dismiss five bob so easily. There was a girl at school he liked and he'd said he'd take her to the flicks one Saturday. He knew if he couldn't put his money where his mouth was another boy would because she was pretty and popular.

'How long's Charlie expecting us to hang about for outside them shops? Gonna be back by about six o'clock, are we?'

'Course we are.' Davy grinned. For all his brashness he craved a bit of back-up on an adventure in unfamiliar territory. He wanted his friend to accompany him and could tell Tom was being swayed towards the pay on offer. 'If you don't want to stop for a fry-up in the caff with us you can catch an early bus back.'

Tom had to admit that the prospect of a free fry-up was almost as tempting to him as five bob in wages. His mother hadn't lavished a dinner of bacon and eggs on him in a long while even though she knew it was his favourite.

CHAPTER TWENTY

'You've come to see your mother again?' Sarah Goldstein flapped her hands at her son. 'You've got me worried, David. I don't see you for months and now you can't stay away? Tell me, what's up?'

'Just passing and thought I'd pop in, Mum.' David smiled, stuck his helmet under an arm.

'Leave the boy alone.' Emo came round the counter and patted David on the shoulder. 'You're mother's just kidding. How are you? Are you coming to young Noah's bar mitzvah next weekend?'

'I think I'm on duty.'

Emo grimaced disappointment. 'Your cousins will all be there. You should ask for the time off and catch up with everybody. We'll have a good time. Plenty of food, and singing and dancing.' Emo gyrated his bulky hips, swaying his hands in front of his face in time to an imaginary tune. 'Of course, your uncle needs to cut down on . . .' Emo raised an open fist, tilting it back and forth, miming a drinker.

David gestured apology.

'It's that wife of his,' Sarah interrupted in a sour tone. 'The woman's enough to send Moses himself to the nearest bottle of whisky.'

David felt a stabbing pain in his gut. Any small reminder of his sin made him wince. He hated using his handcuffs on duty, avoided doing so whenever he could. He hated Jennifer. He was starting to hate Kathy, too. More and more he found himself inwardly raging at his blameless girlfriend when obscene thoughts crammed his mind and he craved her sister's flesh. It was Kathy's fault. If Jennifer weren't her twin sister, if they didn't look alike, he'd never have given the whore a lift home. He'd done his girlfriend a favour that day, hoping to please her, and instead he'd lost his self-respect, and his peace of mind into the bargain.

David grimaced understanding at his father, even as a suppressed sob painfully expanded his chest. Nobody would look up to him or respect him ever again if they knew the truth . . .

'You look nice.'

'Thanks . . . it's not new,' Kathy said quickly, smoothing the skirt of her colourful summer frock with the back of a hand. She didn't want him to think she'd made any special effort on his account.

'Still . . . looks nice,' Nick said ironically as he opened the car door for her. The fresh scent of lavender wafted in his nostrils as she passed him to settle on the leather seat.

'Where do you want to go?' he asked, getting in beside her.

'Don't mind. Not too far. Can't stay out long.'

'Take a drive to Victoria Park?'

Kathy nodded agreement, gave him a smile.

'Thought you might stand me up.' Nick steered smoothly away from the kerb.

'Why?' Kathy darted him a look, immediately wondering if he'd spotted her cycling past earlier in the week when he'd been with his wife.

Kathy had believed she'd gone unnoticed by him. But it was possible Nick had ignored her in the same way she believed David had when he'd driven past her some weeks ago. She'd put that down to her boyfriend being in an odd mood, as he frequently seemed to be lately. Kathy made allowances for him, as he did for her when she'd had a demanding time of it at work; the nature of David's job could be as harrowing as her own.

Kathy had no proof that the woman was Nick's wife but she'd guessed at her identity as they were stationed outside the Goldsteins' shop. The brunette had been embracing Nick and that had also hinted at her being Mrs Raven . . . and Nick being a liar. They'd appeared very affectionate for a divorcing couple.

At the time, Kathy had pedalled away quickly, her heart pounding, determined that she'd never go out with the cheat. Once home, she'd calmed down, realising she'd been acting like a jealous rival. Squabbling with him over a matter that shouldn't concern her wouldn't help Ruby and her kids, so she'd decided to stick to her guns.

Nick Raven was the only person Kathy knew who stood up to Charlie Potter, and she was clinging to a hope that with his assistance Ruby and her children might yet escape the brute to a better life. How such a miracle might be achieved, she had no idea. Nick Raven might lie to her about some things but Kathy sensed his hatred of Charlie Potter, and his concern for Ruby and her children, was genuine.

'I thought your friend David might persuade you to stay away from me,' Nick eventually answered, accelerating away from traffic lights.

'I'm able to make up my own mind on the people I see.'

'You didn't tell him after all, did you?'

'No . . . I didn't . . .' Kathy murmured, piqued by a hint of satisfaction in his voice.

'Why not?'

'Because . . . it would lead to questions. We both know how vicious Potter is and we think something should be done, but if I tell David about our meeting, it'd be sure to open a can of worms. I don't want to lie or put him in an awkward position in telling the truth. He's a decent honest man who has a job to do.'

'You're worried he'd intervene in the Potters' case and make things worse?'

Kathy nodded glumly. 'If he thought the children were at risk he'd see it as a dereliction of his duty if he did nothing. I'd see it as a failure on my part if he did report it.'

'You're really concerned Ruby's gonna lose her family and then do something stupid, aren't you?' Nick gave her a frowning glance.

'Of course . . . that's why I've come out with you . . . to talk about it.'

'I hadn't forgotten.'

The rest of the short journey to Victoria Park passed in silence but Kathy was glad her candid remark hadn't turned him narky. The atmosphere between them remained mild and she relaxed further into the seat when he started to whistle.

'Do you have children?'

Nick turned his head. 'No . . . no kids.'

He'd been leaning forward, elbows on knees while they sat quietly on a park bench, by the lake. They'd arrived in the park just a few minutes ago and had sat down, each occupied with assembling his or her thoughts ready to air them. Now, Nick sat back, looking reflective.

'No need to be downhearted; sometimes it takes a while for babies to come along,' Kathy blurted, unconsciously slipping into her professional mode. 'A patient of mine is overjoyed to be expecting at thirty-six,' she rattled on. 'Not that I think your wife looks that old, of course.'

'How old does she look?'

'Close to your age, I suppose,' Kathy answered, wishing she'd not started this conversation.

'Yep . . . about right . . .' Nick said.

'I saw you together,' Kathy owned up a touch defiantly. 'You were both standing by your car, outside the Goldsteins' shop.'

He nodded, said nothing, frowning at the water.

Kathy felt her temper rising. The least he could do was attempt an explanation or an apology. If he realised she had him down as a liar and a cheat he gave no outward sign of it bothering him.

'Is that why you can't stay out long? Because you saw me with my wife and think I'm lying to you about getting divorced?'

'I can't stay out because I have a lot to do . . . notes to write . . .' Kathy retorted, flushing guiltily; all her work was up to date.

'So let's talk about Ruby and her kids and then I'll take you home to get stuck in. I'm guessing you want my help, so what are you expecting me to do about it all?'

His hardening attitude made her equally snappy in response. 'What *can* you do about it? What can *any* of us do?'

'Hasn't Ruby got a family to lend a hand?'

'Her mother was a widow and passed away a few years ago. She never talks about any brothers or sisters, so if she has some they can't be close.' Kathy frowned. 'Perhaps her in-laws might be decent folk. If they don't know what Charlie's like they'd be horrified to find out.'

'They know what he's like,' Nick said drily. 'Vi Potter's probably been in more fights than that particular son of hers. She had a houseful of them and they're all villains. She won't lend a sympathetic ear.'

Kathy sighed in disappointment. 'I really could shake Ruby sometimes,' she burst out. 'She ought to up and scoot. I've told her so before. Her answer's always the same: no money and nowhere to go.'

'She'd rather suffer Charlie than the Public Assistance Institution.'

'She's frightened the authorities will get involved and she'll lose the kids.'

'Yep . . .'

Kathy felt tears of frustration stinging her eyes and turned her face from his searching gaze. 'It's not fair,' she said huskily, blinking into the distance.

'Hard life, ain't it, for a lot of people,' Nick stated, matter of fact.

'I'm going to speak to Mrs Keiver.' Kathy sprang to her feet, pacing to and fro in front of the bench. 'Matilda will know if any rooms are going in Campbell Road. Ruby can take the kids there; the rent's dirt-cheap. It'll be safer than staying where they are.'

'Even desperate people avoid the Bunk if they can.' Nick sounded dubious.

'She *is* desperate and so long as it's a dwelling, and it keeps her and her kids away from that husband of hers, it'll do, I'm sure of it.' Kathy sat down again. 'Ruby might relish moving from the East End. She's got no friends or family that she speaks about. I don't even think she has much to do with her neighbours.' Kathy felt exhilarated by her brainwave. 'I should of thought of it sooner. Matilda always knows of somebody who needs a char. They might be a rough lot but some of the women in the street can be kind souls when they want to be. I'm sure they'd help with the kids while Ruby earned a little bit . . .'

Nick stroked a long cool finger down her flushed cheek. 'You're getting too involved, and too optimistic, Kathy. You can't make up Ruby's mind for her. Even if she agrees to the move, there's a lot of sorting out to do.'

'Will you help? If Charlie follows her to the Bunk, would you sort him out? You made him leave your mother alone.'

'It's not quite the same thing, is it? Ruby's his missus and I imagine two of the kids are Charlie's . . . could be wrong, though . . .' Nick added ruefully.

Kathy knew he was presenting sensible arguments,

yet she felt disappointed that Nick hadn't immediately agreed to protect the Potter family from Charlie's brutality. Other practicalities began eroding her enthusiasm for the solution she'd found. Peter might want to stay close to his school friends in the East End. If he chose to remain with his father Ruby might not leave either.

'I'd better call in and speak to Ruby soon,' Kathy said. 'She might tell me I'm poking my nose in where it's not wanted.'

She kept her eyes averted, feeling bashful for having been overeager. In the cold light of day there was only a limited chance of Ruby agreeing to her suggestion. The woman might, understandably, consider moving to the worst street in north London as jumping from the frying pan to the fire.

'If the Bunk turns out to be no good for her, I'll find Ruby somewhere local to stay, if that's what she wants. And I'll explain things to Charlie if he comes after her.'

'Somewhere to stay?' Kathy parroted. 'What do you mean by that?'

'I've got a couple of spare rooms in a house,' he said, vaguely amused.

'I don't think she should move in with you,' Kathy choked. 'What would your wife say?'

Nick threw back his head, cursing softly at the clear blue sky. 'There are times, Kathy Finch, when I wish I'd never met you. I can remember being reasonably content.'

'I don't see what's so funny . . .' Kathy retorted, averting her pink cheeks.

'Me neither. I've an empty house. Ruby can move

into a couple of rooms. As for my wife, it won't incon-
venience her or be any of her damn business because
I separated from her over three years ago and, like I
told you, soon we'll be divorced. She's not happy about
it . . .' He shrugged. 'I am.'

'You sound very callous,' Kathy said after a lengthy
quiet.

'Do I?' He turned his head, stared at her. 'That's
because you don't know all that went before, do you?
And don't bother telling me you're not interested in
hearing about it, 'cos I already get the message.'

Kathy flinched from the hard grey eyes on her
profile.

'Has Charlie ever manhandled you when you've been
at his place?'

His abrupt change of subject took Kathy by surprise.
She hoped guilt didn't show in her eyes when she
eventually answered with a shake of the head. She'd
had several scratches on her chin after Potter grabbed
her for threatening to set the law on him for beating
Ruby.

'Right . . .' Nick said. 'Better see what Ruby has to
say about a move to Islington then.'

'It's good of you to offer her shelter . . . thank you . . .'
Kathy said.

Nick stood up and started walking back towards the
path that led to the entrance gate where his car was
parked.

Kathy felt rather churlish. She expected that was his
intention, but nevertheless said something conciliatory.

'I'm sorry about . . . you know . . . you're wife and
everything . . .' she began awkwardly, trotting up behind
him. 'It's sad your marriage didn't work out . . .'

'No, it's not. You still want my help with the Potters, don't you, Kathy?'

'Of course.' She angled her face to read his expression. 'Are you about to change your mind?'

'You keep your sympathy about my divorce to yourself and I reckon I won't change my mind.'

CHAPTER TWENTY-ONE

'Do you want to stop at Ruby's on the way back so you can talk to her?'

'I'm not sure it's a good idea to see her today,' Kathy replied slowly. 'If she jumps at the chance to move but there's nothing for her in the Bunk, I'll have made things worse, not better. I shouldn't raise her hopes before having a word with Mrs Keiver.'

'Head straight over to Islington, shall we, and find out how the land lies?' Nick steered the car to the kerb to wait for Kathy's answer.

'Don't you have work to get to?'

He shrugged. 'Nothing that can't wait.'

'Right . . . no time like the present, I suppose.'

'You could call in and see your mum and dad while we're that way, if you want.' Nick shoved the car into gear. 'Don't worry, I'm not asking for an introduction.' He'd noticed Kathy's startled reaction. 'I'll wait outside.'

'Thanks for the offer but I usually see them at week-ends. Besides, if you knew my mum and dad, you wouldn't want an introduction anyhow.'

'Can't be as bad as all that.' Nick sounded amused as he glanced at her.

Kathy wanted to return him a flippant reply but found she couldn't. She wished she didn't feel shame or pity when thinking of her family. Of course, she also loved them all, even Jennifer, and especially Tom. 'Do you have any brothers or sisters?' She recalled Nick had told her his father had passed away when he was young.

'Nah . . . wish I did have. After me dad died in the Great War, me mum never got together with anybody else. How about you?'

'A younger brother and a twin sister.'

'A twin, eh? Looks like you, does she?'

'Her hair's darker and she's an inch shorter . . . but I think she does.'

'What's her name?'

'Jennifer. And my brother's called Tom. He's leaving school soon and he's driving my mum up the wall, I'm afraid.' Kathy thought it wise to turn the conversation away from Jenny, just in case by some chance Nick Raven had crossed paths with her sister before. God only knew how many clients Jenny had had amongst the men in the East End, or if Nick might be one of them. Kathy believed he hadn't; he seemed too wholesome to associate with the likes of her sister. She wasn't sure whether acknowledging it pleased or depressed her.

'Young Tom's a bit of a tearaway, is he?' Nick grinned.

'Mum doesn't like the company he keeps in Campbell Road because she reckons he'll end up in bad trouble.'

'Your father'll straighten him out, I expect.'

'Mmm . . . hope so . . .' Kathy could have trumpeted a laugh. Her father had never managed to keep himself on the straight and narrow; there was little chance he'd ever set Tom right, no matter how many belts he gave him in an attempt to do so. Kathy understood Tom's lack of respect for the man who would preach one thing and do another.

'Is your sister still living at home?'

Kathy whipped a glance at him. 'No . . . she left home a long while ago.'

'What's she up to? Nursing, like you?'

'No . . .' Kathy could feel his eyes on her profile as he waited for her to elaborate. 'She sort of went off the rails a bit. Mum and Dad lost touch with her.'

'Have you lost touch with her?'

Kathy frowned, wishing he'd take the hint and not ask such direct questions. 'I still see her sometimes,' she admitted quietly.

'Is she married now?'

Kathy shook her head.

'Got work, has she?'

'Sort of . . .' Kathy knew she was sounding snappy and felt ashamed of herself. He was only making conversation so they didn't finish the drive to north London in silence.

'What does Jennifer do?'

'What she shouldn't.' Kathy hoped he'd not heard her mutter beneath her breath. 'Oh . . . that's handy . . .' she burst out, grateful to divert their conversation from her twin. 'Matilda and Beattie Evans are out having a chat with some neighbours.'

They had turned in at the bottom end of Campbell Road and Kathy immediately pointed to some women outside the corner shop. With Matilda and Beattie were two other long-standing Bunk dwellers: Davy's mum, Polly Wright, and Margaret Lovat.

'If you drop me here, I'll just nip over and have a word.' Kathy gave Nick a smile.

The women had spotted Kathy's arrival. Smart cars driving up Campbell Road were a rare sight indeed and caused people to stop and stare.

''Ere . . . that's Winnie's daughter, ain't it, Til?' Beattie nudged Matilda in the ribs.

'That one's a nurse, ain't she?' Margaret Lovat piped up. 'Never found out how the other one turned out.'

'Ain't seen Jenny in years,' Beattie said. 'Sort of just disappeared, didn't she?'

'I heard she's a wrong 'un and that's why Winnie won't have her near nor by,' Polly Wright chipped in.

'Yeah . . . well, if Winnie Finch wanted you lot to know her business, 'spect she'd have told yers more about it.' Matilda had her own ideas as to what had befallen Jennifer Finch but tried not to judge people, or pry into others' secrets. She had hosts of skeletons rattling in her own cupboards and that's where she intended them to stay. Round these parts desperate women did desperate things to keep a roof over their heads when the money and the men ran out. It had been that way for as long as she could remember.

'Bleedin' hell . . . who's that with Kathy? Don't rekernise him as being local.' Beattie smirked, her raised eyebrows signalling she liked the look of the blond fellow lighting up in the car parked across the road.

'I'd take a ride with him any time,' Margaret chortled dirtily.

'They're the ones to watch. Handsome is as handsome does.' Polly Wright nodded sagely. 'My Stan was a good-looker in his day, the mean selfish git.'

Matilda gave her a look. 'Must've been a bleedin' long time before I knew him then, Pol.'

Kathy was aware of the women quietening to watch her approach. Now she was almost upon them she felt unsure how to get Matilda on her own. The little group expected her to blurt out what was on her mind because there was obviously a reason for her turning up out of the blue. But Kathy was reluctant to tell Ruby's problems to all and sundry.

'Hello there, Kathy.' Matilda gave the young woman a welcoming smile, taking pity on her predicament. She guessed Winnie's daughter wanted a private word with her and could guess what about too. That brother of hers was playing with fire and Matilda reckoned Winnie had no idea how badly the little tyke might get burned if he didn't quickly wise up. 'I like your dress. Got it out one of them fancy stores up west, did yer?' Matilda asked. 'Bet it cost a packet.'

'No . . . it was a bargain.' Kathy felt grateful that Matilda had broken the ice. 'It's only off the market. Petticoat Lane . . . loads of stalls to choose from over there.'

'That's a good market,' Beattie chimed in. 'I've been to it meself a few times. Knocks Chapel Street into a cocked hat. Get a better bit of fruit and veg 'cos it's on top of Spitalfields, ain't it?'

'Talking of veg, I'd better get off home and peel a few spuds fer Reg's tea,' Matilda said. 'Got time for a cuppa, Kathy? 'Spect yer over this way to visit your mum, ain't yer?'

As Matilda and Kathy moved away, the trio left behind

looked disappointed to have lost the chance of a gossip and soon dispersed.

'Would your friend like to come in for tea?' Matilda nodded at the car.

'Oh . . . no . . . he's fine where he is, thanks all the same.' Kathy realised Matilda – and the other women too – would be naturally curious about her companion. 'He just offered me a lift.'

'Right y'are . . . He seems familiar to me . . . not sure why . . .'

Kathy darted a glance at Matilda, noticing the woman had her narrowed gaze on Nick. He'd slunk comfortably down in the seat and appeared to be dozing with his hat tipped forward, shielding his eyes from the afternoon glare, a cigarette smouldering between his lips.

'Oh, you might recognise him, actually,' Kathy blurted, remembering something Nick had told her months ago. 'I think he knows your nephews.'

Matilda frowned in concentration. 'That's it. I've seen him in the pub with Rob and Stevie, if me memory serves, 'cos it was a while ago.'

An opportunity to discover more about Nick Raven's past had unexpectedly arisen. Kathy tried to block out her curiosity with thoughts of Ruby's plight but as she followed Matilda towards her doorway the desire increased to ask questions about Nick.

After the blinding Indian summer sunlight the dank hallway of the house seemed gloomier than usual. Matilda led the way towards the rickety stairs, gesturing to Kathy to mind the holes and splinters on the treads as they proceeded up them. The higher they climbed the more Kathy wrinkled her nose against a stale odour of cabbage and damp.

It might have been a few years since Matilda had seen Nick Raven drinking in the Duke with her nephews but the fellow had a presence that wasn't easily forgotten. She'd asked Rob about his blond friend and learned that her nephew thought Nick was a decent bloke despite the fact he often grabbed work Rob wanted. Matilda was proud of her entrepreneurial nephew who ran a small business empire in north London. Nick Raven had a similar outfit in the East End, Rob had told her, and sometimes they worked together rather than as rivals.

Rob Wild had also told his aunt that Nick had started off on his solo career following an enviable stroke of luck. Prior to that he'd been scraping by as a lorry driver. Matilda hadn't enquired too much about it: she knew that such windfalls often came via dodgy means. Her nephew hadn't got where he was being a saint. Matilda had got the impression that Rob admired his friend for outwitting somebody higher up the pecking order and making a packet in the doing of it.

Matilda had spent most of her adulthood in the Bunk living hand to mouth. Tales of people dragging themselves up by their bootstraps to better themselves heartened and fascinated her rather than making her envious. She remembered muttering 'good luck to him' on hearing of Nick Raven's change in fortune.

But there was something bothering her. Rob had also mentioned Nick Raven had recently got married and that the blushing bride was already expecting.

Matilda opened the door to her room, still brooding, ushering Kathy inside. She didn't think Kathy Finch was the sort to mess about with married men so perhaps Nick *was* just a friend giving her a lift. On the other hand, Matilda tended to be a cynic where the opposite sex was concerned: most men – married or not – could be liars and cheats when trying to get pretty young women into bed. Nick Raven might be a nice enough fellow to do business with but it was possible the randy git hadn't owned up to Kathy that he had a wife and family indoors. If Kathy questioned her, she'd willingly tell what she knew. Matilda tended to side with the women; when times were rough they were the people who stuck by you, offering practical help instead of sulking in the pub.

'Take a seat, luv.' Matilda gave the kettle a shake then put it to boil on the hob grate.

Kathy looked around. There was a lot of furniture crammed in the room but few places to sit. The battered armchair had a load of old newspapers dumped on the seat and the bed, shoved up against the wall, was strewn with clothes and other odds and ends. There were two stick-back chairs at the table and gingerly Kathy pulled one out and sat down.

'How are all your girls, Matilda?' Kathy politely enquired. 'Expect you've got loads of grandkids by now, haven't you?'

'Can't hardly hear yerself think when my lot get together Christmas-time.' Matilda turned about to answer Kathy, grinning proudly. 'Lovely it is to see 'em all over at Alice's. We always have a good knees-up, Boxing Day.'

While Matilda rattled cups and saucers together Kathy took a look about. It had been five years since she'd entered the Keivers' home, yet oddly it looked the same. She remembered the spotted old mirror hooked on the wall and the mantel cluttered with oil lamps and frilly candle stumps. On that previous occasion, she'd come calling on Lucy, one of Matilda's daughters.

Matilda put a cup of steaming tea in front of Kathy then sat down opposite. 'So . . . what's on your mind, luv?' she asked. 'Could see something was troubling you soon as you turned up outside.'

Kathy frowned into her tea, marshalling her thoughts about Ruby and a few questions to ask about Nick Raven.

'About Tom, is it?' Matilda kindly prompted. The young woman appeared unsure how to begin.

'Tom?' Kathy echoed. Matilda's concerned expression made her heart plummet. 'Oh, no . . . what's he done now?' The subject of Nick's background fled from her mind.

'Put me foot in it, ain't I?' Matilda took a sip of tea. 'Wouldn't have said nothing to worry you, Kathy, but I thought you might have heard rumours and come round to find out what Tom and Davy have been up to.'

'What *have* they been up to?' Kathy wailed. She was already wondering if she ought to stop off round the corner and see her family after all, before heading back to the East End.

'Seems Tom's getting involved in Mosley's youth cadets,' Matilda announced. 'You know nuthin' gets past Beattie. She's seen him and Davy over Hackney way where her sister lives. They was wearing them black shirts and standing around with the Fascists on their soapboxes.'

Kathy's jaw dropped. 'Tom?' she barked an incredulous laugh. 'Over Hackney? A Fascist? Beattie must be mistaken!'

'Not sure that she is, Kathy.' Matilda gave a sorrowful shake of the head. 'Tom and Davy were seen throwing a stone through the winder of the shop the Belgians

217

own round in Blackstock Road.' Matilda paused. 'Didn't see 'em doing it meself but the winder's broke all right 'cos I've seen it boarded up.'

'Does my mum know?' Kathy whispered.

'Not seen Winnie in weeks, and I wouldn't say nuthin' about it to her anyway. She might be of a mind to let Tom carry on. Lots of people are for the Fascists and it ain't fer me to tell 'em their business.'

'Tom's risking getting himself arrested so he won't be sitting down for a while if they know about it.' Kathy shoved agitated fingers through her hair. Her father would go berserk if the coppers turned up and got a glimpse of the hooky goods stored in the back bedroom.

Matilda regretted giving Kathy something else to fret on. She'd looked as though she had enough on her plate as it was so changed the subject. 'Have you seen yer mum today?'

Kathy simply shook her head too stunned to speak.

'My nephew Rob reckons Nick Raven's a nice chap, I remember him telling me that.' Matilda kept talking while Kathy found her tongue.

'I know he's married,' Kathy said.

'Well, it's good that he's honest. Rob told me about his wife and family, so I ain't going to play dumb on that score.'

'He's not got children . . . he told me that . . . and he's getting divorced.'

'Right . . . well perhaps Rob got it wrong,' Matilda said. She took a gulp of tea. 'On the other hand, I don't think I need to tell a smart gel like you that sometimes men tell you what they think you want to hear.' Matilda laid a rough palm over Kathy's hand, gave it a pat when she saw her colouring up. 'Just thought I'd say me piece 'cos perhaps Winnie ain't yet had a chance to give you her advice.'

'I've got a boyfriend already. His name's David and he's a policeman.'

Matilda withdrew her fingers. 'Well . . . there you are then . . . don't need my opinion after all. Another cuppa?' She shoved back her chair about to get up.

'There was a reason I came over to see you, actually,' Kathy said. She raised her troubled eyes to Matilda's kindly face.

'Ask away,' the woman invited, settling back into her seat.

CHAPTER TWENTY-TWO

'The accommodation would need to be very cheap. I won't speak to Ruby till after you tell me there's a chance of a room.'

Matilda had sat frowning while Kathy recounted the tale of Ruby Potter and her violent thug of a husband.

'How's the poor cow gonna pay the rent with no work and no man to help out?' Matilda asked, ever practical. 'Won't get no cheaper rates than the Bunk but it still costs to live here.'

'I can lay down ten shillings in advance.' Kathy had a small amount of savings and would willingly use them to try to keep Ruby and her children out of harm's way.

'You'd use yer own money on her?'

Kathy nodded, feeling awkward. She didn't want to seem to be acting the martyr.

'Well . . . if you can be generous, reckon I can too,' Matilda said gruffly. 'Got a spare room here that's going begging. Thought about renting it out but never did.'

'What about your husband?' Kathy asked, surprised. 'Reg might not want to share your home—'

'He won't kick up,' Matilda interrupted. 'He's got a good heart when it comes to little kids.'

Kathy had not dared to hope it would be so easy. 'If Ruby agrees to move, I'll pay you for your trouble, promise . . .' she blurted.

'You won't, miss!' Matilda stood up, her eyes suspiciously misty. 'You wouldn't know her 'cos you'd have been toddling when she died . . . but my younger sister, Fran, God rest her, was married to a pig like the one you've just told me about. Me brother-in-law was always using his fists on his wife and kids.' Matilda turned towards Kathy, sniffing. 'Rob and Stevie Wild are his sons – nothing like him, though. Favour my Fran, both of 'em . . . they always did.'

'Did he beat her up *very* badly?' Kathy asked, shocked to hear Matilda's younger sister was dead, and fearing the worst.

'Oh, yeah . . . nearly killed her once . . . Oh, see what you mean,' Matilda said. 'No, he didn't do for her. Fran weren't gonna let Jimmy Wild see her off any more than I was.' Matilda used her knuckles to dry her eyes. 'Spanish flu got her in the end in 1919.'

Kathy knew that such stories of family violence were fairly commonplace amongst London's poor. Ruby's plight was by no means unique but the Potters were the people Kathy felt compelled to help.

'You ask this Ruby what she wants to do then.' Matilda pointed at a connecting door. 'Got a bed in there for her and the kids, if she wants it, free of charge till she sorts herself out. Ain't the Ritz, by no means . . .'

Matilda suddenly burst out laughing at the comparison

and Kathy joined in, giggling hysterically until they were both wiping their eyes and the solemn atmosphere had lifted.

'I'll speak to her . . . and thank you so much.' Kathy stood up, having composed herself after her mirth. 'Best get off now. I suppose I ought to see Mum after what you've told me about Tom. He's getting to be a bloody nuisance!'

'You take care of yerself, dear.' Matilda began clearing away the tea things into the tin bowl.

Kathy was at the door when Matilda said, 'Yer mum and dad are proud of you, Kathy, ain't they?'

Kathy nodded bashfully.

'So they fuckin' ought to be,' Matilda said with feeling.

Kathy emerged from Matilda's hallway into late afternoon warmth and headed straight across the road. Nick had got out of the car to stretch his legs and was pacing aimlessly, apparently undisturbed by a trio of youths who'd appeared to gawp at the Alvis.

'Matilda has offered to give Ruby and her kids her back room rent-free.' Kathy rattled off her news as soon as she reached him.

'Nice of her,' Nick answered.

'Do you mind if I pop in after all and see my parents before we head home?' Kathy asked. 'Matilda's just told me that my brother has been acting bloody daft. I'd better find out if Mum and Dad know what's going on.'

'And if they don't?'

Kathy shrugged, shook her head hopelessly. 'I suppose I should tell them. I don't want to grass him up but if he's not been arrested yet he might be soon, then that will set the cat among the pigeons.'

'What's he done?'

'Apparently, he and his pal are getting involved with the Fascist cadets.' Kathy shrugged bewilderment. 'Doesn't sound like Tom, but Matilda's not one to exaggerate. He and Davy Wright were spotted throwing stones at a foreigner's shop window in Blackstock Road. Now it's boarded up.'

Nick grimaced in sympathy, opening the car door for Kathy to get in.

'If you drive up to the first junction, I'll direct you towards the house.' As they pulled off, Kathy wound down the window to let some fresh air into the car's hot interior.

They had turned into Paddington Street when Kathy spotted her brother and Davy Wright huddled against the wall, smoking.

'There he is! What a stroke of luck.' Kathy's lips tightened into a grim line. 'Would you pull over so I can have a word with him?'

Tom Finch cussed beneath his breath when he saw his sister jump out of the car that had stopped at the kerb opposite. 'Kathy's turned up,' he hissed to Davy, dropping his half-smoked cigarette and stamping on it.

'Ain't scared of her, are you?' Davy mocked, deliberately blowing smoke towards Kathy as she hurried across the road.

Tom had heard his father making complaints about Kathy knocking about with a Yid copper. From what he could see of him, Tom didn't reckon the fellow behind the wheel looked Jewish; nevertheless he feared it was David Goldstein. 'Watch out! That must be her boyfriend with her, and he's a rozzer.'

That information wiped the smirk off Davy's chops.

223

'Bleedin' hell! I'm off home,' he muttered, strutting towards Campbell Road and avoiding looking at the car as he passed it.

'I've been talking to Matilda Keiver,' Kathy announced as soon as her brother was in earshot.

'Bully for you,' Tom mumbled, keeping an eye on the fellow in the car. He had a feeling he was about to hear Kathy knew he'd been causing trouble.

'You've been seen hanging about in Hackney with the Fascists and breaking windows round in Blackstock Road,' Kathy accused, watching her brother for a sign of guilt. She soon got it and gestured in exasperation. 'Have you been arrested? Do Mum and Dad know what you're up to?'

'That old cow Keiver wants to mind her own business,' Tom snarled.

'You're lucky Matilda told me instead of telling Mum and Dad.' Kathy grabbed her brother's arm, hauling him back as he tried to sidle away up Paddington Street. 'They don't know about any of it, do they?'

'I suppose you've blabbed to him, have you?' Tom jerked a nod at the Alvis.

'It's nothing to do with him.'

'No, it ain't,' Tom spat. 'And it's nothing to do with you neither, so piss off.' He gave his sister a shove to try to loosen her grip and was about to give her another when the car door opened. 'It weren't me broke the window, anyhow,' he denied quickly, watching warily as the fellow approached. He was only slightly relieved to see he was in civvies and obviously off duty.

'Did you get arrested over it?'

Tom shook his head. 'Nobody saw us . . .' He realised then that couldn't be right, as Matilda Keiver knew what they'd done. 'We didn't reckon anyone was about. I told Davy it was stupid chucking a brick,' he mumbled before clamming up.

'It's all right . . . I'm fine.' Kathy knew Nick had come over because he'd noticed Tom getting rough with her. 'I won't be a moment.' She gave him a look that pleaded for privacy.

'Keep your hands to yourself,' Nick told Tom in a voice that was bland yet caused the youth to shift uncomfortably. Nick strolled off to wait for Kathy, leaning against the Alvis's bonnet.

'That your schmock copper, is it?' Tom jeered. 'He must be bent as a nine-bob note to afford a car like that.'

'What's happened to you, Tom?' Kathy sensed her anger ebbing away, to be replaced with sadness. Her little brother was unrecognisable in this mood.

'Nothing's happened to me,' Tom muttered sheepishly. 'I've just got a way of earning meself a bit of cash. Mum's always going on at me to bring something in, so I am.'

'If she knew how you were earning it she wouldn't take it.'

'Wanna bet?' Tom sneered. 'She ain't asked where the half-crowns come from fer ages.'

'What did you tell her when she did ask?'

'Got a part-time job working with Davy . . . ain't a lie.' He sounded defiant.

'You're getting paid by Fascists to stir up trouble, are you?'

Tom looked sullen, refusing to answer. 'I'm going home,' he muttered. 'Suppose you're coming 'n' all to grass me up, are you?' He glanced at Nick. 'You'd better keep him out of sight. Dad'll go nuts if you bring the police in.'

225

'Won't be me brings the police in, Tom,' Kathy replied quietly. 'It'll be you if you carry on as you are.'

Feeling defeated, Kathy turned away and walked back towards the car. She knew she'd ask Nick to take her straight home.

'Fancy a bite to eat?'

Kathy shook her head but gave him a grateful smile. 'Thanks all the same but David's coming over later.'

'Right . . .'

'It's true,' she said mildly in response to Nick's sarcastic tone. She felt quite relaxed now, knowing that he fancied her. She realised that she liked him back, despite the fact that, if what Matilda had told her was correct, he'd fibbed about not having any children. She slanted a look at his profile, at the curve of his mouth, wondering if he kissed like David. She knew she'd need do very little to tempt him closer and find out . . .

'We arranged to go to the flicks earlier in the week,' Kathy said briskly, snapping out of a sensual daze. She felt rather shocked at where her thoughts might have led. She believed Nick had separated from his wife but he was still a married man. And David was still her boyfriend.

'Yeah . . . I heard you loud and clear, Kathy. You're seeing David later.' He turned his head, watching through the car window some children noisily playing hopscotch in the street. 'I saw him recently . . .'

Kathy darted her eyes to him. 'Oh?'

'It was the afternoon I waited for my wife after she finished work. He went in the Goldsteins' shop a few minutes after Blanche came out.'

'David sometimes calls in to see his parents when he's

that way.' Kathy paused before blurting, 'Did you speak to your wife about the divorce? Sorry . . . that was rude . . . I shouldn't have asked. I know it's none of my business.'

Kathy felt embarrassed that she'd let curiosity get the better of her. She yanked at the door handle but Nick's long fingers curved on her wrist, preventing her jumping out.

'I was going to tell you anyway what that was all about . . . just wasn't sure how to bring it up.' He frowned. 'Blanche is knocking about with Charlie Potter, so I went over to see her to tell her she's a bloody fool.'

Kathy sank back into the seat, gawping at him. 'Your wife is going out with Ruby's husband?' she parroted in astonishment.

'That's about the size of it.' Nick gave a grim smile. 'Her father asked me to have a word with her because he's worried sick Blanche will end up getting hurt. So I did speak to her . . . but I doubt she'll take a blind bit of notice of anything that was said. I've wasted my time.'

Kathy gasped, nose wrinkling in distaste. She supposed women who liked their men rough and ready might take to Potter. He had a good height, and a certain rugged attractiveness. But she'd not have thought a woman who'd previously been married to a man as nice as Nick Raven would find the uncouth lout appealing. 'Why would she want to have anything to do with someone like him?'

'God knows . . . but they're probably both hoping to wind me up over it. Charlie's got scores to settle with me. Blanche doesn't want me to divorce her. I don't think either of them is bright enough to realise I don't give a toss what they do.' He swiped his fingers over his jaw.

'Well, that's not quite true. I wouldn't like to see Blanche get hurt any more than her father would.' He shrugged. 'But it's her life . . . and if she won't listen there's not much anyone can do.'

'You think Charlie's still mad at you because you beat him up over your mum?'

'He won't have forgotten that, or getting a bucket of water thrown over him.' Nick chuckled at the memory of it.

Kathy moistened her lips, feeling far from amused. 'It must be a great worry for you.'

He smiled, holding her gaze, making Kathy feel warm and comfortable and, oddly, that his wife was an idiot to have lost him.

'You'd better get going if you've got a date this evening,' Nick said.

Kathy nodded, murmuring thanks for all he'd done as she opened the car door. Before he could drive off, she ducked quickly down to speak to him. 'Shall I let you know what Ruby says about moving to Islington?'

'I'll come over Friday evening . . . unless you feel like coming round mine sooner than that, to let me know about it. Want the address?'

Kathy blinked, aware of the challenge in his voice and what lay behind it. She shook her head. 'See you Friday. I'll have finished my rounds by six o'clock, unless there's an emergency.'

CHAPTER TWENTY-THREE

Nick checked his watch, then started drumming impatient fingers on the steering wheel of his car. If George Clark didn't turn up in a minute, he'd get going. The appointment had been for eight o'clock, annoyingly late, but the only time that had suited both of them. Now it was twenty past and Nick was wondering whether the estate agent had been so desperate for a sale that he'd been overoptimistic promising to drive from the other side of town to meet him. The fellow had told him the electricity was still connected to the house Nick was viewing; if it wasn't, Nick knew he'd certainly wasted his time hanging around. He got out of the car and strolled beneath a gas lamp to light up a cigarette, then continued stretching his legs in a stroll along Mare Street. A woman was coming towards him and Nick halted in surprise, thinking Kathy was out doing a late visit. He tipped his hat back on his head but stopped himself calling out to her. Despite a startling similarity this individual wasn't a nurse and she lacked Kathy's grace of movement. Although the facial resemblance was remarkable, the woman was thinner, and her hair a darker blonde. She'd slowed down, eyeing him while lighting up. Throwing back her head so her hair swung about her face, she blew smoke before continuing towards him.

Kathy's sister, Nick realised, was about to offer him her services and he wasn't sure whether to laugh or turn tail in the hope Kathy never found out about it. He recalled Kathy had told him her twin's name and Nick started walking slowly, a morbid fascination to see Jennifer Finch at close quarters drawing him on. He kept going even when he heard a car stop somewhere behind and knew the estate agent had finally turned up.

Jenny had been on her way home but was always on the lookout for punters. She'd quickly assessed the scene the moment she'd clocked him watching her: smart car close by, tall good-looking fellow seemingly at a loose end. She reckoned it was her lucky day. She walked into his path. 'Got a light?'

'You don't need one.' Nick indicated the cigarette smouldering between her fingers.

Without losing eye contact Jennifer dropped the half-smoked stub to the ground, put a toe on it. 'Got a fag and a light?' she asked insolently.

Nick grunted a laugh, pulling out a packet of Players. Jennifer slowly selected a cigarette from the packet, drawing on it immediately before the flaring match had died.

'One good turn deserves another,' she said.

Her voice was unattractively coarse, Nick realised, whereas Kathy had a delicacy to her tone, even when she was telling him off.

'So . . . wonder what you'd like me to do fer you?' Jenny cocked her head at him.

'Nothing . . . got an appointment . . .' Nick began

striding back towards Mr Clark, who looked to be on the point of getting in his car and driving off. He broke into a run, whistling to attract the fellow's attention.

'Sorry, to be so late . . . damn pile-up at King's Cross . . .' George explained his tardiness while resting a pile of paperwork on the roof of his car. He held out a hand for Nick to shake.

Nick muttered something in response, trying to make up his mind whether George had done him a favour in making him wait. He'd now met Kathy's brother and sister, and he could understand why she'd been reluctant to introduce him to any of her family. He took a look over his shoulder to see Jennifer disappearing inside a house.

Half an hour later, Nick was back in his car, having agreed to buy the property at a discount. He raised a hand as George set off up the road, looking pleased with himself. Nick was about to start the ignition when he hesitated, staring at the house he'd seen Jennifer enter. It took just a moment for him to decide not to mention the meeting to Kathy because it was sure to embarrass her, then she might find excuses to avoid him . . .

Nick's eyes focused on the gloomy street scene and instinctively he ducked his head down, swearing beneath his breath as he recognised somebody else he'd come to know through Kathy.

David Goldstein didn't have to wait long for Jennifer to open up and, after a split second when it seemed she might shut the door in his face, Kathy's boyfriend disappeared inside Jennifer's house.

'Do you mind if I go to the party? I ought to show my face. We won't be able to see each other later that evening, though.'

'Of course you must go, and have a good time,' Kathy replied. 'You can't miss it now you've wangled time off work specially.'

'Sergeant Booth'll make sure I get an extra shift next week to make up for it,' David smiled wryly.

David didn't spell out that the invitation to his cousin's Bar Mitzvah hadn't been extended to Kathy. She knew, and whereas once she would have been hurt to be excluded, now she felt hardly a twinge of disappointment. She certainly couldn't grumble that it was unfair rejection by his family: if the Finches had a celebration to attend – which they rarely did, as nothing nice seemed to happen to merit it – she wouldn't be able to invite David along. Her father in particular would be horrified at the idea of a Jewish policeman being introduced to relatives as a possible son-in-law. If her mother insisted David was welcome, simply to show the gossips that one of her girls had caught a respectable man, Kathy would be on tenter-hooks the whole time in case her father made his disgust obvious. Her mother, of course, would be on tenterhooks in case Jennifer's name cropped up . . .

'Penny for your thoughts,' David said, putting an arm about Kathy's shoulders.

'I was just thinking about my sister,' Kathy replied as they settled into a stroll. 'I haven't stopped by to see her recently.'

'Any reason for that?' David asked distantly.

'Not really . . . she was moody last time I went there. I don't know why I bother with her sometimes. But I feel I ought to keep in touch; she is family, after all.'

'She's a big girl. She can look after herself.' David rubbed his hand against Kathy's arm. 'Did you like the film?'

'Did you?' Kathy threw the question back.

They chuckled simultaneously. It had passed the time away, despite being far from the scintillating comedy promised by the advertising hoarding.

'Want a cup of tea?' They'd arrived back at Kathy's and stopped by the gate. 'I'll stick the kettle on. Eunice baked a lemon sponge cake and gave me some.'

'Tempting . . . but better get off. I'm on early shift tomorrow.' David leaned in to slide together their lips. He always gave her a good-night kiss but usually somewhere more private.

'David! You should have come in to do that,' Kathy teasingly scolded. 'You'll scandalise the neighbours.' It was an unnecessary rebuke. There had been no passion in it and Kathy realised he'd not come over amorous in the way he used to in a long while. She accepted that their romance was fading. She still looked forward to seeing him but with the sort of mild anticipation she used to feel when meeting her brother, Tom, in the days before he turned into a wretch.

'One day, I just might scandalise people . . .' David uttered hoarsely, his expression vacant.

Kathy frowned. David's mood swings were unpredictable; at times she worried he was sinking into depression. She put a soft palm to his cheek. 'What's up? Work getting you down?'

'Yeah . . . I could do with a change.' He paused. 'I don't reckon anybody saw me kiss you just then. Don't want the old biddies twitching their curtains and having a gossip. You don't deserve that, Kathy . . . not you . . .'

'Don't be daft! If spying on a couple having a kiss sends people into a tizz, God help them, I say.' To prove to him she'd meant what she said she went onto tiptoe and moved her lips on his. There was no welcoming touch, just a slight flinch of surprise from David. 'Have a good Bar Mitzvah; you must let me know all about it next week.' Kathy walked up the path feeling an odd mixture of sadness and relief creep up on her at their parting.

'For heaven's sake, Jenny! Not again.'

Moments ago, Kathy had fished the key out of Jennifer's letter box where it hung on a bit of string. She'd let herself in to her twin's home to find Jennifer being sick in a bucket. After her sister had suffered the last stomach infection, Kathy had hoped her twin might use the carbolic soap a bit more often. She often nagged her about it, but neither Jennifer's home nor her person ever looked spruce.

'Don't fuss,' Jenny muttered irritably, dumping the bucket down on the carpet. She rolled off the sofa to stand unsteadily, hand clasping her forehead. Having ambled to the sink she turned on the tap and got a cup of water, gargling and spitting into the stained china. Then she sank onto a stool, dropping her head into her hands.

'I'll get you another cup of water.' Kathy approached her. 'You should drink some of it this time . . .'

Jennifer gestured limply that she wanted to be left alone.

Kathy watched her twin for a moment, sensing more than a raging bellyache was troubling Jennifer. She hunkered down beside her but the sickly sweet smell of alcohol made her wearily straighten up.

'Are you hungover?'

'Yeah . . . So what . . .?'

Kathy sighed and automatically began picking up crockery from the floor and dumping it in the sink.

'Just leave it alone!' Jenny snarled. 'I can do the washing up later!'

'I'll do it . . .'

'I don't fuckin' want you to!' Jennifer shrieked. 'Can't you understand? I don't want you here!'

'What's up with you? You've been acting odd – well, worse than usual – for weeks now and I've had enough of it. Who do you think's gonna come by and help you out with food and money, if I don't?'

'You're so very kind to me, aren't you?' Jenny mimicked nastily, eyes blazing. 'You're so nice to everybody, aren't you, Miss Perfect?' She scraped her lank hair behind her ears. 'You always was, wasn't yer? Good little swot at school, good little gel at home fer Mummy 'n' Daddy . . .' She shot up off the seat, pointing at Kathy. 'Well, you make me sick with all that holier-than-thou crap!' She swiped the finger under her running nose. 'Weren't nuthin' left fer me to be but a disgrace, was there, 'cos nobody could ever be as wonderful as you?'

Kathy stared at Jennifer. 'Sounds as though you've wanted to get that off your chest for a long while . . . have you?'

'Yeah, I fucking have!' Jenny raged, her eyes watery. Suddenly her mouth ballooned and, stumbling a few paces to the sink, she was sick on top of the crockery.

Kathy groaned a sigh, then began studying her sister more closely. Jennifer was standing sideways on to her while leaning on the wooden draining board and Kathy could see a tell-tale bump straining her sister's clothes. The reason for Jennifer's nausea suddenly held a very depressing meaning. Given her twin's profession, Kathy suddenly felt daft for not wising up sooner.

'Are you pregnant, Jennifer?' Kathy prayed her sister

would deny it. Her heart leaped to her mouth in the ensuing silence. Doggedly, she repeated her question.

Still Jennifer didn't react in any way. She continued leaning on the draining board with her forehead propped on a braced arm.

'You are, aren't you?' Kathy muttered hopelessly.

'Yeah, I'm expecting . . . gonna help me out, are yer?' Jenny wiped a hand across her mouth, then sent her sister a venomous look. 'You must know how it's done and I could do with a few ideas 'cos the gin ain't shifted it.'

'I hope you're not suggesting what I think you are.' Kathy sounded appalled. It was her job to nurture new life, not destroy it. She would have thought, given Jennifer's occupation, that her sister was clued up on contraception. Of course, however careful women were with their methods, accidents happened.

'See what I mean about you, Miss Goody Two-Shoes.' Jenny gave an acid laugh. 'Wish I lived in cloud-cuckoo-land with you. Don't know nuthin' about real life, do you?'

'I know I'm not a murderer. And if you think I've got an easy ride, you should come with me on my rounds and swaddle a few stillborns. You might be sick of me but, believe me, I'm sick to death of you too! I'm up to the back teeth with your whining and your disgusting habits.' Kathy came to a breathless stop, noticing that Jennifer had let her greasy hair curtain the sides of her face, trying to hide her snivelling. Kathy made no attempt to comfort her. She meant what she'd said and knew she could have told her sister a good many more home truths.

'Have you told Bill the good news?' Kathy snapped sarcastically.

'Ain't seen him in ages. Anyhow, it ain't his,' Jenny croaked.

'Who's is it? Do you even know?'

'Yeah . . . I know,' Jennifer said bitterly.

'Do you want me to have a quick look at you?' Kathy assessed her sister's thickening waist, guessing her to be about three months gone. 'Do you know when it's due?'

'No point in any of that . . . I ain't keeping it. If you won't help get rid of it, I'll find someone who will. Soapy water syringe does the trick, I heard. Already tried pennyroyal and castor oil. They don't work any better'n the gin, so no need to suggest I dose meself with any o' that.'

'I wasn't going to,' Kathy said quietly. 'I was going to suggest you get yourself a decent man. Or a load of johnnies to keep by the bed.'

'That'd make life simple, wouldn't it?' Jenny jeered. She threw back her head, howling a laugh at the ceiling. 'Never get a shilling off none of them then. They'd all do up their flies and get going, including your—' She suddenly clammed up.

'Including my what?' Kathy demanded, again angry and impatient with Jennifer for getting herself into this new mess.

'Nuthin'. Need a bit of fresh air.'

Jennifer opened the back door and stepped out into a warm September afternoon.

'Got any tablets for me head?' she sent back over her shoulder.

'I didn't bring any with me.' Kathy felt like reminding Jennifer she'd just asked for her help, despite shouting at her to fuck off moments ago.

Kathy was aware of the various ways expectant mothers tried to bring on a miscarriage. Thankfully, no

237

patient had ever asked her to end her pregnancy. Most women clammed up on abortion or contraception. They all seemed to have heard about Marie Stopes' Mothers' Clinics but very few would admit to having put a foot inside one, considering it shameful. The poor cows were desperate not to get pregnant, yet seemed to prefer their pills and potions to avoid the risk of another mouth to feed. It amazed Kathy that somehow or other they scraped together the cash to buy such quackery.

Few wives seemed able to persuade their husbands to use a rubber. As a last resort seeking a backstreet butcher seemed simpler than insisting that the man who'd promised to cherish them prove it in that small unselfish way. Kathy understood why Jennifer had mocked the idea of a stranger inconveniencing himself on her account.

'Come inside so we can talk and work out the best thing to do,' Kathy said calmly. 'I'll make some tea.'

'Don't fancy none . . . it'll make me ill. It's too hot indoors . . .'

Kathy knew her sister was choosing to stay outside in the back yard so there'd be no opportunity for them to discuss this new disaster. Neither of them would bring up such a delicate subject out in the open for fear of being overheard by neighbours.

'You might as well get going. I'm all right now,' Jenny said, leaning against the fence. She fumbled in her pocket, drawing out a half-smoked cigarette and some matches. Turning her back on Kathy, she lit up.

'If that's what you want,' Kathy answered as tobacco smoke drifted her way.

'Yeah . . . it is . . .' Jennifer said, without looking round.

The stink of vomit in the sink was overpowering Kathy. She knew her sister would probably expect her to clear the mess up before she left. Kathy avoided looking at the sink as she headed for the door. It was time her sister started clearing up after herself.

CHAPTER TWENTY-FOUR

'Wouldn't mind a drink in the Red Lion for a change. Go on there, shall we, Charlie?' Blanche was directing a poisonous glare at somebody. The pub was crowded yet she was conscious that the chortling coming from an adjacent table was at her expense.

'I'm all right here,' Charlie answered blithely, upending his glass of ale. He knew why Blanche wanted to leave. She and Joyce Groves had been staring each other out from the moment the blonde sashayed into the pub with her brother, Kenny, and a few friends ten minutes ago.

Charlie wasn't bothered that Joyce didn't really fancy him and was only giving him the eye to make Blanche jealous. In his life he had never had so much female attention from good-looking women. Charlie was lapping it up and knew he'd got Blanche pinned beneath his thumb, desperate to keep him sweet. She'd do anything rather than let her rival think she'd got one over on her. Recently Blanche had been telling him no at the end of the evening when his hand travelled under her skirt. He could do without the expense of a room in a cheap hotel but Blanche had put her foot down at doing it against a wall in back alleys. Tonight, though, Charlie reckoned she'd be putty in his hands, whatever he suggested.

Blanche watched Charlie rock back in his chair so he had a better view of the noisy group close by. He winked, smiling lazily at the young woman pouting at him. Blanche gulped her gin and orange, pretending not to have noticed them flirting although she was seething mad.

Lately, she'd been reflecting on what her father and her husband had said about Charlie Potter. At the time, she'd shrugged off their warnings but now realised she'd been stupid to get involved with such a man. But it was too late for regrets. Getting back at the cow who'd turned Nick against her was more important to Blanche than anything else.

Blanche had been cock-a-hoop when she heard on the grapevine that Nick had finished with Joyce. But the solicitor's letters kept coming, so it was obvious he'd not changed his mind about the divorce. Joyce was trying to rub it in that she could also snatch Charlie from Blanche if she wanted to. It was the reason Blanche had stubbornly decided to hang on to him at any cost, even though she feared he was more trouble than he was worth.

Before Joyce started making eyes at him, Blanche had hoped to ease herself away from Charlie by hinting he should spend more time with his wife and kids. There'd been no mistaking the dangerous glint in his eyes when he bawled at her to keep her snout out on that score. Blanche had limited her retaliation to being sworn at in public to a sulky look.

They'd been going out for months and during the early days he'd been on his best behaviour. Shortly after they'd started sleeping together, he'd made less of an effort to impress her in bed or in opening his wallet. But it was his propensity for violence that worried Blanche the most.

Last week a youth had bumped into him in the pub, spilling his pint. Charlie had swung around and clumped him, despite the fellow's rapid apology. Blanche had been horrified that Charlie had lashed out so easily. She sensed it might only be a matter of time before she caught his fist.

No man had ever raised his hand to her. Her father had never physically chastised her although Gladys had often slapped her face for cheek. Neither Nick nor Wes had whacked her, despite quite vicious rows with both of them when things were coming to an end. Nick, especially, had had reason to fly off the handle over her cheating on him. But he'd chosen to walk away and, to Blanche's deep regret, he'd never looked back.

'Need a refill.' Blanche had again caught Charlie winking at Joyce. 'Unless you fancy an early night, do you?' A promise of sex curbed her boyfriend's roving eye, as she knew it would.

'Bit short this week. Ain't got enough fer a room.' Charlie watched for her reaction.

'Got enough for another round?' Blanche sarcastically enquired.

'Yeah . . . got enough fer that.' Charlie suddenly gripped her chin in a way that looked playful yet felt too rough for comfort. 'Same again, gel?'

'Nah . . . can't be bothered now. I've had enough.' Blanche rubbed her fingers over her sore skin.

'How about we find somewhere a bit more private, then, if it's slap and tickle you're after?' He'd leaned forward, breathing alcoholic fumes on her face. 'I'm up for it, if you know what I mean,' He caught one of her hands and brought it to his groin, beneath the table.

'Ain't going down no dark alleys with you so don't bother asking,' Blanche said flatly, pulling her hand away.

'Back to yours, then, is it?' Charlie squeezed her knee, his calloused fingers catching the silk of her stockings as they climbed higher.

Blanche snorted a derisive laugh, tapping away his touch. 'I'm sure me mum 'n' dad would be pleased to see you.'

'Don't need to see us, do they, gel?' Charlie nuzzled her cheek, his first real show of affection since they'd met that evening. 'Got that shed out the back, ain't yer? Got a lock on it, has it, Blanche?'

Over Charlie's shoulder, Blanche noticed Joyce watching them. The idea of doing it in amongst her father's garden tools and pots was so revolting it almost made her burst out laughing, but she knew Charlie was deadly serious. And she knew she wanted to put one in the eye for Joyce.

'Me mum 'n' dad go to bed early most nights, so I suppose I might manage to get the key off the hook and meet you for a nightcap.' She felt ashamed of herself for having promised to bed down with Charlie just yards from where her parents slept. She knew now she'd agreed there'd be no going back . . . he wouldn't let her. He was gulping back his drink in readiness to leave. Behind Charlie's head Blanche raised two fingers at her rival, then stood up with a flourish.

Charlie was grinning, yanking on his trousers and buttoning himself up. It was the first time he'd made

Blanche pant and he was puffed up about it. Ordinarily, he didn't care much about what women liked, he just took what he wanted and if they happened to enjoy it, it was a bonus for them. Blanche was a bit more important because she'd be comparing him with two men who she thought were a better class. Charlie knew that Nick and Wes also reckoned they were his superiors.

Charlie had never liked Raven and he was coming to resent Wes as well. His boss was expecting more work out of him for no more pay, and Charlie wasn't having it. That's why he'd brought in a couple of youngsters on a pittance to do a bit of dirty work for him. Davy was shaping up nicely at it, but his pal, Tom, seemed ready to weasel out when the going got rough. Davy was getting results: the lad had pushed a burning rag through the Butlers' letter box last week and told the draper a pint of petrol would shortly follow if he didn't pay up. Butler couldn't get the till open quickly enough for him after that . . .

Charlie noticed Blanche trying to fish one of her shoes from under the workbench. Gallantly, he used a broom handle to knock it towards her.

'Well, that weren't so bad after all, were it, gel?'

As Blanche bent to retrieve the shoe, Charlie gave her bare rump a slap, making her squeal.

'Weren't so bad?' Blanche echoed in a grumble, gathering up her clothes. 'Bloody good job it's a warm night. Got splinters in me backside now . . . swear I have . . .'

'Get 'em out for you, shall I?' Charlie growled, plunging his fingers between her legs. 'Reckon you liked that so much you're ready for another seeing to, ain't yer?'

Blanche chuckled, pushing him away to continue

dressing. She knew he didn't have another session in him. He'd tried that on a previous occasion, but given up after a few minutes and rolled over to go to sleep.

It was the first time Charlie had satisfied her. Oddly, jigging about against rough wood that smelled of creosote, to find a comfortable position, had aroused Blanche far more than being pumped against a mattress in a seedy guesthouse.

She realised that creeping about stealing the key from indoors had excited her even before Charlie emerged from the undergrowth to haul her inside the shed and start pulling her clothes off. Charlie wasn't a skilled or a patient lover and she'd previously found him a letdown.

He certainly couldn't match her husband's skill, or even Wes's. The first time she'd seen Wes undressed she'd noticed straight away he was different from most men. He'd seen the direction of her gaze and sheepishly told her not to worry about that . . . everything was in working order. Before she could ask questions he'd gone on to say he'd been born with a bit missing. Blanche had known what he meant; it hadn't been the first time she'd played with a cock that lacked a bit of skin.

She'd had a Jewish boyfriend at school and although they'd never actually gone all the way he'd liked her touching him. And she'd liked him touching her. So Blanche had learned that Jewish boys were circumcised when very young, but she'd not let on to Wes about her knowledge.

Wes made no secret of the fact that he hated Jews. He said he was of Irish extraction and rarely spoke about his parents. He'd told Blanche the Hun had seen off his old man when he was a kid and good riddance to bad rubbish as far as he was concerned. It had seemed to

Blanche a callous thing for anybody to say about a parent they'd barely known . . . unless that father had belonged to a despised race that circumcised boys.

'Meet you up the top o' the road on Friday then, shall I?' Charlie was shrugging into his shirt, rolling back the sleeves on his hairy forearms. 'Best get off home to me wife 'fore she starts hollerin' blue murder. Must be close to midnight.'

Blanche carried on buttoning her blouse. Usually, Charlie acted as if he was fancy free and his family didn't exist. He only mentioned Ruby when it suited him because he needed an excuse to get going. Blanche no longer felt bad about seeing another woman's husband; she guessed Ruby was relieved to be rid of him, and couldn't care less where he went or how long he stayed away.

'Might be a bit late Friday 'cos I've got a bit to do for Wes before I'm finished fer the day. So . . . how d'yer reckon I compare to Wes then?' Charlie swaggered over to Blanche handling her breasts beneath her clothes. He hadn't asked before because he wasn't sure he wanted an answer but after his performance tonight he felt confident of having top billing.

'Got it all, ain't yer, Charlie,' Blanche said, returning the favour and probing his balls through his trousers. Oddly, she was feeling horny again already. A moonbeam was slanting through the grimy pane of glass that served as a window. Charlie looked quite young and handsome with his face gilded in silver.

'Perhaps that's what makes the difference when it comes down to it . . . that little bit there on the end . . .' Blanche was rubbing her hot palm on the bulge in his trousers.

'What *little bit* you on about?' Charlie wolfishly asked, unbuttoning himself and thrusting her hand inside. 'Nothing small in there, gel, is there?'

Blanche found what she was after and gave it a teasing pinch. 'Yeah . . . you're much better than Wes, and I reckon poor old Wes must hate being part Jewish . . .'

'When can we leave, Nurse Finch?'

'You're really prepared to do this?' Kathy hadn't detected a hint of uncertainty in Ruby's voice but wanted confirmation the woman understood the risks. 'Please don't think I'm putting pressure on you. But I will help you as much as I can if you're sure it's what you want.'

'I'm sure.'

The two quiet words resonated with Ruby's determination. Her unblinking gaze was so poignantly hopeful that Kathy felt a lump close her throat.

'I'd go with you now . . . sooner the better, as far as I'm concerned. I hate Charlie, but 'spect you know that.' Ruby rocked the pram as Paul snuffled. 'Can't believe you've done this for me. As for the lady over Islington way who's gonna let us stay with her . . .' Ruby gestured amazement. 'She must like you a lot to do a big favour for people she don't even know.'

'She is a kind soul,' Kathy confirmed huskily. 'Salt of the earth, is Mrs Keiver.'

Ruby bit her wobbling underlip to stifle a sob. 'Have to time it right and go when Charlie's not around. But then he's out morning, noon and night most days, thank Gawd.' She paused. 'When he does get in we all wish he hadn't and hope he'll sling his hook again. He don't even come back to pay me wages like he used to on a Friday afternoon. It's a fight getting the rent out of him.'

Ruby gave a gruff snort. 'Ain't gonna be missing no money when I go, that's fer sure.' She glanced about at her chaotic home: washing was hanging over chair backs and a flat iron stood on end on the table ready for use. 'Ain't gonna be missing this dump neither.'

'Campbell Road is no better than this, Ruby; some people would think it far worse,' Kathy quickly reminded her. 'You understand that, don't you?'

'Be a palace, as far as we're concerned, s'long as he ain't in it,' Ruby answered.

Kathy had been taken aback by how keen Ruby was to up sticks. She'd tentatively outlined her plan, wondering if Ruby would consider it an impertinence that Nurse Finch was taking such an interest in her family. But the moment Ruby understood Kathy was being deadly serious about helping her escape her brutal husband she'd looked overwhelmed and pathetically grateful.

Kathy rarely saw Ruby these days without a fading bruise somewhere on her person. She presently had her bare forearms crossed over her thin middle and Kathy noticed purple blotches on her wrists. More worryingly, Pansy, seated on a chair swinging her legs and sucking her thumb, had a sallow shadow on one cheek.

'Yeah . . . he did that.' Ruby knew what had caught Kathy's gaze. 'Pansy was making the baby laugh and they was getting too noisy for Charlie's liking. He's always worse when he's had a drink.'

It was the first time the woman had admitted to her husband's brutality towards the children.

'And Paul?' Kathy asked, her voice little more than a whisper.

'He's always got a fist close to his face, shaking it.'

248

Ruby swallowed audibly. ''S'only a matter of time before he loses control.' She sniffed back tears. 'He threw Paul on the bed the other evening when I was feeding him. Yanked him off me, he did, and said he wanted his tea and damn the Chink.' She cleared her throat. 'That's why I'm ready to go, Nurse Finch. Soon as you say the word, I'm ready to get going with me kids.'

'I have a friend who's going to help on moving day. He's got a car so we won't have to hang about and risk getting spotted waiting at bus stops with your belongings.'

'Would've willingly walked there if need be,' Ruby choked out. She composed herself, using the heel of her hand on her damp eyes. 'Don't reckon it's your boyfriend gonna help, is it? A copper wouldn't put his neck on the line for the likes of me. Don't blame him neither.'

'No . . . it's not my boyfriend . . .' Kathy replied. 'You might remember him, though. He was here the night Paul was born and helped boil up the kettles of water with Peter.'

'Don't remember much about that night!' Ruby grimaced. 'State I was in, it all passed in a blur.'

'That's the best way with a difficult labour . . .' Kathy's levity soon passed. 'Will you tell Peter what's going on before the day?'

'Already thought of that.' Ruby had read Kathy's mind about the secret leaking out to Charlie and ruining everything. 'Won't say a word to nobody.'

Kathy glanced at Pansy; the child's eyes looked huge above fingers curled on top of her nose.

'No need to worry about her . . . she won't say nuthin', will yer, Pansy?'

The little girl solemnly shook her head, then, removing

the thumb from her mouth, she pressed her lips together in a subtle smile.

'I'll see if my friend can make next week. My afternoon off is Wednesday.' Kathy looked expectantly at Ruby for confirmation of the date.

'Suits me as well as any other, Nurse Finch,' Ruby answered, and with a sudden whoop of glee she swept her small daughter into her arms and spun her around.

CHAPTER TWENTY-FIVE

Kathy glanced again at the clock; the hand had been creeping agonisingly slowly towards six thirty. Since six o'clock, she'd been expecting Nick to turn up at any minute and was now impatient to see him. She wanted to blurt out all the exciting news following her meeting with Ruby but also realised, with a feeling of warm surprise, she simply longed for his company.

She had got back on time from her rounds and was praying there wouldn't be an emergency to disrupt their talk about the move next week. She had taken care with her appearance . . . more than she would have done for an evening out with David. In the early days of seeing her boyfriend, Kathy had enjoyed curling her hair and using powder and lipstick to please him. Now she did it mostly for pride's sake. She'd liked, too, the sensation of tingling butterflies in her stomach as the time approached for him to turn up.

At present, the fluttering inside was caused by thoughts of a different man but her exhilaration was being dampened by doubt. She still knew very little

251

about Nick's background yet had come naturally to trust him. She wasn't sure whether that was a good or a bad thing; he might have lied to her about his home life, or Matilda might have been mistaken in thinking he had children. She knew the only way to find out was to ask him.

Kathy moved the curtain to peer out of the front window at the road, letting it drop back as a black car slowed down outside. She didn't want him to think she was pathetically eager to see him and spying on his arrival, even though it was the truth.

Nervously, she clasped her hands together, frowning at the cups and saucers she'd set ready on the table. Perhaps he'd think her a bit mean offering him tea after work. He might prefer a beer or a nip of whisky and she'd not thought to get any . . .

All things considered, a stiff drink was the least he deserved if he agreed to transport Ruby and her family and all their belongings to Islington next week.

Kathy heard the rap on the door and took a quick glance in the over-mantel mirror, smoothing her wavy fair hair before speeding to answer it.

'I hope you won't think it a cheek but . . .' Kathy led the way down a narrow hallway and into her small living room, inviting him to take a seat. She nibbled her lower lip, conscious of his cool grey gaze on her as he settled back against gold upholstery. Kathy thought he looked as well groomed and attractive dressed in casual flannels as he did in a business suit. 'My meeting with Mrs Potter went far better than I imagined it would,' she continued in a rush. 'I was worried she'd think it a dreadful cheek that I'd poked my nose in.' A bashful smile followed the admission. 'But Ruby's grateful I did and wants to escape Charlie as quickly as she can. On the spur of the moment I said you'd help us with the move. Will you?'

'Of course.'

'You don't know when it is.'

Nick shrugged, settled a shoe on a knee as he leaned back in the chair. 'I said I'd help and I will, whenever it is.'

'Thanks . . .' Kathy said huskily, and took the lid off the teapot, about to offer him tea.

'You'd better tell me when it is.' Nick sounded mildly amused.

'Wednesday afternoon.' Absently, Kathy put the lid back on the pot and paced to and fro. 'Ruby said Charlie's never around much these days so we should be lucky and avoid him completely.' She halted by the hearth, then sank to perch on the edge of an armchair opposite him. 'I doubt the family's got much in the way of possessions but there'll be clothes and household bits and pieces to shift. I expect the pram folds down . . .'

'We'll take as much as fits into the boot. Do two journeys, if necessary, if Charlie's not about.'

'Thanks very much . . .' Kathy replied. Her smile soon turned to a frown. 'Ruby had bruises on her arms again and little Pansy had a mark on her face too.'

Nick sat forward, clasped together his hands between his knees. 'I should've clumped Charlie harder when I had the chance that night the boy was born.'

'He's a vile brute.'

'A lot of men whack their kids to chastise them,' Nick stated bluntly.

'Did your father hit you? Sorry . . . forgot your dad passed away in the war,' she murmured. 'My father used

253

to hit us but only when he thought we deserved it.'
Now she knew more about Charlie Potter, she felt guilty
mentioning her father in almost the same breath. Eddie
Finch had been a brutal man at times, to his wife as
well as his children, but he'd never seemed to relish
lashing out in the way that Potter did. Kathy could recall
the sadistic glitter in Ruby's husband's eyes when his
fingers had been digging into her chin, dragging her
upright all those months ago.

'Your father beat you?'

'Sometimes . . . but I got off lightly, so did Tom.
Jennifer wasn't so lucky because she used to drive him
mad. I can understand why he lost control.' Kathy's
laugh was humourless. 'She drives me mad and I often
feel like thumping her to knock some sense into her.'
She paused, sensing he was waiting for her to elaborate
on her twin's infuriating ways. But Kathy felt unable to
tell him anything about her alcoholic drug-addled prostitute of a twin sister who was now carrying the baby
of one of her clients because she hadn't managed to
abort it.

'Mum would box our ears too when we were naughty,'
Kathy resumed, breaking the silence. 'I know she had
a lot to put up with. She always seemed unhappy . . .
she still does . . .' Her voice faded, then sprang again
into life. 'Did you drive Lottie mad?'

'Yeah . . .' Nick chuckled. 'My poor old mum was
always chasing me up the road to clip me ear for something or other I'd done. Bleedin' kids, eh? Who'd have
'em?'

'You?' Kathy blurted.

'Don't have any . . . told you that.'

'Yes . . . you did say that.'

'You don't believe me?'

'I do believe you,' Kathy said quickly, and stood up. 'Like some tea? I'll put the kettle on . . .'

'Why d'you believe me, Kathy? Because you want my help shifting Ruby Potter out of harm's way?'

Kathy swung about by the table, her stare challenging his sarcastic expression. 'Are you lying then?'

'No.'

Kathy knew he was waiting for her to spit out what was on her mind. She knew too he wasn't going to make things easy for her by contributing any facts on the subject.

'Somebody just mentioned to me they thought you were a father.' Kathy let the comment flow over her shoulder as she walked away.

A small kitchenette adjoined the living room and Kathy entered it, twisting the tap to fill the kettle. She closed her eyes, praying there wouldn't be any awkward silences between them now. She should have kept her mouth shut, she told herself, at least until after the Potters had moved to Campbell Road.

'Who told you I'd got kids?' Nick had stationed himself against the doorjamb, watching her at the sink.

'Matilda. She remembered once seeing you in the pub with her nephews. One of them said your wife was pregnant. That's all I heard.'

'Blanche was pregnant. That's why I married her. She lost the baby at about five months, not long after the wedding. I expect you come across miscarriages in your job so know it happens.'

Kathy felt as though she'd shrivelled to half her size. He sounded calm and polite but she knew she'd just been reprimanded, and with good cause. 'I'm sorry to hear about it,' she murmured stiltedly, and struck a match to light the gas stove.

'I was too at the time. But it's all over now . . . water under the bridge . . .'

'Would you like something to eat?' Kathy was desperate to change the subject. 'I've got . . .' She opened a pantry cupboard to hunt amongst the few groceries for something to put in a sandwich, hoping to find a tin of corned beef. But there didn't seem to be much other than a few ripe tomatoes and Bird's custard powder. 'I can pop out and get something,' she offered brightly. 'I need shopping and it's only on the corner . . .'

'Don't worry, it's fine . . . we can go out to dinner, if you like.'

Kathy felt relieved he wasn't about to disappear because the atmosphere between them had cooled. She knew she would like to go out with him but a sense of uneasiness was niggling at the back of her mind, holding back her answer. It was only fair to tell David it was over between them before accepting dinner invitations from another man. She owed him some loyalty.

'If you turn me down, I'll still take Ruby to Islington. Don't feel obliged to do anything you don't want to.'

Kathy swung about but he'd gone back into the living room and was standing by the mantel gazing into an empty grate, his hands plunged into his trouser pockets.

'I'd like to go out with you, but I just want to speak to David first. We've grown apart, so I'm sure it'll be a relief for him too when I tell him it's over. But I owe it to him to be honest.'

'Do you?' Nick said, sounding sarcastic.

'Why d'you say it like that?' Kathy frowned.

He shook his head, turning away. 'No reason . . .

256

just being a prat . . .' Nick had bitten his tongue on telling Kathy that the man she was desperate to protect had been cheating on her with her own sister. He raised his eyes to her face, gave her a rueful half-smile, knowing he'd do anything rather than hurt her. 'You're a good girl, Kathy . . . too decent for me, or him . . . I reckon.'

'I am not!' For some reason, Kathy felt she'd been damned with faint praise. 'Don't make me out to be a prissy madam just because I'm a nurse, or because I don't think it's right to two-time somebody.'

'It was meant to be a compliment, sweetheart,' Nick said gently.

Kathy held her ground as he walked purposefully towards her, his eyes sultry with desire. Cupping her face he touched his lips gently to hers, stroked her cheek with one long finger. 'You tell him then, as soon as you can, and we'll go out next Wednesday, after we've got Ruby and her kids settled in with Matilda.' He paused, looking tormented by indecision. 'I'm going now but I'll see you at one o'clock Wednesday,' he said huskily, putting her firmly away from him. 'Then later at dinner I'll tell you all about myself . . . warts 'n' all.'

Kathy darted to press her lips to his mouth, surprising him. Just as quickly she'd skittered back against the table before he could get a firm grip on her. It was her way of thanking him for Ruby and letting him know she was looking forward to getting to know him better.

'It's good to see you, David. You look well.'

'Nice to see you too.' David gave his past love a smile. Rachel seemed keen to be friendly so he stopped to have a chat. He avoided looking at the little bump of her pregnancy beneath her dress. He sipped bitter, hoping that he appeared blasé about this meeting.

'Where's Sam got to?' David glanced around. He'd not seen his cousin amidst the folk crowding his aunt and uncle's front room for about half an hour.

'Probably talking politics with some of the other men.' Rachel sourly mentioned her husband's pet interest. 'Sam told me that you ran into one another a while ago at a Mosley rally.'

'We did . . .' David thought it best not to elaborate.

'If I tell you something will you promise not to breathe a word to anybody?' Rachel suddenly whispered.

David darted her a questioning look. Her solemn dark eyes were pinned to his face.

'Oh . . . it's not a romantic declaration, David.' Rachel's lips twisted in melancholy amusement. 'Don't look so scared.'

David swirled the ale at the bottom of his glass to avoid her eyes.

'Sam's worrying me,' Rachel stated bluntly.

David frowned, wondering if Sam's political conviction had forced him the wrong side of the law. If so, he'd sooner remain in blissful ignorance of any crime he'd committed.

'It's nothing illegal.' Rachel had read his mind, adding bitterly, 'It's worse than that. He's going off to Spain, and nothing I say will make him change his mind.' Her eyes filled with tears. 'Will you talk to him for me? Please tell him how mean and stupid he's being.'

'Spain?' David echoed, looking mystified. 'What in God's name for?'

A second later, David blew out his lips in a shocked sigh of enlightenment. Civil War had started recently in Spain, and was stirring up people in Britain who despised

Fascist ideology. Sir Oswald Mosley might preach his venom in England but he had his counterparts in Italy and Spain in Mussolini and Franco.

David put a hand on her arm to comfort her, feeling the tremble beneath her sleeve. 'I think he's acting like a fool to even consider it. I'll speak to him, but if he won't listen to you I doubt he'll pay a blind bit of notice to anything I say.'

'Thank you . . . that's kind . . .' She forced a smile. 'I'll move away now in case people think it's you who's upsetting me. If only they knew the truth . . .'

David managed to get Sam alone outside on the garden terrace so they wouldn't be overheard. But his cousin wasn't hiding his irritation at this interference.

'I don't know what you think you're playing at . . . your wife's pregnant.' David gestured amazement.

'I'm not "playing" at anything. It's not a fucking game, is it?' Sam spat, tipping ale down his throat, then swiping the back of his hand over his mouth. 'You wouldn't understand. I bet you're mired up to your neck in corruption every fucking day, doing what you're told, like the rest of them, for a quiet life.'

'Now hang on a minute—' David started indignantly.

'No, *you* hang on a minute. We're Jews so should understand and condemn oppression wherever it's found.' Sam glanced at his family celebrating close by. 'I'm asking you to keep quiet for Rachel's sake 'cos I need some breathing space to get my affairs in order for her, just in case . . .' Sam stared at David, daring him to blab and ruin things.

David gestured defeat. 'I've nothing more to say. I heard you loud and clear: you want to be a martyr.'

'You can hear this too,' Sam snarled. 'You could have kept Rachel if you'd fought a bit harder. It was always you she wanted. Letting me have her was your way of being a martyr, was it?'

Sam strode past into the house, leaving David alone on the terrace.

CHAPTER TWENTY-SIX

'I'm glad we can still be friends, David.'

Despite his gruff reassurance that there were no hard feelings, Kathy had glimpsed shock and sadness in David's eyes when she'd told him it was over. It had brought a lump to her throat so she enclosed him in a spontaneous hug rather than comforting him with words. She'd not thought her news would come as a surprise or that he'd take it so badly.

'Any reason to give me?' David asked as they broke apart. He shoved a couple of fingers along the bridge of his nose, waiting for an answer.

'Apart from our families, you mean?' Kathy remarked ruefully. 'They were never going to approve of us settling down together, were they? You'd made out to your folks that we'd already parted, hadn't you?'

David had the grace to appear shamefaced at Kathy's mild accusation.

She moved away a couple of paces, staring sightlessly at the billboard advertising the film. They'd arranged to meet, as they usually did, by the cinema, but she knew neither of them now wanted to go inside for a final time, and sit together side by side in the dark for over an hour.

'Have your parents made you stop seeing me?' Kathy had mentioned that her father in particular had an aversion to policemen, but so did most working-class men. As a wealthy merchant's son, David had felt confident his prospects would overrule any objections the Finches had to him because of his faith. The Goldsteins were non-Orthodox Jews who'd put down roots in England centuries ago. He wouldn't have proposed to Kathy and risked a rift with his parents, but his ego was bruised by her rejection; he'd imagined them carrying on as they were for the foreseeable future.

'I haven't seen Mum and Dad recently so they don't yet know we're breaking up,' Kathy answered. 'It's not just about our different upbringings and religions, is it?' Kathy gently pointed out. 'There was a spark between us but it's fizzled out. In fact, I've been wondering if you might have had your eye on another girl.'

A guilty look flitted over David's features, proof enough for Kathy that he had been playing around; it explained his moodiness over past months. Kathy had experienced similar inner conflict when trying to banish Nick Raven from her mind. Now she welcomed thoughts of him, accepting that he was the man she wanted.

'It doesn't matter . . . honestly,' Kathy stressed. 'I don't mind if you've got someone else. Actually, I'm glad and wish you both well.'

'You don't know what you're saying, Kathy. If you did, you'd damn me to hell—' David broke off, frowning into the distance. At first, he'd feared Jennifer might blab to Kathy about their affair out of spite. He'd soon realised the slut wouldn't risk losing the regular benefit of her sister's support, or his money. Besides, Jennifer enjoyed the thrill of their filthy sessions as much as he did and wouldn't want them to end because Kathy had discovered they were fornicating behind her back.

Kathy tilted her face, gazing into his eyes. She wouldn't miss his odd cryptic comments, and wondered whether to suggest he buck his ideas up because at times he reminded her of her maudlin sister. 'I'm sorry if I've upset you but things weren't right between us. I'm sure we can both still be happy—'

'Take no notice of me,' David interrupted, shooting her a speculative look. 'Are you keen on another fellow?'

'Somebody has asked me to have dinner with him,' Kathy immediately owned up. 'I'm going out with him next week but I wanted to tell you first rather than do it behind your back.'

A silence developed between them. Kathy realised everything that needed to be said had been said, so changed the subject to something more pleasant. 'Did the Bar Mitzvah go off well?'

David nodded. 'What did you get up to that evening? Did you stay in?'

Kathy knew he was probing to discover if she'd enjoyed herself without him. In fact, she had spent a dismal hour or so that evening with Jennifer, listening to her self-pity. Her sister had hinted she'd find a back-street butcher to get rid of the baby as she'd had no luck bringing on a miscarriage. Mother Nature seemed unwilling to lend a hand, she'd moaned, and as nobody else had offered . . . Kathy had received a hateful stare and had left in disgust once she'd reminded Jennifer she wasn't an abortionist.

'Did you stay in after all?' David repeated.

'I wish I had.' Kathy slowly surfaced from her miserable memory. 'I visited Jennifer but soon wished I'd not bothered.'

'It sounds as though she's unbearable company.' David licked his lips before adding, 'I can't understand why you go there so often.'

'Well, now she's preg—' Kathy pressed together her lips, regretting her slip. Jennifer's condition was constantly weighing heavily on her mind but she'd never intentionally have unburdened herself to anyone, least of all a boyfriend she'd just thrown over.

'Now she's . . . *What?*' David echoed in a peculiar voice.

Kathy shot a look at him, noticing with sinking heart he'd grown pale. There was no denying it was an awkward subject to talk about. But they were both adults and she was sure her sister's ruination wouldn't come as a complete surprise to him.

'Sorry . . . didn't mean to embarrass you,' Kathy sighed. 'Forget I said anything.'

'No . . . you can tell me. I'm not bothered by scandals,' David lied. He forced an insouciant smile to his lips but his gut was writhing in anxiety.

'The stupid fool's got herself in the family way and as I'm a midwife I feel I ought to keep an eye on her,' Kathy blurted.

'Is she getting married?'

Kathy recognised faint hope in David's voice and thought it sweet of him to be concerned. If he knew her family better he'd realise it was far too late to salvage the Finches' reputation by getting a ring on Jenny's finger. 'Not likely,' she muttered bitterly. 'Jennifer says

264

she knows who the father is but hasn't named him yet. I expect she'll tell me in the end, whether I want to know or not. I don't care who the wretch is and neither will my parents. They washed their hands of her years ago.' She gestured sadly. 'If you knew her you'd realise the fellow can't be any good if he associates with Jennifer. It's an awful thing to say about one of your own family, but it's true.' She gazed beseechingly at him. 'You'll keep this to yourself, won't you?'

David grunted agreement.

'You've guessed that my sister's fallen a long way?' Kathy raised her eyes heavenward. 'Sorry, you don't have to answer that. Most people who knew us around the time Jenny left home put two and two together. But they were polite enough to keep their suspicions to themselves. I expect your mum and dad were no different to the rest.'

Kathy knew she'd said too much about her family's rattling skeletons yet felt compelled to offer some mitigation for Jenny's troubled past. 'It wasn't all my sister's fault, though,' she stressed. 'She was just fifteen when an older man led her astray. After that she got into the habit of keeping bad company and letting men take advantage of her.'

'She wasn't a school kid at fifteen, was she? Perhaps she likes that sort of life,' David said hoarsely.

'No, that's not true! She didn't like it at all,' Kathy heatedly championed her twin. 'After she left home, we'd meet up and she'd sob her heart out about her horrible life in Lambeth with the fellow who ruined her. Thing is . . . she couldn't straighten out because Mum and Dad wouldn't have her back. She might have turned out differently if they'd just given her a second chance. But it was always the same with them: you've made your bed so lie on it.'

David nodded, staring straight ahead with his mouth pursed. Kathy felt sure he was finding it difficult to conceal his disgust.

'You won't speak badly of any of us, will you?' Kathy smiled bravely. 'Most families have one bad penny. I bet you've got a story to tell about Goldstein black sheep.'

'Wouldn't want to bore you with our revolting habits.' David laughed, swung about, raking his fingers through his hair. 'But I have got something else to tell you; it's about the Bar Mitzvah.' He placed a friendly hand on her shoulder, urging Kathy to walk with him along the street. 'Let's find a caff, shall we? No point in going in now, the film will have started.'

Glad the atmosphere between them had lightened, Kathy slipped her arm through his as they strolled.

'My cousin Samuel is going to Spain, to fight in the civil war against Franco.'

'He's very brave; his family must be worried about him.' Kathy had read about the uprising in the newspaper and heard it reported on the wireless. The Fascists seemed to be stirring unrest throughout Europe.

Kathy took little interest in politics but she – in common with a good many people – sensed serious trouble lay ahead because of the emerging extreme right-wing views. Sir Oswald Mosley had once passed Kathy in his fancy drop-head Bentley when she was pedalling like fury to a woman in labour. She remembered scowling at him while wobbling and trying to regain her balance because his chauffeur had brought the vehicle too close for comfort.

'I'm going with Sam to Spain,' David announced. 'I

wasn't sure before . . . but now I am. I know it's the right thing to do.'

Kathy came to an abrupt halt, dragging him around by the arm. 'No! You can't do that just because we're breaking up! I won't let you go to war for my sake!'

'It's not just about you, Kathy. I've known for ages I need to change what I'm doing.' David was smiling quite placidly while gazing at a cloudy sky. 'I've been fed up with police work – not just the job but the people too – and something Sam said made me think about my life. He made me feel ashamed . . . lots of things make me feel ashamed, and I want to stop that now.'

'But . . . what about your new girl? Won't she mind?'

'She's not important,' David muttered. 'She's nothing compared to you.'

'Well, what about your parents . . . do they know?' Kathy gasped.

'Don't worry about me, Kathy,' David said, becoming brusque. 'You must see your new fellow and live your life and be happy. And you must let me do what I want.'

'Fighting a foreign war is what you want?' Kathy whispered, bewildered.

'It is . . . for now . . .' David said with quiet determination.

'Crikey! You're a lovely lad, ain't yer, now.' Matilda chucked Paul Potter under his tiny chin, prompting the baby to give her a toothy smile. Matilda withdrew her head from the pram and turned her attention to Pansy. 'And who's this pretty young gel, then?'

Ruby gave her daughter a little nudge, hoping she might answer. But Pansy crept behind her mother, clinging to her hip. 'Her name's Pansy . . . 'Fraid she

267

don't have much to say fer herself.' Ruby ruffled her daughter's hair to reassure her that these strangers were on their side.

'Never mind, then,' Matilda said, leaving the shy child be. She turned to the boy, noticing he looked rather sullen. 'Reckon you must be Peter and you've gotta be twelve if yer a day.'

Peter blushed, secretly pleased. He'd only turned nine a couple of months ago and liked to be thought of as older than his age.

'Strapping lad like you must be a big help to his mum. That right, Peter?'

Ruby's son gave a nod, his red cheeks glowing.

'Go downstairs and help Mr Raven fetch in our stuff, Petie.' Ruby wanted to have a private word with Matilda.

'He'd sooner have stopped in the East End with his father, I take it,' Matilda remarked bluntly as the boy went out and clattered down the stairs.

'Got his pals over that way, that's all it is,' Ruby replied.

'He'll make new pals over this way,' Matilda said. 'Quite a few kids about his age live in the street.'

'Don't know how to thank you,' Ruby blurted gruffly. 'Or Nurse Finch and her friend Mr Raven. You've all been kinder to us than I can ever repay—'

'Gonna stop you there.' Matilda raised a hand. 'Round this neighbourhood, we do favours where we can 'cos we expect 'em back, see.' She grinned. 'Don't get nuthin' fer nuthin' in this life so when you're back on yer feet 'cos yer luck's turned – and it will – you might find I'm wanting summat off you. That's how we repay in the Bunk. Till then you're welcome to stop here.'

'Help you 'n' all, I would, any way I can.' Ruby's voice trembled with sincerity.

'I know, luv . . .' Matilda squeezed Ruby's shoulder. 'I know what it is for a woman to be kicked down by a man. Me sister had a dog's life with the scumbag she married. Had years of it, she did, before she found the gumption to get free of him.' She tapped her temple. 'A lot of it with my Fran was up here. She believed him when he told her she got what she deserved. You make sure you don't get into that way of thinking 'cos it's worse than he's put chains on yer.'

'Charlie's got fancy women, so I hope he'll take one on permanent now I've left. He thinks I don't know about his tarts. Fact is, I don't care what he does s'long as he leaves us be.'

'That's the way, luv . . .' Matilda praised, breaking off as Kathy entered the room loaded down with a cardboard box.

'Take it straight into the back room, if you would,' Matilda directed her. 'Lovely gel, she is . . . diamond . . .' Matilda watched Kathy edge through the doorway with the bulky weight.

Ruby murmured heartfelt agreement, then hurried to help unpack her possessions.

Matilda poked her head round the door, watching the two young women sorting through pots and pans and items of crockery. There was little in the back room. The last time it had been used was when her daughter Lucy had stayed with her when working as a waitress in the West End. The interior looked the same as it had then: a battered old chest of drawers was shoved against one wall and an iron bedstead against the other.

'Got some clean sheets for the bed.' Matilda took an end of the grimy mattress and gave it a shake, sending dust up into the air.

'You keep your'n,' Ruby said, but with a grateful smile for her hostess. 'You might need 'em yerself. I brought bed linen and a few blankets too.'

'Could do with a blanket meself,' Matilda said. 'Nights are drawing in now and the moths made lacework of mine.' In fact, it was a fib: Matilda had pawned her good blanket when Reg ran out of work a few months back. By the time she went back for it, it had gone.

'I've got a spare,' Ruby immediately offered, and started poking about in some of the containers and sacks that her son had just put down. She drew out a faded length of wool, then another. Having sorted out the best blanket, she held it in Matilda's direction.

'Don't mind if I do,' Matilda rubbed a hand over the thick material. 'Reg'll be pleased to see that: won't have to put me freezing feet on his back no more to warm 'em.' Cackling a laugh, she went out calling over a shoulder, 'I'm gonna put the kettle on fer tea. Got some cups in them boxes? We'll need seven in all, by my reckoning, if the kids want a hot drink, so I'm two short.'

CHAPTER TWENTY-SEVEN

'Do you think Ruby and the kids will be all right in Campbell Road?' Kathy was gazing up at the first-floor window of the house she and Nick had just exited. They'd said goodbye to the family only minutes ago, leaving them seated around Matilda's table, drinking tea and diving into the biscuit tin.

'Yeah . . . I do. I've never spoken to Matilda Keiver before today but I reckon she's a good 'un, and none of it bullshit either.' Nick choked a laugh. 'She's a bruiser, though, if ever there was one.'

'My mum would vouch for that. She's known Matilda come off best in fights with men. So watch out.' Kathy's humour dwindled. 'She's wonderfully kind to those she likes but don't get on the wrong side of her.'

Nick turned the ignition then sat back to gaze at Kathy's sweet flushed features. She had a smudge of dust on a cheek that he smeared away with a thumb.

Kathy busily brushed together palms that felt mucky. 'Bet I look a right state.'

"Fraid so . . . can't think what I see in you . . .'

'Thanks!' Kathy feigned indignation, whacking his arm. 'Crikey, I'm tired. My shoulders are aching from lifting those boxes.'

'Need to get you fit, Nurse Finch.'

'I am fit!' Kathy remonstrated. 'You should try riding that bike every day and getting hot and sweaty.'

'Sounds like you need some different exercise,' Nick said. 'I'll have a think . . . see if there's another way we can get you hot and sweaty.'

Kathy felt her cheeks starting to burn and dropped her eyes from his provocative gaze.

'Sorry . . .' Nick said huskily. 'I forget sometimes . . .'

'Forget what?' Kathy sounded prickly.

'Just how lucky I am that a sweet girl like you wants anything to do with a bloke like me'

'What's wrong with you?' Kathy demanded, not wholly joking.

'Nothing much . . . and I'll prove it . . .' He gave her a long steady look. 'You've nothing to be scared of with me, Kathy. We'll take it slow and easy . . . any way you like, for as long as you like.'

Kathy had been frowning at her clasped hands but her mouth softened into a smile, and she wondered how he'd sensed her apprehensiveness. She'd never seriously considered that David might try to get her into bed and into trouble. He'd kissed and caressed her quite passionately in the early days, but had seemed too conscious of his breeding and his parents' feelings to give free rein to his own.

Nick Raven was a different sort of man: the rough edges of his character were still there beneath the gloss of his success. As yet, Kathy wasn't entirely sure whether it might be possible to remove them completely, or if she might prefer they stay . . .

'I'm not a prissy cow, it's just . . .' She sighed, unable to tell him yet about the consequences of her twin sister's slip when she was just fifteen. Forlornly, Kathy realised Jennifer might already be in the gutter but she was heading for the sewer.

'I know you're not a prissy cow, you're young and innocent.'

'You've just made me sound like a prissy cow,' Kathy complained.

'If you were a prissy cow you wouldn't have given up your afternoon to come and spend time with the likes of the Keivers and Potters.'

'Thanks for helping,' Kathy said solemnly. 'It would have been a real slog trying to move everything on the bus.'

'Do it again tomorrow, if you want . . .' Nick tapped the steering wheel with restless fingers. 'So . . . are you hungry?'

Kathy nodded vigorously. 'Starving . . . could eat a horse.'

'Might have to settle for a nice juicy steak. I know a good grill house Wapping way.'

'I'd like to freshen up first.'

Nick nodded. 'Yeah, me too.' He pulled away from the kerb.

Kathy sank back into the seat, relaxed and happy.

'Did you speak to David?' he asked distantly.

'Mmm,' Kathy murmured, feeling drowsy from the motion of the car or she might have tuned into a strange inflection in his voice. The silence lengthened and Kathy blinked open her eyes, realising that Nick was politely waiting for her to elaborate. 'He was surprised, but sort of came clean that he has someone else. I think he might have been seeing her for a while 'cos he hinted they're already cooling off.' Kathy sighed. 'He's jacking in his job with the police and going to fight in the Spanish civil war with his cousin.'

Nick shot a sideways look at Kathy. 'Straight up?'

She nodded glumly. 'I wish he wouldn't; I'm afraid he might get—' She bit her lip unable to utter what was on her mind in case it jinxed David and came true. 'I hope he comes back soon.' She crossed her fingers in her lap.

Nick took his hand off the gear stick, covering hers in comfort. 'Take it from me, he's the sort of bloke who's used to covering his back.'

Kathy thought that Nick sounded callous but let it go. 'I hope David does whatever it takes to keep safe.' She sighed. 'It's a daft idea and I reckon he's depressed, not just about us breaking up, but other things as well. He said he's fed up working for the police.'

'Perhaps his conscience is bothering him,' Nick said. 'Getting shot at by a bunch of mad Fascists should put things in perspective. He'll probably be back behind a desk in Leman Street nick in a couple of weeks.'

'I take it you don't get depressed,' Kathy remarked drily.

'No time, Kath, wish I did, 'cos right now I've got a few things pissing me off.'

Kathy smiled; she liked his odd sense of humour. She also liked him calling her Kath. She was always Katherine or Kathy to her parents. Only Jennifer called her Kath when she was feeling friendly so she hadn't heard her sister use the name in quite a while. 'Oh? What's up then?' she asked, all mock sympathy.

Nick shrugged. 'Property I own in Limehouse got set alight.'

Kathy's jaw dropped. 'Your house got burned down?'

'Not all of it.' A wry smile tilted a corner of his mouth. 'Fire brigade managed to get it under control before it spread upstairs. The tenants renting the place fell akip on the sofa and let sparks from the grate set the rug alight. They all got out safely, so that's the main thing; two kids under five were carried down the stairs by firemen. The other three were able to get themselves out with their parents' help.'

Kathy digested that for some moments. 'Thank God it didn't end in a tragedy. I'm sure those poor people wish they'd not been so careless. They're all homeless now, I suppose.'

'They've moved into the rooms I was going to let Ruby have. Just as well she didn't need 'em after all. That house is in Shadwell and it's a bit smaller than they've been used to. Bit of a squash for them but it'll do fer now till the other one is repaired and they can go back.'

Kathy continued staring at his profile. Suddenly he looked her way, catching her quietly studying him.

'What?' He raised a quizzical eyebrow.

'Nothing,' she said softly, settling back again in the seat and closing her eyes.

'I like a girl with a good appetite.'

'Are you hinting I'm greedy?' Kathy put down her knife and fork, feigning indignation. She'd certainly been enjoying her dinner, and a throng waiting for tables to become vacant was proof that many other people also liked the meals on offer. The grill in Wapping that Nick had chosen was teeming with people yet the atmosphere

275

was buoyant rather than rowdy. Somehow he'd managed to jump the queue; Kathy reckoned it was because he and the Greek proprietor were on first-name terms.

'Eat up.' Nick laughed. 'I'm just saying I like a girl who appreciates good food.'

Kathy again tucked into her juicy steak, wondering if his wife had been a picky eater. She put Blanche Raven from her mind; she'd vowed to herself when Nick called for her earlier that she wouldn't pry about his wife and seem jealous. 'I've no intention of leaving a morsel on the plate,' she said airily.

'You'd like my mum's cooking. She does a cracking Sunday roast.'

'I love roast lamb; not that we could afford to have it very often, but it reminds me of being at home . . . always plenty of mint sauce with it,' Kathy said. 'Mum used to grow a big pot of mint out the back.'

'Roast beef and horseradish.' Nick mentioned his favourite with a slow nod then sat back patting his stomach. 'Not sure if I've got room for apple pie and custard. How about you?'

Kathy sighed. 'Wish I could but I'm full to bursting.'

'Another drink?' Nick crooked a finger and a waiter was hovering close in seconds, pad and pencil in hand.

'Nothing for me, thanks,' Kathy said.

'Sure?'

Kathy gave a smile of confirmation, sipping her port and lemon.

Nick ordered himself another beer and sat back, gazing at her.

'Hope Ruby and the children are settled for the night.' Kathy had been musing on the family while enjoying her blow-out supper, and feeling rather guilty as they

276

were sure to have very little food. Whatever Matilda had she'd share with them, even if it were just bread and dripping. Before leaving the Bunk, Kathy had tried to press a ten-shilling note on to Matilda when they'd been alone. The woman had refused to take it to help out with the cost of keeping the family.

'They'll all be tucked up in bed by now,' Nick said. He laid a hand over her fingers, curled on the tablecloth. 'You've done as much as you can, for now, Kath,' he said softly.

'I know . . .' She felt sorry when he withdrew his stroking touch. 'So you were going to tell me a bit about yourself,' she reminded him.

'What do you want to know?'

'Is there anything I should know?' Kathy returned.

Nick received his beer, immediately taking a swallow, his slate-grey eyes meeting Kathy's over the rim of the glass. He put it down abruptly. 'Do you believe me now when I say I'm getting divorced and don't have any children?'

'Yes . . .'

'That's a good start . . .' He sounded wryly amused. 'I live in a house close to Victoria Park and I've got a work yard off Commercial Road so spend most of my day there or at a storage shed down by the docks.'

'You said you rent properties out to families. Is that your living then?' Kathy asked interestedly.

'Yeah . . . plus a bit of this and that.'

Kathy's ears pricked up at that throwaway comment. It sounded like something her father might say when explaining how he spent his working life. 'By the looks of things, you've been successful at *this and that*,' she remarked a touch acidly.

'Had some lucky breaks along the way. I've not always been my own boss. A few years back I used to drive a lorry for Wes Silver. Heard of him, have you?'

Kathy frowned. The name seemed vaguely familiar and she told Nick so.

'I was driving one of his lorries towards Birmingham when it got hijacked and the load went missing. It was about the same time my wife told me she'd been having an affair with Wes and was thinking of leaving me.'

Kathy blinked, moistened her lips. 'What did you do?' she murmured, astonished that he sounded amused rather than angry at such misfortune.

'I jacked in my job with Wes and kicked Blanche out.' The corners of his mouth had turned down in ruefulness. 'Didn't seem right to carry on with either of them in the circumstances. Anyway, it turned out I did the right thing: I've never looked back on either score.'

'You bounced back from it all that easily?' Kathy asked.

'Yep . . .'

'You're very . . . resilient then.'

'Yeah . . . that's the word. Ready to go?'

Kathy nodded, standing up.

'I'd ask you in for a hot drink but Dr Worth might get to hear about it from the neighbours and . . .'

'Yeah . . . I know.' Nick turned off the engine then tapped a hand idly on the steering wheel. 'Anything else you want to ask me, Kath?'

She shook her head, glancing at him through the dusk. They'd driven home in virtual silence but it hadn't been an uncomfortable quiet she'd felt compelled to fill with aimless chatter. She'd enjoyed the evening but now she sensed the atmosphere between them changing . . . electrifying, if a way that was both exciting and terrifying.

He laughed softly. 'You think I'm a callous bastard for not making an effort to keep my wife.'

'I don't . . . honestly . . .'

'Good . . . because with someone else . . . someone like you perhaps . . . I might have taken it all far more seriously. With Blanche and me it was no great love affair. She makes out now it was, because she wants me back since Wes returned to his wife.'

'You got her pregnant . . . you must have been keen on her once,' Kathy pointed out.

'We lived quite close in Bethnal Green as kids, on Cyprus Street. She's a few years younger but we'd hang about in Victoria Park together. She's an only child, same as me. We'd talk about missing having brothers and sisters to muck about with at home. We didn't have much else in common, come to think of it.'

'You could be a bit more gallant, you know.'

'I was extremely gallant . . . I married her.' Nick stuck a cigarette in his mouth and lit it.

Kathy knew he'd said as much as he was going to about his marriage. Considering this was their first proper date, she couldn't blame him for thinking he'd done more than enough explaining.

She changed the subject. 'Were you hurt during the lorry hijack?'

'Crack on the back of the head from a wrench . . . could've been worse . . . didn't need a long stay in hospital.'

'Did your boss blame you for losing his merchandise?'

'Nah . . . no more than I blamed him over Blanche. Wes knows how it goes: win some, lose some . . .'

He suddenly leaned closer, sliding his fingers around Kathy's nape and easing her against him. He touched his mouth to hers, kissing her with teasing courtesy that was so erotic Kathy pressed into him.

'You taste of port,' he said, savouring his lips as Kathy nestled her face against his shoulder.

'I only had a couple.' Kathy murmured a protest, feeling very content yet aware that neighbours' curtains might start twitching if she sat there, collapsed against him, for much longer.

'You gonna come out with me on your next day off?' Nick spoke against her forehead.

She nodded, liking the silky movement of his lips on her skin. 'I have to go in now.' She'd snapped herself out of her lethargy, sitting straight in her seat, aware of how easy it would be to agree to go home with him. But he hadn't invited her to, and she realised he never would; he'd wait till she suggested it . . .

'I couldn't sail without seeing you one last time.'

'I . . . I thought we'd said goodbye,' Kathy stuttered.

David shoved a hand over his nape, looking hangdog. 'Yeah . . . I know . . . but I've been missing you and couldn't keep away.'

'Oh, David . . . it'll just make things worse for us both.' Kathy sounded torn between exasperation and relief at knowing he was safe and sound for now.

Realising that they were still on the front step, Kathy ushered him inside. 'Of course, I'm glad to see you but . . .'

'But you still want things finished between us,' David completed her sentence. 'I haven't come to beg you to give me another chance. I know you've got someone else. I'm off to Dover tomorrow anyway. Can I write to you from time to time?'

'Yes . . . of course . . . I'd like that . . .' Kathy felt confused; in one breath he said he was missing her, in the next he was sounding martyred because he accepted it was over between them. And as far as she was concerned, it was. To give herself some thinking time she disappeared into the kitchen. 'I'll put the kettle on and make you a cup of tea.'

David followed her, and knowing where the cups and saucers were kept, set them. He cocked his head, assessing her pretty outfit. 'Have I come at a bad time? Are you going out?'

'Mmm . . .' Kathy put the water to boil on the hob, feeling uneasy that her ex-boyfriend had quite naturally made himself at home, rummaging in the cupboards. The guilt she'd felt at throwing him over was niggling at her once more, although she knew it was Nick she wanted. And Nick was soon due to pick her up and take her to the pictures . . .

'Shall I get that?' David went into the hall at the sound of the knock on the front door.

Kathy would rather have made the introduction herself between her past and present loves. But David had moved too fast for her.

'Thought you'd be long gone. Where's Kathy?'

'Who are you?' David demanded, although he knew. A lot of local coppers knew Nick Raven, not through a criminal record but because they coveted his success. His eyes slipped past the tall blond man to the sleek Alvis parked at the kerb. He'd seen that before and fancied owning it.

David gripped at Nick's arm, trying to spin him around on the step, but his effort to send his rival on his way got him nothing but a shove and an impatient glare. David depressingly realised that he had no chance of competing with Nick Raven for Kathy. He'd come with the intention of trying to persuade her to wait for him while he was in Spain fighting the Fascists. David had convinced himself that he'd overreacted to news of Jennifer's pregnancy. She would abort the baby she was carrying. He couldn't be sure it was his – and he guessed neither could Jennifer. She was a working girl and getting knocked up must be a professional risk she'd dealt with before. So he'd now calmed down all round because he was still confident that Jennifer wouldn't betray either of them to Kathy.

'You're the new boyfriend, are you?' David sneered, looking Nick up and down. 'You'd better treat her well . . . or else . . .'

'I'll treat her a damn sight better than you did, no doubt about it.'

David licked his lips. There was something unnerving in Raven's hint he had the means of blackmail. His belligerent stare faltered beneath a pair of contemptuous grey eyes. A stirring of anxiety tightened David's chest; if Raven weren't bluffing . . . the only way he might have come by such information was from Jennifer.

Snippets of clipped conversation reached Kathy and she sighed despondently, knowing the two men were squaring up. Removing the kettle from the hob, she pinned a smile to her lips and went into the hall with a bright, 'Oh . . . have you met . . . or shall I make introductions?' She sent Nick a significant look, hoping to convey that David's arrival had been as big a surprise to her as it was to him.

'No tea for me, thanks,' David said distantly. 'I'm off now. Just came to let you know that I'll be sailing tomorrow.'

'Thanks for coming, David. Take care of yourself, won't you . . .?' Kathy went down the front path with him and gave him a friendly hug by the gate.

'I made a fool of myself just now . . . feeling jealous. Mind if I go and catch up with him to wish him the best?' Nick said smoothly as Kathy came in and shut the door.

'No . . . no, of course not . . . it's good of you to do it.' She went on tiptoe and gave Nick a rewarding kiss on the lips. 'Hope he appreciates your effort,' she added.

'Yeah . . . me too.' Nick was smiling as he went out.

'Goldstein . . .'

David swung about, then plunged his hands into his pockets as Nick approached. 'Come to wish me a safe journey?' he asked caustically.

'Nah, come to tell you to stay away from Kathy – and her sister – when you get back.'

David's back teeth began grinding in resentment. So he'd been right. Jennifer had been blabbing, but it didn't seem Raven was going to elaborate. 'Sounds like we've got more in common than just the one woman, Raven,' David said slyly. 'Been having some pillow talk with Jennifer, have you? I never bothered with conversation with the horny bitch.' He poked Nick in the chest. 'What Kathy'll want to know is are *you* keeping away from her slag of a sister?' David glanced back at Kathy's door. 'If it's a toss up who gets who, guess who I choose . . .'

'You get nobody.' Nick was glad he'd kept quiet long enough to give the prick enough rope to hang himself. 'I had business around Mare Street and saw you going into a house the other evening at about nine o'clock. Didn't look like you were on official business with Jennifer . . .'

David whipped his face aside; he knew exactly the day Nick had referred to. Now, thinking back, it suddenly registered where else he'd recently seen that Alvis parked. If only he'd managed to conquer his lust for Jennifer that last time, he'd be home and dry. 'You planning on telling Kathy?'

'I'm not gonna do anything to hurt her. Neither are you. So stay away, and we'll all be just fine.' Nick patted David's arm. 'Understand, don't you?'

'Oh, yeah, I fuckin' understand . . .' David said bitterly. He strode away, knowing his bridges were well and truly burned.

'You were a while.' Kathy had been pacing, waiting for Nick's return, but had refrained from spying on the two men talking.

'Yeah . . . we had a conversation.' Nick smiled. 'Ready to go out?'

Kathy nodded but couldn't throw off a niggling uneasiness. 'Was David all right when you spoke to him?'

'Yeah, I think so; I reckon he got the message . . .'

'There's somebody outside in the shed.'

'Eh?' Gladys rolled over to blearily eye her husband standing twitching the curtain at the window. 'What d'you say?' she asked, irritated at being woken up. She peered at the small alarm clock on the bedside table, seeing it was past one thirty in the morning.

'There it is again,' Tony whispered.

'What you on about, fer heaven's sake?' Gladys grumbled, struggling upright and craning her neck at him.

'Come 'n' take a look,' Tony hissed. 'Somebody's out in me shed, smoking.'

Gladys swung her stout legs off the bed and pattered over to the window, peering into the dark. She spotted the tiny red dot visible through the shed window and gawped at her husband. She'd thought he was imagining things but she'd definitely seen a light too. She gripped his elbow, shaking it punitively. 'Why didn't you lock the bloody thing?'

'I'm sure I did. I always check it now in case the new mower gets nicked. Someone must've broken in.'

'Better call the police,' Gladys urged. The shiny Qualcast was Tony's pride and joy, and she'd never hear the end of it if it went missing.

'Ain't calling no rozzers.' Tony, in common with most of his ilk, didn't have any truck with the law. He'd sort things out in his own way. He started pulling on his trousers.

'You're not going down there after him?' Gladys squeaked. 'He might be half yer age and crown you.'

'Well, he ain't having me mower, that's fer sure.'

'Might be a tramp just sheltering for the night, Tony,' she wheedled. 'Just leave him be, eh?' Gladys had visions of calling an ambulance as well as the police if her husband insisted on tackling the intruder.

'Ain't leaving him be,' Tony announced, shrugging into his shirt. 'When he's had his forty-winks he might just wheel me mower off down the road with him.' He put a finger to his lips, shushing Gladys because her voice had started getting shrill. 'You'll wake Blanche up, then

285

there's no chance of taking him by surprise. If she finds out we've got a burglar, she'll have bleedin' hysterics.'

'Ain't heard her come in yet.' Gladys was too worried about her husband's planned heroics to give her daughter's whereabouts much thought. She gripped Tony's forearm with two hands and hung on.

'Give it a rest!' Tony finally shook his wife off and pelted down the stairs.

Once out in the garden, he stealthily approached the shed with a wrench in one hand and a heavy torch in the other. He got into position and took a deep breath.

'Right, out yer come! Police are on their way so I'm giving you a chance to get going 'fore they get here.' He took two quick steps forward, then leaped one pace back as he heard scuffling inside the wooden panels.

'Dad?'

Tony's jaw sagged at the sound of his daughter's quavering voice. On instinct, he reached for the door and yanked it wide. The sight that met him caused a grunt of horror to erupt. Blanche had her naked backside in the air while bending over, scrabbling on the floor for her clothes. Charlie Potter was trying to stuff his erection in his trousers and button up over it.

'What the . . .?' Tony could feel his cheeks ballooning in rage and revulsion. 'Get indoors, you filthy little slut!' he roared at his daughter.

Blanche grabbed her clothes to her chest and, whimpering, rushed past her father into the cool night air.

Tony shook his torch at the man sizing him up with a vicious stare while shoving his arms into shirtsleeves. 'You . . . get out of me garden and get going,' Tony uttered hoarsely. He stumbled backwards as Potter strutted towards him, boots swinging in a fist.

286

'Get in the house, you fucking little whore,' Tony ejected through his teeth as his daughter stood in the garden, transfixed, watching them.

Gladys entered the kitchen to be met by a woman's bare back view silhouetted against the open doorway. She flicked the light switch. 'Blanche?' she whispered, clapping a hand to her mouth when her naked daughter swung around, tears streaming down her face.

Tony burst in from the garden, nearly knocking Blanche over. Nervously, he locked the door as though fearing Charlie might try to barge in and create havoc.

Blanche backed against the wall, still guarding her trembling body with her bundle of clothes.

'What's been going on?' Gladys demanded in a faint screech.

Tony seemed momentarily lost for words. 'Tell yer mother what you've been up to with Charlie Potter out in me shed.' He dropped the torch he'd been pointing at his daughter. The wrench followed it onto the floor with a crash. 'I'm going to bed. We'll sort this out in the morning.' He flung himself past the two women and was soon stomping up the stairs.

When he'd set out for work at first light, Charlie had had no intention of going home again that day. Following a late night romp with Blanche, when feeling nice and relaxed, he'd usually be ready for a couple of whiskies and a game of cards before settling down for a few hours' kip on a pal's sofa. Then he'd be up and off to work down the docks just after dawn. Sometimes several days might pass before he again saw his family. Charlie was proud of the fact he could get by on little sleep and still be, in his opinion, an all-round performer at work and play.

But tonight hadn't gone to plan after all. He had an irritating throb in his groin and needed a woman to scratch it for him. It was too late to knock up Wes Silver for a sub on his wages so he could pay for a tart like Beverly, who worked out of the dockside pubs. He'd spent most of his cash on Blanche and she'd been a dead loss so he'd have to go home after all to his wife's bed.

Charlie wasn't bothered about Ruby smelling another woman on him. She knew better than to question him about what he'd been up to. But it was the middle of the week, and the landlord was soon due to do his rounds. For a change his wife hadn't whined about the rent arrears that morning when he'd climbed out of bed but had turned her back on him. Charlie knew they were over a month behind and he was in no mood for a bull and cow with Ruby tonight because she was after money he'd spent. Following the run-in with Tony Scott, Charlie felt ready to swing for somebody and if she started acting up it would be her.

His wife had lashed out last time he hit her and Charlie knew if she did so again he'd really pay her, and smash the place up before he left. He'd remain master in his own home, or there wouldn't be a home. Simple as that.

Charlie slouched round the corner and, with his house in sight, felt annoyed rather than relieved at the prospect of soon entering it. He damned Blanche's father to hell for being a nosy interfering bastard and spoiling his fun. He regretted now not having given Tony a smack but the man had caught him on the hop, then scarpered indoors.

Charlie stuck his key in the lock and booted the door open, feeling too lazy to remove his other hand from his pocket. It was completely dark inside, which was odd because the silly cow usually left a candle stub burning by the baby's pram so she could see to him in the night when he woke up bawling.

It seemed eerily quiet to Charlie and there was a different atmosphere, or rather a lack of one. Usually, some smell of cooking hung in the air, even if it was just burned toast greeting him. He stopped and listened, then felt for the light switch.

Charlie blinked, his expression gormless with amazement. Then his lips drew back against his teeth in a savage snarl. 'You fucking cunt,' he bawled, noticing there was nothing left in the room but the landlord's manky old furniture. 'So that's why you didn't want no rent off me, is it, gel?' He picked up the poker propped against the grate and hurled it against the wall, starting up some hollering and hammering from next door. Charlie flung himself down in the mouldy armchair, sitting legs akimbo and head jutting. 'Told you, Ruby, you go when I say, and not a second before,' he whispered into the silence.

CHAPTER TWENTY-EIGHT

'Fer Chrissake, leave him alone! He's only a kid.'

Davy Wright shrugged off his friend's restraining hand. His eyes had pounced on his prey and were narrowing in excitement. Just a stare had been enough to frighten the boy. But it wasn't enough for Davy. He watched the lad hesitating before swinging around to flee. Immediately, Davy loped after him. Davy was at least five years older and far bigger physically than Mr Butler's son. He slowed down, not wanting to outrun his quarry too soon, spoiling the chase. In under a minute, he was alongside, taunting the child with abuse before swiping out with a foot.

Having crashed into the gutter the boy immediately pushed onto his hands and knees, cowering in expectation of a kick. But Davy stepped back, standing over him while he staggered to his feet. Rather than attempt to barge past his tormentor and make for home, the lad darted in the opposite direction just as a van turned the corner, crashing gears.

Tom had turned away in disgust, not wanting to

observe Davy's bullying, but a screeching of brakes made him swivel about in time to see the boy bouncing off the chrome bumper of the vehicle. The white-faced driver jumped out and began shouting his version of events to a little crowd gathering about the unconscious boy.

Tom raced towards Davy, grabbing him by the arm. 'That was your fault, you bleedin' idiot!' he hissed, careful to keep his voice low. 'I told you to leave the kid alone.' Tom blinked at the people crouching over the motionless boy. One man quickly stood up, then ran towards a shop, shouting over a shoulder that he'd call for an ambulance.

'What if you've killed him?' Tom looked shocked. 'D'you reckon he's dead?' He took a tentative step towards the kerb, angling his head to get a view past the group and see if the casualty was moving.

'He ain't dead, the van weren't going fast enough for that,' Davy blustered. 'Anyhow, it's his own fault fer not lookin' where he was going. Stupid git.' Davy shrugged. 'Ain't nuthin' to do with me. I was just standing here, minding me own business.'

'You were right by him, I saw you . . .' The van driver was pointing at Davy as he broke free of the knot of people to find witnesses to his innocence. 'Why did he hare out in front of me like that?'

'Search me, mate.' Davy sorrowfully shook his head, playing the part of concerned bystander. 'Just seen the kid scoot into the road, that's all I can say. Gonna be all right is he? Silly sod . . .'

'Hope so . . . reckon he's gonna have concussion and his leg looks broken. You see anything, son?' The driver had turned to Tom.

Tom shook his head, swallowing audibly. 'Was up the road . . . never saw nuthin'.'

'His parents need to learn the kid some road sense, letting him run out in front of folk like that.' The agitated driver turned away to find more helpful witnesses.

'I ain't coming over here and doing this no more.' Tom muttered as soon as the fellow was out of earshot.

'You givin' up yer wages then?' Davy jeered.

'Yeah, I am. Tell your uncle he don't need to pay me next week. You can come over on yer own.'

'Charlie ain't me uncle, he's me stepbrother.'

Tom shrugged his lack of interest.

'You turned yeller?'

Tom stuck up two fingers in response to the taunt and started off up the road to catch the bus back to Islington. It wasn't the first time Davy had set about one or other of the Butler boys and both of them were far younger than he was. Nausea was rolling in Tom's stomach and a feeling of dread because the lad didn't just have a bruise or a scratch this time; he might die or be seriously injured, and Tom knew he'd have that on his conscience for ever.

Davy might have been the main culprit in the boy's accident but Tom knew he couldn't get off scot-free. If he'd really tried, he could have stopped Davy chasing him. For weeks he'd been paid to wear a black shirt and hang about outside these shops so the traders would be intimidated and think something bad was going to happen. Well, now it had happened, and shame was making his guts squirm. If that made him yellow, he didn't care. He'd had enough and wished he'd brought a jacket with him so he could put it on to hide the black shirt he was wearing. In Tom's mind, this was far worse than when Davy had poked lighted rags through letter boxes. He'd been anxious then that things were getting out of control but it had been the dreadful incident minutes ago that finally made him determined to go home and take off the shirt so he could burn it.

'You listening to me?' Davy had swaggered up behind to jab Tom's arm. 'Woss up? Lost yer backbone?'

Tom pivoted about, confronting his friend. 'Think you're brave, do you, causing a road accident? Big man, ain't yer, doin' that? Well, I reckon you're a prat. Now piss off and leave me alone.'

'Suit yerself, Finchie.' Davy backed away, sneering. 'But don't come round mine expecting me to lend you when yer skint.'

Tom trudged on, knowing his mum wouldn't like the fact that he'd no money to give her this week. He hung back at the end of the bus queue. He'd noticed Davy's dad in front of him but pretended he'd not. He knew Mr Wright was acting likewise and making out he'd not recognised him either. It suited Tom; he didn't want to speak to anybody right now. He realised that he and Davy wouldn't be pals for much longer. Instead of feeling upset Tom was relieved at the prospect of it. He'd got enough on his plate at the moment: he was leaving school at Christmas and his mother had found out that he'd secretly agreed to start work with his father. Winnie had gone mental, insisting he had to get decent employment. So now he felt responsible for the fact his parents were going at it hammer and tongs most of the time. For a quiet life, Tom reckoned he'd just go down the Labour Exchange and find himself an errand boy job till the war indoors died down. In any case, he wasn't sure now that he wanted to duck and dive for a living like his father.

Stan Wright settled on a seat at the front of the bus. He'd seen his son's mate join the queue and had guessed from the expression on Tom's face that he and Davy had had a bust-up. Stan was cute enough to have seen that coming a mile off. Davy was a loud-mouthed tyke from the Bunk and Tom Finch had seemed a nice polite lad in comparison.

Since Charlie had roped the two youths in on his shenanigans, Stan never saw as much of his son at the weekends. Davy was more interested in collecting his wages than seeing his old dad. Stan was glad his son was earning but he was canny enough to worry about the consequences of what Davy was doing, messing around with Fascist thugs.

Charlie Potter was an all round wrong 'un but Violet wouldn't hear a word against her son. In fact, the more Stan pointed out the pitfalls in Charlie's association with Wes Silver, and how it might bring the coppers nosing around, the more unbearable Violet became. She'd hit him once in front of Davy, and Stan knew his son had been shocked that his father would allow himself to be humiliated. Davy had been embarrassed and he'd made an excuse to catch the bus back home early that day.

Stan understood why Violet was always irate lately: nobody wanted a foreigner's bastard as a grandkid, but he didn't see why he should take all the stick because neighbours were gossiping.

Last week, Charlie had turned up to visit his mother, beside himself with fury, because Ruby had done a bunk and taken the kids with her. Stan would have expected Charlie to be hanging out the flags in celebration. He knew for a fact that his stepson spent more time with tarts than he did with his family. But no . . . because Ruby had gone behind his back, rather than waiting to get kicked out, the big man's ego had been wounded. Violet had been as enraged as her son about the worm turning. Any snub to her kids was taken personally by Violet, so despite never having a good word to say about her daughter-in-law or the brats, as she called her grand-children, she was with Charlie in hunting them down and forcing them back where they belonged.

Stan had come to realise he'd had enough of living with a woman who was a violent nag. So this afternoon he was on his way to visit his ex-wife and put feelers out about moving back to Islington. He was hoping Polly would be grateful that he'd taken the trouble to come over and put her in the picture about their son's antics in the East End. Stan reckoned it was a starting point for rebuilding a bit of trust between them. Then if he managed to get his boots back under the bed for a night, he wouldn't be leaving again in a hurry.

'What you starin' at, yer bleedin' nosy cow?' Charlie spat on the cobbles, glaring at the woman cleaning her windows while sending him dirty looks.

Peggy Mason tutted her disgust and turned back to scrub newspaper over the glass of her front sash.

Charlie was about to storm inside his empty cottage when he hesitated, gave the woman a crafty glance. None of the neighbours had said anything about Ruby leaving him, but they all knew she'd upped sticks. He'd seen a gaggle of women having a gossip at his expense earlier in the week. Now it suddenly occurred to him that Peggy might just know a bit about it all. Ruby had kept to herself because Charlie had made sure of it. But amongst the local women she'd been friendliest with Peggy. He strode over, chest puffed out.

'I'm after finding Ruby 'n' bringin' her back. You have anything to do with helping her run out?' Charlie jutted his chin belligerently.

'Don't you go accusin' me of nuthin'.' Peggy threw down her newspaper and stuck chapped hands on her hips. 'I mind me own business, but I'll tell you this, she done the right thing . . .'

Charlie whipped up a thick finger, pushed it against the woman's blunt nose. 'That don't sound like somebody minding their own business to me. You know something, and if you ain't sayin' perhaps I'll have a word with yer old man.' Charlie glanced at the house. 'Bert in, is he?'

'No, he ain't.' Peggy shifted to bar the door. It was only six weeks ago that Charlie Potter had knocked her husband down because their eldest had booted a ball against his front window. No damage had been done, but Charlie had relished the chance to act top dog.

'I'll make sure I catch Bert when he gets back,' Charlie said menacingly.

Peggy watched him swaggering off, wishing she'd kept her mouth shut. She despised Potter, like most people, but she was wary of him too . . . like most people. Charlie Potter had influential friends and wasn't a man to cross; Peggy didn't want her and Bert getting dragged into a neighbour's domestics.

'Oi . . .' Peggy called, halting Charlie by his front step. 'I do know Nurse Finch was helping Ruby load up the car.'

'Car?' Charlie had visualised Ruby and the kids wheeling off all the stuff in the pram. But he'd suspected that Nurse Finch – damn the interfering bitch – might have had a hand in it all. 'The nurse ain't got a car.'

'Belonged to the feller she was with . . . same one what turned up here the night the little 'un was born.'

Charlie's jaw dropped and he retraced a few steps. 'Nick Raven?' He sounded astonished.

'Don't know who he was,' Peggy muttered, hoping she'd not caused problems for the sweet nurse. But she reckoned Nurse Finch had enough support in Dr Worth, and that policeman boyfriend of hers. Potter wouldn't want to tangle with either of them; nevertheless Peggy reckoned she'd said enough. 'Anyhow, that's all I know about it.' Grabbing up her bucket, she went in and slammed her door.

'What d'you say?' Ruby whispered in her daughter's ear, reminding her of her manners.

They had come out of the corner shop in Campbell Road where Matilda had bought a bag of liquorice. She'd dangled a black string in front of Pansy's face and the girl had gladly accepted the treat but not yet said thank you for it.

Pansy nodded wordlessly, her wide eyes fixed on Matilda's face.

'I know what yer mean, dearie.' Matilda ruffled the child's hair. 'Them big eyes of yourn speak for you, don't they? I can hear 'em clear as a bell . . .' Matilda lilted in a childish squeak, *Thank you, Auntie Matilda, for me liquorice* . . . ain't that right, Pansy?'

Pansy laughed, bashfully poking her tongue into a cheek before tipping back her head and winding the black bootlace into her mouth.

'Here, you take this and make sure you give yer

brother some 'n' all.' Matilda handed the child the paper bag filled with liquorice.

'You don't have to buy the kids sweets,' Ruby began gruffly, absently rocking the pram.

'Know I don't have to . . . just like doing it.' Matilda raised a hand in greeting to a woman across the street. She nudged Ruby's arm as they started a slow stroll back towards home. 'That's me neighbour Margaret Lovat. She's the one does a bit of cleaning for a lady in Tufnell Park. Her lady's neighbour's after a char. Margaret said she can't fit no more clients in or she'd nab the extra work herself 'cos they're all good payers round that way. I'd go for it, but me knees ain't up to it. Think me days scrubbing floors are over . . .'

'I'll take it,' Ruby blurted, her eyes springing to Margaret Lovat. 'Shall we catch up with her and tell her?'

'Bleedin' hell, you're keen,' Matilda chuckled.

Ruby bit her lip. 'Sorry . . . didn't mean to take liberties. Should've checked first that you meant what you said about doing a bit of child minding if I take on a few hours' work.'

'Wouldn't have offered otherwise, would I?'

Ruby was coming to understand, and to like, Mrs Keiver's blunt ways. They'd been living with her and Reg for over a week now and things were turning out better than Ruby had dared hope. Reg had taken to the kids straight away and enjoyed teaching Peter his card tricks in the evening around the table. The food they ate was simple and consisted mainly of bread and jam and biscuits, bought out of Matilda's housekeeping. Ruby was keeping a tally of what she felt she owed and had vowed to repay Matilda as soon as she got herself some work.

Even before she'd asked about employment prospects in the area, Matilda had mentioned knowing of somebody who might put a bit of domestic work her way, if she was up for it. Ruby had been eagerly waiting to hear more about such opportunities but hadn't wanted to pester Matilda for information.

Her husband had never wanted her to work and earn cash to call her own. Mean as Charlie was with his money, he'd sooner give his wife a little bit of it than let her have some independence.

'They're good kids; you won't find them no trouble,' Ruby praised her children. 'Peter can run errands when he ain't at school and Pansy likes to lend a hand, little as she is. She's good with Paul and washes his dirty nappies, bless her heart.'

'Can tell she's bright as a button,' Matilda said, watching the little girl skipping a few paces in front.

'She can talk when she wants to.' Ruby cocked her head, watching for Matilda's reaction.

'Reckon she's got a tale to tell and's waiting fer the right time to open up with it,' Matilda said. 'Don't you worry. They'll all be safe and snug with me while you're out earning.'

'Paul's cutting his teeth so he can be a bit grizzly.' Ruby tucked the pram blanket about her little son, sleeping soundly.

'Had four of me own so know all about teething.' Matilda nodded at the black-haired baby. 'Probably, he'll get a bit of bronchitis with it,' she added knowledgeably. 'My gels all had chests on 'em while cutting their teeth.'

'He has been snuffling . . .' Ruby agreed.

'Heard the poor little mite coughing last night,' Matilda confirmed. She glanced again at the tiny boy. Peter and

Pansy had dark brown hair but their features were not Oriental. Matilda realised that Ruby might have had more than one husband and an earlier partner had fathered the older two.

'Is your husband Chinese?' If Matilda felt awkward asking there was no hint of it in her tone.

'The baby's not Charlie's . . .' Ruby answered after a quiet moment.

'Right' Matilda said. 'So that set him off on a rampage then, did it?'

Ruby snorted a laugh. 'He was a vicious git long before Paul came along. Shame he kept his true character well hid before we got married. I'd've run a mile if I'd known what he's really like.'

'Bein' honest ain't the way men like that carry on,' Matilda returned flatly. 'All charm, ain't they, till they get a woman hooked? My sister, Fran, God rest her, could've told you about their sly ways.'

They walked on quietly for a few minutes.

'Got no family to help you out?' Matilda enquired.

Oddly, Ruby felt no inclination to tell Matilda to mind her own business, and not simply because homelessness might be the consequence of upsetting her. She glanced at the middle-aged woman, her coarse hair pinned in a greying plait on top of her head, her features looking roughened by work and weather. Ruby sensed Matilda Keiver was a person who, in her time, had battled through more bad experiences than most. She felt drawn to Matilda's strength and courage, and it seemed natural to Ruby to want to entrust personal troubles to Mrs Keiver for sharp analysis.

'Got two older sisters,' Ruby answered on a sigh. 'They're both married and live Middlesex way but they keep to themselves.' Ruby turned her warm face away. Her sisters had cut her off when they found out she'd been a working girl at various times during her life. When Charlie went inside Ruby had written to them both to ask for a loan to pay the rent. She'd not heard back. But they were quick enough to send letters calling her a disgrace for showing them up when the news leaked out how she'd managed without their help. 'Mum's been dead for a few years. I was about eight when Dad passed away. He was a lot older than Mum and had been married before. Funny how we follow in our parents' footsteps even though we don't want to. Charlie's a lot older than me and was a widower when I met him.'

'How about your in-laws? Any decent folk amongst 'em?'

Ruby hooted in genuine amusement. 'His mother's a horrible old witch. She's as bad as he is. I lent her me rent one week 'cos she was giving me a hard-luck story. When I called round to ask fer it back 'cos I was brassic she went for me.' Ruby sighed. 'You'd think she'd give a hand keeping her grandchildren clothed and fed but she don't give a toss about anybody but herself and her own kids.'

Matilda could tell that mention of the Potters had agitated the younger woman. 'Your little 'uns are safe and out of harm's way now.' She patted Ruby's arm in comfort.

'Yeah . . .' Ruby croaked. 'Sod the lot of 'em over the East End. I'm here now.'

Matilda noticed Ruby darting glances at her neighbour. Margaret Lovat had come to a halt by Beattie Evans's house and the two women were having a natter leaning on the railings fronting the row of tenements.

'Come on then, we'll have a word with me friend before she disappears.' Matilda gave Ruby an encouraging smile. 'Me eldest daughter, Sophy, is married to Margaret's son, Danny. So we're almost related and go back a very long way. No need to fret; I'm sure the job's yours, if you want it.'

Matilda took hold of Pansy's hand, swinging it playfully. 'Bet your little legs can run faster than my big ones. Have a race, shall we?' Matilda shuffled forwards a few yards then puffed to a halt while the little girl streaked ahead shrieking with laughter, long dark mane flying out behind.

CHAPTER TWENTY-NINE

'I've been expecting you.'

'I bet you have.' Charlie had been spying on Nick Raven for days, hoping to catch him on his own, somewhere deserted. Following their last run-in, when Nick had easily floored him, Charlie had reckoned he might need a bit of an advantage with the younger man. He fingered the blade in his pocket, hoping it would persuade Nick to cough up Ruby's whereabouts before he striped him for good measure.

'So . . . a little bird tells me you've been pokin' yer nose into me business.' Charlie had hoped to unsettle Raven but his opponent was continuing drawing down the shutter on his lock-up, barely glancing at him. The row of warehouses were situated close to the river bank and more than half were disused, due to dilapidations.

'Little bird, eh?' Nick slammed a heavy iron padlock onto a hasp but left it dangling open as he turned about to face Charlie. He knew that Potter was carrying a weapon of some sort. The dip in his right pocket wasn't just from the weight of his hand. He knew, too, that this time, Charlie would have made sure he was sober and in shape for a fight before confronting him.

'Where's me wife gone?' Charlie withdrew the knife and held it out, swaying it slowly to and fro at arm's length. He drew back his lips in a savage smile. 'Been looking forward to this Raven . . . long overdue . . .' He came closer, circling, bobbing his head to and fro on his stubby neck.

Nick stayed where he was.

'Gonna tell me where Ruby is? Make it easier for yerself. Won't need so many stitches in yer pretty face if you act reasonable. C'mon . . .' Charlie made a sudden running lunge but his opponent nipped sideways, the iron padlock in a fist.

'Got nuthin' to say?' Charlie was enjoying himself. He knew that his surprise attack with a knife left Nick at a serious disadvantage. 'C'mon . . . tell me where you took the cow. You'd sooner I ask you than Nurse Finch, wouldn't yer now, Raven?' Finally, Charlie got the flicker of emotion he'd hoped for from his adversary. 'Ah . . . like that, is it?' He nodded his greasy head in satisfaction, stalking the younger man to and fro against the wooden shutters of the warehouses. 'Don't blame yer, son . . . I'd like a go at her too. When you're out of action, I might have a piece of Nurse Finch. Reckon she'd tell me anything I wanted to know once I'd done with her . . .' He growled a laugh, scratched at his balls for effect. With a roar, he suddenly dived forward.

Nick brought up his hand and with split-second aim hurled the iron padlock at Charlie's head. It hit his cheek rather than his forehead but it was enough to make the older man stagger and gave Nick time to nip past him.

He grabbed a piece of pallet leaning against a wall and brought it whistling through air onto Charlie's back.

Charlie staggered against the shutters, the knife still gripped in his sweaty fingers. 'That yer best shot?' he panted.

'Nah . . . this is,' Nick swung the battered lump of wood against Charlie's arm just as his opponent came for him again. This time, Charlie's numbed fingers dropped the knife and Nick darted in to kick it away. He dropped the timber, beckoned Charlie closer. 'You wanted a scrap, so let's have one.' He sneered a laugh as Charlie wiped spittle from his lips and shifted from foot to foot. 'What's up, Charlie? Lost yer bottle now it's fisticuffs?'

Nick's jeer was a red rag to a bull. Despite the pain down his right side, Charlie lumbered forward, head down, hoping to knock Nick over using his weight alone.

Nick sidestepped at the last moment, letting Charlie stumble past to nut the wall. As the older man came upright, looking dazed, Nick gave him a hefty jab and cross that put Charlie onto his knees. A kick under the chin put him on his back.

Nick crouched over Charlie, using his forearm on the older man's windpipe. 'You're too old and too out of condition, mate. Give it a rest . . . give Ruby a rest. And don't ever mention Nurse Finch, let alone go near her,' he added softly. 'Understand?'

Charlie was bubbling at the mouth, squirming and trying to breath but he managed to nod as Nick viciously increased pressure.

'Right . . . things to do . . . sorry to love yer and leave yer . . .' Brushing down his clothes, Nick turned to go. As an afterthought, because of the threat to Kathy, Nick gave Charlie a hefty boot in the guts just as he was crawling onto his knees.

Charlie collapsed onto concrete. 'I'll fuckin' have you back, Raven!' he screamed.

Nick walked off, sticking two fingers up in farewell.

'So . . . how you been then, Pol?'

Polly Wright stuck her wet hands on her hips, running a jaundiced eye over her podgy balding husband. She'd been scrubbing celery in a tin bowl, preparing it to sell door to door off her barrow, when Stan turned up, smiling like a Cheshire cat. They might not have lived together for a long while but Polly remembered that crafty tone of voice he favoured when he was after something. The only time she wanted to see him now was when he was peeling a note out of his wallet for her. Polly reckoned she'd sacrificed the best years of her life struggling to raise his sons alone while he was off gallivanting. Stan ought to show his appreciation with hard cash, not smarmy smiles. She wasn't interested in any of his weasel words either, so if he'd come for any reason other than to weigh her out he could piss off.

'Davy ain't in,' Polly announced. 'He was heading over your way as usual this morning.'

'Didn't come to see him,' Stan said. 'I'm here for you, gel.' He treated her to another soppy smile. 'Keeping all right, are yer?'

'I'm all right . . . so what you up to then?' Polly said briskly. 'Making up for lost time, and brung me some wages over, have yer? Better late than never, I suppose,' she added sourly.

Stan stepped further into the room, choosing to ignore

her sarcasm and her outstretched palm. 'How about we have a brew and a chat about things, eh, Pol?'

'There it is . . .' Polly nodded at the dented metal kettle on the table, letting him know if he wanted tea he could make it himself. 'Needs filling.' She jerked her head at the door. Stan knew where the sink and tap were situated out on the landing.

Stan sighed beneath his breath, turning his back on his wife. But he kept up an air of casual jollity, swinging the empty vessel in a hand as he went onto the landing to get the water for tea. Once out of sight, his expression drooped. He forced on the squeaking tap, letting water splash into the stained sink. He could tell that his idea of returning to live in Islington wasn't going to be all plain sailing. He'd got very little cash with him to sweeten her up. He decided to plump for using his concern about Davy's future to win Polly over.

Having sauntered back into the room with the heavy kettle he stuck it on the hob to boil. 'We ought to have a little talk about what Davy's getting up to.' Stan sucked his teeth. 'Don't want to worry you but I reckon the boy could be heading fer bad trouble if he don't wise up—'

'I know he's joined the Blackshirts,' Polly interrupted.

Stan felt deflated. 'Bet you don't know he's terrorising people for his guvnor, though, do you?'

'And who put him in touch with his guvnor?' Polly immediately accused. 'I know Davy's guvnor is the son of that scummy old bag you run off with.'

'Yeah . . . well . . . we all make mistakes, Pol, I'd be the first to admit it.'

'Taken you a fucking long time to say so, though, ain't it?' Polly crowed. 'You've been gawn ten years.'

Stan started clattering cups and saucers together, his mask of bonhomie slipping, revealing a scowl. 'Charlie Potter's roped Davy and one of his pals into collecting funds for Mosley whether the shopkeepers want to cough up or not. I reckon it's protection money's by any other name. I'm warning you it'll end in tears, if it ain't stopped.'

Polly hooted a laugh. 'That's a bit rich coming from you, Stan,' she scoffed. 'Never had a minute for any of yer sons, did you? Even when two of them went inside fer housebreaking you didn't show yer face. Now you've come over on a Saturday afternoon to drink tea and tell me you're worried Davy and his mate might get their knuckles rapped fer being nasty to folk.' Polly uncrossed her arms and jutted her chin. 'I'll tell you what I know: Davy's earning wages and paying me his keep, which is more'n you ever done. That's good enough fer now. Cross them other bridges when we come to 'em.' Polly snatched the kettle off the hob before it could boil. 'So if you ain't got no money to give me you can sling yer hook. Go back to the East End and put the kettle on for that maggot you set up home with. And make sure you close the door on the way out,' Polly snarled, picking up a head of celery and a scrubbing brush and setting to work.

Stan mooched out from the grim hallway into autumn sunlight, his expression dejected. He stopped by the railings and dug in a pocket for his tin of tobacco, then started on a rollup. He'd got nowhere with Polly, even after emptying most of his change onto the table to tempt her to calm down. All he had left was his bus fare back to the East End.

His wife had made it clear she was in no mood to talk about him moving back in. Even when he'd offered to scrub celery and sell it off the barrow that afternoon, she'd not been swayed to share a pot of tea with him.

Stan stuck a hand on the iron railings, blowing smoke and gazing to and fro at the bustling crowds. Campbell Road never slept; in particular it was a hive of activity on a Saturday when the weather was fine, as today. He could see a small gambling school was in progress: men were crouching on the pavement, or leaning against walls at the junction with Paddington Street. He ambled closer and for a while watched dice being thrown and cards being dealt. It never ceased to amuse Stan that people around here – who were often facing eviction for rent arrears – could raise serious stake money without too much trouble.

The dealer was middle-aged, but a few kids were hanging around acting as lookouts to warn of police approaching. The coppers patrolled in pairs because no local constable, acquainted with the Bunk's dire reputation, would set foot unaccompanied in the street. As Stan eyed the mounds of coins on the floor he understood why Davy had felt bitter about being elbowed out of his job as croupier.

About to stroll on towards Seven Sisters Road, Stan came to a shocked standstill at the sight of somebody he recognised from the East End. Ruby Potter, rocking a pram and holding her daughter by the hand, was just up ahead with a group of local women.

Stan knew Matilda Keiver from way back, and Margaret Lovat and Beattie Evans were two other Campbell Road residents of longstanding who were having a chat with Vi's daughter-in-law. But it was Ruby who recaptured Stan's frowning gaze. It was a very odd turn-up for the books to stumble across Charlie's wife when the fellow had been out searching for her and the kids to drag them home. Stan slunk back against a wall, drawing deeply on the limp cigarette. He reckoned the discovery was worthy of some serious consideration before he carried on to the bus stop. Charlie – and Vi too, for that matter – would be very glad to hear about Ruby's whereabouts. Of course, Vi wouldn't be so happy to know what he had been doing over in Islington, visiting his wife . . .

'I will be different from now on, Mum. I know I've been a disgrace but I can't stand no more of living me life the way it was. I'm finished with men, I swear, so please let me stay 'cos I'm sorry for what I did and it'll never happen again.' Blanche was seated at the kitchen table and she bit into her breakfast toast, gazing up beseechingly at her mother.

'Heard it all before, miss, and you've never stuck to your word for longer than a few days.' Gladys found it hard to look her daughter in the face since she'd come upon her stark naked in the kitchen in the early hours of the morning last week. When she'd discovered from her husband what Blanche had been up to out in their shed, with a local villain old enough to be her father, Gladys had felt physically sick. Blanche had always been a handful, chasing after the boys from when she turned thirteen. Even so, Gladys would never have imagined her daughter would end up acting like a cheap whore for any fellow.

Ever since Tony caught them at it, he had been avoiding coming home at times when he knew Blanche

310

was about. He was so nauseated by his daughter's behaviour he'd sooner eat in the pub than sit across from her at the table.

'I'm off to work,' Blanche muttered, pushing to her feet. She knew her mother didn't believe her when she said she was done with men. But she meant it. She'd had nothing but heartache off her husband because of the divorce, and nothing but trouble off Charlie. She'd never wanted to do it with him in the shed in the first place and felt ashamed at how low she'd sunk. If Nick or Wes ever found out how she'd been caught out with Charlie Potter, they'd think she was some sort of lowlife slut. Not that her father would mention it to a soul, but Blanche couldn't be certain Charlie wouldn't turn vindictive. Blanche knew it would suit her if she never clapped eyes on the creep ever again.

Gladys darted a look at Blanche, noticing her quiet dejection. Her daughter had seemed different lately. She was wearing less makeup and going to work regularly, without moaning. It was far too soon to think Blanche had turned over a new leaf, but the signs were encouraging. 'I'll speak to yer father. Ain't promising nothing 'cos in his eyes you're beyond the pale.' Gladys gave a crisp nod. 'Ain't saying he's wrong, neither. I don't know how he coped with the shock of seeing his own daughter like . . . *that.*' Gladys's face was a study of revulsion. 'But if you're being honest about changing your ways I'll have a word . . .'

'I am! I'm sick of men! They're all selfish bastards only after one thing!' Blanche burst out.

'Yeah . . . well . . .' Gladys cleared her throat, turning back to the washing-up bowl. There was nothing in that bitter statement she could challenge following

311

twenty-eight years of marriage. She'd had to elbow her husband away in bed when he'd tried to climb on top of her the night of the fracas in the garden. If Gladys really thought Tony had been turned on by what he'd seen Blanche and Charlie doing, she'd have screamed blue murder . . .

Blanche set off up the road towards work, hands digging into her pockets, head lowered. She avoided looking at a group of women on the opposite pavement. She knew some of the neighbours had questioned her mother about the reason for the commotion in the garden that night. She'd heard Gladys giving short shrift to the old biddy next door, explaining it all away as somebody trying to steal the new mower. The woman had been complaining about getting woken up by Tony's shouting.

'Yer old man calmed down by now, has he?'

Blanche nearly jumped out of her skin as Charlie stepped out from his hiding place and came up quietly behind her. She clapped a hand to her heart, trying to steady its erratic thumping. 'You frightened the bleedin' life outta me!'

Charlie rubbed a hand over her rump, wedging her skirt between her legs. 'Missed this, gel, like mad. But thought I'd stay clear fer a little while till you sorted things out at home. Bet you've put up with some stick off your mum 'n' dad, ain't yer?'

Blanche sprang away from his touch, wondering why she hadn't realised before just how disrespectfully he treated her. She darted a glance back the way she'd come. The last thing she wanted was her mother turning the corner and spotting him. Gladys would straight away think she'd been lying about leaving the past behind.

'It's all over with us, Charlie,' Blanche announced. She saw at once the spitefulness in his eyes. But she was determined to cut free of him and was, in a way, glad he'd turned up so she could tell him so. If it hadn't been for Joyce Groves giving Charlie the eye, Blanche knew she'd have finished with him ages ago. Well, Joyce was welcome to him.

'You don't mean that,' Charlie lilted, giving her arm a stroke. 'You're just listening to yer old man. I know we got caught out and it was embarrassing. You're a grown woman and can do what you want without asking yer parents' permission.'

'What I want is to keep a roof over me head and not get chucked out. For that I do need me parents' permission.' Blanche crossed her arms over her chest, tilting her chin. 'You've got a wife and kids; it weren't ever gonna work out between us, and you know it.'

'I'm done with Ruby; you're the one I want,' Charlie lied. 'Swear that's true, and I'll prove it to yer. I've come over to tell you we can move in together now I've kicked her out.' Charlie was hedging his bets in case he couldn't find Ruby and drag her back. He needed a woman indoors, providing home comforts when he finished work, more than he'd realised. His preference would be for his wife because she'd grown used to his ways. Charlie reckoned Blanche could end up being a pain in the backside with her demands, and unlike Ruby she had family around her who'd be sticking an oar in if he kept her in line with a slap.

Blanche's jaw dropped; she didn't know whether to laugh or cry. The idea that Charlie seriously believed she'd consider moving in with him was as horrifying as it was astonishing. 'It's over, Charlie,' she said hoarsely.

'Ain't moving in with you ever, so you'd be best off taking your wife back. I'm stopping with me parents. Don't come round here no more after me 'cos if you do me dad's gonna get the law on you.' She hurried past, praying he'd get the message and go quietly without following her.

Jennifer smoothed a hand over her pregnant bump, gazing at it with a mixture of wonder and loathing. She'd got knocked up before, about three years ago. She'd suspected on that occasion Bill had been responsible and had told him so. He'd known there was a fair chance it was his so had sorted her out some money, and the address of a woman who'd get rid of it. Bill hadn't been around in months and Jenny knew even if he had he wouldn't shell out to dislodge another man's bastard from her belly. Bill would tell her it was the culprit's responsibility to come up with the necessary. Jennifer agreed; she was desperate enough now to go and knock on the Jewish bastard's door and demand some support, as Bill wasn't around to hound him for her. Bill would have confronted David if he'd still been coming over on his visits. She should have kept herself prettier for Bill, she realised. She missed him; he'd looked after her in his own way . . . far better than any other man ever had, even her own father.

Jenny stood up from the sofa, feeling restless. She'd not seen David Goldstein in a while and that made her think he'd got wind of her condition from her sister and was keeping his distance. Her mouth slanted angrily. She'd go and nab him in Leman Street police station, if necessary, and show him up in front of all his colleagues.

But first, she'd give him a chance to do the right thing and quietly support her and the kid because she didn't want Kathy to know what a horrible, mean cow she'd been. She'd hooked Kathy's boyfriend on purpose, wanting to get one over on her nice, beautiful sister. She'd never intended it to continue after that first time. But after the first time she'd wanted it to, and she knew to her shame that if David turned up again she'd end up in bed with him.

As Kathy came in from the yard, carrying the mat she'd been shaking out, Jenny bit her lip thoughtfully. 'Been out anywhere nice with that boyfriend of yours?'

Kathy let the mat fall by the back door. 'I'm not seeing David any more.'

Jenny's ears pricked up. 'Oh? Had a bust-up with him?'

'Not really,' Kathy said, rinsing her hands under the tap and flicking them dry. 'We just decided we'd grown apart. Want me to give you a quick examination while I'm here?'

Jenny turned her back. 'No . . . I'm all right . . . don't need no poking around, thanks all the same.'

'What are you knitting?' Kathy indicated the small pale lemon scrap hanging off needles discarded on the settee. 'Is it something for the baby?'

Jenny threw a cushion on top of the tiny cardigan, hiding it. 'Don't know why I'm bothering,' she muttered. 'Social can have it for adoption. I ain't keeping it.'

'You'll feel differently when the baby's born,' Kathy said gently. 'Have you stopped being sick?'

Jennifer nodded, keen to resume their conversation about David. 'The copper's found himself another girl, has he?'

'I think so; but from the way he spoke it didn't sound

315

very serious.' Kathy frowned at her sister. Usually her twin only seemed eager to quiz her over their parents and Tom.

'Typical man, he's thrown you over to go off with somebody else.' Jenny's amusement sounded shrill. 'Give us his address, Kathy, and I'll go round and sort him out for you.'

'Won't do you much good; you won't find him there,' Kathy chuckled, still puzzled by her sister's sudden interest in her social life.

'Where will I find him then?'

'Spain.'

'What?' Jenny croaked.

'David's given up his job and gone to fight in the civil war. He was travelling to France first, then on to Spain. He sailed earlier in the week, with his cousin, Sam.'

Jenny dropped back down to the sofa. 'Made sure he got himself well away then . . .'

Kathy crouched down by Jennifer's seat. Her sister looked shell-shocked. 'What's up? You didn't even know him that well. I'm not upset about us breaking up, if that's what's worrying you.' She took one of her sister's hands between her palms. 'To tell you the truth, I'm seeing another man, and I like him very much, so there's no hard feelings.'

'Well, good for you,' Jenny said bitterly, snatching back her fingers. Her forehead dropped to her cupped palms. 'You told Mum and Dad about the mess I'm in?'

'No . . . do you want me to?' Kathy stood up, sighing. Jennifer slowly shook her head.

'Well, I won't say anything then.'

'Who's the new man you're seeing?'

'I doubt you'll know him . . .'

'If he's from round here, bet your life I'll know him,' Jenny muttered sourly.

Kathy moistened her lips. She'd wondered before whether her twin and Nick Raven might have crossed paths, and now she had a chance to find out. But she wasn't sure she wanted to know.

'Nick Raven . . .' Kathy's heart missed a beat at her sister's reaction to having her boyfriend's identity. 'You've heard of him?' she asked.

'Round here, everybody's heard of him,' Jenny replied. 'Never had the good luck to meet him, though . . . wish I had,' she added. She leaned into the sofa, her head cocked and her smile sly. 'Well, well, well, you don't mess about, do you? Talk about from one extreme to the other. First you want a copper, now you want a villain.' Jenny pursed her lips. 'Good fer you, making the change. Knew you could do better than living off a policeman's poky wages. Bill used to say he'd like Nick Raven's life.'

Kathy hadn't heard Jennifer say anything untoward but something about her sister's attitude was depressing her. 'Nick told me he's a successful businessman who buys up property and rents it out.'

'Yeah . . . he is . . . now. But he used to work for Wes Silver as a lorry driver, before he struck lucky.'

'I know . . .' Kathy said.

'Then one of Wes's lorries got hijacked and all his fags and booze went missing off the back.' Jenny started to laugh. 'Guess who was driving it.'

'I know he was driving it 'cos he told me all about it.' Kathy fell quiet.

Jenny shrugged. 'If he did it, good luck to him, I say. So the copper's gonna be gone for a while, is he?'

'Who knows how long the war will last? Might be ages.' Kathy frowned. 'I hope he keeps his head down and comes home safe.'

'By then, it'll be too late to put things right . . .'

'He knows we're finished. When he comes back, I doubt he'll come and see me.' Kathy went off to boil the kettle for tea.

'Nor me . . .' Jennifer muttered beneath her breath. She felt tears prick her eyes. She'd got no chance of any help from anyone with the baby: her parents hated her; David Goldstein hated her so much he'd sooner get himself killed than have anything to do with her or his kid. And Kathy would hate her, and also abandon her, if she ever found out what a mean selfish thing she'd done sleeping with her Jew . . .

Jennifer found the knitting under the cushion and yanked the stitches off the needles. Wiping her dripping eyes she decided she'd got another use for them . . .

CHAPTER THIRTY

'Police are outside!'

Winnie Finch got a gormless look from her husband for hissing the warning.

'Eh?' Eddie's teacup hovered in front of his slack mouth.

Winnie agitatedly twitched the front curtain again. 'Police . . . and they're heading this way, by the looks of things.'

Eddie sprung out of his chair, and started booting boxes of sheets and pillowcases beneath the parlour table to conceal them. He yanked the tablecloth down so it drooped to touch the floor, hiding the stolen merchandise from view on one side.

'Shit!' he ground out between his teeth as the sound of the door knocker made them both jump. 'I'll nip out the back way,' he mouthed. 'You don't know nuthin' about nuthin' . . . right?' Eddie jabbed with a pointing finger, threatening repercussions.

Winnie gave a single nod, licking her lips and smoothing her pinny. 'They'll know yer about,' she wailed beneath her breath. 'Yer van's out front . . .'

'I've gone fer a bleedin' walk!' Eddie snarled through set teeth.

He bolted into the washhouse and crouched down behind the mangle. He knew if the rozzers spotted the boxes of stolen linen they'd have a good search and come up with all they needed to put him away. The spare bedroom resembled Aladdin's cave. With shaking hands he yanked out a packet of cigarettes and lit one, drawing deeply. After a second it dawned on him that the smell of tobacco might drift in the open kitchen window and he panicked, trying to put out the cigarette so quickly that he burned his fingers. He swallowed his yelp of pain and began waving a hand, frantically trying to disperse the smoke. He strained to listen for raised voices. Then when all was quiet he waited for the sound of a car starting up so he'd know the coast was clear. It came sooner than he expected and immediately he started tiptoeing towards the house. He put his ear to the door, was about to creep in, when Winnie yanked it open, startling him.

'They gawn?'

Winnie nodded, looking uneasy.

Eddie easily recognised his wife's shiftiness. 'Well . . . what d'they want?' he demanded, coming in and closing the door.

'Tom . . .'

'Tom . . .' Eddie parroted.

'I'm gonna kill that Polly Wright and that rat of a son of hers!' Winnie spat.

'What you on about?' Eddie roared.

'Coppers are making enquiries about a kid wot got run over and got a broken leg and his skull fractured over the East End.'

Eddie thrust his face close to Winnie's. No threats were necessary. She knew if she didn't cut to the chase soon, he'd clump her.

'Polly told 'em that our Tom's been over that way with Davy when they're out with Mosley's cadets. Seems a couple of kids in black shirts have been reported by shopkeepers for threatening behaviour.'

Eddie's eyes bulged in fury. If the coppers had spotted his hidden boxes he could have faced a stretch inside because of his own son acting stupid!

'Ain't nuthin' to worry over, Eddie. The constable said the injured kid's gonna make a good recovery,' Winnie babbled, knowing Tom was in for a hiding, knowing too just how savagely Eddie disciplined his kids. 'Just they have to follow things up, they said . . .'

Eddie raised his fist, intending to stop his wife gabbling and discover if the police had mentioned him at all.

They both jumped as the door knocker was used again. Without a word, Eddie scooted back outside.

Gingerly, Winnie opened up to find her son grinning at her.

'Forgot me key,' Tom said blithely, although he found it odd that his mother seemed reluctant to let him in. A second later, his father appeared, shoved Winnie aside and dragged him in by his hair.

'So where you been hiding yerself this afternoon?' Violet looked Stan up and down. He'd been acting odd for a few days. He'd been quieter than usual and keeping out of her way. She knew he usually finished his van deliveries at four o'clock but it was way past that now.

'Had a few hours' overtime come up at work so had to do a run over Kent way.'

'Well, that's all right, we'll have a few extra drinks on it Saturday night.' Violet gleefully rubbed her hands. 'Wouldn't mind an ale right now. Brought any bottles in with yer from the offie?'

A moment after shaking his head, Stan was again immersed in his thoughts. He was thankful Vi seemed to be in a reasonable mood. He'd still not decided whether to tell her that he knew where her daughter-in-law was to be found. Charlie had turned up during the week with a face on him, and mother and son had torn strips off the absentee, then pored over the size of the hiding Ruby could expect if they found her.

'You listening to me?'

Stan focused on Vi's coarse features.

'I was just saying that Charlie's gonna move in with us.'

Stan blinked rapidly, clearing his mind to concentrate. 'Move in with us?' he echoed. 'What you on about?'

'He don't like livin' on his own or wasting rent on empty space,' Violet snapped. 'We've got a spare room and it'll be just like old times having him back home. He was always me favourite.' Her mouth puckered grimly. 'Bleedin' cheek, that Ruby's got, walkin' out on my boy.'

Vi started rattling pots out of the cupboard under the sink then plonked a small sack of potatoes on the draining board. 'Get peeling a few spuds, will yer? Charlie's coming in fer tea with us when he's done his shift down the docks.'

Stan licked his lips, his mind spinning, but he meekly picked up the peeler and set to work. 'There's something I've been meaning to say, Vi.' After days of dithering, Vi's news had prompted him make a snap decision.

'Didn't know whether to bring it up 'cos I know you don't like no interference in yer family's affairs.'

'What you on about?' Vi turned sharp eyes on him while filling a pot with water.

'I know where Ruby and the kids are,' Stan blurted. 'But as I said, you'll have to tell me if I'm speaking out of turn.'

Stan didn't have any beef with Ruby but his philosophy was to take care of number one. Living with Vi was bad enough. Having to put up with Charlie as well as his mother would be an unbearable ordeal.

Violet strode up, staring-eyed. 'You know where Ruby's gawn?' she bellowed. 'Why ain't you said sooner?'

'Only just found out,' Stan howled, ducking her swinging fist. 'Honest, Vi, I only come across her recently. I went to see Davy over Islington at the weekend and spotted Ruby in Campbell Road. She didn't see me,' he speedily added, hoping to pacify Violet. 'I kept out of sight so Charlie can take her by surprise if he wants to.'

Violet crossed her arms over her chest; she felt like taking another swing at Stan for keeping such important information to himself. But as she'd kept something from him, and was continuing to do so, she thought she'd let him off lightly.

When the coppers had turned up looking for Charlie because some lads who worked for him might have caused a road accident, Vi had had no hesitation in pointing them in the direction of Stan's son in Campbell Road. She'd never liked Davy, in any case, and hoped in future he'd stay over his side of town.

Vi grinned. 'So . . . you done us a favour turning up that news, Stan. We'll take Ruby by surprise, all right.'

She rumbled a phlegmy laugh. 'The cow won't know what's hit her.'

'Now you listen to me, Charlie! I know you've got trouble with the missus.' Wes Silver theatrically gave his chest a double-handed tap. 'I've got trouble with my missus. May's in the hospital having an operation on her unmentionables so I've got enough on my plate already . . .' Wes grimaced distaste. 'You understand, Charlie; I don't need no more problems right now.'

Charlie shifted impatiently in front of Wes's desk, trying to control his temper. Like lots of people, he'd heard rumours for years about Wes being part Jewish, but he'd never taken them seriously. But ever since Blanche had brought it to his attention about the circumcision, Charlie had picked up on every mannerism and expression. Wes obviously didn't realise that he spoke, shrugged, gesticulated like the schmocks he despised, especially when money was under discussion.

'Ain't making it your business, Mr Silver,' Charlie said tightly. 'Just asking for a sub on me wages 'cos me rent's due.'

In fact, Charlie had no intention of laying out for any more rent. The landlord and his brother had collared him for half the arrears earlier in the week and nearly cleaned him out. Charlie never liked looking potless in front of other men so he'd pulled out his wallet and paid up to look big. The bastards weren't getting another penny off him though. Charlie was doing a moonlight flit over to his mother's place in a couple of days. He hated the idea of again being under Violet's roof because he knew she'd want to clock him in and out. She'd expect to be told where he'd been, and who with. Charlie was close to turning forty-five and he'd got used to Ruby being the woman running things at home. He'd taught her to mind her own business so he could please himself what he did.

'If everybody in my firm wanted a sub on his wages, where would that leave me?' Wes planted his fists on his desk top, pushing himself upright.

Charlie was accustomed to seeing Wes in expensive suits but today he felt the difference in their status more acutely. Having come straight from his shift at the docks he was in his donkey jacket and old trousers, but they seemed dirtier than usual and the pungent smell of tar was in his nostrils, killing the scent of Wes's cologne. Charlie's insides began churning in resentment because even Wes's expression seemed to him more superior than normal.

He'd helped Wes for over five years build his business, being a general dogsbody for a few quid and a bit of reflected glory. He'd even done six months without complaining, having put a bloke in hospital for crossing Wes. Today, he'd come, cap in hand, for an advance on his wages because he'd not had a woman or a good drink in over a week. None of his workmates would lend him the necessary for an evening out and he knew asking his mother would be a dead loss. Vi might offer to feed him up every so often but opening her purse for him was another matter.

'Can you tell me, Charlie, where does being too generous leave me?' Wes prodded his underling's greasy sleeve. 'How can a man like me survive if all his staff want cash they ain't yet earned?'

'I don't give a fuck, you tight-fisted Yid!' Charlie roared, losing control. He grabbed the lapels of Wes's jacket, tugging him off balance. 'I went inside for you, and what did I get? A few measly quid as compensation,' he snarled into Wes's face. 'I've taken shit off you for years doing yer dirty work and all I'm asking for is a little bit to tide me over.' Charlie shoved Wes back from him, sending his boss stumbling against his desk, before clearing the spittle from his lips with the back of a hand.

Wes was white-faced and trembling, but with rage rather than fear. 'What did you call me?' He straightened the knot in his tie.

'Nothing . . .' Charlie was already regretting his outburst. 'Got a lot on me plate right now, that's all . . .'

'You called me a Jew . . .' Wes locked eyes with Charlie.

Charlie knew he could back down and apologise and it'd probably be back as it was between them . . . or it might not . . .

'Well . . . that's what you are, ain't it?' Charlie sounded maliciously amused. 'Think nobody knows that you've been trimmed up down there, do you?' He laughed softly, nodding at his boss's fly. 'Don't worry . . . yer secret's safe with me.' He cracked his knuckles, wondering why he'd not tried a bit of blackmail sooner to open the miser's fist.

Wes pulled out his wallet and dropped two pound notes on the desk. 'I was born with a defect,' he enunciated icily. 'And I think it bad taste to mock, but different people, different ways. Your sense of humour ain't appreciated by me, Charlie, so no more of it, eh?'

Charlie snatched up the cash. 'Yeah . . . different people, Wes, that's all it is. Sorry if you didn't see the joke . . . 'cos that's all it was. Ruby's giving me the hump lately, winding me up. You know me, loyal as the day's long.'

'Yeah . . . I know you . . .' Wes said, his mouth slanting grimly as Charlie sauntered towards the door. He knew where Potter had got the news about his circumcision: Blanche Raven. Wes had heard about their little fling and had a private snigger. Apart from May and Blanche and a few assorted tarts, only his parents had ever seen him naked.

May was loyal and would stay that way. She'd fought tooth and nail to get him back from Blanche. Wes hadn't thought Blanche was bright enough to make the connection between his lack of foreskin and the Jewish religion. Wes still thought she was a dim floozie so wasn't worried about her blabbing again. Besides, it was only the likes of Charlie Potter who would understand the premium in such information.

Charlie now knew more about him than Wes felt comfortable with. So something would have to be done about that . . .

Charlie strode along towards home, unaware that his boss was still brooding on their altercation. He was already thinking about women. He had hoped Blanche would agree to move in with him. He'd hung around outside the Goldsteins' shop for her earlier in the week, hoping to have another go at persuading her to carry on seeing him. She'd not been any more welcoming than when he'd last ambushed her for a talk. So he'd given up on her.

Charlie was heading towards the café where Joyce Groves worked. He had a feeling she might cut him dead too because he'd seen her snuggling up to one of her brother's pals who'd just got out of prison. Charlie knew he wasn't up to getting belligerent with a felon half his age. He'd have considered having a scrap for Blanche but Joyce Groves wasn't worth breaking sweat for. So he'd give it a go, and if no dice, he'd head off back towards the pubs around the docks and find Beverly or another cheap tart to spend the evening with.

Charlie had been feeling his age lately, and the young-sters he'd employed had taken the weight off him a bit. Davy had been a good help, too, till his mate turned cissy on him. Unfortunately, without Tom by his side, it seemed Davy had turned cissy too. So, they'd had a visit from the police about the Butlers' son getting run over . . . so what? Nobody could prove anything. If the Butlers had done the sensible thing and paid up straight away, nobody would've needed to get hurt. Besides, the injured kid was up and about again and on his crutches, so no problem . . .

'Well it's nice to meet you again.' Lottie enclosed Kathy's hands in her own.

'It's nice to see you too.' Kathy returned pressure to Lottie's warm fingers.

'Sorry if I offended you when you came in the shop with that letter for Nick,' Lottie continued, leading the way to the parlour. 'You see, I didn't realise Nick had started seeing a nice girl.' She darted an apologetic glance at her son, who was closing her front door. 'Sorry . . . that wasn't very tactful,' she said. 'What I meant was that at the time you weren't the one I'd heard about . . .' Lottie frowned. 'I'd best keep my mouth shut from now on so I don't put my foot in it no more.'

'Good idea,' Nick said drily. 'Come and sit down,' he invited Kathy, indicating an armchair in his mother's cosy front parlour.

'I'll make the tea,' Lottie offered brightly. 'It's lovely to be properly introduced. I baked a cake this afternoon after Nick came by the shop and said he'd bring you round later. What I will say, Kathy, is that I've never needed to bake a cake before.' Her son received a twinkling smile before Lottie disappeared to put the kettle on.

'I can tell she likes you,' Nick said with a chuckle.

'I like her too,' Kathy replied, looking around at Lottie's knickknacks on the mantelpiece and cabinets.

There was now wedged between them an unspoken question about his other girlfriends. Kathy realised Lottie hadn't been referring to Nick's wife just then. Kathy had been curious as to his past loves: such a handsome and successful man would have women after him. But as Nick had minded his manners over her relationship with David, Kathy felt she'd no right to be nosy about his previous affairs . . . other than perhaps to make sure all of them were over. She'd hate to think he'd be mean enough to two-time her. She'd wanted to be fair with him and David, and hoped to be treated with equal courtesy.

'Finished with all of them some time ago. I was unattached before you agreed to go out with me,' Nick said. He sat back in the chair, watching her steadily. 'And my solicitor tells me my divorce should be finalised in a matter of days now.'

'Oh . . . sorry . . .' Kathy blurted thoughtlessly, startled that he'd read her mind.

'I hope that's not true.' Nick took one of her hands

in his. 'I wanted us to go out and celebrate when I'm officially a free man.'

'Of course I'm glad you'll be single, but celebrating isn't very kind on your wife,' Kathy pointed out.

'Blanche wasn't always kind on me,' Nick lounged back in his chair again. 'Not that it matters one way or the other any more.'

'Well . . . here's tea,' Lottie announced, squeezing sideways through the door with a tray laden with refreshments. 'Don't think you can beat a bit of jam sponge, do you?'

'My favourite,' Kathy said with a smile.

'Oh, I was wondering if you'd take a look at me kitchen tap while you're here, Nick. Meant to ask you last week.' Lottie put down her cup. 'It's leaking all over the window ledge.'

Nick finished his cake and stood up. He gave his mother a sardonic look as he went out.

'Course he knows I just want to get him out of the way so we can have a girls' chat.'

Kathy smiled, wiping crumbs from her fingers. 'That was delicious cake.'

'I do make a good Victoria sponge. So you're a nurse then?' Lottie launched straight away into her interrogation.

'A nurse and a midwife,' Kathy confirmed.

Lottie looked impressed. 'Bet you have to deal with some rough families round these parts.'

Kathy nodded, the Potters immediately springing to mind. She recalled that Lottie knew Charlie Potter of old. 'Charlie Potter's wife was a patient of mine.'

'I feel very sorry for Ruby being married to him.' Lottie grimaced her disgust for the man. 'I'd like to say he went downhill after his first wife died – Miriam was her name – but he was unpleasant even as a kid.'

'I know first-hand that he's a vile character,' Kathy said. 'Nick told me he came into your shop and caused trouble.'

'He needs locking up, in my opinion. Not that he's been back to bother me since Nick saw him off.' Lottie sat forward, determined to lighten the conversation. 'Another cup, Kathy?' She shook the pot. 'There's enough left and it's still warm.'

'Not for me, thanks anyway.'

'Nick likes you very much.' Lottie beamed her approval. 'Oh, he's not discussed you, don't think that, he never talks to me about . . . such things.' She'd remembered to be discreet.

'I like him very much too,' Kathy said with a shy smile.

'Good . . . that's what I wanted to hear.' Lottie gave a satisfied nod.

'So . . . did she tell you all about my bad habits?' Nick asked as they drove away from Lottie's place.

Kathy laughed. 'I get the impression she dotes on you and probably wouldn't admit you had any bad habits.'

'I don't . . . of course . . .' Nick said, straight-faced, lighting up a cigarette. 'Are you going to introduce me to your folks?'

'Eventually. They might not be the sort of people you'd expect.' Kathy frowned out of the window.

'Families never are, Kath,' Nick said. 'I'd still like to meet them.'

'My dad's a bit . . . dodgy,' she blurted out, then fell

331

silent. 'I don't mean he's been in prison or anything like that.' She sighed. 'But, he could have been arrested at times had he been unlucky.'

'Sounds like a man after my own heart.' Nick smiled behind the cigarette clamped in his lips.

'No . . . he's not; I hope, he's not anyway,' Kathy added vehemently. 'He caused a lot of trouble for us once.'

Nick took her hand from her lap and held it. 'All right, we'll leave introductions for another day.' She felt the light touch of his lips on her hand and turned her cheek to caress his fingers, wordlessly thanking him for his comfort and understanding.

His wife must be kicking herself for losing him . . . the phrase stuck in Kathy's mind as she settled back for the drive home.

Blanche slammed her bedroom door, hoping that her argumentative parents might take the hint and shut up, giving her some peace and quiet to read her book. Half an hour ago, she'd been sitting downstairs in the front room, listening to the BBC National Programme on the wireless, but their bickering had drowned out the music. She'd taken herself off to bed with much huffing, hoping to escape the noise. But their muffled voices had penetrated the ceiling until she'd pulled the pillow over her head, then jumped up in exasperation.

Flopping down again onto her stomach on the mattress, she positioned the novel open on a pillow, but after a moment sighed because she couldn't concentrate. She knew her irritation with her parents – with everything in her life – had escalated when the post arrived yesterday. She snatched at the folded letter she'd been using as a bookmark, skimming it angrily away over the bed coverlet.

As the volume of her mother's shrieked abuse increased, Blanche elbowed herself upright with a curse. She couldn't stand much more of it! She grabbed up the decree absolute and tore it in two, scrunched it in a fist, then lobbed it onto the floor. A moment later, she'd dived after it and pieced the bits together to reread it, even though she knew it word for word.

Just a thought of Nick could make Blanche forget all the other men she'd had, especially Charlie, damn him! That night she'd got caught out with him in the shed had really put her parents at each other's throats. But she didn't feel guilty over it; she blamed them. If they'd been more of a help persuading Nick to take her back she'd never have got involved with Charlie Potter in the first place.

Already Blanche's vow of chastity was wearing thin; a nice-looking fellow had come in the shop with his wife during the afternoon and winked at her. She'd winked right back. Of course, nothing would come of it: he'd looked henpecked when his wife snapped at him because he'd not been complimentary enough about the frock she'd chosen.

Blanche paced restlessly, considering whether to get dressed and go round to see one of her old school friends, just for something to do. Maude Grisham still lived with her parents, just a stroll away. Of course, the Grishams would probably wonder what the hell she was doing calling so late. Blanche looked at her watch; it was nine thirty. Suddenly she was determined to go out, even if it was just for a walk to tire herself out. She jumped up and pulled her skirt and blouse off the chair to get dressed, then hesitated and threw the garments aside. Suddenly she knew where she was going . . . and she wasn't visiting him in those old things. She reckoned she had one last chance to win Nick over, and only one way of doing it . . .

CHAPTER THIRTY-ONE

'What the hell are you doing here?'

'Well, if you ask me in, I'll tell you.' Blanche tilted her head, hoping she looked demure and serious instead of hungry for his touch. She licked her lips, her breathing slowing in excitement. Nick had obviously been getting ready for bed, so she couldn't have timed it better. If she could get inside the house she'd be halfway there . . .

'Don't see the point in this, Blanche . . .'

'Well, I do! I think the least you owe me after getting me pregnant is five minutes of your time now it's goodbye for good.' Blanche lowered her lashes as though blinking back tears and tightened the belt on her coat.

'Five minutes, that's all,' Nick sighed. 'And don't expect me to run you back home afterwards.' Wearily, he opened the door wider.

Blanche hurried inside before he could change his mind and bar her way. In the hall she turned, waiting for him to close the door. She eyed his unbuttoned shirt, pulled out of his trousers in readiness to be removed.

Nick was aware he was under scrutiny, and he suspected Blanche had more on her mind than reminiscing one final time. He'd received a letter yesterday and he reckoned his ex-wife had got one too. She was about to start again on the merry-go-round of them getting back together and was hoping he'd ask her to stay the night.

'Ain't going to work, Blanche,' Nick said, sounding quite sympathetic because she meant nothing to him, and he wished she felt as apathetic about what they'd once had as he did.

'You don't know what I'm gonna say,' Blanche purred, sashaying closer. She ran a single fingernail down his naked throat, close enough now to him to drink in the scent of the citrus soap he liked. 'Can I go in there?' She jerked her head at the open doorway.

Nick looked at his watch, shrugging. 'You've got three minutes left so make it quick. If you think I won't kick you out 'cos you'll have a go at turning on the water-works and waking the neighbours, think again.' Suddenly Nick felt his patience evaporate. He wished now he'd not let the daft cow in. He strode past her and into the sitting room, searching in a pocket of his trousers for a packet of Players. By the time he'd got the cigarette alight and turned back to her, she'd shut the door and taken off her coat.

Nick shook wildly at the match burning his fingers and bringing him to his senses. Blanche was stark naked and from the smug look on her face obviously thought he'd lunge for her. He nearly did, but his hands would have gone to her throat rather than the tits she was thrusting his way.

'You always wanted me, Nick . . . can't say that ain't true. You got me in trouble, remember, 'cos you wouldn't take no for an answer.' Blanche swayed herself closer, tongue caressing her top lip. 'You owe it to me to give it another go . . . and I owe it to you to give you everything you need.'

'Fucking hell . . .' Nick sounded agonised. He wasn't feeling quite so cocksure he could refuse what she was offering. He hadn't slept with a woman since Joyce Groves, because he loved Kathy, had guessed she was a virgin, and was waiting till she was ready to take things further. If Kathy found out he'd slept with his ex-wife, she'd finish with him, no doubt about it. But he was human too, and no man could deny that his ex-wife had a luscious figure on her, and all he had to do was stretch out a hand and get some release . . .

Blanche sensed his steady gaze on her body and rushed at him, winding her arms about his neck and rubbing together their hips. 'The others meant nothing to me, darling. Honest, Nick, every time I was with Charlie, I thought of you . . .' She plunged her mouth upwards, grinding her lips on his.

Nick caught her wrists and forced her back, shoving her away, glad she'd mentioned Charlie Potter just as he'd felt the throb in his groin overtaking his reason. The idea of having a woman Potter had recently been with made him feel sick to his stomach and had killed his desire.

Nick strode to the crumpled coat on the floor and swiped it up before hurling it at Blanche. 'Get that on and get out before I fucking chuck you out, you silly tart.' He carried on into the hall without stopping and flung open the door.

Blanche was almost home before she'd conquered her wrathful weeping. Nick's rejection had been humiliating,

337

but what had really started her bawling was the know-ledge that she couldn't have what she wanted. Nothing in her life was right: she hated her job, she hated living with her parents, and she deserved better. She wanted a man who'd give her nice things and an easy ride, and she'd lost out on two such meal tickets. She now accepted Nick was a lost cause and Wes had gone back to his wife . . .

She sniffed, used her knuckles on her eyes to dry them while thinking of Wes. Once he'd been putty in her hands, until May Silver stuck her oar in. But Blanche had heard that Wes's wife had been in hospital . . . so perhaps poor old Wes might be missing out on his conjugals. Blanche's lips twitched. Her smile grew smug as a couple of youths on the opposite pavement whistled and catcalled. Instinctively, Blanche swayed her hips, knowing they were watching her. She felt so full of herself she was tempted to swivel about, open her coat and give them a flash before turning the corner for home. Laughing to herself, she reckoned that in the morning she'd just pop in Wes's office and tell him she was sorry to hear about his wife being poorly . . .

'Are you hungry, young lady?'

Pansy nodded.

Reg Donovan squeezed the small hand in his. 'Me too. Your Auntie Matilda's getting us a few chips to put in our bread. You'll like that, won't you now?'

Pansy nodded, returning light pressure to the fingers enclosing hers.

'Hope she puts lots of salt and vinegar on 'em,' Reg said.

Reg and Pansy had been to the corner shop for a loaf

of bread and a bag of broken biscuits to dunk in their teas, and were now heading home. Ruby was indoors feeding her baby and Peter was running an errand, fetching a bucket of coal for Beattie to earn himself a couple of coppers. But soon they would all congregate in the front room for a meal when Matilda returned with the hot chips.

At first, Reg had been dubious about having a family lodging with them. He'd feared the overcrowding would lead to friction between him and Matilda: in the past they'd had fiery arguments although their relationship had mellowed in the last few years. Despite them being packed tight as sardines, Reg had to admit to being pleasantly surprised at how much he enjoyed the children's company.

'Hello there, sweet'eart.'

Pansy wriggled her fingers in Reg's hand, dragging back as though to flee.

Reg eyed the man and woman blocking the pavement, sensing trouble. They seemed to have sprung out of thin air. 'And who might you be?' he demanded.

'Tell the paddy who I am,' Charlie taunted his daughter. 'Oh . . . that's right, she can't now, can she, 'cos the cat's got her tongue.' He leered at Reg, revelling in the Irishman's wary expression. 'I wouldn't know that about Pansy, would I, unless I was her pa.' He jerked a thumb at Violet. 'This here's the kids' nan. Peter about, is he? He'll be wanting to see his old man.'

Charlie lunged at Pansy, intending to drag her to his side, but the child scooted behind Reg, hiding from her father.

'You can't take her before I've spoken to her mother.' Reg was doing his best to protect the girl behind him.

He knew that the reason Ruby Potter and her children were camping in theirs was to escape a man who was a brute and a bully.

'Needs some discipline, that one,' Vi snapped, raising a hand, miming a cuff. 'Had too much of her own way fer too long.'

'Don't reckon we've been introduced.' Matilda had come up behind the group, newspaper-wrapped chips under an arm.

She stared at Violet Potter rather than at her male companion. 'Cat got *your* tongue now, has it? Well, I'll start in that case. My name's Matilda Keiver, and this here's me fiancé, Reg Donovan.' Matilda took Pansy's hand, patting it reassuringly while drawing her forward. 'And this little gel's the daughter of a friend of mine. Course, that don't include you.' She pointedly stared at Charlie. 'Reckon you must be the wife beater and this here's yer grannie, is it?'

Vi threw back her head and roared a laugh. She'd seen the woman approaching and had thought she looked tough and mouthy. Vi reckoned she could handle herself with the best of them, even Matilda Keiver, who seemed belligerent and her junior by a few years. She started rolling back her sleeves in a businesslike way. 'You'd best let go of me granddaughter, 'cos she's coming home to the East End. So's that bitch of a mother of hers, soon as I find out where she's hiding herself.'

'Well, that's a shame, 'cos I say they're staying right here with me till Ruby says otherwise.' Matilda locked eyes with Vi.

The standoff ended abruptly when Vi charged, head down, butting Matilda in the chest, scattering her bundle of chips onto the ground. Violet tried to follow up her unusual tactic with another, pummelling at Matilda's breasts rather than her face.

Matilda had had enough scraps with men and women to be ready for anything. The flying assault had winded her but she was strong and competitive. Vi was a couple of inches shorter than Matilda but her body was solid as rock and not easy to shove away. While the woman's head was lowered Matilda took great relish in bringing her knee up and smashing it into her opponent's stubby nose.

Vi howled, tottering back just as Reg sprang to assist his fiancée and earned himself a scolding for his trouble.

'You guard Pansy,' Matilda bellowed. 'I can handle this old maggot with one hand behind me back . . .'

Charlie had no qualms about hitting women and he'd step in on his mother's behalf without a second thought, but his wife must have seen the commotion because she was running up the road towards them with the baby bouncing in her arms.

'You reckon you can handle me, do yer? Let's have a see, then . . .' Vi spat on the ground, circling to get into position to attack Matilda.

Polly Wright craned her neck out of her window to glimpse what was going on in the street. Brawls were commonplace in the Bunk and were appreciated by folk as a momentary diversion from their miserable existence. Polly frowned, having spotted Stan pacing to and fro at a distance from the spectacle. She'd not expected him to be back over so soon. Feeling curious, she set off outside.

'What's that all about?'

Stan stepped on his dog end as his wife joined him.

'Vi wants her grandkids back home. Her daughter-in-law's done a flit over here and Matilda Keiver's been putting them all up. I'm staying out of it.'

Polly looked again at the fighting women. She'd never bothered to go over to the East End and investigate her rival. Now she gave Violet Potter a long stare and chortled, 'Bleedin' hell, Stan, that's an ugly old mare you've saddled yerself with.' She stuck her hands on her hips, assessing the scene: a couple with a baby were having an arm-waving bull and a cow, and Reg Donovan was doing his best to pull Violet and Matilda apart while protecting the crying child. 'Feel sorry for the daughter-in-law; bet she wishes they'd just piss off and leave her alone. How'd her husband find out where she'd skipped to?' After a short silence, Polly turned to Stan. He averted his face.

'You bleedin' weasel,' she said. 'Staying out of it, are you?' she parodied. 'Well, I ain't . . .'

Polly walked towards the action, carefully avoiding slippery mashed chips. She was within a yard of flying arms and legs when Vi swung a hook, making Matilda grunt and stumble. Polly nipped in neatly, sending her husband's lover reeling to the ground with a short sharp jab to her face. 'That's fer sending the coppers after me son, but you're welcome to me old man.'

Matilda held her sides, breathing heavily. 'I almost had her then . . .'

'Yeah, know yer did, Til,' Polly said, shaking her stinging fingers.

'Thanks, Pol . . .' Matilda gasped.

'My pleasure,' Polly said, and strolled, smirking, past Stan on her way back home.

'I'm so sorry, Mrs Keiver,' Ruby mumbled, tearfully.

'No need to be sorry, luv . . .' Matilda was wiping her sweaty face with a hanky.

'I'm going back with him.' The uproar had frightened Paul, and Ruby rocked the baby against her shoulder to try to pacify him.

'You ain't doing no such thing!'

Ruby had seen the graze on Matilda's cheek and the woman's hair, so neatly coiled earlier, was dishevelled, framing her face in faded auburn skeins. 'I have to go back . . . otherwise he'll just keep coming here, creating merry hell.' Ruby made a small futile gesture. 'I'm ashamed you got dragged into it and got hurt.'

'Ain't nuthin' to be ashamed about. A punch-up's par for the course for the likes of us round here.' Matilda managed a grin despite her aching face.

Ruby peeped sideways at her husband. He was standing with his mother, who held a rag to her bleeding nose. They were both watching her spitefully. Ruby had already told Charlie she'd go with him so long as he let Pansy and Peter stay with Matilda until things were sorted out between them. Ruby knew she was in for a hiding, and she'd take it willingly to keep her children safe from Charlie's malice. As for Paul . . . she wouldn't be parted from him; besides, she knew it would be a liberty too far to expect Matilda to care for two children and an unweaned baby.

'Your husband can come back here as often as he likes and bring the old bruiser with him.' Matilda contemptuously snapped her head at the East Enders. 'I can promise them both the same reception as they got today. They won't get no change off us.'

Ruby spontaneously hugged Matilda, careful not to squash the baby between them. 'You've been so kind, but if you'd have the two older kids for me, just for a short while till things calm down and they can come home . . .'

'Do you really believe things will calm down?' Matilda patted Ruby's arm when the woman coloured up. 'It's your life, Ruby, and I ain't gonna tell you how to live it. You come back here any time, and you'll be welcomed with open arms. Understand?'

Ruby knuckled her damp eyes, nodding. 'Would you ask Margaret to tell my lady I can't do her work no more. I'm sorry I mucked her about; hope Margaret won't get into trouble 'cos of me.'

'No need to worry about that!' Matilda clucked her tongue. 'Lots of women round here'll give their eyeteeth fer the position. Job'll be snapped up by tomorrow.'

Miserably, Ruby knew that to be true. She'd lost a good job after only a few days. She'd got on with her client and had found the work and the money gave her a boost. 'I'm off now. Thanks for everything you've done. I'll pay you back . . .'

Matilda quietened Ruby with a finger on her lips. 'None o' that, now. Times like this money ain't important. The kids'll be fine with me. I'll let Kathy know what's gone on, shall I?' She followed the younger woman as Ruby trudged towards the Potters. 'Kathy'll be done up when she finds out you're back to square one.'

'Nurse Finch has been so good to us.' Ruby squeezed Matilda's arm, indicating she shouldn't come further but keep her distance from her belligerent kin. She walked on alone towards her husband, patting Paul's back, but her heart was beating so fast in fear she felt faint.

CHAPTER THIRTY-TWO

Kathy could see her mother was feeling glum, and she guessed that things at home were still fraught for Winnie. Her mother had told her that her brother had got a good hiding off Eddie for bringing the police snooping around. Last time Kathy had seen Tom, he'd been moping in his room with a black eye and both legs striped with weals from Eddie's belt. She had to admit that her brother had been an idiot getting involved with the Fascists in the first place, but Eddie's chastisement was always too harsh. Before she'd left that day, Kathy had told her mother so.

'Has Dad calmed down yet, Mum?'

Kathy was sipping tea by her mother's draining board. Winnie was plunging her husband's smalls up and down in the suds in the sink.

'Needs darning,' Winnie muttered, ignoring her daughter's question and throwing aside a sock. Last time she'd seen Kathy, she'd been full of how she was going after Polly Wright for grassing up Tom, when it was her own son who'd done the bullying and caused the accident.

345

But Winnie had done nothing other than bawl some abuse at Polly, then send the woman to Coventry. She'd heard how Polly had floored an old bruiser of an East Ender, as a favour to Tilly Keiver. Winnie knew that she was no match for Polly even on a good day, and lately she felt dog-tired with depression. So she had avoided going round the Bunk and had given Tom a clip round the ear instead to ease her nerves.

'How's Tom bearing up?' Kathy tried again to find out if there'd been any further blow-up over that particular crisis.

'Little bleeder deserved his punishment.' Before Kathy could follow up the topic, Winnie abruptly changed the subject. 'Bumped into Matilda last week. She said she'd like you to pop in to see her next time you were over this way.'

'I was going to call round to the Bunk anyway,' Kathy replied. 'I look forward to seeing how Ruby and the kids are settling in.

'That little Pansy's a cutie.' Winnie smiled. 'She's taken to Reg. Saw him going for a walk with her. Could be the kid's granddad, he could, way he dotes on her.' Winnie found another holey sock and it joined the other in the darning pile. 'As for the lad, Tom was kicking a ball about with him the other day.'

Kathy smiled, happy to hear the news. 'Just finish me tea and better get going then.'

'You don't mention David Goldstein much lately.' Winnie shot a peek at her daughter.

Kathy put down her cup on the draining board. 'He's gone off to Spain to fight in the civil war.'

Winnie's labouring fingers fell still, dangling two lengths of wet wool in mid-air. Abruptly, she dropped the socks into the bowl and wiped her hands on her pinafore. 'Well . . . that's a turn up fer the books. Are you upset?'

'Not in the way you mean. We'd grown apart so there was no romance left, but I hope he keeps safe, 'cos we parted as friends.' Kathy smiled. 'I've got a new boyfriend . . .'

'Your dad'll be pleased to hear it.' Winnie cleared her throat, realising she'd spoken tactlessly. 'That is . . . you know how your father is with the police. He'd never have liked it if you and David got married.'

'Yeah, I know,' Kathy said wryly. She realised her mother had diplomatically refrained from mentioning that Eddie wasn't keen on Jews either.

'Nice fellow, is he, the new one?'

Kathy nodded. 'Perhaps I'll bring him over one day . . .'

'Mmm . . .' Winnie said with muted enthusiasm, resuming dunking socks. She was already fretting her husband might show her up during the new boyfriend's visit. Eddie Finch could find fault with most people, and to their face, if he was feeling particularly churlish.

Nick hadn't said any more about meeting her parents but Kathy knew she owed him the courtesy of an introduction before long. She had a feeling he might tell her soon that he loved her and she knew she'd fallen for him. She'd been in two minds whether to question him about the lorry hijacking that had happened when he worked for Wes Silver. She should know all about the man she hoped to spend her life with . . . even if some of his past wasn't to her liking. In return he had every right to know about the shameful behaviour of her relatives and she could only hope the truth wouldn't scare him off . . .

Kathy's mind immediately turned to Jennifer. She toyed with her empty cup, brooding on whether to mention to her mum that her sister was carrying Winnie's first grandchild. Jenny had said she didn't want their parents informed, but Kathy knew for certain that her twin yearned to be reconciled with their mother. She hoped her sister had given up on the idea of trying to abort the baby. The moment she'd seen Jennifer's knitting, she'd been relieved that her twin seemed resigned to motherhood.

Without doubt, Jennifer's pregnancy was another calamity to add to those that had gone before. But, in an odd way, the news of a baby – even one born out of wedlock – might melt Winnie's icy heart where Jennifer was concerned. Whether her mother would yet feel able to tell Eddie about their grandchild was another matter. At some time in the future, news that Jennifer Finch had been spotted pushing a pram might leak out. Kathy knew Winnie would sooner hear the scandal from her own daughter than from a neighbour.

Still Kathy hesitated on mentioning the matter. She estimated that her sister was about four months gone. There was still a long way to go and a natural miscarriage could yet occur. She couldn't deny such a solution would be best for all concerned in the circumstances.

As Winnie started wringing out her washing, Kathy said cheerfully, 'Best be off then, Mum, and call round Matilda's before I head for home.'

'Reckernise him, do you?' Charlie had twisted a fist into his wife's tangled brown hair and was forcing her head against the windowpane. 'I reckon he knows you, don't he, gel? Hanging about waiting for you, is he?' Charlie shook Ruby as though he had a kitten by the neck. 'Course, now he's had a butcher's at your ugly mug, he might scarper sharpish.' Charlie shouted a raucous laugh.

'Don't know him . . . never seen him before,' Ruby gasped out. Any effort to talk was agony. Her lips were cut and her left eye puffed up to a slit from the battering her husband had given her the evening after he'd forced her home with him.

But he'd not cowed her. She'd lied to Charlie a moment ago. She couldn't see well enough out of her blurry vision to say for sure if the foreigner was Paul's father. But he had Yan's slight stature and long black hair, and that gave Ruby the faintest of hope that he had come back, as he'd promised he would.

'All look the bleedin' same, don't they, them Chinks?' Charlie dragged Ruby back into the room, shoving her away from him. 'Perhaps he heard you've had his kid and he wants it.' He picked up his donkey jacket from the chair. 'Go and ask him, shall I?'

Ruby tried to outrun her husband to the pram but Charlie knocked her sideways before she could throw herself over the baby and prevent him picking Paul up. 'Perhaps he'll offer me a few quid for the little bastard.' He stuck the howling baby under an arm as though he was so much useless baggage. 'I'd give the little bleeder away free but I ain't turning down a payday. Pikies buy 'em and use 'em as labour. Perhaps the Chinese do 'n' all. Boys can do hard graft as they grow.'

'Put him back in his pram, Charlie,' Ruby pleaded from her crouching position on the floor. 'Please put him back,' she begged. 'He's just a baby, leave him alone. It's me you've got it in for. Please, Charlie . . .' She crawled on her knees towards him.

'Now that's better,' Charlie crowed. 'Seems I'm learnin' you yer duty at last.' He sauntered towards Ruby, Paul screaming under his arm, his tiny face bright red in distress. 'Catch . . .' He carelessly dropped the child through the air onto his wife's lap.

Greedily, Ruby pressed the baby's face to her own, whispering against his skin to soothe him.

At the door, Charlie turned around, his lips thin and vicious. 'If that Chink's still out there hanging around when I get back, I'm gonna ask him a few questions, and if I don't like the answers, you'll pay, and so will he.' He raised a fist, looking at it while shaking it. 'Don't think about running off, will you, Ruby. You know I'll find you just like I did before. Next time, I'll put you in the ground and you won't want me alone with the foreigner's brat, will you, when yer gone?'

'Ruby's a grown woman, Kath. You've got to leave her be now 'cos you've given all the help you can.' Nick drew Kathy into a tight embrace, rubbing her back in comfort as she sobbed.

'I've not helped!' Kathy gurgled, wiping her eyes with the heel of a hand. 'I've just made things worse. I was wrong to interfere.'

'No . . . don't think that! You were right to try to keep the family safe.' Privately, Nick believed Kathy had reason to fear Ruby's lot had worsened the moment she and the kids took off to Islington. Charlie Potter was a vindictive bully and would believe it his prerogative to knock obedience and loyalty into his wife now he'd defeated her escape.

'You told me to leave well alone. But I wouldn't listen. I was stupid and arrogant poking my nose in, thinking

I knew best and making you help too. You must think me a fool . . .' Kathy's voice was shrill with distress.

'Hush . . . I'm proud of you, Kath.' Nick smoothed a tender hand over her tear-stained face. 'I was glad to help. You didn't talk me into it. You just had more courage than me from the start when it came to protecting the family.'

'Peter is trying to put on a brave face but Pansy is so upset without her mum and her baby brother.' Kathy wiped her nose. 'Matilda tries her best to keep them cheerful but they know that something bad's happened . . .' Her words tailed off into a hiccoughing sob.

'Something bad was happening before you got involved, sweetheart,' Nick soothed. 'That bastard Potter needs sorting out once and for all.'

Kathy's wet eyes sprang to Nick's face. 'Don't you go after him, will you?' she whispered. 'If you beat him up again he'll just take it out on Ruby as soon as he gets home.'

'I'm not gonna do anything to make things worse, swear,' Nick vowed softly.

'I wanted them all to have a chance of being happy together, yet all I've done is split the family up.'

'Pansy and Peter are in the best place, staying with Matilda.'

Kathy nodded agreement, but they both knew what Nick had left unsaid: the two older children might be safe but Ruby and baby Paul were again at the mercy of a brute who resented and wanted to punish them.

'Make a cup of tea, shall I?' Nick offered, using his thumbs to dry Kathy's cheeks.

Kathy gave him a grateful smile and sank down on the sofa. She'd got home from Islington just an hour

351

ago. After leaving her mother's house, she'd hurried to see Matilda, anticipating hearing news about Ruby's job and how the children were settling in. Peter had already started school in the area and Kathy had intended broaching the subject of Pansy joining him at Pooles Park, the school she'd attended as a child.

The moment Kathy glimpsed Matilda's face she'd known something awful had occurred, and not just from seeing the woman's complexion was bruised. Without self-pity, Matilda had told Kathy how she'd come by the injuries. She'd added that following the fracas in the street she'd been unable to persuade Ruby to send her husband and his mother packing and stay with her in Campbell Road.

Matilda's philosophy had been much the same as Nick's: Ruby's future was hers to decide and all they could do was promise her help if she wanted it.

'I want to go and see Ruby and make sure she's all right.' Kathy blinked in despair at the ceiling. 'That's a stupid thing to say – of course she's *not* all right – she never will be while she's with him.' Kathy's sadness was being subdued by frustration and anger.

Nick stepped out of the kitchenette, opening a packet of cigarettes. 'Potter will be keeping a close eye on her now. You won't catch Ruby on her own as often as you used to.' He lit the cigarette, drawing deeply on it. 'I heard from my father-in-law that Blanche has finished with Charlie. So that's another reason he might be hanging around indoors more than normal. Promise me that if you're planning on going there you'll tell me so I can come with you.'

Kathy bit her lip.

'Promise me, Kath,' Nick insisted.

'Shall we go tomorrow?' Kathy gazed at him pleadingly. 'I just want to see Ruby and let her know we're still around, keeping an eye on her, ready if she needs us. I won't suggest she leaves him again, I swear.'

'Yeah, we'll do that. If you can get an hour off I'll come over about two o'clock. Potter should still be at work at that time.'

'Mrs Castell is overdue but I'll tell Eunice an urgent private matter's cropped up and she'll have to cover for me if a midwife's needed while I'm out.' Kathy stood up and went to slide her arms about Nick. She closed her eyes, revelling in the warm smoky scent of him as he embraced her. 'Thanks . . . I know you understand 'cos you helped bring Paul into the world, didn't you?' She nestled closer on feeling his mouth warming her forehead.

'Oh, you're back,' Eunice garbled breathlessly. She rushed along the path to meet Kathy, bursting with her news. First, she asked, 'Has Mrs Castell had her baby?'

'Safely delivered,' Kathy announced with a weary smile. 'A little boy, seven pounds eight ounces, and mother and father are delighted . . .'

'Sidney's out . . . an emergency . . . we've had a laying over reported by a mother a couple of hours ago.' Eunice stared sympathetically at Kathy. 'One of your deliveries actually . . . the Potter baby . . . a boy about seven months old.'

Kathy felt her legs weaken. 'Paul Potter?' she whispered. 'What do you mean . . . the baby's poorly?'

'I'm afraid he's dead. Sidney's just been on the telephone. The protesters against the Fascists' march are out in force, making driving difficult 'cos the roads are jammed with police and people, but he's taken the child to hospital. It's just a formality anyhow; there's no hope.'

Kathy's fingers froze on the handlebars of her bike. She felt her head swim and quickly let the bike fall and steadied herself against the shed. 'Are you sure? I was going to see Mrs Potter this afternoon. Are you sure?' Kathy suddenly shouted hysterically.

'Are you all right, Kathy?'

Eunice's concerned features wavered in front of Kathy's eyes.

'You've gone terribly pale. Do you want to sit down? Come inside and I'll fetch you a glass of water . . .'

Kathy snatched herself from Eunice's motherly clasp, acting uncharacteristically churlish. Forcing back her sleeve, she focused on her wristwatch. It was one thirty and Nick was due to come over at two.

She'd been called out at ten o'clock last night to deliver the baby. Everything had gone as it should for Mrs Castell. Kathy had left the happy couple and come back feeling exhausted but elated that they had their longed for family. She'd been sure that it was an auspicious start to the day and she and Nick would go and find Ruby no worse than she had been before making the move to Campbell Road.

'I know it's a dreadful shock to hear such a thing.' Eunice put a comforting arm about Kathy. 'You were fond of the family, weren't you, although they were a rough lot.' She sighed. 'Sidney said that Mrs Potter was in a bad way. Some of those navvies treat their women worse than dogs. They're like animals; but losing a child is a tragedy nonetheless.'

Eunice was being diplomatic. In fact, she suspected, as had her husband, that it might not be a coincidence that a baby was accidentally smothered in bed at around the same time that the mother was beaten. Sidney had said the boy looked unharmed but a post-mortem would be needed to establish the truth.

'Did Dr Worth say if Paul looked injured?' Kathy whispered, her thoughts tracking Eunice's.

'He didn't see any obvious damage,' Eunice replied carefully. 'There'll be an inquest, of course. The father wasn't about for Sidney to question him.'

'I don't suppose he was,' Kathy ejected through gritted teeth. 'I expect he made sure to be absent. I hope the evil swine rots in hell,' she choked.

CHAPTER THIRTY-THREE

Jennifer rolled onto her back with her knees drawn into her aching belly. 'Mum . . .' she whimpered. 'Mum!' she shouted when the searing pain became unbearable. 'You bitch . . . why won't you help me . . . Mum . . .?' Her voice tailed off into a hiccuping sob and she swayed to and fro on the mattress, a blanket held up to her face to try to muffle her cries. Even in her agonised state, she remembered to be quiet because the nosy cow next door might have her ear pressed to the wall.

Her fingers touched the wadding between her legs, then recoiled from the soaked rags. It'll stop soon, she whispered to herself. The bulk of her miscarriage had gone down the outside privy hours ago, and Jennifer had staggered in and poured a measure of whisky, feeling relieved and optimistic that the worst was over. A short while later, lying on the sofa dozing, she wasn't feeling so chipper when a spasm in her abdomen made her jack-knife. She'd dragged herself into her bedroom, taking the Scotch with her, feeling sure that a proper sleep would sort her out. After an hour of tossing and turning, she'd found the energy to wriggle out of her blood-soaked skirt, and just in her slip, had comfortingly cocooned herself in a sheet. As the pain subsided, Jenny held her breath, hoping to keep it at bay with willpower. She rocked onto her side, grabbed at the whisky and upended the bottle against her mouth. With each greedy swallow she savoured the burn in her throat and the soothing muzz in her head. She slid her hand beneath the pillow, snuggling her cheek into it. But it withdrew immediately having touched the instruments of her self-inflicted torture. Hesitantly, her fingers crept back to withdraw cold metal and the sight of the blood-stained knitting needles made unbearable pain again rip her guts.

'What in damnation's going on in there?'

Dot Pearson gave her mother-in-law an old-fashioned look as the older woman thumped on the wall that separated her house from Jennifer Finch's. 'I'll give you two guesses, Ma,' Dot said sourly. 'Could be Miss Finch is overexerting herself doin' her housework, or could be she's overexcited earning herself a few bob. And as she's the local scrubber, won't be putting no odds on which it is.'

'Bleedin' hell!' Marge Pearson breathed, coming to reseat herself at the table. 'Sounds like she's bein' murdered.'

'Wishful thinking, that is, Ma,' Dot muttered, getting up to slam the kettle on the hob. 'Been saying to your son fer months, I can't stand no more of living next to that slag in there. But does he listen?' Dot snorted contempt. 'It's time we moved somewhere better, I've told him . . .' Dot's further complaints were drowned out by a sudden high-pitched scream.

'Don't care how good an actress she is, that ain't a

woman having sex,' Marge said, pushing to her feet. 'She's in trouble, Dot, take it from me.'

Dot chewed at her lower lip. She had to admit she'd never before heard the like coming out of Jenny Finch's. She stared at her mother-in-law. 'D'you reckon she's got a wrong 'un in there with her, beating her up? Ain't gonna call the police out and get on the wrong side of her if it ain't nuthin' . . .'

'Go take a look through her winder, Dot; your eyes are younger 'n' mine,' Marge suggested.

Dot nodded, and the two women trotted into the street. Having ducked to and fro peering through the dirty net covering the glass, Dot straightened. 'She's in there on her own on the bed, far as I can tell.' She spontaneously rapped against the glass and put her lips to the casement. 'You need anything in there?'

A wail met the offer of help.

'Reckon that was a yes,' Marge whispered in shock.

Dot rushed to the door and thrust a hand through the letter box pulling out the key dangling on a string, in the way she'd seen Jennifer's sister do in the past.

'I'll go up the shop and call for an ambulance.' Marge croaked, having taken one look at the awful sight. She knew an emergency when she saw one.

Dot hurried to the bed and gently pushed down on Jennifer's shoulders as she tried to struggle to sit up and wave them out. 'Don't you worry . . . gonna get some help . . . be right as rain, won't yer now . . .' Dot lilted. She barely recognised the ghostly face with huge staring eyes. As Jennifer's lids fluttered shut, Dot guessed she'd fallen into unconsciousness. Dot's glance darted to the knitting needles enclosed limp in one of Jennifer's hands.

Carefully, she removed them. 'Get rid of them then,

shall we?' she murmured, easing the needles from Jenny's cold bloodied fingers. She pulled the blanket up over Jennifer, hoping it might keep her warm till the ambulancemen arrived.

'Ruby . . . will you look at me?' Kathy took the woman's icy face in her trembling fingers, gently turning her chin. Ruby's left profile was swollen and her single-eyed stare met Kathy's wide searching gaze. 'Did your husband smother Paul?' Kathy whispered.

Ruby turned her face to the wall. Since Kathy and Nick had arrived, the woman hadn't uttered a word to them. She seemed to be in shock, as well she might, considering the enormity of her suffering. In a short space of time, Ruby had escaped her sadistic husband, been recaptured and brutalised, and lost her baby son.

Stiffly, Kathy rose from where she'd been crouching by the bed. They'd arrived to find Ruby lying on it, her poor battered features buried in a pillow. For some time, Kathy had been trying to coax an explanation for the tragedy from Ruby but she seemed unwilling or unable to answer questions.

'Perhaps if you wait outside, Ruby might open up to me,' Kathy murmured to Nick.

He nodded, rubbing a hand on his jaw, unsure how to comfort either the bereaved mother or the woman he loved.

'Woss going on?' Charlie stormed into the room from outside. He'd turned the corner expecting to see the loitering Chinaman, but it had been Nick Raven's flash car and his door standing ajar that had fixed an evil scowl on his face. The knot of women staring and gossiping had put the wind up him too so he'd immediately pelted headlong into the house, believing Ruby was plotting to take flight again. He slung a glance between the interlopers, then his eyes pounced on his wife's figure curled on the bed.

'What the fuck you playin' at now, Ruby?' He strode up to her, fists clenching. 'You lazy cow, shift yer arse. What these two doing here? You been blabbin' and ready to stir up more trouble?'

'Go for her again and it'll be the last thing you do.' Nick was immediately beside Charlie at the bed.

Furiously, Charlie elbowed Nick aside so he could tip his wife off the mattress but he'd barely touched Ruby's shoulder when he was punched to the floor. Nick hauled Charlie to his feet and flung him down on the armchair. 'Just sit there and you'll be all right till the police get here.'

'*Police?*' Charlie sprang up. 'What you on about?' He sneered at Ruby, fingering the blood on his lip. 'You've got nuthin' on me. She's me wife and I've every right to discipline the bitch after what she's done. Out searchin' for her and me kids fer weeks, I was. She'd no right to run off like that.'

'You'd left her no choice. And what about Paul?' Kathy asked calmly. 'What right had you to hurt him?'

'Dunno what you're talkin' about, Nurse Finch.' He started towards her menacingly. 'But I do know we was rubbin' along all right till you started poking yer nose in where it weren't wanted. It was you geeing Ruby up from the start.'

Nick spun Charlie around by a shoulder before he could get within arm's reach of Kathy. He ducked as Charlie swung at him but Potter's next tactic was a feint followed by a crafty low blow. Nick folded over but managed to shift out of harm's way, leaving Charlie boxing air.

'Been needing to get you back fer a while, Raven. Reckoned you had me before, did yer?' Charlie leaped after the younger man but Nick jerked upright and nutted him, sending Charlie crashing onto his back.

Kathy's hoarse protest made Nick hesitate then return to the floor the foot he'd got aimed at Potter's ribs.

Breathing heavily, Nick pivoted to the bed to see if the violence had affected Ruby. She hadn't spoken or moved during the brawl.

Charlie dragged himself onto his knees. 'Too quiet in here. Where's the kid, Ruby?'

'As if you didn't know,' Nick snarled.

Charlie struggled to his feet. 'Eh?' He shuffled towards the empty pram and stared in at rumpled blankets. 'You fuckin' whore!' He bounded to the bed but when Nick moved with him he tensed, glaring at Ruby. 'You given the boy to his father?' He sounded outraged. 'You done a deal behind me back? You've had that Chinaman in here while I was out, ain't yer?' He swung around to Nick. 'Been hanging around outside, he has. Tell 'em, go on, that yer fancy man's been back.'

'Dr Worth has taken Paul to hospital. The baby was suffocated.' Kathy frowned. Either Charlie hadn't known about the tragedy or he was a good actor.

Charlie licked his lips. 'It's an accident then. Ain't nuthin' to do with me. She had him in bed with us in the early hours but he was snufflin' 'n' whining as usual. I heard him.' He grunted in sudden enlightenment. 'Ain't a layin' over! I reckon the Chink didn't take to his kid after all and stuck a pillow on the blighter's head. Ask *her* what's gone on.' Charlie wagged a finger at his wife.

Kathy and Nick exchanged a quizzical look. Again, Potter's version sounded reasonable.

'Thought you'd pin it on me, is that it?' Charlie had hit on the peril in the situation. 'Thought you'd get me to swing fer it, didn't yer, so you could take up with the foreigner?' He barked a laugh but his eyes were shifting to and fro and he suddenly bolted for the door, punching Nick in the shoulder to give himself time to escape.

Kathy rushed to Nick as he steadied himself against the wall. 'Are you hurt?'

'Nah . . .' Nick brushed down his clothes. 'Not sure if he's lying about the Chinese bloke or not.' He glanced at the bed. Ruby might have been asleep; she hadn't shifted an inch or reacted to any of her husband's violent accusations.

'Wait outside and I'll try and get her to talk to me.'

Nick touched Kathy's cheek, a tiny smile displaying his agreement.

'Pansy needs you, Ruby,' Kathy said softly, kneeling again by the side of the bed. She took Ruby's stiff fingers between her own. 'Matilda's looking after them well, but you know Pansy wants her mum. I saw her just a few days ago and she's missing you like mad.'

Ruby's eyelids flickered and a tear squeezed through her lashes, trailed to the side of her nose.

'Did Paul's father come here to see you?'

Ruby moved her shoulders in a vague shrug.

Kathy moistened her lips. 'Did he hurt Paul?'

'No . . .' Ruby formed the word with her lips rather than uttering it. 'I had to do it. Had to . . . there was no other way to keep him safe.' Ruby dried her face by turning it into the pillow. 'Did it kindly, see, no pain. Couldn't be sure that Charlie wouldn't torment him if

I wasn't around. Didn't see no other way . . . do you understand, Nurse Finch?' Ruby blinked open her good eye.

'Yes . . . I understand . . .' Kathy finally forced out through the tears pulsating pain into her throat.

Very slowly, Kathy got to her feet, feeling too drained of energy and emotion to loath Charlie for driving his wife to infanticide. At that moment, Kathy felt piercing sorrow but surprise was absent. In Ruby's place, tortured in mind and body, she might have made the same choice to protect a beloved baby from pain.

'Will you tell?' Ruby murmured.

'No . . . I won't tell.' Kathy's vow was barely audible.

'And your fellow outside?'

'He won't tell either,' Kathy said, and almost smiled, so strong was her certainty that the birth and death of a baby boy would be a bond between her and Nick as strong and enduring as their love.

'I'll be better by the morning,' Ruby whispered. 'I'll go over and see the kids tomorrow. Charlie'll calm down now Paul's gone. It'll get better . . .'

Kathy tidied the straggling hair back from Ruby's grazed cheek, tucking it behind her ear, then went outside to find Nick.

'There's no proof that it is anything but a tragic accident.' Dr Worth tapped his mouth with a forefinger, looking at Ruby Potter, still as death on the bed. He had returned from the hospital to check on the grieving mother and found Nurse Finch and Nick Raven at Ruby's house. 'Wretched women take desperate measures with unwanted children, but she is obviously traumatised by her loss rather than relieved.' He shook his head.

'Heaven knows she *is* a poor wretch. Her husband deserves prison for what he's done to her.' Sidney sighed in frustration. 'All her injuries are trips and falls, so she says. It's the way these women are: constantly lying and covering up for their attackers.' He glanced at Nick. 'I'm glad you were here with Nurse Finch. Has Potter been back?'

'Not for long. He scarpered almost immediately,' Nick answered succinctly.

'He must know suspicion will fall on him as he's a renowned thug, and obviously not the dead child's natural father.'

'Was Paul otherwise harmed?' Kathy asked quietly.

'Nothing obvious at all other than teething rash. He seemed small but healthy. Have you managed to get anything out of the mother?' Dr Worth's enquiring gaze fell on Kathy.

'Before he left, Mr Potter confirmed that his wife brought the baby into bed and he heard Paul snuffling.' While giving her careful reply, Kathy kept her eyes steadily on Ruby.

Nick was delving into his pockets for his cigarettes. He lit one while propped against the doorjamb, blowing smoke into the hallway. Kathy knew why he'd distanced himself even if Dr Worth did not. Nick was avoiding answering questions. In the short space of time between Ruby's confession and Sidney's arrival she'd confided in Nick the heartbreaking secret. But Dr Worth seemed satisfied drawing his own conclusions.

'The boy might have been congested cutting his teeth and having trouble breathing.' Sidney paused. 'I'll see if Mrs Potter would like a sleeping draught before I leave. I doubt she will. She didn't want me to fetch a neighbour to sit with her earlier.' He frowned at Ruby's turned back. 'She just wants to be left alone, so she said.'

'Perhaps Mrs Potter knows best.' Kathy knew that Ruby would rally despite her enervating grief. The woman had said she'd be better by tomorrow and Kathy believed she would be, because Pansy and Peter needed her. Ruby's love and duty to her remaining children would make her strong again. Instinctively the anguished mother understood that she needed silence and solitude to heal. Now Charlie had gone – and Kathy doubted he'd show his face for some days – she trusted that Ruby would recover if left alone.

'Would you mind if we drove to my sister's place before heading back to the surgery?'

They'd come out of Ruby's, leaving Dr Worth with his patient. As he got into the car Nick shot Kathy a surprised look. She seemed shattered and he'd guessed she'd want to go straight home. 'No, I don't mind, but it's not going to be easy getting through.' He frowned as Kathy settled beside him.

The Fascist march through the East End had drawn huge numbers of protesters and snarled up roads around the Royal Mint, making them impassable. Police were directing traffic away from the area around Cable Street and sending them into congested side roads.

'Something urgent you need to see her about, is it?' Nick asked, turning the corner into Christian Street.

Kathy had closed her eyes, feeling peculiarly peaceful as though she'd cried too hard and too long and was beyond exhaustion. Yet she'd not shed a tear. She roused herself in the seat, rubbing at her goose-pimply arms, although she was sure she wasn't chilled.

'I just want to see her, today.' Kathy sounded apologetic, giving him an appealing smile.

Nick swore beneath his breath as a mounted policeman clattered in front of the car, making him brake suddenly. 'This is gonna turn nasty, by the looks of it.' He pulled the car to the kerb. 'I'll try another route to the High Street.'

'Sorry . . .' Kathy murmured, yet still felt unable to tell him to abandon the trip to Jennifer's. 'It's worse chaos than earlier when we came the other way . . .' Her remark tailed away as she watched a few bobbies racing to separate fighting men. Elsewhere, people were stacking up furniture in the middle of the road to form a barricade as though a full-scale battle might erupt. 'If David were still around he'd be in the thick of it,' Kathy said as she saw a policeman knocked to the ground. It was the first time she'd thought or spoken about him in some days.

Nick manoeuvred the vehicle carefully, scowling as people banged on the roof in annoyance as he inched forward into their path.

Kathy craned her neck, feeling alarmed as she peered through the throng to see what was going on up ahead. She glimpsed pipe and drum band members kitted out in black-shirted uniform. Mosley's supporters – women were much in evidence, as were the youth cadets – were carrying Union flags and banners bearing the Fascist colours. They looked very smart and well organised, and Kathy realised the police were trying to protect them from the throng of demonstrators rather than disperse the parade.

Eventually, Kathy and Nick reached Mare Street, but, instead of being relieved on reaching their destination,

Kathy felt a jolt of fear. The sight greeting them was eerily reminiscent of what they'd met outside Ruby's house earlier. A group of women were congregated on the pavement close to her sister's front door. They stared as Nick's car drew to a halt.

'Shall I come in or wait here?' Nick asked.

Kathy could tell he also sensed something was amiss. 'Let me see what's going on.' She attempted a smile, getting out.

As she approached Jenny's neighbours, Dot Pearson fiddled with the scarf knotted on top of her head, looking uncomfortable. The other women shuffled into a wider circle, arms crossed over pinafores, leaving Dot as spokeswoman.

'She ain't in,' Dot informed quietly. 'I went in to her, 'cos me and me mother-in-law could hear her crying out. Poor cow was too bad to manage getting help for herself.' Dot jerked her head at the top of the road. 'Rung fer an ambulance from the shop up there. It come and took her about an hour ago.'

'Ambulance?' Kathy breathed. 'What for?' She feared she knew but didn't want to broadcast her sister's condition to anybody in case something else had caused the emergency. Jennifer was still slim and her pregnancy unnoticeable at first glance.

'Haemorrhaging badly, she were.' Dot's tone was sympathetic rather than sly. 'Suspected miscarriage, ambulance man said; they've taken her to Bethnal Green hospital.' She'd lowered her voice respectfully, although it was obvious to Kathy all the neighbours knew what had gone on. 'Your sister was in and out of consciousness but I promised her 'fore they took her away that I'd let you know all about it when you happened by.'

'How long ago, did you say?' Kathy asked, feeling dizzy with anxiety.

'Good hour or so.' Dot suddenly patted her arm. 'Be all right she will . . . young 'n' strong, ain't she? Want a hand clearing up?' Dot tipped her head towards Jennifer's front door.

It took a moment for Kathy to understand the woman's offer of help, then she shook her head. 'Thanks anyway . . . but I'll manage . . .' Kathy's first instinct was to fly to her sister's side rather than sort bloodied sheets for washing.

'Right you are . . . but if you change yer mind just bang on me door.' Dot headed towards home, raising a hand to her cronies. She'd told them most of what had gone on, but not about the knitting needles. Dot had two children but she'd been pregnant three times. Two children were all she was having till her husband agreed to move them out of this dump and somewhere better. Then this afternoon she'd learned that her and Jennifer Finch had more in common than she knew, so she didn't regret for one moment throwing the knitting needles in the dustbin before the ambulance had turned up. Wasn't the first time she'd done that, after all . . .

Dot disappeared inside her house and, aware no more gossip was to be had with the invalid's family present, the other women dispersed.

Kathy got back into the car, too distressed to speak immediately.

'What's happened?' Nick enquired softly.

'My sister's been taken to hospital . . . a miscarriage,' she blurted.

'Do you want to go and see her?' Nick suggested gently.

Kathy nodded fiercely, keeping her face lowered towards her lap. But her shoulders started shaking with huge silent sobs.

Nick drew her into his arms. 'Never rains but it pours,' he murmured against her hair, soothing her with stroking fingers.

'I can't stand any more . . . I can't! Why all today? Why this as well today?' Kathy keened against his shoulder.

''Cos tomorrow's gonna make up fer it.' Nick murmured comfort against her moist cheek. 'You'll see, Kath . . . it's all gonna come right for us tomorrow.'

CHAPTER THIRTY-FOUR

Charlie hung back in the shadows till he saw Beverly saunter out of the dockside pub. He swore beneath his breath in thankfulness. Under normal circumstances, he'd have strutted inside and straight up to the bar to find her, but following the recent uproar at his place he couldn't be sure the coppers weren't out with a warrant for his arrest. His haunts were well known so he was keeping his head down in case he'd been falsely accused of murdering Ruby's brat. Charlie was incensed that suspicion would naturally fall on him. He'd never clumped the boy, much as he'd been tempted to every time he looked in the pram at that sallow face.

He didn't want an inquisition from people who'd seen Ruby's bruises and so judged him a baby-killer. As far as Charlie was concerned, he'd been entitled to teach his wife a lesson for leading him a merry dance. Ruby was numb with shock at losing the kid but she might be the first to point the finger once she perked up. Charlie knew she was his alibi and if she lied to frame him he'd take her down with him, one way or the other . . .

370

The Chinese weren't a rare sight in London by any means, but Charlie reckoned that the fellow he'd seen was Ruby's boyfriend. His bowels clenched in possessive jealousy. It was possible Ruby had invited the Chink in to introduce him to his kid while he was out earlier. If they'd argued the foreigner might have turned on the bastard he'd left behind on his last visit.

Ruby idolised her children and no man would ever compete with them in her heart. If the boyfriend had done it, Ruby would be screaming blue murder to the police; instead, she seemed to be blaming herself. So perhaps it had been an accidental laying over like Nurse Finch had said.

Charlie's expression turned vicious on thinking about that prissy little bitch. He knew she had been stirring things up for him; but he hadn't known until it was too late that Nurse Finch and Nick Raven were so close. He hadn't finished with Raven, and Charlie made a solemn vow that first chance he got he'd pay the bastard back for again making him look a berk in front of his own wife . . .

Charlie was startled from his rumination by the sound of cats fighting close by. He slung a look over a shoulder, slinking further under the dripping brick arch, then peered into darkness to see if the noise had disturbed Beverly. She was still smoking and slouching.

The sudden yowling had set Charlie's heart racing and he knew he was jittery and must calm down. He needed a good few ales inside him, and Beverly under him all night long.

He peered into the dusk, watching the tart glancing to and fro, cigarette clamped in her mean mouth. A short fat fellow stumbled drunkenly off the pavement and Beverly strolled up to him. He pushed her back, then weaved on his way, oblivious to the two fingers she'd stuck up close to his head. Resting her rear against the wall, Beverly looked resigned to waiting for another likely punter. Charlie wanted it to be him and was ready to reveal himself.

The fat fellow looked like he'd had a change of heart. He turned around and barked something indistinct, but Beverly seemed to understand him and eagerly trotted over.

Fired up with frustration, Charlie reckoned he'd have to take it out on somebody or drive himself nuts. He swore beneath his breath, ambling off towards his mother's house. He didn't want anybody to spot him and know his whereabouts, but he'd trust Vi with his life . . . Charlie's brooding was interrupted by the sight of a motorcar purring around the corner. He turned his face to the wall and, almost level with a shop doorway dived into it, out of sight.

The last person he wanted to see was Nick Raven. Charlie knew he'd drag him to the police station, and laugh while he was doing it. Charlie hovered in his shelter, gazing from beneath his brows but the car didn't disappear; it slowed down then parked up on the opposite side of the road by a house sporting an estate agent's board. From his hidy-hole, Charlie watched Nick get out of the car, then heard a set of keys jangling. A moment later, he watched a weak light come on in the hallway before Raven closed the door. Charlie pursed his lips, a foxy twist to his mouth. Glancing to and fro, he reassured himself nobody was about . . . nobody had seen him . . . not even Beverly, and there might never be a better opportunity to take the flash git by surprise.

It had started to drizzle and Charlie turned up his coat collar, gazing left and right. He'd had enough of lurking in the shop doorway and wondered if Nick was in there for the night. He lit a cigarette and shuffled impatiently. He'd give it a few more minutes then get on his way. He stroked the blade in his pocket. He'd been carrying it with him ever since he'd gone on the run. A noise alerted him to his quarry's reappearance and Charlie felt sweat soaking his forehead and his heart pumping with excitement.

After he'd seen to Raven, he'd go and give Beverly another try. Her room in Poplar was a shithole but Charlie didn't care; he'd bunk there with her willingly until things had died down and he could go home.

Charlie crept forward, knife in hand. If he were to swing for a murder it might as well be this one, was his philosophy. Aware he was within striking distance of Raven's spine, he tilted back his head to take one celebratory drag on his cigarette, blowing smoke skywards, barely aware of a shadow closing in behind. He hardly felt the blade slip across his throat either, or the hand diving into his pocket, and crumpled quite gracefully to the ground.

Nick swung about at the thud, preparing to defend himself because he'd glimpsed a moving figure. A slim dark-haired man politely inclined his head in a way that seemed to Nick distinctly oriental. The next moment, the fellow had melted away into darkness.

Crouching down, Nick tilted his face to see the dead man's features although he'd already guessed his identity, and that he'd been Potter's intended victim. He'd noticed the knife gripped in Charlie's fingers but suddenly withdrew his hand without touching it.

'Fucking hell, Charlie, bet you never saw that

coming . . .' Nick muttered, straightening slowly. 'Well . . . don't know his name, although I reckon Ruby does . . . but I do know I owe him a drink. What do you reckon, mate?' He shook his head at Charlie's corpse, allowing himself a grim smile, then quickly got into his car and drove away.

'You speak good English.'

'I know, sir.'

Wes studied the fellow, thinking for a Chinaman he was good-looking, all cheekbones and shiny black hair. He was polite too. Wes had liked that about him last time they'd spoken. Not that much had been said apart from essentials. He'd no more desire for a social conversation now.

'It's done.'

'Proof?'

The Chinese man held out a wallet.

Wes took it, fingered the worn brown leather before dropping it in a pocket. He didn't need to look inside for Charlie's union card to recognise it as his.

'Put him out of action for a while, have you?'

'He won't be bothering anybody.'

Wes thought there was something quite sinister in the young man's Mona Lisa smile. He pulled cash from his inside pocket and held it out.

In an instant, the money was gone and so was the Chinaman.

Wes hesitated beneath the gas lamp instead of turning directly for home. He snapped himself out of his odd mood. Charlie had deserved to be put in his place. It might teach him not to blackmail him – even slyly. Nobody went against Wes Silver and got away with it . . .

374

Wes plunged his hands into his pockets and turned to walk back towards the spot where he'd parked his car. Idly, he wondered if Charlie had caught a glimpse of his assailant's slitted eyes before he hit the deck. He knew Charlie hated the Chinese, and with good reason.

'Now that's a joke, Charlie . . .' Wes said softly. 'And I do hope *you* saw the funny side of it . . .'

EPILOGUE

Two Weeks Later

'Somebody outside wants to see you.'

Jennifer glanced up from her magazine, open on the starched coverlet. 'Not brought Dot in to see me, have you, Kath?' she enquired in a sarky tone that gladdened her sister's heart. Despite her pallor, the old Jennifer was fast reappearing, making Kathy certain her twin was well on the road to recovery.

Kathy had only moments ago arrived on the ward and now perched on the chair by her sister's bed. 'It's not Dot; but that woman has been a diamond and she sends you her best, as always.'

'Probably just being nice so she can have all the gory details when I get home,' Jenny grumbled.

'Mum's outside.' Kathy's eyes glistened as a poignant mixture of hope and disbelief lit Jenny's expression. Her twin's gaze had jumped to the entrance, anticipating Winnie's arrival.

'Mum's come to see me?' Jenny whispered in awe.

Kathy nodded. 'She's waiting outside; she wanted me to ask you if she could come in. I said you wouldn't mind but she insisted on having it from you. It's been such a long time . . . I expect she's composing herself.'

Jennifer smoothed her hair, as a child might in readiness for maternal inspection. 'Does she know . . . about everything?' Jenny's apprehensive eyes darted to her sister.

'She knows as much as me.' Kathy paused. 'Mum asked who the baby's father was . . . I didn't know what to say, Jen. She'll ask you the same question. She probably wants to hear he was a decent sort of boyfriend . . .'

'Well, he wasn't and he's not important, he never was.' Jenny agitatedly flicked closed the magazine, rubbed together her palms.

'Just thought I'd warn you that she'll ask about him,' Kathy soothed.

'He was a no-good two-timing bastard, that's all he was.'

Kathy smiled wryly. 'We'll all be glad to forget about him then,' she said cheerfully. 'Mum'll want to wring his neck, same as I do.' She patted her sister's hand. 'Ready?' At Jennifer's quick nod, Kathy stood up. 'I'll fetch her in.'

'Kath?'

Kathy turned back to her sister to see a peculiar expression on Jenny's face.

'I do love you, y'know, even though I don't show it. I know I'm a horrible cow. I want to be better . . . honest. So thanks for everything and I'm really sorry for what I've done.' Jenny swallowed, blinking back tears. 'I'm gonna be different now, Kath, swear I am. Ain't asked you to sneak me in a drink, have I? I'm done with it fer good . . . done with all of it. I know you've got every right to hate me, Kathy, the way I've behaved . . .' Jenny suddenly covered her face with her hands and started to sob.

Kathy stooped to hug her sister, kissing the top of her head. 'Don't be daft. You're my sister and I love you too, no matter what.'

'No matter what?' Jenny gasped, burrowing her head against Kathy and gripping her sister's arms tightly.

'No matter what!' Kathy said vehemently. She showed her sister two crossed fingers. 'Like that, you 'n' me, Jen, even before we were born.' She wiped her sister's tears. 'Always have been, always will be.'

'You're happy with Nick Raven, aren't you?'

Kathy nodded, her smile soft. 'Yeah . . . happier than I've ever been.'

Following all the recent commotion, she'd not found the right moment to broach the subject of the lorry hijack with Nick. With sudden clarity, Kathy realised she no longer cared to do so. Nick Raven might have made his luck through thieving but he was a good man now, who'd proved his worth many times over and, even if he weren't, Kathy knew she'd still love him and want to be with him. Dodgy deeds and shameful secrets might lurk in both their pasts but they were unimportant; they had the future to look forward to.

'You deserve him,' Jenny said. 'Can't wait to meet him. Find out if he's got a brother fer me.'

Kathy laughed, affectionately touching her sister's face. 'He's an only child, I'm afraid. Now buck up! I'm fetching Mum.' She waited for Jennifer's smile before setting off.

Kathy walked back past patients in iron beds holding low conversations with their visitors, feeling quietly content. When she'd told her parents the harrowing news that Jenny had nearly haemorrhaged to death following a miscarriage, they'd been devastated. Eddie had burst into tears; Winnie had gone green but, ever practical, had wanted to go straight to the hospital and take charge. She'd started getting into her coat, despite Kathy saying that the doctors wouldn't yet allow Jennifer any visitors. In a matter of minutes, the shock of almost losing a child had healed a rift of over five years' duration.

No mention had been made by anyone of whether the miscarriage had been self-induced. Kathy had tormented herself wondering whether her refusal to help Jennifer end the pregnancy had made her twin sink low enough to risk her life. Jennifer wasn't saying. And now she was on the mend, nobody was asking. But when Kathy had cleaned Jennifer's flat following her haemorrhage, she'd noticed the knitting, and the needles, had disappeared.

Kathy pushed open the door to see her mother prowling the corridor. Winnie caught sight of her and delved inside her shopping bag to check the contents, as she always did when nervous.

'Jenny wants to see you, Mum.'

Winnie sniffed, cleared her throat. 'Well, I want to see her too,' she said briskly in a way that peeled back years and reminded Kathy of the scoldings they'd get at home. 'I've got a few things to say to yer sister, I can tell you . . .'

Three Weeks Later

'Did you go to the funeral?'

'No . . . stayed well away. I let his mother deal with it all.' Ruby shifted her shopping from one hand to the other. 'I went to the cemetery when they'd all gone;

had a few things to get off me chest and say to Charlie. All done now so won't be going back there no more.' She gazed into the distance. 'If the kids want to go and see their father's resting place when they're older, I won't stop 'em. Peter's asked after him. Pansy knows he's gone but don't care to find out rather than won't ask.'

Kathy and Ruby were walking back from Smithy's shop in Campbell Road, having bought some milk and a twist of tea so they could sit and have a cuppa with Matilda. Kathy peered ahead to where Pansy was squatting on the kerb outside the Keivers' house. A small fair-haired girl was crouching beside her, holding out a skipping rope.

'I see Pansy's made a friend.'

'Yeah . . . met her at school,' Ruby explained.

'Pansy's going to school?' Kathy sounded delighted.

'Matilda thought Pooles Park might suit her, so that's where she's started. She looks forward to it,' Ruby said sheepishly. 'Peter goes there 'n' all, but he likes to play with his pals on the way home. Matilda picks Pansy up for me on afternoons I'm doing me cleaning job, and brings her in.' She paused. 'I always knew you was right; it's important Pansy learns her lessons. Want her to be clever and get a good job, like you.'

'You were worried she'd get bullied, though, weren't you?' Kathy said.

'No chance of that if Matilda's with her.' Ruby snorted in amusement. 'Pansy don't wanna talk, she don't have to, so far as Matilda's concerned. I reckon she'd clip the ear of anybody who'd got something different to say, including the teachers.'

'She's a forceful woman.' Kathy chuckled. 'And she's a wise woman . . . you did right to listen to her.'

'She's a wonderful woman,' Ruby said simply. 'Been the saving of me . . . and so have you . . .'

'It's good to hear you laugh, Ruby,' Kathy interrupted the woman's gruff gratitude. 'Will you go back to the East End when you feel up to it?'

Ruby shook her head, her expression determined. 'Nothing there fer me now, Nurse Finch. This is me home, this is where me family is . . . me new family. Me kids call Matilda "Auntie"; I like that.' She grimaced. 'I know the Bunk's a dump, but it's my kind of dump. Course, we can't live with Matilda for ever, though she says we're welcome to, and I reckon she means it. Want me own little place so we can spread out a bit. Now I've got me job back I can put a bit by in a kitty for rent on a couple o' rooms.' Her top lip curled in loathing. 'Never took to me mother-in-law and she never liked me, or the kids. Now she blames me for Charlie getting robbed and murdered 'cos he wouldn't have stayed out if he hadn't been upset over . . .' Ruby abruptly bit her lip, unable to utter the name of the little boy she'd loved and lost.

'Have the police caught who did it?'

Ruby shrugged. 'Only come to see me the once and the constable reckoned it was unlikely they'd find him. All the people comin' 'n' goin' on the boats and so on, he could be halfway round the world by now, he said.' Ruby's words faded away as a host of hateful memories flooded back. 'Not gonna pretend I didn't wish Charlie dead at times, but he was me husband and I wouldn't have wanted him to go like that.' She blinked back tears. 'But for it happening a few days sooner, I'd still have the little 'un. Me punishment, that is, for being wicked . . . and I'll torment meself over it every day of me life . . .'

'Hush . . .' Kathy put an arm around Ruby's shoulders, turning the woman to face her. 'Did Paul's father come to see you that day, Ruby?' The matter of the loitering Chinese fellow had been puzzling Kathy and it seemed the right time to solve it.

'Charlie wasn't lying . . . there was a foreigner outside for an hour or so; it might have been Yan . . .' Ruby nibbled her lip. 'Last time we spoke, he told me he'd come back for me and I believed him at the time. That's why I didn't do nuthin' when I found out I was pregnant with his baby. He was nice . . . gentle . . . spoke good English too.' She gave a bitter laugh. 'Six months later and no sign of him, I was having second thoughts. But it was too late then 'cos the baby was moving about and I couldn't do it. Anyway, I'm glad I didn't . . . I'm glad I had Paul . . . just for a little while . . .' Her voice tailed off into a choked sob.

Kathy embraced her in comfort.

'Anyway, with me eye being so swollen,' Ruby resumed gruffly, 'everything was blurry so I couldn't tell if I recognised the fellow outside. Charlie made me stand at the window so he probably got a good look at me all bashed up. Whoever he was, I never saw him hanging about in Fairclough Street again.'

Ruby raised a hand and waved to her daughter, who'd just spotted her. The child jumped up and tore towards her mother diving straight for her legs, burrowing into her skirt. 'Funny thing is, when I was over the cemetery with a posy for Paul – oh, his grave ain't nowhere near Charlie's, made sure o' that – there was a few flowers already laid down. Saw a man in the distance with black hair. He looked familiar, but too far away to tell, and there's a lot of Chinese about . . . Ooh, mind out, Pansy, you'll trip me up,' Ruby said as her daughter continued to cling to her, getting under her feet.

'You're going to school then, young lady?' Kathy asked, ruffling the child's long dark hair.

Pansy nodded bashfully.

Kathy crouched down, so her face was level with Pansy's. 'I went to that school. My teacher was called Miss Timmings.'

'Miss Milton . . .' Pansy whispered.

'Your teacher is Miss Milton?'

Pansy nodded.

'Is she nice?'

Again the child slowly wagged her head before racing away as her friend called her.

'Don't want you to lose yer job over me,' Ruby blurted. 'You're a good midwife.' She sounded distressed again. 'I ain't prying, but Matilda bumped into your mum, and Winnie told her you're giving up nursing. Ain't because of me, and what went on, is it?'

'No . . . honestly, it's not,' Kathy reassured. In truth, she knew keeping Ruby's secret – as she would till the day she died – was no greater burden on her conscience than the guilt she felt over refusing Jennifer help when she'd begged for it. It was her job to nurture new life, yet recently she'd had her cut-and-dried beliefs tested and the doubts haunting her mind were not yet quietened.

'It's just . . . a crossroads in my life and I need to have a breather and decide about the future.' Kathy paused. She'd not yet told anybody that Nick had asked her to marry him, and she'd said yes. She'd wanted to save the wonderful surprise till they'd been shopping for a ring at the weekend. But Ruby needed something to ease her anxieties. 'I'm getting married, Ruby . . .'

Ruby laughed, throwing back her head in delight and relief. 'You're getting married! Ain't no better reason to stay at home than that. I'm guessing the copper's off the scene and you've caught that smashing Mr Raven.'

Kathy nodded, and as Ruby dropped her shopping bag to spin her around, she allowed her inner joy free rein, whooping with abandon as loudly as was Ruby.

'Well, good for you!' Ruby said breathlessly as they broke apart. 'He's the sort of bloke every gel wants but can't have. He'll look after you.'

'Our secret!' Kathy put a finger to her lips. 'I've not yet told my mum and she'll crown me if she's last to know.'

'Our secret . . .' Ruby echoed. 'Right . . . reckon I'm ready fer that tea.' Briskly, she picked up her shopping. 'Come on, Nurse Finch, let's get Matilda to put the kettle on.'

'I think you should call me Kathy now . . .'

'Right, I will . . .' Ruby said, and, linking arms, they walked on down the road.

Tell us about the real Campbell Road?

The construction of Campbell Road, Islington, began in 1865, on land known as the St Pancras' Seven Sisters Road Estate. The initial properties that appeared were intended for sale or rent to respectable tenants, but unfortunately, building along the street was done piecemeal and took a long time. Over a period of years, the demand fell for houses like those springing up in Campbell Road and poor people, unable to afford to buy or rent a whole house, started taking rooms in the properties. As more undesirables arrived, the rents fell even lower and the clerks and artisans fled to better areas. In 1880 a lodging house was opened at 47 Campbell Road, licensed for 90 men. It was the first of many such establishments in the road and by 1890 Campbell Road had the largest number of doss-house beds for any Islington street. The poorest of the poor continued to colonize the area, and Campbell Road gained the reputation for being the worst street in North London. The Bunk, as the slum came to be nicknamed, had been born, and during its heyday it flourished as a magnet for rogues, prostitutes and vagabonds. In 1937 the name of the road was changed to Whadcoat Street in a vain attempt to dilute its bad reputation. Slum clearance started in 1952 finally putting an end to the street, and in its place was built a council estate. All that now remains of the notorious Bunk is the name Whadcoat Street on a brick wall.

What inspired you to write about it?

My grandmother was born in 1901 and remembered moving into Campbell Road when she was still an infant. Her family lived there in cramped rooms in various dilapidated tenement houses until she was a grown woman. She finally escaped when she married in 1922, but oddly came back to her mother's house in The Bunk to give birth to my mum. My great-grandmother, Matilda, remained in the street for many more years, until her death in a rather mysterious accident during World War II.

I, and my siblings, grew up in Tottenham, North London. We always knew that our maternal grandmother had had a 'hard' life. It was some while before we fully realized, from a book published about Campbell Bunk, how dreadful had been her upbringing in an Islington slum.

In the 1970s/80s a historian, Jerry White, began researching the social history of Campbell Road. He contacted ex-residents of the street and my grandmother was interviewed and her recollections incorporated into his study. On the book's publication, my nan was presented with a copy.

When my beloved mum died we discovered amongst

386

her belongings the Campbell Road book, and some pages of a novel she'd started to write that had been inspired by her mother's wretched early life. My dad wondered whether it would be possible to finish the novel as a tribute to her and my grandmother. I considered it a privilege to take on the task, and *The Street* was published in 2011, the first in the Campbell Road series.

The characters are so vivid – are any of them based on real people?

I never knew my great-grandparents, Matilda and Jack, as they had died before I was born. Jack perished in the Great War, still a young man. However I had heard about Matilda from my mum and nan. I knew she was a hard-drinking bruiser of a woman who earned her living in The Bunk as a rent-collector and as a bookie's runner, amongst other things. I based the character of Matilda Keiver on her, and hope my great-gran would approve of her alter ego. In *The Street*, and in some of the sequels, the character of Alice is based on my nan, who provided us all with a wonderful insight to her pluck and resilience in the interviews she gave for Jerry White's study on Campbell Bunk.

Where do you get your inspiration for all of the gritty dialogue?

Dare I say it . . . from my roots in Tottenham, and from my husband who harks back to the East End. His mother's family came from the Brick Lane area, and his father is from Bethnal Green. I've overheard relatives use some very colourful language and slang! That apart, I tend to be an observer and store away memorable jargon to recycle in my books.

When did you start to write?

When my sons were in infant school I decided to try my hand at writing a novel. My writing career took off to a good start in the early 1980s when a North American publishing house accepted my first work. The book was a Regency romance and I continued writing in the genre for twenty-five years, both for the American market and for a British publisher, before turning my hand to Sagas. I started work on *The Street* in 2009 and was delighted when HarperCollins took it on and it became a success two years later.

What books inspired you?

Jerry White's study of The Bunk, incorporating my nan's reminiscences, had a huge influence on my decision to write *The Street*. It is a wonderfully detailed social history of Campbell Road, from its birth in Victorian times to its demise in 1952. I would recommend it to anybody who has an interest in that particular area of Islington, and hasn't already read it.

Do you think that the disappearance of streets like Campbell Road is a good thing or a bad thing?

Personally, I would give my eye teeth for the opportunity to walk the road that has fascinated me for so long. Campbell Road has become part of me, and in my mind

I can see and smell the dank buildings and hear the residents as they go about their daily lives. Practically, of course, the buildings were riddled with decay and many had been abandoned by the time the demolition started in 1952. Clearing the area to provide modern, sanitary housing was no doubt the right thing to do. Campbell Road wasn't meant to be a museum piece; it was of its time. And in its time became both a curse and a blessing for people who were desperate enough to need its shelter.

Despite its reputation for lawlessness and dilapidation, The Bunk could boast a community spirit and camaraderie that united residents in a way that justified its existence.

What do you think helped women like Tilly Keiver and Ruby Potter to get through life?

In a word: women. Wives and mothers provided invaluable support to one another, despite living hand-to-mouth in such a slum. Whatever was needed, whether it was child-minding, the loan of small amounts of food or money, or shelter from an abusive husband or father, the assistance came from female relatives and neighbours. The pudding basin whip-rounds for the desperately needy were a regular occurrence in Campbell Road; money donated by people struggling to survive themselves.

Will we see Tilly Keiver again?

I certainly hope so. She's far too young and lively to be put to rest!

Want to know how it all started? Read on for a thrilling
extract from Kay's first book in the Campbell Road series

THE STREET

ONE

'Shut that brat up or I will . . . fer good.'

'You don't mean that, Mum. Little 'un's hungry. I've been waiting up for you to come home so's you can feed her. Why do you say horrible things?' The small girl's expression was a mixture of contempt and sorrow as she challenged the woman swaying on her feet. In fact she knew very well why her mother turned mean and brutal: it was due to the amount of Irish whiskey she had tipped down her throat in the hours since she'd left this squalid hovel that was their home.

Tilly Keiver narrowed her glassy gaze on her daughter. 'You got too much o' what the cat licks its arse with, my gel.' The words were slurred but menacing. Unsteadily she shoved herself away from the doorjamb. 'If I weren't dog tired you'd feel the back o' me hand and no mistake about it.' She raised a fist raised to emphasise it was no idle threat. Slowly she let the hand fall so it might aid the other in grappling with the buttons on her coat. Irritably she shrugged the garment off and left it where it fell on rag-covered floorboards. Small, careful steps took Tilly on a meandering path towards the iron bedstead. It was the dominant piece of furniture in a room cluttered with odd, dilapidated pieces.

Alice Keiver watched her mother, listening to her swearing beneath her breath as she bumped into a stick-back chair and sent it over. Then her ample hip met the wardrobe. If Tilly felt the hefty contact there was no sign: the volume of cursing remained the same. She was soon within striking distance and Alice shrank back into the armchair. She'd been huddled within its scratchy old embrace for two long hours whilst awaiting her mother's return. Her thin arms tightened about the fretful infant wriggling against her lap. To soothe the hungry baby and quieten her mewling she again stuck the tip of her little finger between tiny lips. Little Lucy pounced on the fruitless comfort and sucked insistently.

Alice knew that once her mother had reached the bed and sunk onto the edge she was unlikely to rouse herself to retaliate, whatever she heard in the way of complaints. Soon that moment arrived.

'You're not tired, you're drunk as usual.' Despite Alice's frail figure her accusation was strong and she lithely sprang to her feet, clutching the precious bundle of her baby sister protectively against her ribs as she paced this way and that.

'Get yerself in the back, 'fore I use this on yer,' her mother slurred, showing her a wobbling fist. But Tilly's chin was already drooping towards her bosom.

Alice made a tentative move forward, and then tottered quickly back as her mother snapped up her head but, as she had correctly assumed, Tilly made no move to rise from the bed once she'd settled into the comfort of its sagging edge.

'You're a bleeding nuisance, you are. Worse'n all the rest put together. Now git! Let me get meself to bed. Cor, I'm all in.'

Tilly Keiver was a big-boned woman with a florid face

392

topped by reddish-blonde hair. Usually she kept her beautifully thick mane under control: plaited and coiled in a neat bun either side of her head. But a night of roistering with her cronies in the Duke pub, and a painful stumble on the way home, had resulted in her crowning glory resembling a fiery bird's nest. She yanked out two pins from one side of her head and a thick plait uncoiled sinuously onto a shoulder. She left it at that. The other side was forgotten.

After a few quiet minutes Alice thought her mother had dozed off where she slouched. But before she could act, Tilly managed again to rouse herself and, having folded forward, her callused fingers began pulling at her footwear.

Tilly's new boots had been got, against fierce competition, just that afternoon from Billy the Totter. Carefully she tried to unlace them but the fancy double bow she'd fashioned when sober got the better of her. In a frenzy of impatience she used toe against heel to squash down the leather and prise them off. The last one freed was tossed from her foot against the wall in a fit of temper. Even in her inebriated state Tilly regretted rough-handling her prized possession. Her frustration resulted in coarse cursing that continued as she fumbled with her heavy skirt. She managed to work it to her ankles and shake it away. Done with undressing, she swung her feet up onto the mattress and momentarily lay quiet and still; the only sound from that side of the room was the settling bedsprings.

Alice moved quietly closer to help her mother cover herself. But Tilly's flopping hand had finally located what it sought. After a few attempts she managed to swing the solitary blanket high enough to drift about her body.

'Don't go to sleep yet, Mum. Lucy needs feeding,' Alice pleaded in a whisper. 'And there's no milk left. There was only a drop that'd gone sour and Dad put it in his tea before he went off to work.' She gently shook her mother by the arm to rouse her.

Alice knew her mother was conscious but choosing to ignore her pleas, so now she must wait. In a very short while Tilly would sink so deeply into sleep that she'd hear and feel nothing. Alice gently placed little Lucy on the bed a safe distance from her mother's twitching, and started to tidy the room. She must loiter until she heard her mother snore.

She picked up Tilly's best coat from the floor, shook it, and draped it across the end of the bed. The small-back stick chair had been made even more rickety by rough treatment; nevertheless Alice moved it to neatly join the three still pushed under the table. The precious boots were collected and placed together out of sight beneath the bed. A rumbling sound drew her back, on tiptoe, to her mother.

'Mum?' she tested quietly. There was no response. Even when baby Lucy let out a wail Tilly stirred only to suck in another ragged breath. Alice tested her mother's consciousness again, this time with more volume to her voice. Tilly snored on.

Quickly Alice's nimble fingers unbuttoned her mother's blouse. Deftly she positioned the baby close to a plump breast to nurse. Alice froze stock still, her fingers covering the baby's mouth to stifle her whimpers. One of her mother's hands had fluttered up as though she might swipe them both away, but after a moment, hovering, it fell back to the mattress.

Little Lucy's face had become crumpled and crimson as though she sensed imminent comfort slipping away. But Alice was sure now that her mother was sufficiently stupefied. With furtive care she guided the baby close then snatched away her fingers, allowing the baby to latch on and feed.